BALLAD of SWORD & WINE

QIANG JIN JIU

3

BALLAD of SWORD & WINE

QIANG JIN JIU

WRITTEN BY

Tang Jiu Qing

ILLUSTRATED BY

St

TRANSLATED BY

XiA, Jia, amixy

Seven Seas

Seven Seas Entertainment

Ballad of Sword and Wine: Qiang Jin Jiu (Novel) Vol. 3

Published originally under the title of 《将进酒》 (Qiang Jin Jiu)
Author© 唐酒卿 (Tang Jiu Qing)
English edition rights under license granted by 北京晋江原创网络科技有限公司
(Beijing Jinjiang Original Network Technology Co., Ltd.)
English edition copyright © 2025 Seven Seas Entertainment, LLC
Arranged through JS Agency Co., Ltd
All rights reserved

Cover & Interior Illustrations: St

Seven Seas press and purchase enquiries can be sent
to Marketing Manager Lauren Hill at press@gomanga.com.
Information regarding the distribution and purchase of digital editions is available
from Digital Manager CK Russell at digital@gomanga.com.

Seven Seas and the Seven Seas logo are trademarks of
Seven Seas Entertainment. All rights reserved.

Follow Seven Seas Entertainment online at
sevenseasentertainment.com.

TRANSLATION: XiA, Jia, amixy
ADAPTATION: Dara
COVER & MAP DESIGN: M. A. Lewife
INTERIOR DESIGN: Clay Gardner
INTERIOR LAYOUT: Karis Page
COPY EDITOR: Jehanne Bell
PROOFREADER: Kate Kishi, Hnä
EDITOR: Kelly Quinn Chiu
PREPRESS TECHNICIAN: Salvador Chan Jr., April Malig, Jules Valera
MANAGING EDITOR: Alyssa Scavetta
EDITOR-IN-CHIEF: Julie Davis
PUBLISHER: Lianne Sentar
VICE PRESIDENT: Adam Arnold
PRESIDENT: Jason DeAngelis

ISBN: 979-8-88843-312-6
Printed in Canada
First Printing: January 2025
10 9 8 7 6 5 4 3 2 1

TABLE OF
CONTENTS

76 Casting the Net   13

77 Dispute   27

78 Individual Servings   39

79 Clues   51

80 Bride Price   63

81 Shadows   71

82 Debt Collection   81

83 Scenery of Spring   91

84 Wealth   105

85 Assignment   115

86 Old Manor   125

87 Imperial Heir   135

88 Imperial Preceptor   149

89 Cracks and Booms   161

90 Veteran General   171

91 Libei   183

92 Anxiety   195

93 General   207

94 Raging Waves   219

95 The State   227

96 The Fall   235

97 In Pain   249

98 On the Run   259

99 Thank-You Gift   269

100 Latent Threat   279

101 Treasure   291

102 Cizhou   299

103 Beauty   309

104 Elder Brother   315

105 Cunning   323

106 Crude   331

107 Odd   341

108 Silver   351

109 Jingzhe   361

110 Son of a Concubine   369

111 Mother   377

112 Chasing the Stars   387

APPENDIXES

•   Character & Name Guide   401

•   Glossary   415

CASTING THE NET

THE LAST OF THE NIGHT rain was fading, but the humidity of their bodies lingered in the bedding.

The little cottage by the hot springs on Mount Feng had been newly renovated; although it was small, it contained all the necessities. Xiao Chiye, robe draped over his shoulders, got up and fed the horse and gyrfalcon. The only sounds on Mount Feng at daybreak were the soft *plinks* of water dripping from the eaves. He basked in the mountain breeze for a moment, his robe casually open, until the chill of early spring calmed the sharp edge of excitement that had persisted through the night. He had sobered from the wine, but his passion had grown more intense and vicious, followed by the kind of languid tenderness that came only after being sated.

This was the pleasure of indulging in desire.

Xiao Chiye removed the saddle on Snowcrest's back and gestured to Meng, who spread his wings and flew out of the eaves into the forest.

When Xiao Chiye ducked back inside, the close heat of the place hadn't yet dissipated. Shen Zechuan lay face-down on the pillow with the blanket drawn over him, making it impossible to tell if he was asleep or awake. Dangling from his half-exposed right ear was that jade earring. Xiao Chiye took it off for him and, in passing, rubbed his earlobe where it had turned red from the pressure of the clasp.

Shen Zechuan moaned. He hadn't yet sunk into a sound sleep, and after another moment of stillness, he opened his eyes to look at Xiao Chiye.

"We should go," he rasped.

Xiao Chiye lay down beside Shen Zechuan and met his eyes. "It's a day off today. It's still early."

Shen Zechuan hummed. "There's still work to be done in the Imperial Prison."

"Such a busy man." Xiao Chiye laced their fingers together and pulled Shen Zechuan closer. "In just one day, you rose to the position of northern judge, and then to vice commander. Those you'll be facing now are noble descendants with hereditary ranks. They won't be easy to manage; someone is bound to try to trip you up with some underhanded trick."

"Serving at the emperor's side is never easy," Shen Zechuan said.

It was in this way Shen Zechuan lay: expression open, body soft and satiated. They locked eyes, then, like the gentle breeze after a rainstorm, came their kiss, light and slow. They had earnestly bared their hearts to each other in this humble thatched cottage, as if in these few scant hours away from Qudu they could cast aside the strategy and prudence politics demanded and become no more than two young men.

"This place is too small," Xiao Chiye whispered. "The view of the sky is blocked by vermilion walls, and the mountains and plains are hemmed in by cities—Snowcrest can't run to his heart's content. Someday, when we return to Libei, I'll take you riding through the Hongyan Mountains."

Shen Zechuan rested his head against Xiao Chiye's chest. "Is the moon in Libei as round as the moon in Duanzhou?"

Xiao Chiye answered only after a long pause. "I've already forgotten. Is the grass in Duanzhou as tall as the grass in Libei?"

"I've already forgotten."

They burst into laughter, dispelling that cloud of melancholy. Shen Zechuan breathed in Xiao Chiye's scent as Xiao Chiye pressed his chin against the top of Shen Zechuan's head.

"Let's go together," Xiao Chiye said.

"Home?"

Xiao Chiye tightened his arms around Shen Zechuan. "Home. Let's ask Ji Gang-shifu to come with us. Libei is vast; there's plenty of space for him."

Shen Zechuan laughed and lowered his lashes. "Shifu wants to return to Duanzhou. I'm afraid we won't be able to go together."

Xiao Chiye looked down at him. "As long as we can get out of Qudu, we'll go together, even to the ends of the earth."

"The wolf pup should be in Libei." Shen Zechuan found Xiao Chiye's eyes again. "It would be a pity if the poor thing grew complacent with a life of leisure."

"Libei has my eldest brother, and the Libei Armored Cavalry has my father," Xiao Chiye answered evenly. "Riding is the only thing that suits me."

Shen Zechuan lifted Xiao Chiye's chin and looked into his eyes. "Talents bestowed by the heavens will find their use; it's only a matter of time. Ce'an, Ce'an—all the hopes of Libei lie in this name."

Xiao Chiye let out a booming laugh and rolled over to pin Shen Zechuan to the bed. He pressed his forehead against Shen Zechuan's. "Do you want me or not?"

After a lazy stretch to ease his aching muscles, Shen Zechuan squeezed the back of Xiao Chiye's neck and answered huskily, "Will you give yourself to me or not?"

Xiao Chiye dipped his head to kiss him and pulled the blanket up over them both.

After that rainy night, the days grew warmer in Qudu.

The Grand Secretariat demanded Pan Xiangjie's dismissal from his position as Minister of Works, and the Chief Surveillance Bureau submitted more than ten memorials in a row impeaching him. The daily arguments in the imperial court grew so heated Li Jianheng's ears ached. Wei Huaigu, the Minister of Revenue, and other high-ranking ministers from the other noble clans stuck together; they wouldn't abandon one of their own at the first hurdle. In the end, even minor officials like Fu Linye were only demoted with a reduced salary, and were allowed to remain in the capital.

After the fall of Hua Siqian during the coup at the Nanlin Hunting Grounds, Hai Liangyi had assumed the position of the Grand Secretary of the Grand Secretariat. Although he entrusted Xue Xiuzhuo, a man from the Eight Great Clans, with heavy responsibilities, he had also promoted several low-ranking officials from common households one after another—most conspicuously the current Minister of Justice, Kong Qiu. The two sides fought a bitter war against each other, both before the court and in the shadows.

However, this recent case was a matter of grave importance. Someone had to take responsibility for the clogged ditches: the noble clans couldn't push the blame onto a scapegoat this time. If Pan Xiangjie wasn't impeached, then Wei Huaigu would have to go.

The Ministry of Revenue was obviously of greater importance to the noble clans than the Ministry of Works—the manual laborers could be cast aside, but control of the treasury must be retained.

To this end, Pan Xiangjie wasn't the only member of the Pan Clan on the chopping board. His eldest son of lawful birth, the Vice Minister of the Ministry of Revenue, was also set to be suspended from his post to await impeachment.

Li Jianheng no longer spoke his mind so readily before the court. After adjourning for the day, he called for Xiao Chiye to stay behind. They took a stroll around the garden to take in the spring views.

"I heard you rode out of the capital in the middle of a thunderstorm some days ago." Li Jianheng held back the sleeve of his bright yellow imperial day robe as he offered half of his candied fruits to Xiao Chiye. "What were you up to?"

"The Imperial Army's drill grounds are close to Mount Feng. I worry whenever it rains; it's been only a few days since the flooding in the public ditches. I rushed over that night to take a look," Xiao Chiye replied breezily, as if he hadn't registered that Li Jianheng was keeping tabs on him. He smiled. "Your Majesty knows all about that military drill ground. It cost the Imperial Army an arm and a leg. If the rain were to damage it, those twenty thousand men of mine would have to go squeeze in with the Eight Great Battalions."

"If you marched the Imperial Army to the Eight Great Battalions' military grounds tomorrow, the Ministry of Revenue would allocate the funds for your drill grounds' repair immediately." Li Jianheng tossed the candied fruit into his mouth. "They have their guards up around you—I've noticed that much by now. They would rather keep you as far away as possible."

"We're all merely doing our duty. Where do they get such outlandish ideas?" Xiao Chiye said self-deprecatingly.

Recalling the last time Xiao Chiye was besieged and attacked on all sides in court, Li Jianheng promptly answered, "They're full of foul notions, and sly as old foxes. Every one of them speaks with such eloquence, but in truth, their words are traps meant to set others up. Never mind you, they even had the gall to pull one over on *us*. Take Pan Xiangjie: his dereliction of duty almost led to our death. And look—who should enter the palace last night to keep the empress dowager company but Commandery Princess Zhaoyue? The empress dowager knew better, of course; she said she wouldn't interfere in state affairs and sent the princess away. Now, how would a girl who's about to be wed know the ins and outs of these political matters? No doubt the Helian Marquis put her up to it. The two families are in-laws, after all!"

Xiao Chiye followed Li Jianheng down the steps and beneath the fresh green buds of the branches. "Has Your Majesty made up your mind to punish Pan Xiangjie then?"

"Of course. We mustn't let him off easily," Li Jianheng said. "Cen Yu submitted a memorial just a few days ago with a drawing of the disaster victims from the low-lying district; it's devastating. We are the emperor; we're confined within the imperial palace. It's just as the secretariat elder said: all our information comes through others. But that drawing—Pan Xiangjie's negligence and tardiness in clearing up the public ditches led to untold suffering. He must be punished. The secretariat elder thinks so too."

Having tasted the sweetness of dishing out rewards and receiving praise from the grandmasters of remonstrance within the Chief Surveillance Bureau, Li Jianheng next wanted to make an example of Pan Xiangjie.

"I happen to disagree with the secretariat elder," Xiao Chiye said unexpectedly. "Pan Xiangjie deserves punishment, yes, but he shouldn't be so peremptorily removed from office."

Li Jianheng frowned back at him. "After such a blunder, you propose we keep him around so he may make another?"

Xiao Chiye cast a glance at the clear skies overhead. Remembering what Shen Zechuan had said about how blame would be laid at Pan Xiangjie's feet, he laughed. "Of course Your Majesty must punish him. But if you dismiss him from his post, it'll be the end of his career. Pan Xiangjie is advanced in age. He's made some worthy contributions in his position as Minister of Works over the years. Your Majesty, the blockage of the public ditches caused sewage to flood the streets and destroy buildings, but the embankments of the Kailing River remained as solid and secure as an iron wall. In previous years, when other regions have flooded, very few dams and embankments have held up so well. The minister clearly put some effort into the construction and didn't cut corners."

"But his negligence of the public ditches is a fact as well. Why should we let him off easy just because of the Kailing River?"

"Your Majesty," Xiao Chiye said. "The court assembly this morning discussed the allocation of funds for the spring plowing. The Ministry of Revenue has been wrestling with the provinces over this. They've been at an impasse for half a month; if it drags on any longer, it'll be too late."

"What's that got to do with dismissing Pan Xiangjie?" Li Jianheng was none too pleased. "Even if we retain him, the Ministry of Revenue will not allocate the funds. Wei Huaigu's subordinates are all smooth-tongued; not even the secretariat elder wastes his breath arguing with them. Only those from the Chief Surveillance Bureau can draw with them in a verbal match."

"All the capable officials within the Ministry of Revenue at the moment are Wei Huaigu's protégés; where he leads, they'll follow. But Pan Lin, Pan Xiangjie's son, happens to hold the post of Vice Minister in the Ministry of Revenue. If Your Majesty employs a light touch with Pan Xiangjie this time, their Pan Clan will re-member Your Majesty's kindness. Their loyalty will be as assured as if Pan Xiangjie's son is Your Majesty's own. When Your Majesty deals with the Ministry of Revenue in the future, you'll have a man on the inside willing to speak up on your behalf. What's more, if Pan Xiangjie is dismissed and prosecuted, the Ministry of Works will have to nominate someone to take up his vacated post. His replacement may not necessarily be as loyal." Here Xiao Chiye paused to let Li Jianheng think for himself.

Li Jianheng took a few steps. "But if he's not dismissed," he said, hesitant, "there must still be some punishment that will appease the masses."

"Pan and Fei are related by marriage, while Fei and Xi have long been on close terms. None of them lack for money. Your Majesty can fine Pan Xiangjie—have him cover all the expenses incurred from the dredging of the public ditches, then hand him a more corporal punishment of flogging."

"Flogging?" Li Jianheng blurted. "At his age, wouldn't that kill him?!"

Xiao Chiye smiled. "How shall he mend his ways and shed tears of gratitude if you don't give him a taste of his own mortality? Let the grandmasters of remonstrance give him a verbal lashing as well until they're satisfied. By the time Your Majesty summons him again for an audience, he'll be grateful even if Your Majesty instructs him to bark like a dog, let alone cover some civic expenses."

Delighted, Li Jianheng circled back. "As expected, you're always the resourceful one!"

"Wei Huaigu himself ran the audit on the whole expenditure. I worry he may have, out of impure intentions, doctored the accounts.

Your Majesty should act with prudence and have the case gone over again."

Sure enough, Li Jianheng hesitated. "This is a job for the Ministry of Revenue. Where do we find the man for the job? The other ministries can't interfere in this matter either."

"Then find someone in the Ministry of Revenue. Perhaps the official at the top can't give a clear explanation, but the minor officials at the bottom are all men who serve Your Majesty honestly." Xiao Chiye brushed aside a branch and seemed to think things over before continuing, "I met a competent official at the Temple of Guilt during the flood. It was he who kept the records and accounts for all the medicinal herbs the Imperial Army collected from the local apothecaries. Even the secretariat elder was full of praise for him. Perhaps he's just the man you're looking for."

"If even the secretariat elder praised him, we can't go wrong!" Li Jianheng said, overjoyed. "What's his name? Let's go with him!"

Xiao Chiye's voice was steady. "His name is Liang Cuishan."

Xi Hongxuan had been taken into custody shortly after the flood. He'd originally thought—with Li Jianheng's protection and Xue Xiuzhuo's efforts—he would be quickly released. But days passed in prison with no word from the outside world. Something, he guessed, had gone wrong somewhere between the throne and his cell.

When Shen Zechuan arrived at the prison, he showed his authority token. As the fastest-rising, newly appointed official who had so recently shared drinks with the Minister of Justice Kong Qiu himself, he had little trouble finding his way in—Qiao Tianya only needed a few catties of wine to talk the warden around.

The moment Xi Hongxuan saw him, he scrambled up and approached the bars. "How is it? Why has there been no news?

Has Pan Xiangjie been punished? If so, then it's about time for me to be released!"

Although Shen Zechuan's authority token was swinging from his waist, he hadn't appeared in his official robe. He was dressed instead in a dark gray day robe with the collar tightly secured. The dim light obscured his features as he entered, and against his dark clothes, his skin looked uncommonly pale, almost frosty.

"You're still waiting for Pan Xiangjie to be prosecuted?" Shen Zechuan asked. "There's been no word of him these days."

"He's the head of the Ministry of Works. How could the court not punish him after the disaster with the public ditches? Even His Majesty couldn't justify it." Xi Hongxuan clenched his fists. "What went wrong?"

"Wei Huaigu, attempting to shirk responsibility and shift the blame, tried everything to drag Pan Xiangjie down. But as you know, pushing too hard can backfire; even rabbits will bite when backed into a corner, let alone the long-suffering Pan Xiangjie. The Pan Clan has offered to cover all expenses related to this incident. The porridge stall over at the Temple of Guilt has yet to be dismantled, and the womenfolk of the Pan Clan have been going every day to hand out porridge to the disaster victims. They've made quite the show of humbling themselves, as if ready to accept any physical and verbal abuse—as they say, not for the sake of the monk but for the Buddha. Even the secretariat elder has had to take this into account when considering Pan Xiangjie's punishment."

Solemnly, Shen Zechuan continued, "Meanwhile, the Ministry of Revenue's repeated delays in allocating funds for the ditch maintenance cannot be covered up. If Wei Huaigu was smart, he'd do everyone a favor and admit his mistakes; he'd endure his scolding and get it over with. Yet he's too oblivious; the man doesn't know when to bend. Second Young Master, if Pan Xiangjie isn't dismissed and Wei Huaigu isn't punished, I'm afraid the only one left on the chopping block is you."

Xi Hongxuan was silent a moment. "Wei Huaigu is too money-minded. He's trying to paper over this matter because he's afraid once he admits any wrongdoing, the gap in the Ministry of Revenue's accounts will be exposed, and Hai Liangyi will gain leverage over him. Knowing him, if he can't shove Pan Xiangjie forward as a scapegoat, he'll make me fork over the money instead. No matter what, he won't let himself suffer. Fuck, that wily old fox!"

When the noble clans had ganged up on Xiao Chiye over the assassination incident, they had wanted a share in the Eight Great Battalions. But instead of knocking down Xiao Chiye, they were now fighting among themselves. Xi Hongxuan was indignant. He had already spent a hefty sum making amends for his brother, Xi Gu'an, after he fell from grace. Fortunately, he had the family salt mines, so silver was still flowing in, and the imperial court had no window into the Xi Clan's private accounts. But if Wei Huaigu wanted money, that was a different matter. The Eight Great Clans knew their own. The Xi were a family of salt merchants who did business by sea and kept a large fleet of ships in the Port of Yongquan—the other seven clans knew this all too well.

"Money that wards off a calamity is money well spent," Shen Zechuan said earnestly, his face grave. "With you behind bars, you'll need someone on the outside to handle this business for you. You're transferring money from private accounts at a great distance. If the Wei Clan wants some ten thousand taels, transportation alone poses a significant risk. There must be someone you can trust to organize this on your behalf. This is of utmost urgency; you must see that it's done as quickly as possible."

"Ask Yanqing!" Xi Hongxuan blurted, then hesitated.

Although Xue Xiuzhuo knew the ins and outs of the Xi Clan, Xi Hongxuan didn't fully trust him not to get some other ideas in the process. The Xi Clan's accumulated wealth was something previous generations had risked their lives to hoard, and they owned a string of connected shops and businesses in Juexi and Hezhou. If it was money Wei Huaigu wanted, Xi Hongxuan could afford the expense, but there was no one to whom he could entrust the task of transferring such a sum. Since Xi Gu'an's death, the few Xi Clan concubines had been clicking away at their abacuses, making their own calculations about the Xi Clan's fortune. If he wasn't careful, he'd meet his end at his family's hands before he died in prison.

"Lanzhou," Xi Hongxuan said abruptly. "You've been promoted to vice commander of the Embroidered Uniform Guard, and you're managing the Imperial Prison. You have special rights to enter and exit Qudu on official business. This matter may be inappropriate for Yanqing, what with him now in the Court of Judicial Review. His position will make him too conspicuous; he's sure to draw scrutinizing eyes. How about you handle this matter for me instead?"

Shen Zechuan looked taken aback. "I've neither managed accounts nor dealt with Wei Huaigu before, and I'm not familiar with your businesses outside Qudu. How could I be trusted to handle this?"

But that unfamiliarity was just what Xi Hongxuan needed; it made Shen Zechuan perfect for the job.

"I have managers in the salterns. They know their business, so you won't need to worry about arranging for the money," Xi Hongxuan explained. "But the transportation of a large sum like that will be troublesome. Tens of thousands of silver ingots would pile up into mountains if loaded onto carts. But we can't go the water route; all my family's established routes are on the sea. As far as the inland waterways go, the Hua Clan of Dicheng has the final say in the north, while the Yan Clan of Hezhou calls the shots in the south. We must go overland, but that means passing through the thirteen cities of Juexi... Fucking hell! I hope all this silver crushes Wei Huaigu to death! In any case, there's nothing you need fear while passing through Juexi, save for Jiang Qingshan—that man is a tough one. You'll want to watch out for him. If he catches on, I'll be skinned alive!"

"This is too important," Shen Zechuan continued to protest. "You should first discuss it with Xue Xiuzhuo."

"No." Xi Hongxuan's mind was made up. "Yanqing isn't suitable for something like this. It would put us at cross-purposes if he were to get involved. Just tell him to continue to plead my case in court. Perhaps His Majesty is hesitating over my case now, but when I get out of here, I'm going to serve him Wei Huaigu's head on a platter!"

He smiled at Shen Zechuan. "Don't panic," he added. "I know you've no experience with business and trade. I left a bookkeeper in my Qudu residence; his name is Xi Dan, an old hand in my employ. Bring him here if you can... I'll give him all the necessary instructions."

Xi Hongxuan was a shrewd man. He didn't dare put his trust in Shen Zechuan just yet. Ji Lei's death was still stark in his mind; Xi Hongxuan was determined to be different, so he had insisted on seeing his own man before withdrawing any money. The location of the Xi Clan's keys was known only to Xi Hongxuan himself, and none of the Xi Clan's vaults would open without them.

"Give me a few days," Shen Zechuan said softly. "I'll bring him right to you."

DISPUTE

AMID THE CHAOS at court, Pan Xiangjie had been
suspended from his post as he awaited impeachment. He had
received a flogging in punishment and was back at home,
sighing and moaning as he lay on his stomach, nursing his injuries.
His son, Pan Lin, who was implicated as well, had endured the
rebukes of the Chief Surveillance Bureau every day during court.
A few days later, he too was suspended from his post, and was now
under house arrest.

Xiao Chiye, having been promoted to the rank of marquis,
organized a banquet in celebration and specially invited the
Helian Marquis. But after the ill-fated matchmaking attempt with
Commandery Princess Zhaoyue, the man was too embarrassed
to appear before him. The marquis feared Xiao Chiye, flush with
success and notoriously tyrannical, would humiliate him before his
other guests. After thinking it through, the Helian Marquis sent his
son to attend on his behalf.

The young marquis was called Fei Shi and was another well-
known figure on Donglong Street. He had gone drinking with
Xiao Chiye in the past, but none of the petty tyrants like himself
were anywhere near as domineering as that little dictator from
Libei. Fei Shi feared the Xiao Clan. He no longer caroused with

Xiao Chiye, and whenever he saw Xiao Chiye with Li Jianheng, he always gave them a wide berth. Faced with the prospect of attending Xiao Chiye's banquet, he first wilted by half, then changed course and headed to the Pan manor to persuade Pan Lin to join him.

"Come with me. It's better than being bored!" Fei Shi had scurried over with such haste he still gripped the hem of his robe in both hands. "The banquet is right on the Kailing River. There'll be loads of people there."

Pan Lin's son was just a month old. He teased the baby with a handkerchief before saying, "Not going. I've been in a foul mood these last few days."

"What fun is there in sitting at home and playing with a baby?" Fei Shi squeezed in front of the hovering nanny. "I can't skip it this time. My father made his instructions clear: *Go have some fun and make friends with him.* I heard he's friends with Cen Yu, the Left Censor-in-Chief of the Chief Surveillance Bureau. Think, if Xiao Er steps forward and intercedes on your behalf, you won't have to endure those rebukes anymore."

"Seriously?" Pan Lin tossed the handkerchief aside. "Cen Xunyi's been more brutal than anyone in reprimanding me! Xiao Er only advanced in rank this time because of his friendship with His Majesty. What's he going to say to Cen Yu? I'm not going. Do you think I want to embarrass myself?!"

"Look at you, you're such a stick in the mud!" Fei Shi was wracking his brain to coax him out the door. "Xiao Chiye is old friends with His Majesty. If he can put in a few good words for the Pan Clan before the throne, would you be in such a sorry state? Come on, let's go. I've had a drink or two with him before. I'll introduce you!"

Unable to rebuff Fei Shi, Pan Lin found himself dragged out of the house and into the carriage, trundling toward the Kailing River.

Xiao Chiye's banquet filled all the gaily painted pleasure boats on the Kailing River. Now that he was famous, the brothels and taverns along the riverbanks also benefited by association with a boost in business. Tonight, money flowed through hands like water. Xiao Chiye didn't even have to open his mouth; all around him, the crowd practically elbowed past each other to be the first to show him their generosity.

But in this world, there was no such thing as a free lunch. If Xiao Chiye accepted their money, he would owe them a favor. If not today, there would be plenty of pretexts for them to lean on him in the future. Xiao Chiye knew this all too well and didn't accept a single coin. Every copper for this grand occasion had been paid out of his own pocket.

Chen Yang clicked away at the abacus in the back corner. The more he tallied, the slower he became. Eventually, he tossed away the abacus and said to Ding Tao and Gu Jin, "The palace has rewarded us with so many fields and mansions. Let's sort them out and find an auspicious day to sell the lot."

Xiao Chiye had just stepped out of his chamber. He cut an imposing figure, outfitted in a golden crown, brocade robe, and coal-black boots, but when he heard Chen Yang, his countenance shifted. He lifted a hand to the money pouch at his belt. "Am I so poor?"

"We have too many expenses at the start of spring. The country estates are largely self-sufficient; they'll bring in some money. But most of the manors in Qudu sit empty. They were bestowed by the palace, so we can't rent them out, but we still have to arrange for their upkeep. Both the prince's manor and Plum Blossom Manor are permanent residences, and we employ three hundred or so people between them. The monthly salaries, monetary rewards, and—"

"And Ding Tao's candy allowance," Xiao Chiye added. "You eat an entire frontier reconnaissance squad's worth of rations each year. We've spoiled you rotten."

Ding Tao didn't dare make a fuss; he merely snatched up his little notebook and mumbled, "The princess consort gave special permission for it back at home..."

"You've grown up," Xiao Chiye said callously. "You don't need so much candy anymore. It's bad for your teeth."

"I'll hold off on calculating tonight's expenses for now." Chen Yang gripped the table, feeling a little dizzy from the numbers. "I'll finish tomorrow morning."

"A man's gotta spend to get things done!" Gu Jin said succinctly.

"Do a proper audit of the accounts for those country estates," ordered Xiao Chiye. "I hardly go there, and Dage is too busy to manage them on his end. Leave those subordinates unchecked too long, and they may start to get ideas." He took a long stride out, then turned back. "Calculate those expenses now! It won't be more than a couple thousand taels. There's...someone...managing this account."

Gu Jin watched him stalk away. "Who? Who in our household could be managing how our Er-gongzi spends his money?"

Chen Yang fetched the abacus back and flicked at it intently before muttering something noncommittal.

Ding Tao rubbed one boot against the other and leaned forward to whisper, "I know who it is."

Despite the extravagance of the preparations, not many officials were invited to the banquet. No court officials of the fourth rank and above escaped censure from the Chief Surveillance Bureau if they gathered for private feasts. Xiao Chiye was also the supreme commander of the Imperial Army, so to avoid any appearance of favoritism, he couldn't invite the important military officials who worked with him. The feast Cen Yu had held after the public ditches incident was also a private feast. On that occasion, he had first presented a memo to the Grand Secretariat, and it was only after Hai Liangyi had given his approval that Cen Yu invited his guests. This was how it was properly done. Even then, Kong Qiu, who had indulged to the point of inebriation, had been censured and made to sit through a lecture from Hai Liangyi after the fact.

The censors of the Chief Surveillance Bureau, as their title implied, were the grandmasters of remonstrance. They could rebuke the emperor at the top and denounce the lower officials at the bottom. Hai Liangyi himself might receive censure for any negligence: during the public ditches incident, Hai Liangyi, who had held the posts of the Grand Secretariat's Deputy Grand Secretary and Grand Secretary in succession, would've borne the blame if disease had spread. Even the emperor was not beyond their reach. In the beginning, when Li Jianheng had just ascended, he'd found the dragon throne in Mingli Hall so hard his buttocks ached if he sat for too long. He had griped about it to his attendants; only a few days later, he had received a diplomatic rebuke from the censors. To date, he had never dared bring up the matter of padding the throne again.

So Xiao Chiye could invite authorities neither political nor military, but he could invite nobles, or more specifically, the distinguished nobles. As long as a person was of hereditary noble rank, he invited them all. Most of these rich young masters with titles but no real power had someone in their family to fund them, so they could have all the fun they wanted with perfect peace of mind. Fei Shi was a prime example of such a man. His father was alive and in good health, and his elder sister was poised to marry a man from the Han Clan. He didn't have to worry about trivialities like meals and clothing. He wasn't a good student either; he'd barely learned anything. His only vocation was loafing around.

The moment Fei Shi stepped out of the sedan, he headed straight for Xiao Chiye, dragging Pan Lin behind him. "Your Lordship, congratulations!"

Xiao Chiye laughed. "I'm honored Your Little Lordship has graced me with your presence tonight. Please, drink to your heart's content."

Seeing how approachable he was, Fei Shi felt much more at ease. "Your Lordship is generous. I shall not leave sober tonight!"

Xiao Chiye turned a genial gaze on Pan Lin. "And Vice Minister Pan, please enjoy yourself too. Is your father Lord Pan feeling better these days?"

Pan Lin, whose heart had been in his mouth, relaxed and returned the greeting. "I thank Your Lordship for his concern. My father's health is much better. It's just that he feels ashamed in the face of His Majesty's graciousness; he's been facing the wall these days, reflecting on the error of his ways."

"Lord Pan is a veteran minister of three reigns." Xiao Chiye sighed with feeling. "He's a prudent man, and conscientious in his handling of state affairs. What a pity for him to have met with such unexpected misfortune."

Pan Lin had suffered setback after setback in recent days. He had pleaded with a great number of people to intercede on his family's behalf, that their sentences might be reduced. Other than the Fei Clan, who still had the heart to help them out, the others came up with all sorts of excuses to turn him away. Pan Lin had been born a legitimate descendant of a noble clan, and his career had been smooth sailing. It was only recently that he had gotten a taste of the real world and learned how fickle and hypocritical society could be. Xiao Chiye's words left him both surprised and greatly touched.

"My father..." Pan Lin seemed to choke up, then politely forced a smile. "Forget it. I'm here tonight to celebrate Your Lordship's happiness, so let's not speak of other things. Your Lordship, congratulations!"

"I'm blessed that His Majesty sees fit to shower kindness and favor upon me. All I did was crawl around in the mud. I can't compare to the vice minister and Lord Pan, who worry about the state all day long. Chen Yang," Xiao Chiye called over his shoulder, "invite His Lordship Fei and Vice Minister Pan onto the boat and serve them well."

Chen Yang bowed and led the pair onto the pleasure boat. One side of the ship's interior was draped with sheer curtains, and the sound of the pipa flowed into the night. The seats were arranged according to seniority; Chen Yang led them both to seats of honor. Everyone at this table was a descendant of the noble clans.

Pan Lin saw a few acquaintances but didn't greet them. Sensing the unfriendly atmosphere, Fei Shi stood at once to mediate.

"Why if it isn't Eldest Young Master Xue? What a rare sight!"

Xue Xiuyi was Xue Xiuzhuo's elder brother of lawful birth. He had neither talent nor intelligence, and had for years relied solely on his birth to trample Xue Xiuzhuo whenever possible. He was an ambitious man, and now, as he saw the Pan Clan on the decline, he had begun to give Pan Lin the cold shoulder.

"Hmph." Xue Xiuyi sipped his wine. "And how is the Little Lordship Fei doing?"

Fei Shi produced a fan and waved it a few times. "Me? Not too bad. What has the eldest young master been up to lately? You ought to come out and have some fun with us one of these days!"

Chin raised haughtily, Xue Xiuyi said, "I've been busy studying some books that are the only extant copy from the previous reign."

"My, my." Fei Shi smiled. "The eldest young master is a man of great achievements. So how is it that you have time today?"

All this while, Xue Xiuyi had turned his profile to them, unwilling to look Pan Lin in the eye. "I heard Yao Wenyu has returned to the capital. I thought I might see him here tonight, so I came. There are a few things I'd like to talk to him about."

Pan Lin had been tolerant of his attitude until now, but at these words, he sneered. "Hard to say if you'll ever get the chance. The queue of people wanting to pick Yuanzhuo's brain is lined up in order of their learning and accomplishments, and stretches from here to the Hongyan Mountains. I fear even if the eldest young master hangs around waiting all night; it's still far from your turn!"

The thing Xue Xiuyi could least tolerate was others making digs at him for his lack of talent and shallow knowledge. He slammed down his wine cup and said frostily, "Fine. Perhaps I'm not worthy, but at least I'm aware of my own limitations. I know whether or not I deserve to sit in this position!"

At this double-edged remark, Pan Lin surged to his feet.

Xue Xiuyi had a sharp tongue. He laughed mockingly when he saw Pan Lin's flushed face, but didn't let up. "Come now, Chengzhi, take a seat. Why aren't you sitting down? Are there nails on the chair? Everyone on the boat is looking at you. You're basking in glory tonight—your Pan Clan has indeed impressed everyone lately, even more than when you managed to sire a son!"

Pan Lin's first wife had died of illness, and his concubines' few pregnancies had all ended in miscarriages. Seeing that he was over thirty and still without a son, Old Madam Pan had abstained from meat and prayed to Buddha, searching high and low for prescriptions to increase her son's virility. The old madam shoved one woman after another into his bed in hopes of begetting a boy, making such a ruckus that everyone soon knew about it. All the wagging tongues of Qudu mocked Pan Lin behind his back for his unmentionable affliction.

Trembling with rage, Pan Lin jabbed a finger at Xue Xiuyi. "You, you..." He sputtered, so furious he was gasping for breath. "Who the hell do you think you are?! You let your brother of common birth beneath you take charge and manage your clan. You're just, just—dumb as an ox!"

Xue Xiuyi slapped the table and rose as well. "Shut up! You're a disgrace to the educated class! You don't know dogshit!"

"You're worse than a beast!" Pan Lin countered.

Caught in the middle, Fei Shi clutched his teacup as he was speckled with spittle. He closed his eyes and yelled, "What the hell?! Eldest Young Master, Chengzhi, stop! Why ruin a good banquet—"

"Don't you dare put me in the same category as him," snapped Xue Xiuyi. "He's a disgrace, not even worthy of carrying my shoes!"

Pan Lin looked left and right, then picked up his teacup and smashed it.

The table erupted into chaos. Fei Shi sat helpless as these young masters wrestled with each other with no regard for their dignity.

Xue Xiuyi rarely appeared in public. He was naturally frail, and had no skill in fistfights or boxing. It didn't take long for Pan Lin to shove him to the ground. Xue Xiuyi clutched his bruised side and wailed, "Ow, ow, ow! You dare to strike me, you—!"

With nothing left to smash, Pan Lin removed his shoe and swatted Xue Xiuyi's face. "I'm teaching you a lesson on behalf of Old Master Xue! Who the hell do you think you are? Someone ought to slap that foul mouth of yours!"

Voices rose around them. Dodging the shoe, Fei Shi cried, "Stop! Stop fighting! Men, men!"

Xiao Chiye lifted the curtain, his expression grave. Chen Yang led the guards to break the pair apart.

Xue Xiuyi had been smacked so hard there were red shoe prints on his cheek. He covered his face and stretched out a leg, still trying to kick Pan Lin. Straining his neck forward, he spat hatefully, "We aren't done yet. This isn't over!"

Pan Lin was a sorry sight as he came back to his senses; he had never intended to humiliate himself so in public. Avoiding all the eyes on him, he endured his misery and said resolutely, "Even if I, Pan Chengzhi, should starve to death in the future, I'll never sit at the same table as you, Xue Xiuyi! Even if our Pan Clan of Dancheng is on the verge of death, I'll never beg your Xue Clan for help!"

He tossed the shoe to the floor. When he raised his head, he didn't look at anyone but merely turned to Xiao Chiye, cupping his hands before his chest. "Your Lordship, please allow me to compensate you for spoiling the fun," he said, loud enough to carry. "I'll pay you back double for anything I've broken, and I'll even cover the expense of this entire Kailing River banquet. Your Lordship, please enjoy yourself tonight. I shall take my leave and call on you another day to offer my sincerest apologies."

He kicked off his other shoe. In nothing but white socks, he stepped over the mess on the ground and brushed past Fei Shi as he made his way out.

"Your Excellency, wait," Xiao Chiye said, unhurried. "Chen Yang, help the vice minister change his clothes."

"Right, right, Chengzhi!" Fei Shi chimed in. "Let's get your clothes changed first!"

When all was said and done, Pan Lin was a young master of a noble clan. His words might be unyielding, but if he really were to step out into the streets in such a state, the humiliation would be too great; death might be preferable. At the repeated urging of Chen Yang and Fei Shi, he relented and followed them.

Xiao Chiye turned to address Xue Xiuyi. "Eldest Young Master," he said, beckoning Gu Jin over with a finger. "You too."

INDIVIDUAL SERVINGS

P AN LIN WAS THE PICTURE of misery as he sat on the settee near the window in his fresh change of clothes. Guilt-ridden, Fei Shi sat before him and made several attempts to speak, only for the words to die on his lips.

"You don't have to say anything." Pan Lin stared out the window at the brilliantly lit courtyard of an old brothel on the riverbank. "It's just my luck to have run into a lowlife like him tonight."

"If you know he's a narrow-minded lowlife," Fei Shi said, "then why let him get to you like that? Chengzhi, he's not worth it."

Pan Lin barked out a self-deprecating laugh. "Has the Pan Clan fallen so far that I should forsake my integrity for a meal? If I have to sit there and allow him to mock me like that, I'd rather die."

Seeing him like this, Fei Shi began to realize the social snubbing from these last few days had genuinely hurt him. Fei Shi might be a spoiled young master, but he was an optimistic one. He reassured him, "As long as the green hills remain, one needn't worry about firewood—where there's life, there's hope. His Majesty hasn't even issued the edict yet! Chengzhi, didn't His Lordship say so too? Lord Pan is a veteran minister of three reigns. That still carries some weight in His Majesty's heart."

At that moment, Gu Jin lifted the curtain, and Xiao Chiye bent his head to enter. Fei Shi and Pan Lin rose as one to bow.

Xiao Chiye raised a hand. "Gentlemen, no need to stand on ceremony. Lord Pan, please take a seat."

Pan Lin sat and said solemnly, "Not only have I spoiled Your Lordship's fun tonight, I've also held Your Lordship up from enjoying his own feast. I deserve a beating."

Xiao Chiye didn't really mind, though he didn't rush to say so. Gu Jin served him tea, and he sat and took a few sips before speaking. "I've long heard of Your Excellency's talents, but never had the chance to strike up a conversation. It could be said fate and luck brought us together here tonight."

On hearing this, Fei Shi smiled and threw Pan Lin a speaking glance. Pan Lin hurriedly got up and bowed.

Xiao Chiye motioned for him to sit again. "I was the one who dredged the public ditches, so I'm intimately acquainted with this matter. The public ditches on Donglong Street were old and haphazard to begin with; they were dug long before Lord Pan took up his post as Minister of Works. Frankly, there are too many aspects of this incident that don't make sense. The blame for the flooding shouldn't fall entirely on Lord Pan."

Warmth surged in Pan Lin's heart. "A few years ago, my father specifically asked someone to draw up a plan for improvements. But that was back when the Zhongbo troops had suffered their defeat, and the state treasury was empty. The Ministry of Revenue refused to disburse the funds, so the plans had to be set aside." He heaved a sigh. "Who could've known!"

"To think there were such plans." Xiao Chiye covered the teacup with its lid. "But Wei Huaigu didn't mention a word of this before the emperor. Aren't your families on good terms?"

At Pan Lin's silence, Fei Shi hastened to say, "Your Lordship, it's obvious why Wei Huaigu's going all out to curry favor. He wants to climb the ranks. He's served so long, and he's finally qualified for a promotion just in time for the review this year. He's waiting for the reviews to be submitted so he can be promoted to Deputy Secretary; he plans to stand toe to toe with Secretariat Elder Hai on the imperial court in the future. No one expected the public ditches to clog so disastrously at this critical juncture. Of course he wishes to disassociate himself with the issue. He's not willing to shoulder the responsibility in the slightest."

"Is that so." Xiao Chiye's face showed mild surprise. "I've noticed the accounts of the Ministry of Revenue seem to have been in good order the past few years; I really thought Wei Huaigu deserved a promotion. To think he'd turn out to be such a vile person who so shamelessly seeks personal gain? Lord Pan's situation is truly unfortunate."

Fei Shi couldn't miss the note of regret in his words. He plucked up his courage and said, "Everyone's been tight-lipped lately. Your Lordship, Chengzhi and I have asked a number of people, but no one will say what punishment His Majesty has agreed upon for Lord Pan with the Ministry of Justice. If His Excellency were to be sentenced...would he be assigned out of Qudu?"

Heart racing, Pan Lin looked at Xiao Chiye.

Xiao Chiye gave his thumb ring a few turns. Only when he had them on the edges of their seats did he speak. "It's hard to say. His Majesty seems to be hesitating."

"As long as the imperial edict hasn't been issued," Fei Shi said, "there's still a chance to turn things around. Your Lordship is now a true official in the Son of Heaven's inner circle! I hope Your Lordship can put in a few good words with His Majesty regarding this issue."

"I won't put in a good word for Lord Pan." Seeing their faces fall, Xiao Chiye continued smoothly, "I'll only speak the truth. His Excellency is a talented minister and has made great contributions to the state. Even if he's committed a minor blunder, it doesn't merit execution—or banishment. I'll speak to His Majesty again tomorrow. If all goes well, the pardon will arrive at your residence within the week."

The rims of Pan Lin's eyes were red with emotion when he stood. He didn't dare overstep and touch Xiao Chiye, so he grasped his own sleeves and dropped to his knees as though transplanting rice seedlings. "Many thanks—*many* thanks to Your Lordship for saving our lives!"

"Gu Jin, quickly, help the vice minister up," Xiao Chiye said with a smile. "I'm only doing what's right. There's no need for Your Excellency to take it too much to heart. When you return today, tell Lord Pan to rest well. He's still needed for plenty of state and governmental affairs in the future."

Fei Shi, who was frank by nature, said, "If there's anything we can do for Your Lordship in the future, just say the word! Chengzhi, let's go. We must head back and tell His Excellency the good news!"

Pan Lin thanked Xiao Chiye again and said sincerely, "Please let me know if I can be of assistance to Your Lordship in the future. Libei is too far; I'm afraid I won't be of much assistance to you there. But as long as it's in Qudu, Your Lordship only needs speak and I, Pan Chengzhi, will do my utmost!"

"Please, we're all friends here," Xiao Chiye said. "You mentioned earlier that Lord Pan had found someone to draw up plans for the public ditches a few years ago. It just so happens that I've been worrying about those repairs myself. Could I trouble you to ask Lord Pan if he could lend me the plans for a look?"

"There's no need to ask. I'll send someone to deliver them to Your Lordship's manor the moment I return home," Pan Lin said.

Xiao Chiye offered a few more comforting words, then watched as Gu Jin saw them off the boat. He listened to the music of reed pipes for a moment before turning back to Ding Tao. "Tell the cook to go ahead and dish up whatever you like. Once you've eaten, prepare some sweet and spicy dishes, then get the cook to grill some fish and deliver it to your Shen-gongzi. Do it quietly."

Ding Tao ran off, notebook bouncing in his little bag. Chen Yang stepped up to Xiao Chiye's shoulder and murmured, "Master, Xue Xiuyi won't stay put for long; he's still waiting to see Yao Wenyu. Are we going over?"

"Yes. Of course we are." Xiao Chiye looked back with eyes like chips of ice. "Xue Xiuzhuo used the Quancheng silk to plant a trap for me. I owe him one. Tell the attendants to open a few more jars of good wine. Xue Xiuyi is of great use to us."

The Imperial Prison, under the charge of Kong Qiu, was strictly monitored. No information made its way to Xi Hongxuan, and he couldn't get a word out. He had been neatly cut off from the world, and the longer he waited, the more anxious he became.

One night, he woke and found himself in isolation; he had been moved into a windowless room as he slept. Xi Hongxuan was an obese man; he couldn't squat down to the slit at the bottom of the door. All he could do was bend over and call out through the gap to the warden delivering his food, "What's happened? Sir! Boss! At least tell me *something*."

That warden paid him no mind as he shoved rancid rice and leftover soup through the flap and left.

"Hey, buddy, please hang on!" Xi Hongxuan raised his voice. "I still have some silver in my pocket. You've been working so hard these past few days, why not take it to buy some wine? Consider it a show of my respect for you!"

The warden turned back and spat at him.

Snubbed, Xi Hongxuan sagged back on the straw mat in a daze, leaving his meal untouched. He had barely slept in these days of waiting. He turned his circumstances over and over in his mind, but he didn't know where he had gone wrong. As time stretched in the darkness, so too did his uncertainty. This kind of powerlessness was simply too much to bear.

This room was damp, with no ducts to admit air and no windows to admit light. As someone who disdained sleeping on even bamboo mats for the way they pinched his skin, his current predicament was pure torture. Moreover, rashes had broken out on his back, but he couldn't reach to scratch them.

It seemed like years later when Xi Hongxuan heard movement at the entrance. The door creaked open, and Shen Zechuan strode in. Behind him, Qiao Tianya, disguised as a stoic-faced young man, lit the lamp.

Xi Hongxuan struggled to get his legs under him. "What's going on? Why am I locked up in here? Was this Kong Qiu's idea? I've never heard of such a room in this prison!"

"It's not like you're a veteran convict; it's no surprise you don't know about this place." Shen Zechuan pulled off his cloak and handed it back to Qiao Tianya. "Come; the food here isn't fit for human consumption. I've had some dishes specially prepared. Eat, and we'll talk."

Cloak draped over one arm, Qiao Tianya opened the food box with the other and served up the delicacies they had bought on the way over.

Xi Hongxuan sat on the straw mat and watched Qiao Tianya's movements in silence. He let out a burst of laughter, and his expression grew cold. "This looks like a last meal."

"This case doesn't merit a death sentence; why scare yourself?" Shen Zechuan sat on the bench Qiao Tianya had dusted clean.

When he noticed Xi Hongxuan hadn't moved his chopsticks, he gestured for Qiao Tianya to produce another pair. He picked a few dishes for himself to eat before sampling a mouthful of the wine.

Finally, Xi Hongxuan reached for the food.

Shen Zechuan set down his chopsticks and watched him, smiling. "We are brothers. Must you be so guarded against me?"

Xi Hongxuan picked up a steamed twisted roll and gobbled it down. Only after his hunger pangs subsided did he reply. "It's an unusual time. If you were in my shoes, wouldn't you do the same? How did it go with the business we spoke of before? Have you seen Xi Dan?"

Finishing the wine in his cup, Shen Zechuan nodded to Qiao Tianya, who opened the door and led in another man.

"Second Master!" Xi Dan nearly pounced on Xi Hongxuan; as soon as he got a look at him, he lowered his head and wept. "You've suffered!"

Steadying his hand, Xi Hongxuan drank the last drop of his wine and said, "Oh, get up! Don't make a fool of yourself! It's not time for me to meet my maker yet!"

"During these last few days," said Xi Dan, wiping his face, "since the second master wasn't home, I've instructed the shopkeepers to manage their accounts carefully. I'm keeping a close eye on them. But you're the pillar of our clan; our businesses can't run without you."

Xi Hongxuan ate his food in silence. After a long while, he said, "Tell me what's going on out there."

"His Majesty wants to assign responsibility for the ditches incident, but neither the Ministry of Revenue nor the Ministry of Works will shoulder the blame," Xi Dan replied. "Pan Xiangjie is suspended, and has already received a flogging. When I saw the direction things were headed, I went to plead with Lord Xue myself. But he's busy with his official duties; I didn't manage to get to see him at all!"

"Yanqing wouldn't see you?" Xi Hongxuan threw his chopsticks down and looked at Xi Dan through narrowed eyes. "Are you telling the truth?"

In the face of his disbelief, Xi Dan rushed to assure him. "Second Master, why would I lie about this? To find out the truth, you'd only have to ask him yourself as soon as you're released! I wouldn't dare speak falsely! Hasn't His Majesty just issued a general amnesty? The Court of Judicial Review is working with the Ministry of Justice to delve through all the old cases. Lord Xue is neck-deep in the files with Kong Qiu and the others. I didn't dare to stop his sedan chair, so I never got a chance to meet him."

It was only when Xi Dan explained it this way that Xi Hongxuan was inclined to believe him. "What rotten luck to be framed with this kind of timing. Lanzhou, who instigated His Majesty to leave the palace? Is there still no update regarding this?"

"There are only so many people around His Majesty, we need only to go down the list," Shen Zechuan said. "But it's obvious His Majesty is reluctant to allow any investigation. He's trying to protect the other party."

"Mu Ru is the only one His Majesty would go this far for." Xi Hongxuan clenched his fists. "Whores like her are ruthless. She must have had some reason for it. You have to be careful. She'd better not have an imperial heir in her belly and be planning to play regent from behind the screen!"

"Since she's in Xue Xiuzhuo's camp, I doubt she'll conceive so easily." After a moment, Shen Zechuan reminded him, "Your transfer to the Bureau of Evaluations was Xue Xiuzhuo's idea as well. If it's indeed the case that Mu Ru means you harm…what is Xue Xiuzhuo thinking? I don't get it."

On the day Xi Hongxuan abducted Qi Huilian, Shen Zechuan had likewise mentioned that it was Xue Xiuzhuo's idea for him to enter the Bureau of Evaluations. Half a month later, the implication of his words had taken on a different undertone.

Xi Hongxuan pondered a while. "Let's set these matters aside for now. Lanzhou, our first priority is to get me out of here. What did Wei Huaigu say? How much does he want? Whatever it is, I'll give it to him!"

Shen Zechuan held up four fingers.

"Four hundred thousand?"

Shen Zechuan didn't move.

"Four *million*?!" Bracing himself on the table, Xi Hongxuan rose to his feet. The dishes and bowls slid and clattered. Xi Hongxuan's expression was ghastly under the lamplight. He flung the wine cup down and seethed, "Good one, Wei Huaigu—well-played, Wei Clan! So, four million…"

He began to laugh grimly. "This is the total military expenditure of Great Zhou; it's almost as much as the cost of rebuilding Zhongbo! That's so much money. Fuck. How does he think he's going to move a mountain of silver? Transporting it from the west, even in batches, would take half a year! And it'll cost extra to convince people at each of the passes and checkpoints when the money is crossing territory borders! Even if the silver actually gets to Qudu, where will he store it? There's simply no way to hide this much money!"

Shen Zechuan shrugged. "What he's doing now is ripping you off by making such an exorbitant demand. What does he care about the logistics? The Embroidered Uniform Guard has heard news that the

Wei Clan has its sights set on Zhongbo. Think about it. Wei Huaigu controls the Ministry of Revenue. If he manages to take control of the six prefectures of Zhongbo as well, then this sum really will be used on military expenses. When the Wei Clan has their own troops—with the backing of the empress dowager—then the Xi Clan will be at their mercy."

Xi Hongxuan whipped his head around to look at Shen Zechuan. "When you advised me to join forces with the rest of the Eight Great Clans back then, did you ever think this would happen? Lanzhou! These people are vicious beasts one and all; their greed knows no bounds. The moment they have us in their clutches, you and I will never get back on our feet again!"

"Back then, when I advised you to join forces and kick out the Yao Clan, you hesitated," Shen Zechuan reminded him. "The Yao Clan was a good target; you could have made an example of them. Since you missed that chance, the situation you're in today was only to be expected. Xi Hongxuan, if you don't make them bleed, they'll think of ways to cut you out." Shen Zechuan's tone turned sorrowful. "The situation is changing rapidly. It's unlike days gone by, when everyone could still talk reason. Within the Eight Great Clans, one clan will rise when another falls—it's a wearing down from within. You should have already swallowed up the others and declared yourself the victor."

Xi Hongxuan's breathing quickened. He did regret his past inaction. His palms were drenched in sweat as he faced the flickering candlelight. "Lanzhou—when I get out of here, I swear I'll heed your advice in all future plans! But it's already come to this; we have to think of a way to get the four million first..."

"Four million is too much," Shen Zechuan said. "There's simply no way for that much money to pass through Juexi without drawing

Jiang Qingshan's eyes. Wait a little longer. I will negotiate with Wei Huaigu."

At this point, waiting was his only option. Suppressing his impatience, Xi Hongxuan said, "We have to hurry. The situation in the imperial court changes by the day. His Majesty is indecisive; he has no mind of his own. The moment Xiao Er or Mu Ru wins him over, it'll be too late."

Shen Zechuan couldn't stay long. As he swept his cloak over his shoulders, he asked, as if as an afterthought, "That's right. If you're in prison, then what about Qi Huilian? He's important too; we can't let anyone see him."

Xi Hongxuan parted his lips to speak but seemed to change his mind a breath later. He said, his voice soothing, "Don't you worry; Qi Huilian won't starve to death. I've found someone to watch over him, and the place is well-concealed. I'll return him to you once I'm out of here."

In the soft darkness, Shen Zechuan turned slightly to glance over his shoulder, the sliver of a smile curving the corners of his eyes. He fastened his cloak and said softly, "Sure thing."

A cold draft blew through the open door, making the hair on Xi Hongxuan's neck stand on end. He rubbed at his arms, thinking to say a few words more to reassure Shen Zechuan. But the man was already gone.

CLUES

>>> ———————— ✦ ❀ ✦ ———————— <<<

A CACOPHONY OF HUMAN voices drifted over the Kailing
River. Xue Xiuyi sat cross-legged on the settee, cracking
peanut shells and drinking wine. When Xiao Chiye entered, he hurried to brush his robe clean and stood to pay his respects.

Xiao Chiye sank into the chair across from Xue Xiuyi as Chen
Yang stepped forward to pour wine for them both. Xue Xiuyi kept
his fingers pressed to his sides, nervously wiping his hands on
his robe. "That's enough, that's quite enough, thank you—Your
Lordship, too much wine is bad for your health!"

Cup in hand, Xiao Chiye smiled. "The eldest young master is
conscientious. You must be diligent about your health at home."

"Only a little." Xue Xiuyi didn't dare sit back down without permission. He was short and slight to begin with, and with his back
still hunched in a bow, he appeared all the more humble and lowly
before Xiao Chiye.

"Please sit," Xiao Chiye said pleasantly. "I'd like to seek the eldest
young master's advice."

Perched at the edge of the settee, Xue Xiuyi demurred, "I wouldn't
dare presume to offer any."

Just from the look of him, Xiao Chiye could see that Xue Xiuyi
was poles apart from his brother Xue Xiuzhuo. If Xue Xiuzhuo had

to defer to an elder brother like this, of course he wouldn't take it lying down.

"It's been some time since I last saw Lord Yanqing." Xiao Chiye paused to drink his wine. "I hear he's been busy investigating cases with Minister Kong. I imagine it's been hard on him."

"He's only basking in glory now because the secretariat elder promoted him." Xue Xiuyi had long disliked Xue Xiuzhuo; he had made things as difficult as possible for this common-born brother of his, but regrettably, striking Xue Xiuzhuo had always been like striking cotton: absorbing any damage and bringing all Xue Xiuyi's efforts to naught.

"He's the eldest young master's younger brother of common birth. According to custom, the one leading the way in joining the ranks of court officials should be the eldest young master. Yet it seems to be the other way around in your household."

Xue Xiuyi had accepted the wine Chen Yang poured, not daring to refuse it. After a few cups, his sense of propriety began to slip; he could feel the earth spinning under his feet. He gripped his cup harder and snorted. "Well, he's just that capable, no? Your Lordship wouldn't know, but ever since he was a child, he's always been the type to ingratiate himself with those in power. He's always been a shrewd one! There was heavy snow the year he was born. Alongside our generation name, Xiu, he was supposed to be named Gui, promising a life of wealth and prestige. But a Daoist priest predicted he would meet a prestigious benefactor in his lifetime, and his name would hinder that destiny. His birth mother was a resourceful woman who fawned upon the old master of our clan in every way. She pleaded for him to be named Zhuo—*excellent*—instead, to signify the cultivation of virtues and outstanding capabilities, with the courtesy name Yanqing, suggesting fairness and purity. He sure lives a charmed life..."

Xue Xiuyi's eyes dimmed as he spoke; by the end, his expression was grim.

"Eldest Young Master, why contend with him?" Xiao Chiye said kindly. "You're the lawful heir of the Xue Clan; you're far more esteemed."

His words had struck a nerve. Xue Xiuyi set down his cup and heaved a long sigh. "Your Lordship..." This deep in his cups, Xue Xiuyi grew bolder. "You're the second lawful son of the Prince of Libei, with no son of common birth to pose a threat to you. You don't know what it's like. People like us fear having a capable younger brother like him back home—he's of lowly birth, yet he's somehow a notch above me. Whether it's at home or outside it, who doesn't praise him to the skies? How can I hold my head up like this? Look at the Eight Great Clans—which of them has a son of common birth at the helm? How is it only the Xue Clan that's produced a Xue Xiuzhuo?!"

It was because of Xue Xiuyi's own selfishness that he so detested Xue Xiuzhuo. But it was because of Xue Xiuzhuo that the Xue Clan had made a comeback in recent years and secured its position among the Eight Great Clans. The lawful sons born to the principal wives of the Xue Clan numbered in the hundreds, and beneath them were the countless common sons of concubines. All expenses for momentous family occasions—marriages and funerals, monthly salaries and monetary rewards, expenses for living in separate manors, as well as taxes and sundries for the country estates—flowed from the Xue Clan's coffers.

Initially, Old Master Xue had planned to prop Xue Xiuyi up and let this eldest son of lawful birth take charge of managing family affairs. But Xue Xiuyi was either too engrossed in cultivating the mystical path to immortality or busy lavishing money on undeserving impostors and swindlers. It was precisely as the empress dowager had once said: the current generation of the Xue Clan was a worthless lot. Other than the common-born Xue Xiuzhuo, no one else was worthy of notice.

Xue Xiuzhuo presently held the position of Assistant Minister in the Court of Judicial Review as well as acting as head of the Xue Clan. In just a few years, he had managed to halt the family's decline and help it find its footing among the noble clans. He had plenty of brothers at home who loafed around and contributed nothing, as well as both paternal and maternal uncles who spent their days devising schemes to cheat the clan of its money. All of them lived off Xue Xiuzhuo even as they spat on him, shamelessly reaping the benefits of his efforts while cursing him as lowborn.

Xiao Chiye knew all of this already. He and Shen Zechuan were of the same opinion: if not for their uncertainty regarding Xue Xiuzhuo's loyalties, who had all along been hiding behind the noble clans, they—valuing talent—would have tried to recruit him to their camp. The Quancheng silk incident was the crux. It had altered Shen Zechuan's opinion of Xue Xiuzhuo and turned him into a person they must guard against: a man astute enough to tie thousands of puppet strings as precautions, long before events were set in motion, was unlikely to put himself at the disposal of another.

Running his fingers along the rim of his cup, Xiao Chiye considered. "Everyone has times when they're down on their luck. The eldest young master oughtn't be too anxious over it. In any case, Xue Xiuzhuo appears to be acquitting himself well beside the secretariat elder and Minister Kong. He's not known to drink or fool around either; he's a decent man who knows his place."

Xue Xiuyi immediately grew agitated. He fell into wine-induced hiccups and had to cover his mouth to compose himself before blurting out, "That's all just an act! Your Lordship, you know of the Twin Flowers of Donglong Street, right? Ouhua Pavilion and Xiangyun Villa! Well, a few years ago, Xue Xiuzhuo bought a bunch of young men and women from Xiangyun Villa and hid them in our manor to train up!"

Xiao Chiye's gaze sharpened at the mention of Xiangyun Villa, and he lowered his voice. "Xue Xiuzhuo bought people from Xiangyun Villa?"

"He did!" Xue Xiuyi held up ten swaying fingers. "He bought more than this many...boys...and girls... All from Xiangyun Villa!"

After a moment of silence, Xiao Chiye rose. "Chen Yang, keep the eldest young master company. I'm expecting Yao Wenyu to arrive any moment. I'll go welcome him."

Xue Xiuyi sat straight up at the mention of Yao Wenyu's name and stuttered his agreement, not daring to pester His Lordship any further.

As soon as Xiao Chiye stepped out the door, he shouted, "Gu Jin!"

Gu Jin dropped down from his station on the roof and went to one knee. "Er-gongzi!"

"When I told you to investigate Xiangyun Villa before, how could you miss that Xiangyun sold over ten people to the Xue Clan?"

Stunned, Gu Jin didn't dare to raise his head. "I beseech Gongzi to punish me!"

During the assassination case, Xiangyun had betrayed Xiao Chiye and provided false testimony that he'd accepted bribes. The entire incident remained strange; to date, their investigations had uncovered nothing explaining why Xiangyun would suddenly throw Xiao Chiye over for the noble clans. Xue Xiuzhuo was no lecher, yet he'd bought so many people from Xiangyun Villa and hidden them in his manor without anyone the wiser. What secret lay buried there?

Shen Zechuan was right.

Even when Xue Xiuzhuo wasn't directly involved, his name appeared in every incident since the Nanlin Hunting Grounds— perhaps even in everything that happened before that pivotal night.

"No shit you should be punished. You've been drinking since we arrived in the capital. Have you crawled so deep in that jug those sharp eyes of yours have gone blind? Incompetence and dereliction of duty—no doubt you should be punished for both. Go ask Chen Yang for a whipping yourself!"

Gu Jin began sweating profusely.

Xiao Chiye had entrusted Gu Jin with this job because he appreciated the man's meticulousness; Gu Jin was by far the most skilled at this kind of reconnaissance work. As a former scout in the Libei Armored Cavalry, he had never made such a blunder. What Xiao Chiye said was true: Gu Jin had stayed in Qudu too long and taken his duties too lightly.

"I'll give you two days to get to the bottom of this. I want the number of people Xiangyun sold to Xue Xiuzhuo, their names, places of birth, ages; I want to know who their parents and distant relatives are." Xiao Chiye strode past him and said in frosty tones, "One more oversight like this and you needn't remain in this position."

Gu Jin kowtowed silently, then rose to his feet and streaked off toward Xiangyun Villa.

When Chen Yang, finally freed of entertaining Xue Xiuyi, came out, he saw Xiao Chiye's dark expression. Hoping he was delivering better news, he said, "Master, Xue Xiuyi is taking a rest."

"Get someone to escort him home tomorrow morning." Xiao Chiye turned and cast a glance back into the room. "There's a set of rare books in Plum Blossom Manor. Send someone to fetch them; you can give them to him on his way out."

"Those are part of the Yao Clan's collection," Chen Yang reminded him. "Should we inform Yao-gongzi?"

"Yao Wenyu sold Plum Blossom Manor to me with everything in it; he's already decided he doesn't want them. He spends most of the year out traveling in foreign lands; he's not worried about these dusty old books." Xiao Chiye'd had more than a few cups tonight, but he didn't seem drunk. He tossed aside the handkerchief he'd used to wipe his hands. "Besides, even if he returns to the capital, he's elusive; it's hard to catch even a glimpse of him. There's no way he'd attend a banquet like this. He is not an easy man to pin down."

"If Yao-gongzi hadn't declined to join the ranks of officials in the imperial court, I fear Xue Xiuzhuo wouldn't have had a chance to shine as he has."

Xiao Chiye's look of displeasure hadn't eased. "The turbulence of politics can't be equated with engagement with academia. Yao Wenyu might not necessarily fare any better in court than Xue Xiuzhuo. They're an interesting pair—opposites in every way."

"When all's said and done, Yao Wenyu is Secretariat Elder Hai's student. If Xue Xiuzhuo is a traveler of the secular world, Yao-gongzi is an immortal who transcends it." Chen Yang pondered this. "But Secretariat Elder Hai appears to cherish Yao-gongzi all the more for it."

"You're right. Hai Liangyi imparts his knowledge to Yao Wenyu without reservation. He didn't hesitate to break his own prejudices with regard to the noble clans to accept him as his student. This alone shows how he values him. Xue Xiuzhuo's political achievements are enviable, yet Hai Liangyi still won't afford him the dignity of accepting him as his official student. And what's more, in all these years, Hai Liangyi never made the slightest attempt to force Yao Wenyu into politics."

Xiao Chiye sighed and continued. "Yuanzhuo, Yuanzhuo—
a precious stone in its primordial form. It was out of fatherly love
that Hai Liangyi bestowed this courtesy name on Yao Wenyu. Such
closeness between teacher and pupil is not something anyone can
compete with. Yao Wenyu is a young master of a noble clan, directly
descended," he pointed out to Chen Yang. "Going by their logic,
he's even more legitimate than those so-called 'legitimate heirs' of
the Pan, Fei, and Xue Clans. The Yao Clan is righteous and distinguished. In the past, even the eligible young ladies of the Hua
Clan found it hard to marry into this clan. By Yao Wenyu's time,
mountains of gold and silver cannot compare to the wonder of a
bowl of wild vegetables."

Chen Yang had seen Yao Wenyu only a handful of times. Even
when he bought the estate, he had but one brief encounter with him.
He remembered the man as a scholar with nothing on him but a
book pouch who shunned horses and sedans, and instead kept a
donkey.

"Is Ding Tao back?" Xiao Chiye asked abruptly.

"...He hasn't left yet."

"Let him play." Xiao Chiye strode into his own room and traded
the brocade robe he was wearing for a set of casual clothes. "The
banquet has gone on long enough, and I've already shared a toast
with all those with whom I ought to keep company. There're still a
few hours before daybreak. I'll be back soon."

Shen Zechuan stepped out of the alleyway, and Xi Dan followed;
he didn't dare overtake Shen Zechuan and so simply stood behind
him awaiting orders, his head lowered.

After looking him over for some time, Shen Zechuan said, unexpectedly gentle, "You spoke well tonight."

Xi Dan hastily bowed. "It is this lowly one's greatest aspiration to help Your Excellency out of any frustration or difficulty."

"Xi Hongxuan is suspicious by nature; we won't trick him out of real cash with a few words," Shen Zechuan commented. "Are you familiar with his businesses across all the various regions?"

"Yes, yes, I am!" Xi Dan nodded. "His accounts, large or small, are always sent to his estate in Qudu each month. The sixty-eight shopkeepers under him are all sons of domestic servants; the lives of the parents, wives, and children of these people are all in his hands. They were raised specifically to manage his businesses. They can't hide any activity in the storefronts from his eyes, no matter how minor; he knows the score. That's why his business empire has run so smoothly all these years."

"If Xi Hongxuan wants to withdraw these four million taels, he must hand you the key and instruct you to take the money from the vault," Shen Zechuan said. "My only question is: How will the money be transferred?"

Xi Dan made a few mental calculations. "It's true that there's a huge risk traveling overland. The carts must contain some cargo as a front to conceal the silver. This is four million taels we're talking about. Without a long-standing business to serve as cover, Jiang Qingshan, the Provincial Administration Commissioner of Juexi, will see through it in an instant. And Your Excellency, if we travel by land, we must first pass through the thirteen cities of Juexi, followed by Dicheng. These are all difficult checkpoints. Most importantly, Xi Hongxuan is right; there's no place in Qudu that could conceal this sum of money."

These were silver ingots they were discussing, not paper notes. Even if one had a vacant courtyard in which to hoard them, it wouldn't likely be able to accommodate the full four million. On top of that, there was the headache of spending this much money once it was in hand.

Shen Zechuan considered as he looked into the night. "This sum will not enter Qudu."

Xi Dan didn't dare make a sound, waiting for Shen Zechuan to continue.

Sure enough, he did. "The shipment will be subjected to inspections in Juexi whether it is transported by land or sea. Four million is too large a sum. Even if we're thorough in our planning and hide the shipment from prying eyes, we can't count on every man who carries out our orders to be so meticulous. And it's all pointless if the money can't be spent when it comes. No, this money won't reach Qudu."

"What Your Excellency means..." trying to follow the line of Shen Zechuan's thoughts, Xi Dan ventured, "is that we should trick the money out of him, keep it where it is, and circulate it through trading?"

"Half of it will be handed to you to do just that," Shen Zechuan said. "I'll come up with something for the other half. Be prepared. The Xi Clan's businesses are extensive, and they can't operate without a manager. When Xi Hongxuan falls, you'll be next in line."

Xi Dan swiftly agreed.

Shen Zechuan climbed into the waiting carriage alone. He still had to return to the Imperial Prison to sift through the files of all the cold cases within the last two decades for clues, and didn't have time to go home and sleep.

When the horse carriage reached the Imperial Prison, Ge Qingqing, who was on night patrol, had given the order to open the gates and waited for Qiao Tianya to drive in. As Shen Zechuan stepped down, Ge Qingqing came closer and whispered, "His Lordship the marquis is here."

Shen Zechuan reached for the clasp of his overcoat as he strode onto the front porch and nodded toward Ge Qingqing, who took his leave. Pulling the coat off, he draped it over his arm and pushed open the door.

Xiao Chiye had spent the evening indulging in wine, and the scent of alcohol lingered on him even after a change of clothes. He slumped in Shen Zechuan's chair, an open book covering his face. At the sound of the door, he lifted the book but didn't move.

"Come sit here." Xiao Chiye tossed the book onto the table.

Shen Zechuan shut the door behind him and hung his coat on the rack, unfastening more clasps at his throat as he went. Meeting Xiao Chiye's gaze, he swung one leg over Xiao Chiye's thighs, looking him in the eye as he shifted closer. Xiao Chiye reached out to wrap his arms around Shen Zechuan's waist, their soft lips meeting as they kissed to their hearts' content.

80

BRIDE PRICE

❯❯❯ ———◆——— ✿ ———◆——— ❰❰❰

THIS PASSIONATE EMBRACE lasted a long time, kisses heating up, a taste of the forbidden fruit that awakened an insatiable hunger for more. They were accustomed to testing each other's limits in the dark. As their affection deepened, a kiss was no longer sufficient to settle them. Desire, primal and raw in the primes of their lives, was laid bare between them. Such cloying and clingy intimacy was a gift unique to lovers, since it was a rare luxury to share each other's company without a moment apart. With so many eyes and ears in the Imperial Prison, this kiss was unspoken compensation for all the time they lost.

When they broke apart, Xiao Chiye asked, "Where did you go?"

Shen Zechuan settled into Xiao Chiye's lap, his thighs grinding against Xiao Chiye's. He took his time to slow his breathing, and with a hint of seduction in his half-lidded eyes, replied, "Counting money."

Xiao Chiye pinched him. "Do you get off on counting money?"

Shen Zechuan let out a husky laugh. "I get off on being pinched by you."

The sound of that laugh made Xiao Chiye restless. He grabbed Shen Zechuan's chin with one hand to hold it in place. "Keep going with this seduction of yours."

Shen Zechuan's collarbones peeked out from his loosened collars, and the stark bite marks from their last assignation had yet to fade. Paying them no mind, Shen Zechuan wet his bitten lips with his tongue. "I have something to discuss with you."

Xiao Chiye pulled him up against him. "What a coincidence. I have something to discuss with you too."

Shen Zechuan's mouth went dry under the heat of Xiao Chiye's gaze. He had to swallow before he could say, "Libei's military supplies for this year will have to wait until the fourth month to be dispatched from Juexi. I need to borrow the Northeast Provisions Trail."

It took only a moment of thought for Xiao Chiye to see what he was up to. "Supplies shipped via the Northeast Provisions Trail are personally escorted by the Libei Armored Cavalry. There are no inspection checkpoints along the way. You can use it to transport the silver, but it'll be subject to my brother's approval."

"If the money belongs to me, the Heir of Libei won't agree to it. But if this sum of money is yours, he surely will." Shen Zechuan raised his chin slightly in Xiao Chiye's hold. "Consider this a bride price. Hold onto it for me, Er-gongzi."

"Only that for a bride price?" Xiao Chiye laughed as he freed up one hand to pull the meal box on the table closer. "I'll have to think about it."

Shen Zechuan sniffed. "There's grilled fish."

He promptly forgot all about bride prices and pulled the chopsticks from the box with single-minded focus. Xiao Chiye watched as he ate. In the blink of an eye, the bowl of rice was half gone, and there were only bones left of the fish when it returned to the plate.

Xiao Chiye didn't care for fish. He'd lost his mother at a young age, and his family, unlike the Eight Great Clans, wasn't one to spoil their children. Although he'd had a nanny and maidservants to see to his needs, he had been left to feed himself as soon as he learned to hold his chopsticks. He was a spirited child, and there were plenty of toys he'd rather play with than waste his time picking out fish bones. After choking on them enough times, he had lost all taste for the dish.

"Is it good?" Xiao Chiye asked, eyes still on him. "Apparently, the chef is from Hezhou, and even harder to hire than the chefs in the palace."

Shen Zechuan's chopsticks nimbly picked out the bones and fed Xiao Chiye the cleaned flesh. Xiao Chiye tasted it and gave his critique: "Passable."

Having eaten his fill, Shen Zechuan set down his bowl. "What did you want to discuss with me?"

Xiao Chiye handed him a handkerchief. "Our earlier investigation of Xiangyun missed a key piece of information. A few years ago, Xue Xiuzhuo bought a group of people from Xiangyun Villa and kept them in his manor. I'm afraid not even Xi Hongxuan knows about this."

As expected, a shift came over Shen Zechuan's expression. "Xue Xiuzhuo's not the type to keep private prostitutes. He usually keeps his distance even in Ouhua Pavilion. His behavior is far from normal."

"I agree, it's strange." Xiao Chiye leaned back in his chair. "I have a hunch this has something to do with Xiangyun's false testimony."

"But if this is true, he bought them years ago." Shen Zechuan furrowed his brow. "If this was a means to bring Xiangyun under his control, then this move was planned *very* far in advance."

"Why would this give him leverage over Xiangyun? If placed too early, some pawns won't stand the test of time. I have a feeling

he didn't make such a move solely to get a handle on Xiangyun."
Xiao Chiye cocked his head, sorting out his reasoning. "He couldn't
have predicted you plotting the assassination attempt. Any subsequent developments would've been hard for him to guard against."

Xiao Chiye picked through this tangle of strings, one at a time.
His wolfish intuition told him this matter wasn't so simple.

"Improvisation." Shen Zechuan cupped Xiao Chiye's face and
eased it upright. "You're right. The puppet string tied to Xiangyun
wasn't specifically intended to deal with you. Her perjury in the
assassination case was merely an opportunity seized. That he could
so readily throw Xiangyun under the wheels shows she was of little
significance. There's some other reason he bought those people;
Xiangyun was merely a convenient pawn that came with it. What's
more, she's a pawn he couldn't wait to discard."

Xiao Chiye was just a step behind. "Then, the key to understanding his purchase of those people lies—"

"—in the group of people he bought," Shen Zechuan finished softly.

They looked at each other, caught yet again in a labyrinth of
unknowns. Xiangyun Villa was a brothel. Who there could be of
such great importance to Xue Xiuzhuo?

"He bought over ten people to obscure the truth—there's no
knowing who among them was his intended purchase. I doubt even
Xiangyun herself knows," Xiao Chiye said. "I need to convince Xue
Xiuyi to probe into this again. His status in the Xue Manor allows
him free access to the estate. Xue Xiuzhuo might deny entry to
outsiders, but he can't refuse his own brother."

This piece of information was critical, but at present, Shen
Zechuan could make neither heads nor tails of it. Part of the reason
he had moved on Xi Hongxuan now was out of apprehension about
Xue Xiuzhuo, who already had Xi Hongxuan dancing to his tune.

Rather than becoming more clear and decipherable with the passage of time, this person had, contrariwise, become increasingly obscure and unreadable.

"There's still time." Shen Zechuan seemed to be thinking aloud. "The moment we get overly anxious and begin to second-guess ourselves, it'll cost us any advantage we have. If he hasn't made his move, it must mean the time is not right yet—this is an opportunity we can exploit. Right now, we're the ones moving in the shadows, while he's out in the open. We stand to learn some crucial information if we simply follow the clues. Xi Hongxuan has always been friendly with Xue Xiuzhuo. Even if he didn't know Xue Xiuzhuo purchased those prostitutes, he'll know something others don't. I'll question him again later."

"After all this talk, you still haven't let Er-gongzi in on the details." Shen Zechuan made a move to get up, but Xiao Chiye pinned him on his lap. "How much silver did you swindle out of him?"

Shen Zechuan snapped out of his thoughts and pursed his lips slightly. He raised four fingers, just as he had before.

Xiao Chiye grasped those fingertips tight. "That much? I accept. Put it down as my bride price, quick."

"At least pretend not to jump at the first offer. Four million is too little."

"You're being too generous," Xiao Chiye said. "A starting price of four million? Since you're so good at making money, Er-gongzi will take whatever price you offer."

That made Shen Zechuan laugh. "I told him Wei Huaigu wanted four million taels. He didn't hesitate for a moment. Four million is clearly a drop in the ocean to the Xi Clan."

Seeing how happy he was tonight, Xiao Chiye made no further mention of Xue Xiuzhuo. He bounced Shen Zechuan a little on his lap.

"Only the Xi Clan themselves know precisely how much money they have. Everyone else can only see the salterns and copper mines they operate. But their business ventures aren't limited to the entirety of the empire; they stretch all the way into foreign lands. The common rich young masters make their fun visiting brothels and gambling dens, but Xi Hongxuan's idea of a good time is running them. That broker on Donglong Street belongs to him too; their account books implicate plenty of bigwigs in the imperial court, all of whom have fields and businesses down as collateral. They have no choice but to keep Xi Hongxuan happy. This time it's four million—how much will you get out of him next time? The Northeast Provisions Trail is only open twice a year. How to hide and spend that much silver— these are problems you'll have to give some thought to."

"No one has ever broken into the Xi Clan's vault. Simply keeping the money where it is would be the most secure method. If we were to spend the money now, it'd be too hard to escape the eyes of the imperial court. Even the accounts of your twenty-thousand-strong Imperial Army have to be gone over with a fine-tooth comb. If this sum is not spent and disposed of perfectly, Er-gongzi will find himself in jail awaiting quite a trial."

"Spending money, huh?" Xiao Chiye said, his curiosity piqued. "What do you have in mind besides play and fun—or are you saving it for Zhongbo?"

"No destination in mind yet." Seeing that their time was almost up, Shen Zechuan stood and refastened his collar with one hand. "Er-gongzi doesn't handle household affairs, so how would you know the value of daily staples like tea, rice, oil, and salt? Even if we can't spend it right away, we'll have plenty of uses for this money in the future. There's no harm keeping it on hand; it's better to prepare for all contingencies."

So intently did they discuss Xi Hongxuan's household finances and assets, as if they already belonged to them, that it was clear they were bent on extorting every last copper.

Xiao Chiye still had to return to the banquet on the Kailing River, and could only stay for a few words. He had rushed over as soon as he had a free moment to see Shen Zechuan, and now that he'd fed the man, he couldn't afford to linger.

He'd already mounted his horse when he recalled something else and tugged on the reins. "The officials' review will happen in the next few days. The Grand Secretariat has proposed a candidate for the Provincial Administration Commissioner to oversee the six prefectures of Zhongbo. Jiang Qingshan, the current Provincial Administration Commissioner of Juexi, is already on his way to report to Qudu on imperial orders. My guess is it's him."

"I've long heard of his name and reputation. He displayed courage and foresight when he handled the relief efforts for the thirteen cities of Juexi six years ago." As he spoke, Shen Zechuan recalled that this man was also on good terms with Xue Xiuzhuo and couldn't help but pause.

Xiao Chiye guessed the turn of his mind. "Even if he's friendly with Xue Xiuzhuo, it doesn't necessarily mean he's in Xue Xiuzhuo's camp. When he enters the capital, you should meet him and try to get a read on him. He comes from a common background and doesn't rely on the noble clans for support. When the time comes, decide for yourself if he can be used." Seeing Shen Zechuan hesitating on the steps, Xiao Chiye raised a hand to beckon him.

Shen Zechuan stepped forward, ready to hear him out. But Xiao Chiye kept silent and merely reached out to ruffle his hair. A moment later, Snowcrest reared back and broke into a gallop.

Ge Qingqing pushed the gates open, and without another word, Xiao Chiye sped away into the night.

SHADOWS

THE FOOD in the prison was filthy and rotten. Xi Hongxuan's constitution had already been weakened by the pox, and now, with his stomach roiling, he was in abject misery. His mental state was crumbling; he fell often into a lethargic sleep and woke always in darkness. Gradually, he lost track of time.

Without any window to let in a breeze, the air in the narrow cell was foul and stale, and a musty smell hung in his nose. No ordinary man would be able to stand it.

Xi Hongxuan was gravely ill; what was more, he couldn't turn or stretch freely in the cell. All he could do was lie paralyzed on the rough straw mat and let his consciousness drift amid the damp and cold.

As usual, the warden slid open the door flap and shoved some rice through. Hearing no movement from inside, the man looked in through the hole. All he could see was Xi Hongxuan's drooping arm. Fearing his prisoner was dead, the warden opened the door and shone the lamp into Xi Hongxuan's face.

Xi Hongxuan struggled to open his eyes. Through dry and cracking lips, he rasped out, "S...sir, please spare me some water."

The warden poured the bowl of water he'd brought onto Xi Hongxuan's face.

With great effort, Xi Hongxuan opened his mouth and gulped the water, careless of his dampened collars. After several swallows, he managed to pull himself together. "Thank you, thank you!"

The warden threw the bowl away, grabbed the oil lamp, and made to leave.

With an unexpected burst of strength, Xi Hongxuan surged up and grabbed hold of the warden's clothes. A strained smile split his round face as he said through hacking coughs. "Hey, pal, tell me. This—this isn't the prison at all—am I right?"

The warden swatted Xi Hongxuan's hand away. Xi Hongxuan burst into hoarse laughter, gasping violently as he lay on the straw mat. He pulled at his soaked lapels and slid his gaze to the pitch-dark ceiling. "This isn't the prison," he murmured. "I should've realized a long time ago! It's been days and days. Even if Kong Qiu hasn't come to interrogate me, officials from the Ministry of Justice ought to be making their rounds. Too quiet... It's far too quiet in here..."

Xi Hongxuan fixed his unblinking stare on the warden. "I've done some calculations. You deliver food every day at precisely the same time; you even push the tray into exactly the same position. Pal, the average warden isn't nearly this rigid! In the last few days, not one man came to exchange shifts with you in guarding the prison door. You wouldn't accept my money, and these sleeves of yours... they're pristine, without so much as a speck of dust! You're tall and muscular, discreet and meticulous—you're from the Embroidered Uniform Guard, aren't you?!"

The warden's face was devoid of expression as he carried the oil lamp out and closed the door behind him. Xi Hongxuan listened to the sound of metal chains winding around the handle, then pounded his fists down on the straw mat under him.

"Shen Zechuan...Shen Zechuan!" Xi Hongxuan struck the ground until his knuckles were red, then shouted at the top of his lungs, "Plotting against me! To think you'd scheme against me! You out there. Tell him. Tell him to come!"

There was no reply from the darkness.

Xi Hongxuan dug his fingers into the mat. His head was spinning as he spat, "He wants money, doesn't he? Call him over. As long as he lets me out...as long as he lets me out..." He struggled to swallow a mouthful of saliva, then pulled at his hair and gasped, "I'll give him the money! I can't fucking stand it anymore!"

The warden sat down in the hallway beside the oil lamp and popped a few broad beans into his mouth, which he washed down with wine. The metal door that held Xi Hongxuan had been well made; all he could hear from within were faint sobs and whimpers, like the wind sighing in the dead of night.

Xi Hongxuan's vision grew dim and murky. He didn't dare sleep again for fear that he would never wake. By the time Shen Zechuan next showed himself, Xi Hongxuan had reached a state of exhausted calm.

Shen Zechuan remained on his feet as he observed Xi Hongxuan.

Many years ago, Xi Hongxuan had narrowly escaped the jaws of death while out at sea. Since the day he had clawed his way back to life, he had never been in such a sorry state. He was different from other descendants of the noble clans—he wasn't afraid to take risks, nor was he afraid of looking wretched, if it meant he would survive. He let Shen Zechuan look as his parched throat constricted around a disconcerting laugh. "Lanzhou, you've got some balls! Four million. I nearly met my end being fleeced by you."

"It wasn't easy to find this place. Neither too conspicuous nor too far away." Shen Zechuan let out a soft sigh. "I really wasn't expecting you to be so discerning in your observations."

Xi Hongxuan pointed with a shaking arm. "Birds die for food, and men die for money. Brother, I'm more than willing to give you this sum! But don't tell me you want my life for this piddling bit of money." His voice was weak and unsteady, but even starvation and illness couldn't strip him of his adaptability. "Lanzhou...I could've continued pretending to be oblivious. I'm the only one who knows where the Xi Clan's keys are kept. I could've run you in circles and extracted myself from this place through trickery. But see, I didn't. I still hold our bit of brotherhood close to my heart. Lanzhou! We joined hands to kill Xi Gu'an and Ji Lei. Today you're the target of envy in the Embroidered Uniform Guard. If you screw me over and kill me now, you'll lose the Xi Clan's support forever! The higher you climb in the Embroidered Uniform Guard, the narrower your path will become. You know what it feels like to be stuck in circumstances so thorny you can hardly move a step forward, don't you? Which of those old men with their hereditary positions would ever be willing to submit to you? You're an ambitious man—but wasn't it only on my account that Han Cheng tolerated you? If you kill me, you will become the target of all!"

Shen Zechuan crouched down, a handkerchief between his fingers as he looked at Xi Hongxuan and asked seriously, "Then, in your opinion, what should I do?"

Xi Hongxuan had seen this expression on Shen Zechuan count-less times before; Shen Zechuan's intent to kill flashed in his eyes like a blade. Xi Hongxuan dripped with cold sweat as he locked eyes with him. "You and I haven't reached the point of no return. Shen Zechuan, I lost this time. I concede! Suffering defeat in business is part of the game; it's no disgrace. Why should I make a scene and fall out with you over a trivial matter like this? I'll tell you the truth—I'm afraid of you! But it's because I fear you that I want to keep working alongside you. Think about it. Kill me now and you'll have the four million. But if you have me on your side, you'll have the Xi Clan's mountains of gold and silver. I admit defeat! So why stain your hands with blood? We still have all the days ahead of us to lord over Qudu!"

"That's a fair point," Shen Zechuan said. "But it's a tad too easy to dismiss me with words like *admit defeat*, isn't it? I've heard the second young master has sixty-eight keys. How about we split them, forty-sixty? I can't tell you how it'd set my mind at ease."

Xi Hongxuan slowly levered himself up. The look he turned on Shen Zechuan was ferocious. "I'll give you the keys. But once you take them, you can't ask for Qi Huilian again. How about it? Are you willing?"

Shen Zechuan slowly raised his fingers before flicking the handkerchief as if bored stiff. "You think Qi Huilian is worth all that? Naturally, I'll take the keys."

"If he's worth nothing, it's pointless to retain him. I'll kill him then!"

Shen Zechuan began to laugh. "You think I don't know where he is? Look where we are now; you still want to test me?"

"Who's testing whom?!" Xi Hongxuan dragged himself toward Shen Zechuan, face finally twisting. "I understand you, Lanzhou. You won't fool me with the same trick twice. Every word you speak is designed to deceive; the more you pretend not to give a damn about someone, the more important they are to you. You lied to me that day in the courtyard, and now you intend to tell the same lie again. I may not be a man of brilliant intellect, but I'm not *that* dumb. You don't know where he is. If you knew—ha! You'd have killed me the second you laid hands on the money! So how did it go, Shen Zechuan? Still couldn't find him despite searching all over Qudu, could you?"

Shen Zechuan's grip on his handkerchief tightened.

Xi Hongxuan smoothed aside his matted hair. "Eloquent you may be, but you've forgotten one thing: your careful concealment of him was enough to make me suspicious. Even when I think you're speaking the truth, I still have to be on my guard. The thing I fear when dealing with you is that any time you turn around, you might stab me."

Shen Zechuan's eyes were hard as he looked at Xi Hongxuan. "What do you want?"

"I want to get out of here." Xi Hongxuan pointed at the door. "I want to walk out of here unscathed. If I'm not out tonight, expect Qi Huilian's corpse to be cooling on your doorstep tomorrow morning. Do you believe me? Go ahead and try me. Xi Dan, that rat bastard who betrayed his master for money, must've told you all the men under my command are the children of servants in our clan. Hundreds of people rely on me for their safety. Even from in here, I have plenty of ways to dispose of Qi Huilian!"

"You're lying." That grim ruthlessness within Shen Zechuan surged up as he stood and took a few steps back; the dimness settled in from all sides, morphing his cold face into that of a behemoth lurking in the dark.

"This place is isolated; there are no outsiders. How could you pass on any message? Your death is so near at hand, yet still you're trying to play games with me?" Shen Zechuan's tone was icy and sharp with the shadow of a smile. "Sure. Let's play. I'll escort you out."

"I had my doubts about you; why wouldn't I take precautions?!" Xi Hongxuan was drenched in cold sweat; he could feel this chance slipping through his fingers. His voice rose with every word. "I told the guards I'd head down once every two weeks. If I don't appear, they'll dispose of him. You asked me last time if I dared believe your words. Shen Zechuan, this time I'm asking you: Do you dare to believe mine?!"

Shen Zechuan didn't make a sound.

Xi Hongxuan mellowed his tone, as if soothing his captor. "If you already bought Xi Dan, you must know I'm the only one who knows where Qi Huilian is. I've long understood that no one in this world can be trusted; I left myself countless escape routes. Lanzhou, why must we both lose here? Fighting like this will benefit neither of us. Aren't you making all these moves in the hope of gaining something? There's no profit in killing me; surely you won't go through with it. Whatever it is that you're lacking, I have it—I'll give it to you. Only lend me your guts and your wits, and we can flourish together in Qudu. Look at Li Jianheng. He's a good emperor—those are few and far between. For men like you and me, he's our ticket to success. This is a meteoric rise we're talking about, Lanzhou! Do you imagine Xiao Er will take you in if you kill me and offend the noble clans? How long can the Xiao Clan's infallible reputation and unmitigated success in battle continue? Xiao Fangxu is old. If Xiao Jiming should die too, then what is Xiao Er good for alone? They are doomed to fail and fall!

"Lanzhou." Xi Hongxuan seemed to lament, yet continued to persuade. "We've both suffered under other people's thumbs. How can you choose to submit to Xiao Er and be at his beck and call? The only things in this world that will never abandon you are money and power! Join forces with me, and I'll give you the money. Help me keep the Xi Clan intact, and we can bring our business to the next level. When that day comes, no one jockeying for power will be able to knock us from our pedestals! You wanted me to swallow up the other clans and proclaim myself victor. So why would you bind yourself now with any constraints?!"

He continued without pause, "And think about the six prefectures of Zhongbo. Don't you want to rebuild Zhongbo and avenge your past humiliation? Shen Wei's name may be mud, but you can smash the gates to Zhongbo open with silver. They're so poor there and in such dire straits that they're eating their neighbors' children. You could be their savior. After that, who would dare stand in your way? Who would dare curse you? Put money in the right hands, and all this can be yours. Can the empress dowager promise the same? Can Xiao Er promise the same? Lanzhou, why do you hesitate? We can still join forces and climb our way to the top, just as before."

Shen Zechuan appeared moved by his words. He no longer brimmed with murderous intent, and even his tone had lost some of its edge. "Had you been this candid earlier, we wouldn't have ended up here. You're right. By joining forces, you and I can save ourselves a lot of trouble."

"To a merchant, profit is king. If our collaboration didn't yield sufficient benefits, would I waste my breath?" Xi Hongxuan's back prickled. His wound from the building collapse had scabbed over, and it itched so fiercely these days that it hurt. He took a few breaths, then continued, "Then there's no time to lose. Release me now. Once I'm out of here, we'll sit down for a proper chat."

More than ten martial arts experts were waiting in the Xi manor in Qudu. Xi Hongxuan had spent a pretty sum hiring them to intimidate Shen Zechuan the last time, and had kept them on out of caution. In truth, he was burning with anxiety; he still couldn't figure out what Shen Zechuan was thinking. Yet this only solidified his intent to kill. He'd burn any bridges he had to in order to fight to the end. And no matter what, he had to get out of here first—only when he had his freedom could he find some variable to exploit and turn the tide.

He wanted Shen Zechuan dead—he wanted it so much he couldn't wait for tomorrow, much less sit here wheedling him like this. Two people who'd worked together a long time were usually evenly matched: they could sit down and trade barbs as equals. Xi Hongxuan felt that he and Shen Zechuan had already lost this balance; while Shen Zechuan bounded his way up the official ranks, Xi Hongxuan found himself fettered in shackles of Shen Zechuan's making—chains that rendered him incapable of controlling the situation as he had at the outset.

Xi Hongxuan still didn't know where it had all gone wrong. But he had a businessman's instincts; he saw now that he had been walking in circles like a man under a spell, and knew beyond a doubt that Shen Zechuan was to blame.

They had been in cahoots until now, but other than killing Xi Gu'an to get his hands on the Xi Clan's keys, every sweetness Xi Hongxuan had tasted had been fleeting. Of the two of them, only Shen Zechuan had truly climbed to greater heights, power firmly in hand.

Xi Hongxuan knew he had been made a fool of, but he maintained a careful look of docility, as if he worshiped the ground Shen Zechuan walked on, yet feared him to the point he dared not move against him.

Qiao Tianya cracked the door open and held up a lamp for them. The skin of Shen Zechuan's exposed wrists was pristine. With his side profile bathed in lamplight, he looked no different from the way he appeared in the daytime as he said politely, "After you, please."

Xi Hongxuan breathed a silent sigh of relief.

82

DEBT COLLECTION

T HE XI MANOR was located along one of the winding inner streets of Qudu, on the south side of the city. In comparison to the sprawling Pan and Fei manors, its grounds were significantly smaller. It was also very near the manor belonging to Prince Qin of the Guangcheng Emperor's reign. Although the Xi Clan had special permission to expand, the first few clan heads had been cautious and didn't dare expand or embellish their mansion beyond the standard regulations. The interior architecture of the manor was more in the style of Juexi, while the pavilions and terraces were restrained and common-looking.

Xi Hongxuan was on tenterhooks the entire journey back, but once he heard the ringing of horses' hooves come to a stop, he knew he was safely home. Still wary, he bunched up the soaked, wrinkled hem of his robe and hurried off the carriage. Shen Zechuan was already standing outside, sizing up the Xi manor.

"It's an old mansion." Xi Hongxuan kept his tone light, as if this was any other day. "We've talked of renovating it for years, but never had the time. Come over in a few days when the weather warms up and I'll show you the new plans."

Shen Zechuan turned his eyes toward the estate next door. The green-glazed tiles peeking over vermilion walls were standard flourishes on a prince's manor, but the overgrown trees obscuring the view made them eerie.

Xi Hongxuan followed his gaze. "Prince Qin's manor. The prince suffered from consumption and passed away a year before the Xiande Emperor ascended the throne. No one's lived there since. I imagine it'll be bestowed on someone as a reward eventually."

Shen Zechuan didn't shift his gaze away. "It looks even more imposing than Prince Chu's manor."

"Of course." Xi Hongxuan jerked his thumb heavenward. "The current emperor wasn't favored by the Guangcheng Emperor as a child. It was the crown prince, Prince Qin, and the former emperor who stood out among the imperial heirs. What a pity—the crown prince slit his own throat in the Temple of Guilt, Prince Qin passed from illness in this very residence, and the former emperor lingered for years on his deathbed."

He suddenly smiled. "But of course, how would our current emperor have had the chance to sit on the throne otherwise? Prince Qin was a rather pitiable figure himself. He had a close relationship with his father during the Guangcheng Emperor's final years, and the emperor visited him often. But someone in his employ beat a few villagers to death at his country estate. An official complaint was lodged against him, and the Guangcheng Emperor sentenced him to house arrest in that manor. It was during this period that Prince Qin contracted consumption. When he heard his son was so ill, the Guangcheng Emperor made a special trip down to visit him. No one knows what they talked about, but they parted on bad terms. After that day, Prince Qin fell out of favor. The emperor's mandate to self-reflect behind closed doors dragged on and on, keeping him a prisoner until his death."

Shen Zechuan tucked this information away but remained silent. When Xi Hongxuan saw he had no inclination to discuss the topic, he raised a hand to wave off the servants swarming over to them. "This manor of mine is not as big as the manors of princes and other aristocrats, but there's still some distance to walk. Lanzhou, I'm weak as a kitten, and I stink to high heaven. It'll be faster if we ride."

The servants from the Xi manor rushed to prepare sedan chairs. Xi Dan was the head steward of the household, but he didn't dare show himself now. It was instead Xi Hongxuan's eldest sister-in-law who came out to welcome them.

Xi Hongxuan loved this woman, or so he claimed. Shen Zechuan had heard him repeat countless times that his desire to kill Xi Gu'an was born of the hatred he bore his elder brother for stealing his intended bride. Yet his expression was indifferent as he watched her descend the steps. He didn't ask for her help supporting him either, but dismissed her with a perfunctory wave as he took his seat in the small sedan.

Shen Zechuan, lifting the curtain of his own sedan with an out-stretched finger, saw it all clearly. Qiao Tianya, walking alongside, opened his mouth to speak; a slight shake of Shen Zechuan's head stopped him.

The sedans entered the Xi manor grounds and made several turns before arriving at the courtyard where Xi Hongxuan made his quarters. His courtyard was markedly different from the rest of the estate. It was tastefully decorated, and the long corridor connected Xi Hongxuan's rooms to a row of brightly-lit offices with windows and doors thrown open—supplemented, at this hour, by a row of brightly lit lanterns. The clacking of abacuses mingled with the rise and fall of various regional accents in a noisy confusion. A woven awning stretched over a tea table on the open ground before the front hall, and seated and standing in its shelter were various shop-keepers and bookkeepers who had come from all over, seeking the master of the house.

At the sight of Xi Hongxuan, this milling crowd stood and crowded around the sedan. Those who were here to report expenses, prepare stock, demand payments, and make greetings mobbed him at once, creating quite a din.

Xi Hongxuan stepped down and bowed to the crowd. "This humble one has only just returned. Look at the state I'm in; I can't do any work just yet. No need to be anxious. Wait here and someone will call you into the office on that end. I merely spent the past few days having some fun; nothing of importance. Business continues as usual. Oh, as for the shopkeepers here to demand payment, fret not. When has the Xi Clan ever missed a deadline or defaulted on a debt? As long as you have the memorandum with you, I'll pay your claims in full!"

Anxious to keep Shen Zechuan steady, Xi Hongxuan pushed aside the crowd and called for the attendants to hurry over and serve up tea for those waiting. Politely cupping his hands to his guests the entire way, he finally managed to chivvy Shen Zechuan into a relatively quiet hall at the back of the courtyard.

"Lanzhou, take a seat. I'll go wash up a little and change." Xi Hongxuan shook his dirty robe for emphasis before instructing the servants to prepare refreshments.

Shen Zechuan took his seat and drank the proffered tea. By the time the food and wine were served, Xi Hongxuan had returned in a fresh silk robe the color of oxblood. He took his seat and personally filled Shen Zechuan's cup with wine.

"Sorry to have kept you waiting!" Xi Hongxuan touched the flesh on his neck and chuckled. "It's good to be home. That cell was awfully damp. I can't tell you how refreshed I feel after washing up.

Here, Lanzhou, drink! You showed no mercy this time, did you? A few more days in there and I'd have been dead meat!"

"I wouldn't go so far as that," Shen Zechuan said with a smile. "All this was only to give you a little scare. We're friends; how could I deal you such a vicious blow?"

"And yet you caused me so much grief!" Xi Hongxuan groused, smiling bitterly. "The state of my back is frightful; I'll have to call for a physician to take a look later. Could you not have simply told me you were in want of four million? Ay, you had to go around in such a big circle!"

The two men chatted merrily over wine, showing no signs that they had been at daggers drawn a mere hour ago.

The wine was excellent, as were the dishes. Xi Hongxuan wiped his mouth with a napkin and spread his arms to sprawl back on the chair, satisfied. "It's not that I'm unwilling to give you the keys. But Lanzhou, you can't have your cake and eat it too. If I return Qi Huilian to you, I'll lose my insurance. I can't hand the keys *and* the old man over to you."

Shen Zechuan had only picked at the food before setting down his chopsticks. "I've done you a disservice, it's true. But Second Young Master, there are some things I didn't fabricate. Make a few inquiries and you'll know that Wei Huaigu truly wishes you ill; he didn't want you out of there at all."

"They all have their own ulterior motives." Xi Hongxuan wiped the fine beads of sweat at his temples. "But if you were able to smuggle me out of prison without anyone noticing, the court must've decided to go easy on me. I have His Majesty to thank for this, I assume?"

"His Majesty went to great pains to protect you, so the prison can't overstep their authority to investigate further. But you've been temporarily suspended from your post and sent home; you won't be able to carry out your duties in the Bureau of Evaluations." Shen Zechuan changed the topic. "I've brought you home as you asked. We can renegotiate the matter of the keys, but I want to see Qi Huilian now."

Xi Hongxuan threw aside the napkin and smiled as he rubbed his full stomach. "If you want to discuss the keys, we have to come to an understanding now. Lanzhou, you've never had dealings in business before, so you don't know how it works. It's not any simpler than being an official. You can hold the keys and carry out the ingots, but that silver is dead weight. If you take it out, sooner or later you'll spend it all. Why not leave it where it is and let me continue to invest it in our businesses? Isn't it wonderful to let your money beget more money? However much you need in the future, only give me a number."

He sat unmoving in his chair. The earlier clamor outside had faded without them taking notice. The windows and doors in the hall were wide open, and the weeping willows outside, shrouded in inky darkness, looked like a row of hanged ghosts crammed at the windows looking in. The night was still and quiet, and the candle wicks popped in the silence. Even the servants that had been waiting on them seemed to have vanished. It was as if the two of them were the only ones left in the estate.

Shen Zechuan eased himself back in his chair. "How quickly your tune has changed. After stepping out of that prison cell, it seems the second young master has found his courage."

"My stomach is full; I'm much more comfortable now." Xi Hongxuan looked at Shen Zechuan and pointed to his own head. "Even better, I'm still sober. I'm telling you, it's not a choice between Qi Huilian and the keys. You may take Qi Huilian; you may not have the keys. Give the nod, and you can have him tonight."

Shen Zechuan let the silence stretch. He slid the little bamboo fan out of the pocket in his sleeve and held it for a moment, as if to weigh it. "That's not what we discussed."

"The world of business changes at a rapid pace," Xi Hongxuan answered gruffly. "Earlier, you held all the bargaining chips, and now I do. The terms of our discussion naturally must shift accordingly."

Shen Zechuan smiled. "And if I insist on both?"

"Then it will come to naught." Xi Hongxuan patted his belly. "Lanzhou, let me offer you a piece of advice: don't be a greedy son of a bitch. People are happiest when they're content with their lot. You've got your four million. I won't pursue it further. This is an adequate gesture of goodwill, is it not?"

"The money has yet to be delivered into my hands." Shen Zechuan didn't divulge any details about his plans to use the Northeast Provisions Trail to transport it in two shipments. Instead, he said, "It's not easy to move that much money. You know that better than I do."

"I have my own channels for escorting goods. Jiang Qingshan is sharp, but he can't keep an eye on everything." Xi Hongxuan spoke with confidence now, sensing he'd gained the upper hand. "I can get the money to you. I said it once, and I'll say it again: Lanzhou, I'm willing to give you the four million. But you have to tell me the truth. Were these incidents—the collapse of my Ouhua Pavilion, the flooding, and the pox—your doing?"

"Of course not," Shen Zechuan said. "What I told you was the honest truth. If you want to know more, you'll have to ask Xue Xiuzhuo. I see you're keeping a tight grip on the keys, so I won't insist. You said it yourself—we must work together if we want to rise. Now, can you give me Qi Huilian?"

Xi Hongxuan pushed his chair back and stood. "I sent someone to fetch him ages ago. You've already waited so many days; what's a little longer now?" He paced back and forth, belly-first, to aid digestion. Looking thoughtful, he made his way to the door and took a step out to shout, "Where is he?"

The servant outside murmured something in reply.

Straining to hear, Xi Hongxuan took a few more steps down the stairs. The courtyard was dead silent. When he was well clear of Shen Zechuan, he jerked around and bellowed, "Shut the doors!"

At once, the wide-open doors of the hall swung shut, and planks were secured over the windows with a symphony of thuds. The hall was sealed in the blink of an eye. As the rustle of night wind sent the grim willows swaying, several figures materialized out of the dark to stalk the edges of the hall.

The affable mask had fallen; Xi Hongxuan gritted his teeth in rage. "Shen Zechuan! You dare to ask for Qi Huilian back? How greedy can you be—you're a snake trying to swallow an elephant! You think you can treat me like a fool and push me around? I'll take your life tonight!"

He retreated a few more steps. "Bring forth that double-crossing Xi Dan. We'll show him what happens to those who bite the hand that feeds them!"

Xi Dan was led out, back hunched and hands securely bound. On seeing him, Xi Hongxuan gave him a kick to the face that sent the man toppling to the ground, then stomped violently on him.

"The balls on you, to sell your master out for money! Despicable bastard—rotten piece of shit! You forgot your parents are in my hands. I'll see that your whole family follows you to the grave tonight!"

His eyes blazed with hate.

"Fetch my sister-in-law up here too. Does she think I don't know she's screwing this lowlife behind my back? Xi Dan, you don't have the guts to betray me on your own. But lust is like a blade hanging over your head, isn't it. You have only yourself to blame if you let someone exploit your weaknesses and end up betraying your master for money. Scum!"

He kicked Xi Dan until the man rolled over and howled in pain. More men hauled over the lady of the house, whose knees buckled the moment she saw Xi Hongxuan. She knelt before him, wailing and pleading without cease.

Xi Hongxuan let her hug his thigh and looked down at her, grim-faced. "Did you know he meant me harm? You knew, and you still chose to help him. Were you planning on running off together? I've never treated anyone better in my life than I treated you. I gave you all my love and most of my life, and this is how you repay me."

Eyes red-rimmed, Xi Hongxuan hauled his sister-in-law up by the arm. "Xi Gu'an snatched you away, and I snatched you back. I accorded you the same honor and prestige you've always enjoyed; I showered you with gold and jade so you wanted for nothing. I held you in cupped hands like my most precious treasure. You...oh, you!" Xi Hongxuan was so consumed by hatred he could barely speak; his heart was dripping blood. "You can leave this earth with him. I'll send you both on your way tonight!"

Xi Hongxuan shoved her down and spat on her. "Draw your blades!" he called with a fiendish smile. "Mince up these heartless and ungrateful creatures, and we can save on the dishes that accompany our wine tonight! Second Master has got money to spare!"

He fished out a handful of gold and silver ingots from his lapels and sleeves and scattered them over the ground, where they rolled in all directions. Amid the clatter of money colliding, Xi Hongxuan stumbled back a few steps and burst out laughing, tears streaming down his face until his shoulders shook with sobs.

"Everyone in this world is driven by self-interest. With my money, I will have no shortage of true hearts—for money, a person will kill their closest kin, their flesh and blood, even their own beloved!" Standing amid his discarded gold and silver, Xi Hongxuan raised his arms high and shouted himself hoarse. "Do it! I'm here to collect my debt!"

The men drew their blades, and cold steel flashed in the night.

SCENERY OF SPRING

DARK CLOUDS SHROUDED the moon, offering only flickers of ghostly shadows. The scrape of blades unsheathed was like silk ripping in the wind, a rending that warned of imminent peril.

From inside the hall came three taps of the bamboo fan. Shen Zechuan was as composed as ever as he picked up the jug to pour himself another cup of wine.

"You're right." Shen Zechuan lifted the cup to his lips. "We do have scores to settle tonight."

Xi Hongxuan lowered his arms and watched with cool detachment as the crowd of fighters swarmed toward the hall. "Clever as you are, if you'd only been obedient, you would've suffered far less."

"The moment you enter Qudu, you become a caged bird in a pavilion, oblivious to the danger of the spreading blaze ahead," said Shen Zechuan. "You're both fortunate and unfortunate. Back then, you fought the waves for a chance at life, and for that, I toast to you." As he spoke, he poured the wine over the ground, as if to honor someone already dead. "You and I both understand that those trapped by their circumstances are least likely to be obedient. Nine out of ten people who meekly obey will not survive until heaven opens its eyes and lends them a hand."

"I fought against the battering waves; you're fighting against the very same thing. Human lives are the most worthless thing of all. Shen Zechuan, I toast to you too! You survived despite all the torture and torment you endured back then. But tonight, you're going to topple like a toy boat capsizing in a drain!" Xi Hongxuan snickered, then smoothed his features into indifference. "Between the two of us, only one may live."

"You've taken your bath and had your wine." Shen Zechuan dropped his wine cup and rose to face the doors. He grasped the hilt of Avalanche, his thumb pressing down on that white pearl as he chuckled. "Do you really not intend to reveal Qi Huilian's whereabouts before I see you off?"

The courtyard was suddenly illuminated by a burst of fiery light. Xi Hongxuan turned; flames had sprung up on the building behind him. He bellowed, "Don't let him draw you into a fight! Whoever can take his head will have a hundred taels of gold and silver!"

The doors and windows splintered as the men lurking in the shadows pounced like wolves. Shen Zechuan's blade sprang free of its sheath. He took two steps forward, and blood splattered from ground to roof, following the arc of his sword. The long blade that was Avalanche seemed forged from ice and cast from snow as flesh parted under its edge, so fast not a drop of blood stained the blade even as the paper in every window was dyed with sprays of red.

Avalanche was the same as Wolfsfang. Each blade lay dormant in Qudu, collecting dust, the waist ornaments of refined young masters. But when they were given the chance to be drawn from the sheaths that restrained them, the bloodthirsty ruthlessness of the blades reflected their masters in every cold glimmer.

The tongues of flame came furiously licking at the walls, and within seconds, half of the Xi manor was engulfed in fire.

Qiao Tianya leapt from roof to roof, knocking the killers who sped after him off the eaves with flying kicks, then flipped onto the roof of the central hall and flashed Shen Zechuan's gold-plated authority token.

"The Embroidered Uniform Guard is investigating a case on imperial orders! The Xi Clan has privately assembled more than a hundred gallant martial arts masters right under the Son of Heaven's nose. Our investigations point to the presence of fugitives and outlaws among them. Xi Hongxuan's traitorous intentions are plain to see. He ought to be executed for this!" Qiao Tianya's voice rang clear over the courtyard. "This pertains to the incident at Ouhua Pavilion and concerns the safety of the Son of Heaven. Anyone involved is to be taken into custody in the Imperial Prison. The Scarlet Cavalry has surrounded the Xi manor. I advise you to surrender without a fight!"

"Don't listen to him!" Xi Hongxuan shouted. "I'm a bosom friend of the Son of Heaven; we've faced death together! The Embroidered Uniform Guard attempts to murder loyal ministers to cover up their crimes. Those who aid me tonight are the upright heroes of our nation! You can follow me to the palace gates tomorrow morning to receive your reward!"

The burning rafters collapsed with a thunderous crash. Xi Hongxuan stood amid the waves of heat, not taking a single step back, as he stared fixedly at that flashing figure in the hall.

"The eunuch faction has only recently been eradicated. His Majesty encourages everyone to voice their views; what he hates most are treacherous officials like Shen Zechuan who abuse their power to deceive the masses *and* the throne! Gentlemen, the one who slays him tonight will be a hero. His meritorious deed will go down in history for the ages!"

Out of sight, Qiao Tianya spat. This Fatty Xi's silver tongue was second to none. If they couldn't gag that mouth, he would convince these people that black was white. Qiao Tianya tucked away the token and leapt down, drawing his blade to face his enemies head-on.

The wet sheen of blood sparkled against the blaze in the courtyard. In the outer buildings, the manor had descended into chaos, the air ringing with the shouts and cries of shopkeepers, bookkeepers, and servants trying to escape the inferno. The Scarlet Cavalry outside moved swiftly to block off the gates.

A hulking figure stood silhouetted in the door to the hall. Xi Hongxuan looked on indifferently as that figure leaned back, straight as a ramrod, and toppled over onto the stairs, streaming blood from his gaping throat. Shen Zechuan returned his blade to its sheath, then strode over the corpse's outflung arm and walked down the stairs, step by step.

Xi Hongxuan burst out laughing, cackling until he shook all over. "So, I still can't hold a candle to you. Even His Majesty wouldn't dare blame you for killing me with this kind of justification."

Shen Zechuan tipped his head back to survey that raging fire. "You weren't meant to die this early."

Xi Hongxuan looked up at the sky and heaved a sigh. He was remarkably calm; those demented peals of laughter and furious curses had all vanished. "Whether I die early or late, I still die being played for the fool by you. What kind of fucking justice is that! I'm not ashamed to lose to you, Shen Zechuan; I concede defeat—but I can't take it lying down. You think yourself steel tempered in the crucible of hardship? You've got a long way to go. I meet my end tonight because I underestimated my enemy. But there are plenty of people in this world who see you as the thorn in their side. They're all lined up, waiting their turn. You may kill one, then another, but you will never be able to kill them all. But the real tragedy...."

He gazed silently at the night sky. "You and I weren't born to walk an easy road. Things that are readily available to others, you and I must fight for with our lives. The prejudice between children of principal wives and those of concubines is deep-rooted. How absurd is it that I was born a lawful son, yet have lived a life worse than the common-born brats of other clans? My life is worth nothing, and yours even less. You want to charge ahead, to fight, to seize what power you can—but who knows what will happen in days to come?"

Xi Hongxuan spread his arms wide, as if asking both heaven and Shen Zechuan at the same time. "There is no end to strife. Who will succeed and who will fail? Will your victory be secure when I'm gone? You will kill the others, and the others will kill you!"

He laughed again, wild and unbridled. Then he crouched to pull a blade out of a corpse on the ground and stumbled toward Shen Zechuan.

"I'm a man of the Xi Clan. In this life, I've triumphed thrice over Xi Gu'an; I'm not inferior to him! My parents were blind! I gave my heart to the wrong woman and exhausted all my love and hatred. I—" Xi Hongxuan brandished the blade and brought it to his own throat; hot blood sprayed across Shen Zechuan's chest. The blade tumbled to the ground, and Xi Hongxuan pulled at Shen Zechuan's sleeve as he sank to his knees alongside it, slurring his final words through a rictus smile. "I...will wait for you...on the path to the underworld..."

Shen Zechuan watched Xi Hongxuan collapse at his feet. Warm blood trickled down his fingers. He stood in silence for a very long time, silhouetted against the backdrop of the roaring flames, then flicked his fingers to shake off those lingering droplets of blood.

The Xi manor had burned to ash, and the Embroidered Uniform Guard escorted the survivors to the Imperial Prison. In his audience with Li Jianheng, Shen Zechuan submitted a memorial regarding Xi Hongxuan's misdeeds, detailing how he amassed a private fighting force and resisted arrest.

Li Jianheng was shocked, but the evidence of Xi Hongxuan gathering men in his estate was irrefutable; the Embroidered Uniform Guard had even thoroughly checked their backgrounds through the Ministry of Justice. The matter was handled impeccably, with no loose ends; even the censors of the Chief Surveillance Bureau could find no fault with it.

Wei Huaigu was sly indeed. Upon seeing this play out, he hinted to his pupils to first denounce Xi Hongxuan as a treacherous villain who had poisoned the Son of Heaven's mind and led him astray, before next decrying Xi Hongxuan for putting His Majesty in harm's way; the collapse of the Ouhua Pavilion, he announced, had in fact been entirely staged by this man. The Wei Clan went all out to absolve themselves of blame, and the Xi Clan's former allies turned their backs. Such was the fickle nature of power: when the guests had all left, the abandoned tea grew cold.

Yet, even after Ge Qingqing led men to search every street and alleyway of Qudu and examine all entry and exit documents, they found no sign of Qi Huilian and Ji Gang.

"They're assuredly still in Qudu." Shen Zechuan closed the records on his desk. "He intended to use Xiansheng to threaten me. Sending them out of Qudu would have made it harder for him to use them."

"Xiansheng is an old scholar, but Shifu is a worthy opponent with few equals," said Qiao Tianya. "I've already deployed men to keep searching for them in secret. Surely that will yield something."

Shen Zechuan said nothing, sinking into his thoughts.

Seeing him unresponsive, Qiao Tianya had moved to take his leave when Shen Zechuan called out, "Since there's no other business tonight, I'll make a trip to Plum Blossom Manor. There is much to discuss. Go ahead and wait for me there. Ask Gu Jin what kind of people Xiangyun Villa sold to Xue Xiuzhuo."

Qiao Tianya acknowledged the orders and took his leave. When he stepped outside, a few people were resting in the courtyard. They were all seniors in the Embroidered Uniform Guard of the fourth rank and above; among them, a few were noble sons whose ancestors held titles and properties, and who had the right to don python robes bestowed by the emperor and carry the Xiuchun saber. Ge Qingqing had led his own men to rest on the other side. Although everyone belonged to the Guard, there was a clear divide between cliques.

Shen Zechuan had advanced through the ranks too rapidly within the last six months; it was inevitable that he would draw envy. He rubbed elbows with men in power on all sides, and had taken over the mantle of northern judge, which established him as a top dog among the upper echelons of the Embroidered Uniform Guard's command. The web of connections with the Guard was labyrinthine; pick anyone at random, and they would have their own privileged background and title. When a new commander came in, it was customary for him to swap pointers with the veterans. Shen Zechuan had been too busy with official duties, and hadn't yet had time to try to get closer to his men. But once the busy spring planting season passed, they were bound to see each other one way or another on their subsequent missions.

Standing between these two unspoken factions, Qiao Tianya's heart sank slightly. He let the curtain fall behind him and left ahead of Shen Zechuan.

Xiao Chiye had yet to return from the drill grounds at Mount Feng, and only Gu Jin remained at Plum Blossom Manor. Qiao Tianya drank half a cup of wine with him and inquired into the matter of Xiangyun Villa.

"A total of sixteen people of similar ages. All boys and girls under the age of twenty." Gu Jin and Qiao Tianya sat on the railing along the veranda. The weather was fine, with green buds and sprouts everywhere they looked. "As for their backgrounds and origins, I've already told Tao-zi to write them out and hand them over to my master. Your master will see them soon, I'm sure. But this isn't an easy matter to investigate. These people are a motley crew, like a cluster of weeds. There's nothing that connects them other than their ages."

"Isn't that just the problem?" Qiao Tianya picked the little porcelain cup, half the size of the usual, off the tray and sipped his wine. He frowned as he rolled it over his tongue. "The harder these people are to investigate, the more important they may be. This wine is pretty good, but why are you using such a small cup? It's scarcely the size of my thumb."

"Drinking gets in the way of work. If you reek of wine when the masters return, you'll be in for a scolding." After the dressing-down he had received from Xiao Chiye, Gu Jin didn't dare to drink as liberally as he had done. He simply sat with Qiao Tianya for a moment. The patrols in Plum Blossom Manor were under his charge, so he departed a short while later and left Qiao Tianya to entertain himself.

Qiao Tianya sat alone on the veranda and drank his wine, appreciating the spring scenery. Content to keep his own company, he remembered his seven-stringed qin was still here and toyed with the idea of taking it out to play. He rose and made a detour, tray in hand, passing under a veil of verdant branches, when he suddenly heard the notes of the seven-stringed qin. Qiao Tianya followed the sound in search of it. He didn't rush out, but instead brushed aside the trailing branches and glanced around for the source of the music.

The long walkway was bathed in sunlight, and a brightly illuminated man sat cross-legged in the center. He wore only a hairpin of aged wood in his inky hair; his sky-blue, wide-sleeved robe was adorned by a jade ornament and a small flat pouch hanging from his waist.

Qiao Tianya couldn't get a clear look at his face; all he could see was the man idly plucking away at the strings. He played a tune, then stopped. A music score was laid out beside him. He was pondering it when a kitten the color of smoke and clouds sprang onto his back and clambered around his neck to bat its paw at a stray lock of his hair.

The man plucked the cat off and tucked the little creature into his sleeve, his mind still on the qin that Qiao Tianya recognized as his own. He stepped forward slowly, and the man's face gradually came into view.

The willow catkins of the fourth month drifted down around them, while green velvet buds hung out to dry in the dazzling sunlight. The man was fair. While Shen Zechuan's fairness brought to mind the stark white of frost, this man was like smooth white jade placed under the warm green sunlight of spring. He had none of Shen Zechuan's sharpness, nor did he have Shen Zechuan's breathtaking allure, yet he was in a class of his own—ethereal and unforgettable.

Qiao Tianya, once a young master from a family of officials, recalled a poem his eldest sister-in-law had once recited:

Such is the mountain hewn from jade; as is the forest of jadeite pine. His unrivaled beauty, one of a kind; second to none, a man divine.[1]

Though they had never conversed, Qiao Tianya knew who he was.

"Truly the epitome of a man of leisure." Qiao Tianya swung his legs over the railing and set the tray on the ground. "There's no need to study the score for this tune. If you're keen to learn, I can teach you."

The man looked up at him and laughed. "I think of wine, and the wine appears. I seek the tune, and the musician arrives. My friend, you're truly my lucky star."

"The springtime view in the gardens of this estate is excellent. A pity no one appreciates it. It's fate that I've encountered you while enjoying the scenery of spring. And it's pure serendipity that I happened to hear this melody. Kindred spirits are hard to come by. I'm not good at much besides playing the qin. If you pass me by, you'll find no one else here who's up to teach you." Qiao Tianya poured wine for himself while standing. After drinking a cup, he tilted his chin at the man. "So, how about it?"

"Serving one's teacher is akin to serving one's father."[2] The man laid the qin on the ground and dangled his jade pendant to tease the cat, saying in a composed and deliberate tone, "To be acknowledged as someone's teacher, you must first convince the student of your worth."

---

1   From "Tune of Master Whitestone," a folk song included in Anthology of Yuefu Poetry, a Song dynasty poetry anthology by Guo Maoqian. Jade and pine are often associated with beautiful men, and are used here to signify one whose appearance is beyond compare.
2   From Lü's Spring and Autumn Annals on Learning, a compendium of philosophies of the Hundred Schools of Thoughts, compiled around 239 BC under the patronage of Qin dynasty chancellor Lü Buwei.

Qiao Tianya stroked the light stubble on his chin. "I, Qiao Tianya, never lie. Acknowledge me if you're willing to believe me. Forget it if you aren't."

The man let the jade pendant fall into his lap and looked at Qiao Tianya again. After a moment, he smiled. "I believe you."

By the time Xiao Chiye returned, Meng on his shoulder and reins in his hand, it was past dark. It was only as he was leading the horse through the gates that Chen Yang remembered and said, "Master, there was word a few days ago that Yao-gongzi has returned. Although he avoided the banquet, he will call on us when he can."

"He's a hard man to track down. Who knows when he'll feel like paying any calls?" Xiao Chiye peeled off his dust- and sweat-soiled outer robe as he strode through the door. "If he comes, tell the kitchen to prepare some light dishes for him. He's been with Secretariat Elder Hai so long he's grown accustomed to the man's tastes; he rarely eats meat these days."

After coming out to greet them, Gu Jin followed Xiao Chiye inside. Xiao Chiye stroked Meng, still resting on his shoulder. "Bring in some boiled meat and fresh water. Meng's had a tiring day too—is he here?"

Gu Jin nodded. "He arrived a little less than an hour ago. He's handling official affairs in the study."

"Has he taken his meal?"

"No," Gu Jin replied. "His Excellency told the kitchen he'd wait for Gongzi to return so you could dine together."

Xiao Chiye gave him a look as he turned his thumb ring around. Gu Jin got the hint and averted his eyes, not daring to stare longer at Xiao Chiye. But his master's mood seemed to have taken a turn for the better. Before he went farther inside, he took off Wolfsfang and tossed it to Gu Jin.

"Give the sheath a wipe down." Xiao Chiye pulled at his collar and took a sniff. "Send it in later; I'll sharpen the blade myself. Have someone keep an eye on the serving at dinner. There's plenty to discuss tonight, but be sure to prepare enough hot water. Where's Qiao Tianya? Make sure he takes his master's python robe to the laundry room and scents it with incense before morning court. That's all for now. You're dismissed."

Gu Jin nodded and withdrew, and Xiao Chiye pushed the inner door open.

Shen Zechuan had been listening from inside for quite a while. He dipped his brush in ink without lifting his head. "What admirable domestic virtue. Er-gongzi is truly a man after my own heart."

WEALTH

>>> ———◆ ✿ ◆——— <<<

ONSCIOUS THAT he reeked of sweat after a day running around the drill grounds, Xiao Chiye didn't go around to Shen Zechuan's side of the table but instead pulled out a chair on the nearer side. Stacks of case files covered the table's surface, many still sealed with the Ministry of Justice's memorandum slip. From the date inked on top, Xiao Chiye could see they were all from a very long time ago.

"You're investigating old cases." Xiao Chiye draped one arm along the chairback and picked up Shen Zechuan's little bamboo fan from the table, flicking it open and closed. "The Imperial Prison's cases alone took you weeks to go through. Why are you looking at the cases from the Ministry of Justice now too?"

"There was a gap in the Imperial Prison's records in the four years before the Xiande Emperor ascended the throne." Shen Zechuan looked at the files. "At the time, Ji Lei had the backing of Pan Rugui; I doubt he was so lacking in connections that he didn't take up a single assignment. But the Imperial Prison has no case records from this period. The cases from those years must have gone through the standard judicial process of the joint trial of the Three Judicial Offices instead of the Embroidered Uniform Guard. Ji Lei could only follow the Ministry of Justice's lead, assisting them as necessary."

"What I mean is," Xiao Chiye murmured as he blocked Shen Zechuan's view of the files and tipped up his chin with the open fan, "why are we looking into old cases?"

"It was in this room that we once discussed the fall of Zhongbo." Shen Zechuan set down the brush. "I spoke of making a distant friend while attacking a nearby enemy. Do you remember?"

Xiao Chiye closed the fan and rose to his feet. He sidestepped the table and walked toward the inner end of the bookshelf, and emerged at length carrying a map scroll. Shen Zechuan pushed aside the documents on the table, and Xiao Chiye flicked the scroll to unroll it across the surface. Both looked down at the detailed military topography spread out beneath them.

"This is a treasure I keep stashed away for special occasions." Xiao Chiye used the fan to sketch a circle around the six prefectures of Zhongbo. "Of course I remember what you said. You're referring to the fact that someone used the Biansha Horsemen to knock out the six prefectures of Zhongbo, which lie close to Qudu. This is attacking a nearby enemy. Then the Hua Clan fell into decline, and the empress dowager was forced to marry Third Lady Hua to Qidong. This is making a distant friend. If we put the two together, we can guess both were meant to weaken Libei, leaving it isolated with neither support in close proximity nor assistance from afar."

"But playing out a game like this takes too long, and the variables are innumerable. If the player wants to ensure he makes no moves in error, then he must maintain a position from which he can view the entire board." Shen Zechuan rose from his seat and slid a finger across the map, crossing Zhongbo and coming to rest on Qudu. "He has to be here. The Xiande Emperor had only reigned for three years when the Biansha attacked—too short to hatch a plot that would see Zhongbo fall. We must look further back. Many things happened during the Guangcheng Emperor's era of Yongyi that shifted the situation. Our mastermind has to have involved himself somewhere within those events. I'm hoping, if I look through these old cases, that I might find some clues."

"It's hard to get the full picture from files alone." Xiao Chiye looked down at the map. "You need to find someone who was involved, or someone who knows the details."

Placing his palms on the table, Shen Zechuan looked at him sidelong. "We don't have such a person."

Xiao Chiye held out the fan to Shen Zechuan. "On the contrary, I do have a candidate to recommend...but what will you bribe me with?"

Shen Zechuan smiled and grasped the other end of the fan, but didn't pull it away. He looked at Xiao Chiye across the bamboo frame. "Let me guess. The one you want to recommend is Yao Wenyu, am I right?"

"He's a member of the Yao Clan. He would know about many of the incidents that occurred during that period. Plus, he later went on to acknowledge Hai Liangyi as his teacher. Hai Liangyi served in the Ministry of Justice and the Ministry of Personnel before the Grand Secretariat. He would know the details better than anyone." Xiao Chiye drew the fan closer, and Shen Zechuan's hand with it. "Or do you not care to meet him?"

"I've heard his reputation, of course. Whether he's truly capable or all form and no substance, I'll know after meeting him. And I do want to. But when will I have the chance? After today, I'll be tied down with work for the latter half of the month."

"Everyone else is queuing up with high hopes to present their visitation cards to him. But of course, which of them can match the prestige of Lord Shen?" Xiao Chiye smiled.

"He might be a banished immortal who has fallen from heaven, but if he's not a tool meant for me to use then even if I use all my powers of flattery, it'd be futile." Shen Zechuan was telling the truth. He had indeed heard much about Yao Wenyu. But if they were to line the man up next to Xue Xiuzhuo, he would rather work with the latter. What they were investigating were worldly affairs; there were simply too many sordid matters here. Even if such an otherworldly, divine being were praised to the skies, Shen Zechuan had little inclination to woo the man to their side.

As the saying went, scholars were useless in all things practical. The work of an official was no more carefree than the courtesan selling herself in a brothel: flattering those above you and stepping on those beneath you; ingratiating yourself with others; taking a beating with a smile—each of these acts was an art. That Hai Liangyi didn't drag Yao Wenyu down into this mundane world spoke volumes about Yao Wenyu's temperament. Who could bear to hold an immortal down in the mire? Let him remain free and happy among the clouds.

Xiao Chiye thought differently, but he was in no hurry to say so. "I'm merely a casual acquaintance of his. He has friends all over the world, but those who can truly sit with him for a chat are few and far between. His manner is courteous but distant—he's similar to you in that respect. You could just meet briefly and make an impression on each other. Should need arise in the future, you could at least name him among your nodding acquaintances."

Hearing him put it this way, Shen Zechuan didn't object further. Xiao Chiye wouldn't recommend a person without reason. Shen Zechuan made a mental note of it—he'd get Qiao Tianya to help him free up some time to meet Yao Wenyu later.

Xiao Chiye had gone to speak with Shen Zechuan the moment he arrived. He felt warm, and the sweat he had worked up riding had yet to dry. Seeing the sweat at his temples, Shen Zechuan said, "Go take a bath and change your clothes. By the time you're done, it will be time for dinner. We can discuss any other trivial matters later."

"Now who's being virtuous?" Xiao Chiye lifted a leg to push the chair aside and bent to hoist Shen Zechuan over his shoulder. "But speaking virtuous words is only half of it—it must be followed by action. Let's bathe together. We can save time, economize effort, and conserve water."

Shen Zechuan reached out to straighten the brush that had been knocked askew, but Xiao Chiye was already striding toward the bath. The water was heated quickly, and once the curtain was pulled, it remained so for close to four hours. No one dared interrupt the flow of firewood. Chen Yang, being the most tactful, could read the situation best—the moment he saw Xiao Chiye would bathe, he had instructed the kitchen to prepare ingredients for the dishes and then wait; there was no hurry to serve them just yet.

Shen Zechuan had come to understand one thing very well: he could starve anyone but Xiao Chiye. Xiao Chiye couldn't endure it in the slightest. He would count every last day Shen Zechuan owed him and claim his due, demanding repayment as he held him in his grasp. He was full of youthful vigor, and whatever wiles Shen Zechuan possessed simply couldn't compare to Xiao Chiye's diligence and thirst for learning.

"I already know about everything." Xiao Chiye reached a hand out to rub Shen Zechuan's right earlobe and leaned in close to murmur, "We don't have to discuss Xi Hongxuan tonight. You've sent Ge Qingqing scouting around lately; are you looking for Ji Gang-shifu?

The Imperial Army is standing guard at the city gates. If they spot anything strange, I'll send someone to notify you."

Shen Zechuan's skin bloomed red under his touch. He leaned back against Xiao Chiye's arm and closed his eyes to catch his breath, exposing his fair neck. His chest was heaving.

Xiao Chiye fastened the earring for him. "Er-gongzi will discuss nothing else tonight."

Shen Zechuan leaned forward, pushed against the edge of the pool yet inseparable from Xiao Chiye. The waves built up, crest upon crest. He trembled as his climax crashed over him; in Xiao Chiye's embrace, the sensation of being filled tipped him from pleasure into the thrill of abandon. It threw his consciousness into chaos; he could do no more than murmur vague words under his breath.

The sounds sent tingles through Xiao Chiye's body.

Between them, there was no setting aside the cups after taking a sip of wine; there was only drinking to their hearts' content. They were desperate for true and undisguised desire, and could only find it in each other. They craved the headlong rush of their bodies clinging to each other in bed—first the storm, then the gentle rain. All their worries could be washed into oblivion by their mutual passion. They never whispered sweet nothings in the most intense moments, when burning lust was drowned by the desire for love. Their intimacy lay in the unspoken agreement of their need; impassioned kisses stood in for words they couldn't say. This was their conversation: a kiss for their desperation, a kiss to mark their climax, and a kiss for the tender silence of the moments between.

By the time Xiao Chiye was sated, he had lost all track of time. He brushed Shen Zechuan's dripping hair from his forehead and caressed his wet cheeks. Shen Zechuan lifted his fair neck and pulled him closer, tongue darting out to wet his lips.

Xiao Chiye had yet to pull out. He kissed Shen Zechuan again and picked him up.

Shen Zechuan let him kiss as he felt his way to the mess of their spend and drew it across Xiao Chiye's stomach with slender fingers.

After they were done, Shen Zechuan ate a little porridge while Xiao Chiye fed him mouthfuls of steamed twisted rolls. Shen Zechuan had changed into a clean inner garment; with Xiao Chiye's outer robe draped over his shoulders, he watched Xiao Chiye eat his meal.

Xiao Chiye had an astonishing appetite lately, and ate intently. Shen Zechuan didn't know what he was doing over at the military drill grounds at Mount Feng, but he sensed Xiao Chiye's mood was poor.

Lifting his head, Xiao Chiye glanced at Shen Zechuan. "Go sleep on the bed. You'll catch a cold if you fall asleep like that."

Shen Zechuan moved a fish to his own bowl and began to pluck out the bones. He was so tired he was dozing off, but he took his time to say, "The repairs and renovations on the drill grounds have just concluded, and your funds are sufficient to cover the costs. Is someone making trouble for you?"

Xiao Chiye, his face impassive, chewed for a moment. "I want to add firearms to the Imperial Army's arsenal."

Ah. That would be tough.

He instantly knew the reason for Xiao Chiye's displeasure. At present, firearms were only allocated to the Eight Great Battalions. This was valuable stuff, and the Ministry of War wouldn't hand it out to just anyone, much less to Xiao Chiye. But Xiao Chiye had long had his eyes on them. The Eight Great Battalions had let the brass muskets gather dust in the arsenal. Xiao Chiye had played with one the last time he was there, and it was there he began plotting to acquire some. But Xiao Chiye knew his request would hit a wall at the Ministry of War. Not even Li Jianheng had any say in this matter; because it was of great significance to the balance of martial forces in the nation, the decision lay firmly in the hands of the Grand Secretary of the Grand Secretariat—Hai Liangyi himself.

Shen Zechuan considered for a moment. His chopsticks moved to grasp a piece of fish, and he held it out to Xiao Chiye. "Your intentions are too obvious. You want the Imperial Army to test the waters in preparation for introducing firearms in the Libei Armored Cavalry. Considering how wary the court is of Libei, Hai Liangyi will no doubt refuse you."

Xiao Chiye usually avoided fish, too impatient to pick out the bones, but now that he tasted it from Shen Zechuan's chopsticks, he found it to be acceptable. He ate everything Shen Zechuan fed him and only spoke when they were finished. "Let him. I'll think of some other way to get my hands on them. Libei has its own military craftsmen. If I can find a way to get the designs, they should be able to copy them—like drawing a tiger with a cat as a model."

"These designs won't be easy to come by." Shen Zechuan rinsed his mouth from the teacup in Xiao Chiye's hand. "Hai Liangyi keeps a tight watch on those."

But Xiao Chiye was determined to have them, for reasons Shen Zechuan understood more than anyone.

Hua Xiangyi would be married to Qidong soon. Qudu's strategy of making a distant friend while attacking a nearby enemy was already taking shape. Libei must respond, and quickly. The Libei Armored Cavalry wasn't an invincible force; the reason it remained infallible was because its two successive commanders were resourceful and swift to adapt to changing circumstances. If the Qi Clan really fell out with Libei as a result of this marriage alliance, then in addition to strategies for confronting the Biansha Horsemen, Libei would also need to consider tactics for confronting the Qi Clan's infantry.

"The Minister of War, Chen Zhen, comes from the same hometown as Kong Qiu. We should consider him one of Hai Liangyi's people. This man's been friendly enough with my father in the past, but he wouldn't necessarily even do my eldest brother a favor. And now that it's come to me..."

Recalling yesterday's frustration, Xiao Chiye paused. "There's another way."

Shen Zechuan snuffed the lamp. They lay on the bed together, sharing a pillow.

"It'll be hard to go through Chen Zhen," Shen Zechuan said. "If he's from the same hometown as Kong Qiu, that means he's from Qidong. If it's a question of Qidong or Libei, he'll be biased in favor of the former. Firearms... The Embroidered Uniform Guard might have the designs."

Xiao Chiye drew him into his arms and closed his eyes. "Xi Hongxuan is dead, and those keys have become a gold mine without a master. Everyone's watching you; they're all dying to rip you apart and search for them themselves. And you've incurred enough of your colleagues' envy. Don't trouble yourself with this—Er-gongzi has a way."

Shen Zechuan smiled and said nothing.

Xiao Chiye slowly opened his eyes. "Those two million taels will not enter Libei. I've already spoken to my brother. The money will stop in Cizhou. You can retrieve the silver whenever you go back there. But you can't do anything with four million taels. Er-gongzi will give you even more."

The two of them were trapped in Qudu, yet the way he said it was so genuine and sincere. Xiao Chiye had told his share of lies in the past, but in this moment, it sounded as if he had never believed anything more. He was like a wolf pup collecting the stars, hoarding them all just to stuff them into Shen Zechuan's hands, like that little jewelry box of pearl and jade earrings.

He spoke through his actions more than his words.

Shen Zechuan looked back. "Actually, it's not just the four million. Xi Hongxuan did keep his keys securely hidden. But he's no sage. It's inevitable that he divulged a word or two here and there to those close to him in unguarded moments. The affair between his eldest sister-in-law and Xi Dan had gone on for some time, and both were tricking secrets out of him all along. He had sixty-eight keys, thirty of which I know—"

Xiao Chiye, who was so strapped for cash he was on the verge of selling his manors, was fuming. He flipped over to cover Shen Zechuan's mouth, biting him until Shen Zechuan gasped lightly for breath.

"Xiao Er," Shen Zechuan hissed through stinging lips. "You're—"

Xiao Chiye pinched his chin to stop him from saying it. They tumbled into the bedding, trading urgent kisses.

Ding Tao was on the rooftop feeding a sparrow he had begun to tame. Hearing the thump of the pillow sliding off the bed inside the room, he clutched the sparrow tighter, wanting to peek in but too timid. Looking around, he saw his many gege staring determinedly into space. He gulped. "I-I, uh—I guess I'll tell you a story. My father wrote about it in his little book. There was this—"

Qiao Tianya and Gu Jin hissed in unison, "Oh, shut up."

ASSIGNMENT

GREAT MISFORTUNE had befallen the Xi Clan. As Xi Hongxuan had no children to take up the mantle, his shops all over the Zhou empire temporarily suspended operations. Their shopkeepers sent letters to Qudu and prepared to travel, ready to set up a mourning hall in their old home of Chuncheng and discuss plans for the future. From the chair in his office, Shen Zechuan instructed, "This journey is a long one, and you're bringing women with you. I worry for your safety. Xiao-Wu, lead a few of our men to escort Xi-dage there."

Xi Dan knew Shen Zechuan's true intent in sending him with a minder. Nevertheless, he hurriedly kowtowed to show his gratitude.

"There's only the eldest mistress left to head the Xi Clan now." Shen Zechuan glanced down at the account books spread out before him. "Be attentive when you go back. Other matters are less pressing; stabilize the business first. Don't lose your head. The deal we discussed a few days ago can be set aside temporarily as well. Once you obtain the keys, keep a low profile and check the entrances to the vault. A man's wealth becomes his ruin if he rouses greed in others. Now that you have to look after such a large enterprise and manage the money as well, you're bound to encounter some trouble."

Xi Dan understood that he relied wholly on Shen Zechuan for protection now. He was a smart man who, having worked for Xi Hongxuan for years, knew very well how to assess a precarious situation. He had decided to go all out under Shen Zechuan precisely to prevent himself from being regarded as one of this man's expendable game pieces.

"After receiving such guidance from Master, this lowly one wouldn't dare be sloppy. Rest assured that I'll do my best to maintain the business for Master when I return to my hometown."

"Xi Hongxuan put so much trust in you because you have every necessary capability. But he was overbearing and only willing to put you to work on the accounts. There's someone new in charge now; I'm giving you the chance to show your mettle." Shen Zechuan pushed the account book aside without looking up. "Be honest in your work and play by the rules, and there will be plenty of chances for you to lead in the future. But I warn you now: speak a single word of deceit, and I will claim that traitorous tongue."

He said it breezily, but Xi Dan felt chilled to the marrow. He kowtowed again, not daring to look at Shen Zechuan this time.

It was noon when Shen Zechuan dismissed Xi Dan. Ge Qingqing had just returned; he entered and removed his blade, and an attendant came over to serve him a cup of tea, which he gulped down.

"No luck." Ge Qingqing pulled out a chair and sat. "The Xi Clan's manors in Qudu have all been thoroughly searched. There's no sign whatsoever of Xiansheng or Shifu."

Shen Zechuan leaned back in his chair with a scowl.

"Could they be in one of the Xi Clan's countryside estates?" Ge Qingqing wiped sweat off his brow. "The Xi Clan has plenty. Who knows, he might really have hidden them outside the city."

"It's been so long. Shifu is still strong; if he could, he would surely have thought of a way to come back and see me. But he hasn't." Shen Zechuan's heart sank. "So he's trapped somewhere; he can't make it out."

Qi Huilian didn't have the strength to truss a chicken, but Ji Gang was different; almost no one in Qudu was his match. Perhaps there was a skilled expert among the martial artists Xi Hongxuan had hired at some astronomical expense. But now that Xi Hongxuan was dead, those hired fighters should have scattered, fleeing the pursuit of the imperial court. Why on earth would they still care about two detainees?

"Call Fei Sheng over," Shen Zechuan said. "I have a mission for him."

Ge Qingqing was momentarily stunned. When he could speak, he said, "These people—will he be willing to take it on?"

Shen Zechuan raised his eyes, his gaze cold. "Since he is registered to serve in the Imperial Prison, then it makes no difference whether he is willing or not. If these men cannot be useful to me, then leaving them at loose ends will only lead to disaster."

The Embroidered Uniform Guard didn't lack for talent, but scouts like Gu Jin, whose eyes and ears were exceptional, were few and far between. Fei Sheng was a son of common birth, born of a concubine; he had inherited his father's old post and was now an assistant commander. He was the most outstanding among the Guard for this kind of work, but had been previously overshadowed by Qiao Tianya. Still, he'd hung on until he reached his eighth year, when he could be considered for promotion, and made many trips to his clan lands to pay respects to the Helian Marquis. He'd fancied himself a natural choice for the position of northern judge. Who would've expected Shen Zechuan to drop out of the sky? This man had completely dashed his prospects, leaving Fei Sheng stuck in his original post, standing around awaiting orders from a man who had been his junior.

Fei Sheng was fundamentally different from a man like Ge Qingqing. He knew more about the convoluted circles of court officials than Ge Qingqing, who came from an impoverished background. Ge Qingqing had a strong friendship with Ji Gang— Fei Sheng didn't give a damn about him. He could strike up a casual conversation with Han Cheng himself, who was by far his superior, and could even be considered halfway to being Han Cheng's disciple. For now, he was at the forefront of the Embroidered Uniform Guard members who stood against Shen Zechuan. When Shen Zechuan had been at the height of his glory a few months prior, Fei Sheng had laid low and avoided him, but the friction between them had built inevitably in recent days.

Shen Zechuan had spent too long examining old cases, in part because half his time was wasted on people who thought of him the way Fei Sheng did. They heeded only some of the instructions he handed down to them, and were sloppy in locating and gathering the case files. Shen Zechuan had been unable to match all the records to the correct reigns and had to personally make a trip to the Ministry of Justice before he could put everything in order.

The tension between the two sides was at a breaking point. Ge Qingqing knew Fei Sheng and the others were capable, but still choked with resentment to be bested by them. Still, when it came to searching the city, Ge Qingqing understood his skills were inferior. Finding Ji Gang and Qi Huilian was top priority. Ge Qingqing bit back his objections and rose to call Fei Sheng.

He ducked out from behind the office's curtain and walked across the courtyard. Fei Sheng was there, drinking wine and playing the finger-guessing drinking game with others. Ge Qingqing stood in the doorway and said stiffly, "Assistant Commander Fei, please make your way into the central office. His Excellency has need of you."

Fei Sheng seemed not to hear him; with one foot on the chair, he shouted loudly as they played. It was an astonishing display of disrespect, making such a ruckus in broad daylight.

Ge Qingqing never lost his temper with these men. He had been tagging along on missions with his old man since he was young and had seen all sorts. He was adept at taking care of others and had a strong sense of propriety. Most importantly he was likeable and could make the acquaintance of everyone from the squad commanders standing guard to attendants far below him in rank. No matter how uncomfortable he was, it wasn't his way to show his displeasure. He strode through the door and took up the wine jug on the table to personally pour a cup for Fei Sheng. He said courteously, "It's nothing major, and it's not a mission on His Majesty's orders either. It'll just take a moment."

Fei Sheng tossed a handful of peanuts into the air and caught them in his hand. "If it's not on His Majesty's orders, go grab one of my subordinates. Why's he singling out someone of my rank for nothing major? That doesn't make sense, does it?"

"His Excellency makes his own arrangements. Whether or not you take up the assignment can be negotiated." Ge Qingqing poured for himself and clinked cups with him. "Going over those old cases the last few days has been tough on everyone. Assistant Commander Fei has worked hard and achieved much. Here's a toast to you. Capable men are always rewarded with more work. The vice commander is waiting."

It was no secret that Fei Sheng didn't care for Shen Zechuan. He boasted that he was Shen Zechuan's senior with many more years in the Guard, and that Shen Zechuan was unqualified to order him around. But when all was said and done, they had to work together.

He couldn't afford to make a scene without good cause; if news of his defiance were to make its way to Han Cheng, it would reflect poorly on him.

So Fei Sheng drank the wine and smiled mirthlessly at Ge Qingqing. He didn't deign to answer, but collected his authority token from the table and turned to leave.

Given such a pointed cold shoulder, Ge Qingqing could only set down the wine and cup his hands to the surrounding Embroidered Uniform Guard—all varied in their expressions—before he left. The moment he stepped out, his own men, waiting outside, stood up.

Ge Qingqing wiped his mouth. "What are you standing for? Skip the formalities between us brothers. Sit."

Xiao-Wu, who was of similar age to Ding Tao, had yet to learn not to wear his heart on his sleeve. "Look at that Fei Sheng with his nose in the air," he fumed. "He swaggers around like a tyrant, puffed up with his own importance. Karma's gonna hit him in the face someday. What kind of an honorable man acts like such a snob? Bah! Qing-ge, why do we put up with him? Remove his token and drag him out, then cover his head with a sack and give him a good thumping. That'll teach him to behave!"

"Watch what you say," Ge Qingqing rebuked him. "If news gets out that we beat up our own people, we'll all look like fools!" He eyed every one of them in turn. "We are all doing our duty here. We mustn't leave any misunderstanding or unhappiness to fester. How else can we watch each other's backs when we're out on a mission? If they look down on us, we'll just work harder to prove ourselves."

Fei Sheng lifted the curtain to the office and sloppily paid his respects. The reek of wine on him was so strong Shen Zechuan caught a whiff of it from the far side of the desk.

Without lifting his head from his work, he said, "Drinking on duty is punishable by a deduction of your salary, yes?"

Seeing that Shen Zechuan didn't get up to greet him, Fei Sheng pulled over a chair. But before his backside touched the seat, Shen Zechuan glanced up and smiled. "Sit."

Fei Sheng couldn't tell what he was up to. He sat. "I hear Your Excellency's looking for me. What can I do for you?"

"I have an assignment no one can accomplish but you," Shen Zechuan replied.

At this, Fei Sheng relaxed. He fished out a pipe from his sleeve pocket and lifted his chin haughtily. "Is it an assignment from the prison? If it's an order from the chief commander, pass me the official paperwork and I'll get started."

Shen Zechuan tapped away the excess ink on the tip of his brush. "It's not a prison assignment, and it's not an order from the chief commander."

Fei Sheng struck his flint and bit down on the pipe as he laughed. "Then it's an order from Your Excellency? I can do it, but I'm on an ongoing mission to track and record these days. Aren't we just about to enter the fourth month? I have to keep an eye on the price fluctuations of Qudu's daily necessities."

The Embroidered Uniform Guard was indeed tasked with acting as the emperor's eyes and ears in the city. They tracked and recorded a number of major and minor civil matters, including the prices of grain, rice, noodles, and tea—these were reported to Li Jianheng and Hai Liangyi whenever necessary. But this assignment certainly didn't require Fei Sheng's personal attention. He was a fourth-rank assistant commander, and the only assignments for which he might be directly dispatched were arrests and assignments outside of the capital.

Claiming he was tied up with this mission was simply a way of refusing the assignment.

"Why use an ox-cleaver to kill a chicken? An assignment like that is a waste of your talent."

"I fear my abilities have always been mediocre. I can't compare with such a naturally talented hero as Your Excellency. A third-rank vice commander at such a young age, and even His Majesty looks upon you favorably. What's more, you're a man of poise and elegance." Fei Sheng blew out a few puffs of smoke. "Men like me can only hope to scrape by. We don't dare to dream of glorious work, and we don't dare act the hero either. Wait a few days. I might free up some time after that."

"This assignment cannot wait."

Fei Sheng cleared his throat and leaned forward, fixing his gaze on Shen Zechuan. "What can I do? Everything has its priority. I have to finish the task at hand before I can take on your assignment. This was the rule set by Ji Wufan when he was commander, and it's not one I can break. You'll have to wait."

Shen Zechuan didn't blink as Fei Sheng's smoke washed over his face. He observed Fei Sheng's defiant expression as Fei Sheng knocked the ashes onto the edge of the table.

Feeling he'd won, Fei Sheng pushed the chair back and prepared to bid him farewell.

Pale fingers flashed out to pin a slip of paper onto the desk before Fei Sheng. "I can wait," said Shen Zechuan. "But can the assistant commander? You're up for promotion this year. Coincidentally, the Provincial Administration Commissioner of Juexi, Jiang Qingshan, is on his way to the capital to report on his duties. Surely you understand the Grand Secretariat's intent in this. He will take charge of Zhongbo, and he lacks an inspector-general from the Embroidered Uniform Guard at his side. So tell me: Is Assistant Commander Fei still busy?"

Jiang Qingshan was an outstanding provincial governor. It was under his administration that Juexi had become the Zhou empire's granary; the provisions for the armies of both Libei and Qidong all flowed from him. This was a man not even Xiao Jiming or Qi Zhuyin could afford to offend. Working for him as good as guaranteed one's prospects would be bright.

Fei Sheng couldn't advance any further up the ranks without help. Although he was a member of the Fei Clan, one of the Eight Great Clans, he was a son of common birth born of a concubine; he didn't grow up alongside the lawful sons of principal wives like Han Jin, Fei Shi, and Pan Lin. Without their connections, he couldn't rise any further. Being stuck frustrated him to no end, and he took his dissatisfaction out on Shen Zechuan with sarcasm and mockery.

He immediately extinguished the pipe and rubbed his palms on his robes to clean them. Bending closer, he said with a smile, "Look at me, not knowing what's good for me! What's the assignment? Please tell me."

"I need you to scour all of Qudu for two men," Shen Zechuan said.

"Shall I search openly, or..." A glance at Shen Zechuan and he understood. "Ah. That's easily done. I'm good at this. Give me their descriptions, Your Excellency. Five days. I'll find them for you!"

Shen Zechuan lowered his voice. "I'm giving you two."

Fei Sheng looked at the slip of paper, clenched his teeth, and accepted.

OLD MANOR

HUA XIANGYI AND Qi Shiyu's wedding was set for the
eve of Grain in Ear³ in the fourth month, when the
wheat was ripe for harvest and the rice was ready for
planting. The Ministry of Rites had long made their preparations
and submitted them to the empress dowager for her approval. The
internal affairs of the palace were numerous and complex, and the
key government offices couldn't afford to be short-staffed for such
a major event.

Fuman had originally thought himself the perfect candidate for
the position of Director of the Seal at the Directorate of Ceremonial
Affairs. He had attended the Eunuch School, where he'd learned to
read and write, and now managed the affairs in the Grand Secretariat
and Mingli Hall. He possessed both qualifications and experience.
Furthermore, after their encounter during the epidemic scare, he had
Xiao Chiye to vouch for him. Eyes on this promotion, he'd lately
been even more discreet and fastidious than usual as he attended to
his official duties.

Unexpectedly, when the imperial edict came down, the position
of Director of the Seal instead landed on Fengquan. Fengquan was
young and had almost no experience to speak of; he'd never studied

---

3   芒种 (mangzhong) is the ninth of the twenty-four solar terms, starting around June 5th or 6th
on the Gregorian calendar.

in the Eunuch School. What was more, he was a junior eunuch who had entered the palace at a later age than was customary and shared a damning connection with Pan Rugui and Ji Lei. To hand this man a post comparable to that of an inner-palace minister—Fuman didn't know if he should sob or sigh.

"The promotion of an outer-court official is dependent on his family's social standing, origins, and the teacher or master he studied under. I thought, when it came to promotion, inner-court eunuchs like us wouldn't face this hurdle of family background and status. But damn." Fuman set down his teacup and heaved a sigh. "It's the same everywhere you go!"

"What family background does he have?" Xiao Chiye took a leisurely sip of his tea. "He's only riding on his elder sister's coattails."

Fuman slapped his knee and lamented, "Your Lordship, why don't *I* have a sister?!"

Xiao Chiye snorted with laughter. "If the seal isn't available, there's still the brush. The Director of Writ also manages the Eastern Depot. Lao-Fu, by letting him run out at the head of the pack, you'll escape the spittle of grandmasters of remonstrance."

"His Majesty's treatment of me can't compare to the former emperor's favor toward Pan Rugui, and the Eastern Depot isn't as influential as the Embroidered Uniform Guard." Fuman hesitated a moment. "Your Lordship, considering how favored Imperial Concubine Mu is at present, if she produces an imperial heir in the future, wouldn't Fengquan secure his position for life? It'd be one thing if he simply didn't know his place, but I fear he harbors some ulterior motive. Who's to say he won't break the court's laws and throw the state into chaos? Wouldn't that make him a second Pan Rugui?"

Fuman greeted Fengquan with a smile when he saw him in the palace, but in truth, he was sick with jealousy. Fengquan had Mu Ru propping him up within the inner court. If Fuman, who had already been so neatly supplanted, wanted to stand with Fengquan as an equal in the Directorate of Ceremonial Affairs, he had to win over the outer-court officials.

"He's young, and he'll still have to rely on you for plenty of things. You're familiar with the ins and outs of the Grand Secretariat, and even the Grand Secretary knows who you are. If one were to compare, he's merely a lad who takes what doesn't belong to him. He's unworthy of mention," Xiao Chiye said, comforting him. "With us looking out for each other from within and without, he's not someone we need to fear. How are things in the palace lately?"

"Second Young Master Xi is dead. His Majesty still thinks of the tune he had yet to complete; he's been upset about it for days." Fuman looked sidelong at Xiao Chiye. "But Your Lordship, while I was serving tea to Their Excellencies in the Grand Secretariat, I heard Minister Wei saying that he still wants to investigate the Xi Clan's accounts. The Xi Clan ran so much of the commerce at the Juexi ports, but there's no head of household left. That business is like a piece of fatty meat before the dogs—they're all eyeing it!"

"Isn't some of the family still alive?" Xiao Chiye and Shen Zechuan had already discussed the next stage of their plans for the Xi Clan. All those keys that had fallen into Shen Zechuan's hands were, in Xiao Chiye's eyes, Shen Zechuan's trousseau—but for now he was biding his time. "Xi Hongxuan's eldest sister-in-law and his various cousins all have experience managing their businesses, and they've committed no crimes. If Minister Wei digs through their accounts without cause, he'll be accused of kicking the family while they're down."

"Yes, and His Majesty didn't agree to it. But the Grand Secretary seems..." Fuman propped an arm on the table to move closer to Xiao Chiye. "...He seems intent on pursuing the accounts too."

Hai Liangyi had his own considerations. The Xi Clan had far too much silver squirreled away. Rather than let the noble clans plunder this carcass for themselves, he had likely calculated that he might as well claim that money for the state treasury and let the imperial court manage it. But if he wanted the money, Hai Liangyi would have to fight the noble clans for it.

"It comes down to His Majesty." Xiao Chiye thought for a moment. "His Majesty is a wise ruler, and he's committed to governing with benevolence and righteousness. Just last month he granted a general amnesty. Wouldn't searching and seizing the Xi Clan's assets without good reason run contrary to the intent of the amnesty? His Majesty must also see this. Lao-Fu, Fengquan will no doubt take Minister Wei's side on this matter. If you go along too, you'll look like you're blindly following. Next time you're serving His Majesty, why not take the opportunity to tell him in detail why it would be inadvisable to pursue those accounts at present?"

The gears turned in Fuman's head. "Won't this offend Minister Wei?"

"Whether it's inside or outside the palace, there's but one true master—His Majesty." Xiao Chiye smiled. "Pan Rugui was powerful too, but he didn't throw in his lot with the emperor—I'm not at all surprised he ended up executed. And besides, does Mingli Hall tolerate wagging tongues? How would Wei Huaigu know what words you say in private to His Majesty? His Majesty likes sentimental people. You don't have to push; just mention it in passing."

"I shall take Your Lordship's advice." Fuman was all smiles, warm and affable. "In any case, this money won't land in either of our pockets. We might as well put it out of everyone's reach!"

"Speaking of our pockets, the Ministry of Revenue has been tabulating the Imperial Army's expenditure on the medicinal herbs used at the Temple of Guilt for quite a number of days. I wonder how it's going—have you heard anything?"

"They finished just recently; it's already been submitted to His Majesty's desk. Everything is in good order." Knowing that Liang Cuishan, the Ministry of Revenue official entrusted to handle the accounting, had been nominated by Xiao Chiye himself, he said, "Lord Liang really is something to have kept those ledgers in such good order. There was nothing he couldn't answer readily when the Grand Secretary questioned him on it. Looks like he's on his way to a promotion too!"

With that, Xiao Chiye had no further questions. As Fuman left, Chen Yang handed him a block of new tea from Hezhou, prepared in advance. It sank too heavily in Fuman's hands to contain merely tea. He politely declined; it was only after Chen Yang's repeated exhortations that he finally allowed himself to accept.

The next day, after court was dismissed, Xiao Chiye waited outside Mingli Hall to be summoned. Shen Zechuan stood just a few feet away. The two of them maintained an appropriate distance— not too far, not too close.

"There are people everywhere probing into the Xi Clan's affairs." Xiao Chiye removed Wolfsfang in its sheath and handed it to Shen Zechuan, taking the opportunity to grasp Shen Zechuan's hand around the hilt as he did so. "Your Excellency ought to move quickly."

Shen Zechuan seemed to have something on his mind. He lifted Wolfsfang in his grip. "He's already left Qudu and is rushing back to Chuncheng with the coffin in tow. There should be news next month."

"Hai Liangyi is unlike the others. He's made up his mind to claim the Xi Clan's wealth for the state treasury. No matter how your man hurries, he'll still lose the first-strike advantage." Finding Shen Zechuan distracted, Xiao Chiye released his grip.

Shen Zechuan's arm sank, barely able to hold up the blade. "No matter how fast Hai Liangyi is, he still has to play by the rules."

Xiao Chiye cast a wary glance down the walkway of Mingli Hall. "What's wrong?"

"We've been searching," Shen Zechuan replied. "Shifu is still missing."

"As long as no passage document has been issued, he's still in Qudu. The Eight Great Battalions wouldn't have dared let people in or out without authorization during the epidemic. And the Imperial Army took over patrol of the gates right after. If Ji Gang-shifu had left, I would have heard news on my end."

"I also think he's still in Qudu." Shen Zechuan paused. "Xi Hongxuan was only after Xiansheng. Shifu went along for the sake of protecting him. He shouldn't have been held up this long. But if Xiansheng is in danger, Shifu can't leave on his own."

"Xi Hongxuan is dead." Xiao Chiye shifted his gaze to the other side of the walkway. "Time to get someone to check that gentleman's house."

Shen Zechuan followed the line of Xiao Chiye's gaze. Xue Xiuzhuo, dressed in official's robes, was approaching with Jiang Qingshan at his side.

Xue Xiuzhuo's looks were plain, but he carried himself with a scholarly and refined bearing. He differed from Kong Qiu, Cen Yu, and their sort: he was gentle toward others, and made a favorable impression on those he met. Jiang Qingshan, beside him, wasn't at all what one would expect; despite the rumors, the formidable heavyweight of Juexi looked quite a bit younger than his real age.

As they drew close, the four men exchanged polite greetings.

When Jiang Qingshan had come to Qudu to report on his work in the past, he had merely seen Xiao Chiye from afar at the Court Officials' Feast, and it was his first time meeting Shen Zechuan. But he had little interest in social connections in court, so he was neither overly warm nor coolly pretentious toward them.

"Many old cases were closed this year, and it's all to the credit of Assistant Minister Xue and the other gentlemen from the Ministry of Justice." Xiao Chiye nodded to Xue Xiuzhuo with a smile. "His Majesty is certain to lavish praises upon you when we meet with him today."

Xue Xiuzhuo smiled too, shaking his head slightly. "It's all due to Minister Kong's insight and wisdom that the cases could be closed. I merely assisted him as I could; I hardly made any contribution at all. On the contrary, it's Vice Commander Shen who waded through that mess of disorganized case files and set them to rights. It must have been hard on him."

"It was only a matter of checking the Imperial Prison's archive," Shen Zechuan said. "This is something even a common clerk would be able to handle."

Xue Xiuzhuo's expression betrayed nothing. Other than Jiang Qingshan, the other three were all feigning civility. Jiang Qingshan seemed as though he didn't want to get involved; he stood to the side and said nothing.

Fuman lifted the curtain and stepped out to call their names, and the four men entered Mingli Hall together. As Shen Zechuan strode in, he caught sight of Fengquan, who was serving beside Li Jianheng's dragon throne.

Meeting his eyes, Fengquan smiled.

Fei Sheng prided himself on his skill in conducting searches. There had never been a person he couldn't find. Yet after two days, even after combing every inch of Qudu, he had turned up no trace of Ji Gang and Qi Huilian.

Ge Qingqing had followed him every step of the way. When he saw that Fei Sheng had lost his arrogance and fallen silent, he asked, "Do you think they've been taken out of the city?"

Despite his attitude, Fei Sheng was serious when it came to his official duties. He squatted at one end of the Xi Clan's burned veranda, his gaze distant. "It's unlikely. One of them is an extraordinary martial artist; only by taking them in a single strike would no traces be left behind. For an endeavor like this, the greater the commotion and the more complicated your plans, the easier it is to be exposed—removing them from the capital would involve too many moving pieces."

Ge Qingqing took a few steps back and surveyed the Xi manor with its spacious halls and sprawling gardens. "But if he hid them here, how could it have escaped the searches of our brothers? We've been over this estate from top to bottom."

"Although I never associated with Xi Hongxuan, I've heard something of his temperament." Fei Sheng rose. "He was suspicious by nature. The more important a thing was to him, the closer he would've kept it. He didn't trust anyone. If these two men are so important, he wouldn't risk them being far away..."

Fei Sheng trailed off. He climbed up the scorched wall and pushed aside blackened branches to peer over into the manor next door.

"That's Prince Qin's old manor." Ge Qingqing had climbed up after him and crouched down to look inside.

"Deserted for many years..." Fei Sheng dropped down on the other side of the wall and took a few steps into the painted corridor of the abandoned manor: it was peeling and drab with age, and covered in cobwebs. He used his Xiuchun saber to knock off the thickest cobwebs and tried pushing on the doors, which were pasted over with paper seals.

"That's right. No one's lived here since the Guangcheng Emperor's time." Ge Qingqing looked around. "You think he hid them here?"

As soon as Fei Sheng touched the door, he knew something was off. "An abandoned manor, yet the seals are merely covered in dust—no cobwebs or weathering. Something's fishy!"

He took half a step back and kicked the door open.

IMPERIAL HEIR

THE DOOR PANEL fell to the ground with a loud thud, kicking up a cloud of dust. Fei Sheng covered his nose and mouth and strode in.

This was the former manor of Prince Qin. Although it had fallen into a state of severe neglect, hints remained of its former grandeur. After checking all corners of the courtyard, Fei Sheng lit a candle he carried on him, extinguished his bamboo firestarter, and headed into the inner chamber.

Ge Qingqing lifted the bed curtain and looked inside. "This curtain and bedding are all new."

"There were still people staying here as of a few days ago." Fei Sheng stopped beside the table and lifted the teapot lid to reveal tea stains within. "They drank spring tea from Baimazhou of Juexi. Xi Hongxuan didn't exactly treat them poorly."

When he glanced back at the bedding, Ge Qingqing saw dark stains; his heart began to pound. He lifted the quilt and took a sudden step back.

Hidden beneath was a putrid-smelling corpse with obvious signs of decomposition. Whoever it was had obviously been dead for days. Fei Sheng held up the light to inspect the body.

"This man was strangled to death." Fei Sheng pointed to the corpse's neck. "His throat was crushed."

"There are bloodstains," Ge Qingqing said. "He took a blade to the back before he died."

"Not only that. Look at his neck. There are two sets of strangulation marks—the first attempt didn't kill him. How could the men Xi Hongxuan hired be capable of forcing this shifu of yours into such a corner?" As Fei Sheng spoke, he flipped the body over with his saber. "There's no anomaly in the way the blood has settled in the corpse, so he wasn't likely poisoned. Look—these gashes on his back are a mess. A layman who knew nothing about swordsmanship hacked away at him. The blade missed all the vital points; that's why they had to choke him to death. They probably joined forces to kill this man. I suspect Shifu was injured. Perhaps he was too weak to finish the job, and Xiansheng had no choice but to take up the blade himself."

The more Ge Qingqing heard, the more alarmed he grew. "The corpse was laid out in such an orderly manner here—does that mean Xiansheng and Shifu haven't reached the point of panic yet? As long as—"

"It's possible the corpse was arranged by someone else." Fei Sheng surveyed the room again. "There are no traces of a fight here. I'm guessing Shifu was injured and couldn't display his true prowess, which is why he needed Xiansheng's help. But wherever they were taken after this, it wasn't arranged by Xi Hongxuan. None of those hired martial artists would have dared set themselves against the Embroidered Uniform Guard after his death just for a bit of money. Whether or not this corpse belongs to one of those hired hands remains to be seen. If it isn't—"

Fei Sheng ground to a halt. He had been willing to take this assignment for Shen Zechuan on the promise of a lucrative post. If Xi Hongxuan hadn't kidnapped the men he sought out of personal grudge, then it must involve court strife. Unwilling to put himself in the middle of it, he didn't finish the second half of his thought: If the dead man wasn't a hired martial artist, then a skilled expert like this could only have come from the imperial palace. This corpse was possibly one of the Embroidered Uniform Guard's own.

Ge Qingqing understood his concerns anyway. They fell into a silent impasse for a moment before they roused themselves; in a house this eerie and ill-omened, standing idly by wasn't wise.

Fei Sheng drew his blade back from the corpse. "In any case, the men we're looking for are most certainly still in Qudu. The houses and manors of officials and princes all have their own guards. Their doors are tightly shut, and most contain a secret passage or two. Hiding a few men is too easy. My apologies. This humble one is unlearned and of little talent. I can only search so far for Lord Shen!"

He cupped his hands toward Ge Qingqing and headed out the way he'd come in. He mounted his horse and headed back to turn in his report.

Ge Qingqing stood in the room after he'd gone, looking at that trail of blood. Noticing that it dragged off the bedding and onto the ground, he knelt to look under the bed. The shadows here were even deeper, but it looked as though something was there. Ge Qingqing extended an arm to fish it out. It turned out to be a handful of ashes; when he blew them away, a fingernail-sized piece of paper remained in his palm—the remnant of a note Qi Huilian hadn't thoroughly burned away.

Shen Zechuan closed his eyes. Pinched between his finger and thumb was that piece of paper, burned a crackling yellow. Only a few words remained on it, yet they were ones he was intimately acquainted with.

Qi Huilian's notes touched upon quite a number of subjects. Most were treatises on contemporary politics, which he had discussed with Shen Zechuan in the Temple of Guilt back then. Every little thing he had taught Shen Zechuan—every inside story about the eunuchs he had known when he served as grand mentor—all of it was in these notes. During the epidemic, Qiao Tianya had transferred everything to the new house for Qi Huilian's personal safekeeping.

To foil prying eyes, Qi Huilian had his own ciphers for recording his notes, which varied according to the treatise. All were his own inventions, created during his time at the temple. If one were to read the notes normally, they would appear to be simply a jumble of words, like the ravings of a lunatic—entirely incomprehensible.

Yet he had burned them. Was it because he was forced by circumstance, or because he feared his captor would be able to read them?

Qiao Tianya, who had been leaning against the wall, straightened up when he saw Shen Zechuan step out. Shen Zechuan swept down the steps. "Prepare the carriage."

It was already late in the day; Qiao Tianya didn't have to ask where he was headed. The inconspicuous carriage set off, circling twice on Shenwu Street before reaching Plum Blossom Manor.

"Where is His Lordship?" Shen Zechuan asked as he got out of the carriage.

Seeing him so solemn, Ding Tao didn't dare mess around and replied honestly, "His Lordship has just stepped out to invite Eldest Master Xue for a drink. He will return later. Your Excellency, shall I call His Lordship back? He's just a few streets away."

Xiao Chiye was probably trying to probe deeper into Xue Xiuzhuo's dealings. The Xue Manor was a tough nut to crack. Relying on an insider like Xue Xiuyi was far more convenient than sending someone to grope around in the dark for clues.

Shen Zechuan strode into the courtyard. "Just say I'll be resting here tonight. Tell him to come back when he's done drinking and not to stay out all night, but there's no need for him to rush back. Xue Xiuyi isn't someone easily dismissed."

Ding Tao murmured an acknowledgment and took off. Qiao Tianya, following Shen Zechuan, asked, "Why the sudden hurry?"

"Xi Hongxuan didn't trust anyone, but he trusted Xue Xiuzhuo." Shen Zechuan climbed the stairs under the dim light of the lantern. "The last time, when Xi Dan bluffed him, he was quicker to suspect a member of his own family than to suspect Xue Xiuzhuo. He always had to ask Xue Xiuzhuo about everything. It's the same with Xiansheng—Xi Hongxuan wouldn't have had the guts to act on his own."

Before his death, Xi Hongxuan had been absolutely certain Shen Zechuan would ultimately fail. *Why?* He must have known something Shen Zechuan didn't. Xi Hongxuan's promotion to the Bureau of Evaluations was Xue Xiuzhuo's suggestion. He had heeded him in every particular—why had he been so receptive to Xue Xiuzhuo's advice?

Shen Zechuan's feet paused in their steps.

The Xue Clan had been on the decline for a long time. Xi Hongxuan would never put himself at the disposal of someone he considered down and out. He wasn't easily won over by anyone. The two had come to associate through the solidarity and friendship between fellow students. Due to marriages between their clans in previous generations, they also had some ties of kinship. But how had Xue Xiuzhuo maintained his hold over Xi Hongxuan?

Xi Hongxuan put profit above all else. Even his own brother might be disposed of on a whim. Whatever minuscule blood relationship he shared with Xue Xiuzhuo, it wasn't enough for Xue Xiuzhuo to gain his utmost trust.

Apprehension crept over Shen Zechuan. He looked up to the eaves. The shadows they cast resembled a menacing beast, jaws stretched and brandishing its claws, holding his body between its sharp fangs. These elusive clues were like the first rustle of tall grass that, in the darkening night, brushed against his hands and legs, alerting him to the danger.

When Xiao Chiye looked up from drinking with Xue Xiuyi and saw Ding Tao step inside, he knew Shen Zechuan had returned to the manor. Without turning from his conversation, he gave Ding Tao a slight nod in acknowledgment.

Xue Xiuyi was half-drunk again. He'd thought to call a few prostitutes down for company, but Xiao Chiye didn't suggest it, so he refrained from rashly requesting them. Wine cup in hand, he hiccupped at Xiao Chiye, "He... Xue Yanqing! That flock of fledglings he's raising in his estate—he settled them in a big courtyard, and even hire...hi-hired a teacher and set up some kind of private school. If you ask me, he d-doesn't seem to be raising any prostitutes."

"Is that so?" Having downed several cups of wine, Xiao Chiye showed no sign of intoxication. Beside him, Chen Yang filled Xue Xiuyi's cup to the brim again. Xiao Chiye casually clinked rims with him. "Then what did he buy all those people for? There must be some reason."

"There's something odd about that Xue Xiuzhuo!" Xue Xiuyi swallowed a mouthful of wine and continued, "If not for Your Lordship's reminder, I would have never thought about it. The people he bought are of a similar age, all good-looking, with boys and girls both p-pleasing to the eye. There are a fair number of people in the imperial court who prefer men. All those male prostitutes on Donglong Street are delicate and supple. They're in no way inferior to r-real women! Maybe he thinks the ones in the brothels are unclean or will run their mouths and open him up to gossip and ridicule, so he's raising his own on the sly to share with friends."

Xiao Chiye let him prattle and toasted him again. "If that's his plan, he's going to have to put in a lot of time and effort. Those renowned male courtesans on Donglong Street have proven worth; their patrons spend cold, hard cash on them. Besides, you said he bought both boys and girls. Is the teacher he hired only teaching the boys?"

"That's the odd thing!" Any gentlemanly refinement Xue Xiuyi possessed had been lost several cups ago. He hung his head until his hiccups stopped before speaking again. "Your Lordship, he let those girls learn music, weiqi, calligraphy, and painting—all the four arts! And why not; what man wouldn't like a pretty lady as a study companion? Yet he also lets those boys study essays on current affairs."

Xiao Chiye's eyes cut toward Xue Xiuyi. "He lets those boys study essays on current affairs? Is that all they learn?"

Xue Xiuyi shook his head hard. He extended a wavering finger. "He set up a real school in that little courtyard. I've even seen him go in there to teach them personally. Your Lordship, do you know what he taught? They were all proper classics. Just the other day, he was teaching these boys...contemporary politics!"

When Xiao Chiye returned home, long past midnight, he saw the lamp was still lit in his room—Shen Zechuan was waiting for him. Chen Yang had dismissed the attendants, leaving only a few guards to stand watch over the courtyard.

Xiao Chiye stepped inside. Only a single glazed lamp burned on the small table. Shen Zechuan sat before it, looking through his cases. He had removed his hair crown, and with Xiao Chiye's large robe loose on his shoulders, he looked as he always did before he retired for the night.

Draping himself across Shen Zechuan's back, Xiao Chiye tilted his head to kiss his earlobe. "Just leave a note if you need to tell me something and get some sleep. Whether we discuss it now or tomorrow morning, it's all the same."

Shen Zechuan hummed in acknowledgment and turned to look at him.

Rising, Xiao Chiye removed his blade and outer garment, then settled down cross-legged beside Shen Zechuan.

Shen Zechuan's fingertips pinched the page of the book, but he didn't turn it. "Some things must be discussed in person; they can't be explained in a jotted word or two."

Xiao Chiye finally relaxed and started unfastening his collar. "Let's take turns. You first, or me?"

Seeing him struggle with the clasps, Shen Zechuan raised his fingers to undo them for him. After thinking a moment, he said, "There are many things I have yet to wrap my head around. You go first."

Propping his elbow on the small table, Xiao Chiye fished out another book from the cabinet behind them and handed it to Shen Zechuan. As Shen Zechuan opened it, he said, "Among the group of people Xue Xiuzhuo bought, the eldest is eighteen years old, and the youngest is fourteen. Boys and girls both, mixing in the same courtyard. The only thing they might be said to have in common is that they're pleasing to the eye."

"Eight cities. Zhongbo. Juexi." Shen Zechuan ran his finger across the names. "He didn't look at their place of origin when he bought them."

"Or this might have been done to obscure the truth, so that others wouldn't know where to start looking even if they wanted to." Seeing Shen Zechuan's finger pause over a name, Xiao Chiye moved in closer for a look. "You've seen this name before?"

"Ling Ting..." Shen Zechuan looked at that name again. "I've heard this name at Xiangyun Villa."

"They're all Xiangyun's people," Xiao Chiye said. "She likes sharp and canny children; that's why she used Ling—*smart*—as a surname and changed all their names."

"You had a drink with Xue Xiuyi earlier tonight. Did he mention anything?"

"He said something strange." Xiao Chiye paused. "He said Xue Xiuzhuo brought this group of people back to the manor, where the girls learn everything the high-end brothels teach, while the boys attend proper school. Xue Xiuzhuo hired a teacher for these boys. They're educated not only on essays on current affairs from the Imperial College, but discourse on contemporary politics as well."

Shen Zechuan considered this in silence.

"If it was students he wanted, he could've picked them from decent households," Xiao Chiye continued. "There are plenty of young men from the Imperial College who'd jump at the chance to acknowledge him as their teacher. Yet he's teaching boys he bought from a brothel. Even if these kids really accomplish anything in their studies, they can't become officials due to their low status. So what's in it for him? Does he intend to raise a bunch of over-educated retainers and kept poets?"

"Xue Xiuzhuo." Shen Zechuan's attention had drifted, lost in contemplation. He swiftly organized his thoughts. "If he wants to raise intellectual hangers-on, there are better candidates. We missed a key point earlier. Xue Xiuzhuo and Xi Hongxuan were on good terms. It's not as if Ouhua Pavilion couldn't afford to give him the flock of brothel fledglings he wants. Yet, he specially bought them from Xiangyun Villa—he had set his sights on a specific person all along."

Images flashed through Shen Zechuan's mind. Although he didn't have Ding Tao's eidetic memory, he mulled over every word and gesture in his interactions with others. He remembered them all; he wouldn't forget any details.

As long as Li blood runs in him, he's an imperial heir.

Grand Mentor Qi's words were a thunderbolt that cleaved apart the fog in Shen Zechuan's mind. Once this phrase surfaced, more followed. He sat up, scattering the papers on the small table with his sleeves.

"The former emperor." Shen Zechuan grabbed Xiao Chiye's arm, his voice gradually steadying as he arranged his thoughts into words. "The former emperor reigned for a little more than eight years, and his chronic illness never improved. He had no heirs, and the only one who ever fell pregnant was Imperial Concubine Wei. During the Nanlin Hunting Grounds incident, when the Hua Clan rebelled, Hua Siqian had the guts to make his move precisely because of this child in Imperial Concubine Wei's belly. But Imperial Concubine Wei was found drowned in a well the next day when we returned to the capital. At first, I suspected you. But later I thought it had to be the old-guard ministers from Hai Liangyi's side who'd struck first—remove Imperial Concubine Wei and sever the noble clans' wishful thinking about other heirs to pave the way for Li Jianheng's smooth ascent. Now that I think about it, that can't be right either. Even if Imperial Concubine Wei was with child, there was no knowing if it was a boy or a girl. The nobles couldn't pit an unborn child against Li Jianheng, who already had the support of Libei. For Hai Liangyi, killing Imperial Concubine Wei would have been an unnecessary move.

"Tracing back further," Shen Zechuan went on, "the Guangcheng Emperor occupied the throne before the Xiande Emperor, and the crown prince of the Eastern Palace slit his own throat in the Temple of Guilt when the imperial grandson was still an infant. Had he survived, he would be twenty-six this year. This plot was jointly handled by Ji Lei and Shen Wei. Ji Lei couldn't have been too careless if he wanted to defect to Pan Rugui—he would have had to show his value. It's unlikely he left such a seed of disaster behind. In that case, the only one in this world who can still claim to be an imperial heir is..."

Xiao Chiye gripped Shen Zechuan's icy cold hand and continued, low-voiced, "The eldest is eighteen, and the youngest is fourteen. If there's truly another imperial heir, then only the Guangcheng Emperor fits the timeline. The Eastern Palace was massacred in the thirtieth year of Yongyi. For nearly a decade after, no imperial concubine carried a child to term, thanks to the empress dowager's watchful eyes. Although the Guangcheng Emperor was suffering from illness at that time, he wasn't *that* frail. Unable to break free of the Hua Clan's hold over him, he must have turned outside the palace."

"Other than me, the only one who knew the stage floor of Ouhua Pavilion had been hollowed out and filled with vats was Xue Xiuzhuo. The collapse was an attempt to kill Li Jianheng; I just couldn't figure out why. But if he really has an imperial heir in hand, everything else makes sense. He killed Imperial Concubine Wei, then tried to kill Li Jianheng." That lurking unease in Shen Zechuan's mind was growing more and more distinct.

Xiao Chiye looked stricken. "If that's true, then the imperial heir is among that group of people."

They faced each other. Shen Zechuan spoke at a whisper. "This imperial heir—"

"—must not live." Xiao Chiye pinched Shen Zechuan's chin and closed the distance between them. His eyes were deep and grave. "Lanzhou, we cannot let a single one of these people live."

He spoke slowly, his killing intent like a raging whirlpool in the depths. In an instant, a thousand thoughts flashed through their minds: What did it mean if there was another imperial heir? If it was true, all their present plans would be overturned; they would suddenly be forced on the defensive. A noble clan who controlled the imperial heir would be nigh impossible to defeat. Think of the empress dowager, who ruled the court behind a screen for twenty years—the Li Clan, in her hands, was a puppet. The power and influence of the noble clans would rise again, and Hai Liangyi would be beaten back into obscurity.

A sharp knock rang out from the other side of the door, shattering the heavy atmosphere.

"Speak," Xiao Chiye called.

"Master." It was Qiao Tianya, speaking urgently. "The men who have been hurrying all night to catch up with Xi Dan are back."

Shen Zechuan stood at once, gathering his robe, and opened the door. Qiao Tianya stepped aside to reveal Ge Qingqing, waiting on one knee in the courtyard. Shen Zechuan walked down the steps. "What is it?"

"Your Excellency." Ge Qingqing looked up. His voice quavered, hoarse. "Xi Dan opened the Xi Clan's vault, but it...it had already been emptied."

The leaves on the branches in the courtyard rustled in the wind. Meng cocked his head, looking askance at Ge Qingqing. Moonlight smeared the ground as white as a blanket of frost. In the thick silence, Shen Zechuan turned his head back toward Xiao Chiye. "Er-lang, we've been played for fools."

His tone was gentle, yet upon hearing it, the entire courtyard of guards lowered their heads.

IMPERIAL PRECEPTOR

>>> ———— ◆ ❀ ◆ ———— <<<

DESPITE THE PLEASANT BREEZE, the night had a chill
that made one shiver with terror.

Xiao Chiye's earlier murderous aura was largely dis-
pelled by that intimate *Er-lang*. He stayed silent some moments,
bathed in the pleasant coolness as he found his calm.

Shen Zechuan looked back at Ge Qingqing and said evenly,
"They couldn't have transported so much in such a short time; this
must have been in the works for a while. No matter how thorough
he is, he can't cover his tracks completely. Gather some men and
head out of the city tonight. Go to Qinzhou first; make detailed
inquiries along the way. Note down any transactions between Juexi
and the northeast within the past two years involving large or bulky
goods. Send someone back to give me a detailed account."

Ge Qingqing's heart had been heavy with worry after receiving
the news. But when he saw how unruffled Shen Zechuan was, he
couldn't help his relief, and composed himself as he nodded.

"Chen Yang." Robe still hanging off his shoulders, Xiao Chiye
motioned for him to step forward. "Take the men to the Envoys'
Hall in Qudu first. Say a bandit is on the run in Juexi. Request a few
medium-grade horses and show them an official writ of arrest for a
notorious bandit leader. Tell them the Imperial Army must stay close
to the capital, so the task has been entrusted to the Embroidered

Uniform Guard instead. I'll make a trip to the Ministry of War and the Ministry of Justice tomorrow morning personally and submit a report."

The city gates had closed for the night; they couldn't leave without good cause. The Embroidered Uniform Guard happened to be entrusted with the important responsibility of arresting wanted criminals, though they were expected to report to the Ministry of Justice and Chief Surveillance Bureau and wait for official approval before leaving the city for fieldwork. Xiao Chiye was giving Ge Qingqing a reason to take men out of the capital tonight without being called to account by the Ministry of Justice.

Ge Qingqing prepared to leave immediately upon receiving his orders. Chen Yang threw on his robe as well and led the way, and the two left the residence ahead of the rest.

Xiao Chiye led a thinly clothed Shen Zechuan back inside by the hand. Seeing Shen Zechuan still deep in thought, he said, "Xue Xiuzhuo is no doubt behind what happened to Xiansheng. If he's willing to move him, Xiansheng is still of some use to him. He won't rashly kill him. There are too many secrets hidden in the Xue manor. I'll have to think of a plausible reason to obtain a special search-and-arrest warrant from His Majesty."

"Deploying the Imperial Army will require a major case with ironclad evidence. We'll have to rely on the Embroidered Uniform Guard a little longer." Shen Zechuan didn't settle back into his original seat. It was already very late; knowing he wouldn't rest tonight, he poured himself a cup of strong tea. Yet he took merely a sip before he handed the rest to Xiao Chiye.

Xiao Chiye drained the cup. "Xue Xiuzhuo is cautious in everything he does. He never accepted the ice bribes officials outside the city offered him upon their return to the capital. Throughout his tenure as Chief Supervising Secretary, the imperial censors from the Chief Surveillance Bureau all regarded him as the most upright and uncorrupted official. He's rarely impeached. Even the Embroidered Uniform Guard will be hard-pressed to find an excuse to investigate him."

"Investigating him openly will alert our enemy." Shen Zechuan fiddled with the teacup, his mouth filled with the bitter aftertaste of the tea. "He's out in the sunlight, while we're in the shadows. As long as we keep the pawn that is Xue Xiuyi concealed, we are still on the offensive. We can handle anything that happens outside the palace, but we must be even more vigilant when it comes to affairs within it. Xue Xiuzhuo has already shown his intent to kill His Majesty, and Mu Ru and Fengquan are helping him. He knows every one of His Majesty's moves the moment he makes it. Under these circumstances, we must stay on our toes."

Xiao Chiye thought for a moment. "Wasn't Fengquan just named the Director of the Seal of the Directorate of Ceremonial Affairs? Given his service record, he's sure to be scorned by both inner and outer courts. Fuman, who ranks beneath him, is already itching for a fight, while Hai Liangyi detests all eunuchs on principle. And Fengquan's authority, even as the Director of the Seal, can't compare to Pan Rugui's during his time in office. If Fengquan's being squeezed from both inside and out, unable to fend for himself, he won't have the capacity to do any favors for Xue Xiuzhuo."

"It's of pivotal importance that His Majesty's position is secure," Shen Zechuan said. "No word of the imperial heir must get out."

Since Li Jianheng's ascension, he had been castigated constantly by the imperial censors and met with mishap and danger at every turn. He had no outstanding record of political achievements, and the common citizens didn't view him as favorably as they had his predecessor. If any whisper of another imperial heir were to leak, it would no doubt stir up public sentiment. No matter how one looked at it, it would be a threat to stability.

"Regardless of whether Xue Xiuzhuo holds a real or false dragon in his hands..." Xiao Chiye pressed the pads of his fingers to his thumb ring and stared into the glazed lamp. "The emperor of our Great Zhou can only be Li Jianheng. Any crown prince named in the future must be Li Jianheng's son."

The Xiao Clan, at present, had prevailed over the Hua Clan and managed to hold onto their power. Xiao Chiye had gained his footing, and Xiao Jiming's defenses in Libei were solid as well. Zhongbo and Qidong had become battlegrounds for their rivalry with the noble clans in Qudu. The mediation of outspoken ministers like Hai Liangyi and those beneath him had kept the fight from escalating further. So far the Grand Secretary had managed, with some difficulty, to prevent things coming to a head between the two tigers fighting over the mountain.

But Hai Liangyi's greatest shield was Li Jianheng. Li Jianheng respected and trusted him greatly, and acknowledged his unyielding loyalty. He was willing to lay all major and minor affairs of the imperial court out on the table for discussion with him. It was his trust in Hai Liangyi that had kept Li Jianheng from immediately turning to the empress dowager for support in this tug-of-war between Libei and the Eight Great Clans, and it was also this trust that had allowed Hai Liangyi to secure his position as the Grand Secretary of the Grand Secretariat at the start of the new reign.

Li Jianheng, as a man, wasn't important. But after he ascended the throne, Li Jianheng as the Tianchen Emperor became crucial. He was the eye of the political storm; the center of all covert and overt attacks, the shackles the three factions each used to restrain one another, and the dagger the three factions each used to stab one another.

Now that Xue Xiuzhuo had surfaced, Shen Zechuan couldn't help but wonder—even as he looked for a breakthrough—if there wasn't yet another powerful person hiding behind Xue Xiuzhuo.

A few days later, it rained during Xue Xiuzhuo's day off.

His sky-blue robe of fine-woven silk fluttered as he strode through the drizzle to formally call on Qi Huilian. In the little tower where he was being held, Qi Huilian was eating his meal in great bites; he didn't spare Xue Xiuzhuo a single glance.

Xue Xiuzhuo didn't take a seat at the table, but stood and bowed low, in the manner of a pupil to a teacher. He spied Ji Gang sitting before the window polishing a stone and said to the servants attending them, "Elder Ji has yet to recover from his injuries and ought to avoid spicy food. Ask our chef from Duanzhou to prepare the dishes again."

"Don't bother." Ji Gang blew away dust and said solemnly, "I'm not eating."

Xue Xiuzhuo made no reply, and the attendant withdrew to give the chef his instructions. The Xue Clan was prominent in the city of Jincheng; they knew little of the local flavors of Zhongbo. He had hired this chef hailing from Duanzhou specifically for Ji Gang.

The drizzle outside pattered down among the apricot blossoms of spring, beating the pink and white petals strewn across the ground into mud. After eating and drinking his fill, Qi Huilian wiped his mouth and rose to look out at the bleak scene in the courtyard. His chopsticks, shoved aside on the table, rolled to the floor. "Don't waste your time," he said, his back to Xue Xiuzhuo. "Ji Gang is obstinate. If he says he's not eating, he's not eating. Have them prepare some steamed buns and pickled vegetables for him to allay his hunger."

Xue Xiuzhuo smiled. "How could I be so irreverent with both elders in my house as guests?"

"Then open the doors." Ji Gang carved a nose and eyes into the stone. "We can find our own way back."

"The spring air has a chill to it lately," Xue Xiuzhuo said with no change in expression. "Vice Commander Shen is still without a place to settle down; how could he provide proper accommodation for the elders?"

"Drop the politesse and just say we're your prisoners." Qi Huilian walked a few steps; the iron chain on his ankles clanked with his movements. "I've been a prisoner most of my life, and I'm reaching the end. I'm old, and he's disabled. What are you trying to do holding two old, weak, and sick men captive?"

Xue Xiuzhuo bent to pick the chopsticks up off the ground. Wiping them with a handkerchief, he said, "In the past, Xiansheng was a brilliant man of great stature. You should've enjoyed the posthumous honor of being enshrined and worshiped within the Imperial Ancestral Temple after death. What a pity you threw in your lot with the wrong man and ended up feigning insanity in the Temple of Guilt for twenty years. Today, I would like to ask you to take up the title of Imperial Preceptor once again. You can finally lay to rest your regrets at never seeing the crown prince you taught enthroned back then. Moreover, it will redress the injustice you suffered and afford you a fresh start in the imperial court—you can once again stand before the masses with all the dignity you deserve. Are these two reasons not sufficient? I am someone who greatly respects and admires Xiansheng."

"Become the Imperial Preceptor again." Qi Huilian took a step backward, dragging the iron chain at his heels. A laugh escaped his throat. "You want me to become the Imperial Preceptor again? What arrogance! The empire is at peace, and the current emperor is legitimate—the rightful ruler of our Great Zhou. He has Hai Renshi to watch over him, so why does he need Qi Huilian? I'm a crazy old fool. To think I could assume such an important post is pure fantasy!"

Xue Xiuzhuo set the chopsticks back on the table. "Xiansheng only suffered as you did because you were slandered. During the years of Yongyi, the empress dowager controlled state affairs, upsetting court order and discipline and encouraging rampant corruption among officials. It was even worse during the years of Xiande. Hua and Pan colluded to stir up trouble in Qudu, the eight cities, and the entirety of Great Zhou, visiting untold suffering upon the common folk. After that, the troops of Zhongbo suffered their defeat, and desolation and despair ruled the six prefectures as bodies of the starved littered the roads. Xiansheng wasted twenty years in the Temple of Guilt—yet it seems you've lost your heroic spirit after coming out. Have you no will to compete for glory with Hai Liangyi?"

Qi Huilian turned back to the window, hands on the sill as he watched the rain pelt the apricot blossoms. After some silence, he said, "Twenty-five years ago, I did want to compete with Hai Liangyi and determine who was superior. We both took the same imperial examinations. He was so unremarkable, while I ranked first at the provincial, metropolitan, and palace level. But having climbed so high at such a young age, I didn't know how to navigate official circles with tact. I was framed and demoted out of the capital. Too ashamed to face the people of my hometown, I hid myself away, depressed, for several years. Later, Hai Liangyi was promoted, and he rose through the ranks. Yet the crown prince didn't take him as his teacher; he instead welcomed me back to Qudu as the Grand Mentor of the Eastern Palace. At the same time, I assumed the post of Minister of Personnel. Hai Liangyi came second to me his entire life. But he is a gentleman. When the Eastern Palace fell, the crown prince was condemned by all. Only Hai Liangyi believed there was still hope in him—that he wasn't beyond redemption. On the basis of this alone, I cannot compare to him. Between us, there is no superiority or inferiority, only mutual appreciation. But alas, heaven is blind. Though we share the same path, we cannot walk it together. I've been out of the world for twenty-five years. You're right. I no longer have the drive nor desire to compete with him."

Xue Xiuzhuo was silent, leaving only the patter of rain and the soft scraping of Ji Gang carving and polishing stones. The rain grew stronger, and the apricot blossoms fell from the branches in a chaotic mess, forming a patchwork of pink atop the muddy water.

"In this lifetime, I've taught only two students. Both times I imparted to them all the knowledge I learned over the whole course of my life. The first time, I thought too highly of myself and was unwilling to compromise, and it was precisely through this pride that I caused my student such great harm." Qi Huilian gazed at that dirty water covered in tattered petals as if looking at the unfortunate echoes of his life. "I, Qi Huilian, am not an immortal. Two students are enough. I'm not up to teaching another."

Ji Gang burst into a fit of violent coughing. He covered his mouth with a handkerchief and grumbled, "Close the windows!"

Qi Huilian shut away the pitiful scene outside and looked back at Xue Xiuzhuo. "That's all I have to say. Don't pester me! Be gone; don't stay where you're not wanted."

Xue Xiuzhuo didn't move. There was no resemblance between him and his brother, Xue Xiuyi; he scarcely looked like a noble clan's descendant at all. He lacked the haughtiness of men like Pan Lin and Fei Shi. The unhappiness he had endured over decades as the son of a concubine had polished him into an individual of unobtrusive yet sophisticated elegance.

"I esteem Xiansheng's talent and learning, and more than that, I admire Xiansheng's ideals. I have called on you here thrice to beseech Xiansheng to come out of obscurity and return to politics, all because I understand Xiansheng's aspirations. Xiansheng, Hai Liangyi is a gentleman of integrity, but what gentleman has ever been able to co-exist with petty men for long? The current emperor isn't given to the study of the classics, and he hasn't the benevolence to treat men of virtue with the respect they're due. He's merely a frail lifeline everyone grasps as our Great Zhou teeters on the brink of collapse. He cannot become a wise and virtuous ruler. How much strength and energy does Hai Liangyi have left in him? Entrusting the safety of the state to him—this is a complete reversal of hierarchy, and a poor judgment of priority."

"It has always been the duty of ministers to assist the sovereign in governing the state," Qi Huilian replied. "Hai Liangyi is doing his best to salvage the deteriorating situation and mediate between factions. He's a loyal subject. Don't tell me you'd rather he be a traitor who overthrows the Li Clan and incites a change in regime?"

"The conflict between the noble clans and common households has raged for hundreds of years. To cure this age-old societal ill, one must have the determination to cut off all means of retreat." Xue Xiuzhuo rose to his feet. "If Li Jianheng can't do it, there are others. Our Great Zhou is the empire of the Li Clan. As long as a Li sits on the throne, why not exchange one for another if it will help us weather this crisis?"

On this point, Qi Huilian fundamentally disagreed with Xue Xiuzhuo. Thus he merely treated him as any other descendant of a noble clan abusing his power and refused to engage in further conversation.

Xue Xiuzhuo let the silence stretch before saying, "Xiansheng and I, too, are travelers on the same path. It's a pity Xiansheng doesn't trust me. Even so, I must tell you this—Shen Zechuan is a vestige of evil. He drags out a feeble existence nursing his hatred. There is nothing else in his heart; he exists solely for revenge. He's a vicious man, and narrow-minded—poles apart from the late crown prince. When Xiansheng teaches him with the heart and mind of tutoring a sovereign, it's no different from helping a villain. Even if he achieves great things in the future, he won't be a good ruler."

Ji Gang slammed his carving knife down and glared furiously at Xue Xiuzhuo. "What do you know about Chuan-er? You call him a vestige of evil, but the way I see it, the greedy vestiges of evil are all of you! Shut your trap and leave!"

Xue Xiuzhuo bowed. "Should Xiansheng have second thoughts, I'll be waiting."

He left, and the curtain dropped behind him.

Xue Xiuyi was wandering within the estate when he spied Xue Xiuzhuo approaching from afar. Holding his umbrella, he made his way to the veranda, only to bump into the students from the brothel who had just been dismissed from classes.

He tossed the umbrella to the maidservant behind him and looked them over as each of the students paid their respects to him. "Is this path yours to walk on?" the maidservant scolded. "How impertinent you are, blocking the way of the eldest master!"

The students hung their heads and shuffled aside to make way. Noting an especially fetching girl of around seventeen or eighteen at the back of the group, Xue Xiuyi tugged her sleeve caddishly and said, "Are you one of the little birds Yanqing brought back? What's your name?"

The girl cast a glance at Xue Xiuyi without answering.

At just that moment, Xue Xiuzhuo happened to appear at the other end of the walkway. Stepping forward to block Xue Xiuyi, he smiled. "Did Dage just get back? Better return to your courtyard. It's really coming down; careful or you'll get drenched."

Xue Xiuyi slapped his hand away. "I know!"

He took a few steps; the students behind him were all bending their heads, addressing Xue Xiuzhuo as "Xiansheng." He craned his neck for another look and found the girl from earlier looking back at him.

Her gaze revealed neither fear nor trepidation. Even after Xue Xiuyi caught her looking, she didn't avert her eyes. Instead, she held his gaze until Xue Xiuyi couldn't help but turn away first.

The wind and the rain lashed at his face. Xue Xiuyi shivered and hurried off, his arms wrapped tightly around himself.

CRACKS AND BOOMS

G E QINGQING HAD BEEN GONE from the capital a little less than half a month. One after the other, the Xi Clan's vaults turned up empty; fortunately, money was still flowing in from the shops in the various regions, now managed by Xi Dan. Coupled with the four million taels of silver Xi Hongxuan had signed over to him already, Shen Zechuan didn't come up totally empty-handed.

The two million he'd sent via the Northeast Provisions Trail at the beginning of the fourth month had arrived safely in Cizhou. When word of it arrived in Qudu, Ding Tao handed the letter straight to Shen Zechuan.

Wiping sweat off his brow, Shen Zechuan waved the sealed letter at Xiao Chiye, who was similarly drenched and already stripping off his clothes to take a bath. From the other side of the screen, he said, "Just read it out to me."

Xiao Jiming's message was concise: the silver had arrived in Cizhou without a hitch, and the military provisions for the Libei Armored Cavalry this summer and autumn had arrived at the warehouse shortly after.

"Soon, Jiang Qingshan will be transferred to Zhongbo to take up the post of Provincial Administration Commissioner. Does that mean these army provisions from Juexi were prepared by someone else?"

Xiao Chiye sank into the bath. As he scrubbed down, he answered, "They were jointly prepared by the Assistant Administration Commissioner of Juexi, Yang Cheng, the vice prefects under him, and Juexi's various vice magistrates. They're all old hands under Jiang Qingshan's command and the most efficient when it came to the preparation of military provisions in the past."

Shen Zechuan set the letter on the desk. He thought of saying that, since the provisions hadn't undergone Jiang Qingshan's personal review, they ought to be properly inspected before distribution. But when he considered Xiao Chiye wasn't managing Libei's military affairs, he thought the better of it. Xiao Jiming knew his business; an outsider like him needn't interfere. He let the idea drop.

Xiao Chiye slipped a dark, wide-sleeved robe over his inner garment. He could hold his own against these solemn colors; even with the robe hanging loosely over his shoulders, he cut an imposing figure. He picked up a cup of tea that had gone cold. "Gu Jin went to the Xue manor last night. Xiansheng and Shifu are most likely detained in one of the small towers."

"No common place could trap Shifu." Shen Zechuan touched the brush on the desk. "I want to see for myself."

"Xue Xiuzhuo is vigilant. If he discovers us and transfers Xiansheng and Shifu elsewhere, we'll really be looking for a needle in a haystack." Xiao Chiye removed Shen Zechuan's crown and let his hair fall loose. "I've set some men to watch the Xue manor on rotating shifts. We need to think of a safer method."

"There's one thing I still can't figure out." Shen Zechuan let Xiao Chiye comb his hair for him; his strokes were clumsy, not at all like one would expect from the popular second young master. "How did he empty out the Xi Clan's vaults? Ge Qingqing didn't find anything in Qinzhou either."

Xiao Chiye met Shen Zechuan's eyes in the mirror. "Can't figure it out? I already did."

Shen Zechuan looked back at him, waiting.

"It doesn't matter if they're transported by land or water; as long as they were transported through established trade routes, those four million taels of yours would all be subjected to inspections at various regional checkpoints. He knows this too. So there's no point in checking the trade routes." As Xiao Chiye spoke, he plaited a little braid the width of a finger into Shen Zechuan's hair. "Every government post Xue Xiuzhuo's held throughout his career is a key position. A Chief Supervising Secretary audits the accounts in the various regions, and when it's close to the Court Officials' Feast, he must deal with the Transport Office, which is responsible for organizing and transporting the local taxes and tributes paid to the imperial court. No position could make it any more convenient for him to smuggle the silver in and out of Qudu."

Suddenly enlightened, Shen Zechuan wondered aloud, "But where did he hide it all? The Xue manor is larger than the Xi manor, but the family is less established in Qudu; they don't have as deep a foundation as the Yao Clan, in either sense. Even if he dug, he can't hide that much money."

"That depends on how he plans to use it." Xiao Chiye withdrew his fingers, and Shen Zechuan's inky hair cascaded down like water. It was soft to the touch, possessing not an ounce of the hostility of the rest of him. He pressed down on Shen Zechuan's shoulders from behind, and their faces appeared in the mirror together. "His hometown is Jincheng, and Hezhou is just south of it. The Yan Clan dominates Hezhou's waterways, and they have business dealings with the Xi Clan's ships in the ports of Juexi. Now that we've removed Xi Hongxuan from the equation, Xue Xiuzhuo will have to find people who can manage money as well as Xi Hongxuan if he wants his silver to start moving again—and that is none other than the Yan Clan of Hezhou. If I had to guess to whom he entrusted this silver, it's the Yan Clan."

Shen Zechuan had never been to Hezhou, but he'd heard of the formidable Yan Clan. Unlike the Xi Clan, where legitimate sons of the principal wife ruled the roost regardless, the Yan Clan prized ability. It didn't matter whether one was of lawful or common birth as long as they had talent. During the first year of the reign of Xiande, the Yan Clan made their fortune trading tea in Hezhou. They rarely entered Qudu other than to pay tributes. Shen Zechuan knew very little about them.

He thought that Xiao Chiye was likely right, but he couldn't go without poking a little fun. "Er-gongzi's braids are so prettily done. Truly a cultured man of many talents."

"This Er-gongzi has had plenty of practice," Xiao Chiye teased in return. "Aren't Snowcrest's little braids pretty? I plaited all of them."

"I put my heart and soul into saving up for a betrothal gift," Shen Zechuan said, "yet you think me the same as Snowcrest?"

Xiao Chiye bent lower and jested into the mirror. "A horse, hm?"

All sorts of expressions danced in Xiao Chiye's eyes. Pressed tightly like this, back-to-chest, Shen Zechuan remembered the last time they'd ridden the horse on that rainy night. Although the marks of those love bites no longer lingered on his smooth neck, it blushed nearly as red when Xiao Chiye whispered into his ear.

Shen Zechuan lifted his chin, exposing the exquisite curve of that neck. It shone like the crescent moon in the dim light: softened by shadows, innately smooth and lustrous.

He whispered, "Am I?"

Xiao Chiye fell under his spell. His lips brushed the corner of Shen Zechuan's eye, then curved in a smile as he stared at the man in the mirror. "How could I bear to think so? You are the master of me. I only want to take you riding."

The anxiety that had weighed on Shen Zechuan for days dispersed, just a touch, in Xiao Chiye's arms. When he smiled, it carried a hint of seductive allure that even he himself didn't notice.

The temperature in Qudu rose precipitously in the fifth month. They'd scarcely enjoyed the refreshing coolness of spring when the summer heat crashed over them. The lower-ranking officials weren't permitted to take sedans as they went about their tasks, so they all hiked up their robes and fanned themselves whenever they could. They were drenched in sweat as they entered their offices and drenched again as they exited, lips peeling and faces red under the blazing sun.

After receiving a succession of rapid promotions in the wake of his audits of the Imperial Army's accounts, Liang Cuishan had finally caught his breath. He was now working under Pan Lin, the Vice Minister of the Ministry of Revenue, handling the task of auditing the taxes of the various regions outside Qudu.

Pan Lin, for his part, was overwhelmed with gratitude toward Xiao Chiye. Not two days after he returned home from the river banquet, Li Jianheng had granted his father, Pan Xiangjie, a pardon for his offense in the matter of the ditches. Instead of being banished to the frontier as they'd feared, he received a salary suspension pending investigation and was excluded from this year's annual review.

Xiao Chiye had never publicly vouched for or recommended Liang Cuishan for promotion, but those officials were all astute men who knew Liang Cuishan was someone Xiao Chiye had personally spoken of to the emperor. Thus, though Xiao Chiye said not a word, Pan Lin had taken Liang Cuishan under his wing, sparing him from Wei Huaigu's reproach.

"It's the grand Hua-Qi wedding next month. We'll need to familiarize ourselves with the processes the Ministry of Rites sent over, and the expenses must all be clearly calculated so we can give a flawless answer when the empress dowager inquires after the wedding banquet." Pan Lin drank his chilled green bean soup. He was so hot his back was soaked in sweat.

Although Pan Lin was some years younger than Liang Cuishan, he had joined the imperial court earlier, and his rank was high. Whenever Liang Cuishan didn't refer to himself as *this humble subordinate* before him, he still had to say *this pupil*.

Liang Cuishan was warm too, but they were in the office compound and had to satisfy the demands of etiquette. He couldn't strip off his robe as he liked; the censors from the Chief Surveillance Bureau would most certainly chastise him if they saw. He dabbed his forehead with a handkerchief and nodded. "This humble subordinate shall heed Your Excellency's instructions; not a single line shall be left off this account."

Pan Lin gave him orders on a few other matters before stepping out to get on a sedan—there were still some details to verify at the Ministry of Rites.

Liang Cuishan was painfully aware of the debt of gratitude he owed Shen Zechuan and Xiao Chiye for their recognition of his worth. He didn't dare be shoddy in his work and promptly set about reconciling the accounts. Yet he had sat for only a moment when he heard someone barge in.

It was midday, and few people were about in the office. Liang Cuishan hurried down the steps to greet the visitor. Encountering an unfamiliar face, he asked, "Can I help you find someone?"

The man was sweating profusely as he shoved a missive into Liang Cuishan's hands. "This humble subordinate is an official from the Northeast Provisions Trail Postal Relay Station! Your Excellency, this is an urgent report dispatched from Baimazhou last night. It comes with the authentication tally belonging to the Provincial Administration Commission of Juexi. This is a matter of extreme urgency!"

The Northeast Provisions Trail!

The moment Liang Cuishan heard this name, he knew the dispatch must concern Libei. He accepted the missive and demanded, "Why was this delivered to the Ministry of Revenue? All communications from Libei are considered military reports; they should be delivered to the Ministry of War!"

"This is an urgent report dispatched from Baimazhou," the man repeated. "It bears the tag of the Ministry of Revenue! Your Excellency, please present it to the minister's desk, quickly. The consequences of delaying this express report aren't something you or I can afford to bear!"

Liang Cuishan ran back inside with the relay report under his arm and hurried over to Wei Huaigu's office, only to find him out. An attendant accepted the documents in his place but seemed to barely take note of them. He told Liang Cuishan not to wait, saying the minister would handle it later.

Something about this wasn't right. How could an express relay report be handled so flippantly? Wei Huaigu's people were clearly stalling for time! Liang Cuishan's heart was pounding as he retreated. Instead of returning to the compound, he lifted his robe and raced to the office of the Embroidered Uniform Guard.

It was a blisteringly hot day, and Liang Cuishan was panting by the time he arrived. Without even taking a moment for a sip of water, he burst into the courtyard and requested to see Shen Zechuan.

"What's the matter?" Qiao Tianya asked as he led him in. "Did Your Excellency run all the way here?"

"It's urgent!" Liang Cuishan had no attention to spare for Qiao Tianya; when he entered and saw Shen Zechuan, he blurted, "Your Excellency! This humble subordinate has an important matter to discuss with you!"

Shen Zechuan gestured for Qiao Tianya to serve tea. Setting aside the documents on his desk, he fixed his gaze on Liang Cuishan. "What's wrong?"

Liang Cuishan didn't dare sit. He took a deep breath. "This humble subordinate received an express relay report earlier at the Ministry of Revenue, dispatched from Baimazhou in Juexi. It concerns the Northeast Provisions Trail! This humble subordinate delivered the report to the top, but never saw Minister Wei and could only pass it to an attendant. This assuredly concerns Libei. Your Excellency, I fear there's been some accident with the military provisions sent to Libei last month!"

Shen Zechuan rose to his feet. "Go to the Imperial Army's office and inform the marquis at once. Take my horse. Tell anyone who asks that you're on an urgent mission for the Embroidered Uniform Guard—spur the horse all the way there!"

Although the preparation of the military provisions—supplies of rice, wheat, and millet—was handled by Baimazhou in Juexi, the inspection of them was the responsibility of the Ministry of Revenue.

The military provisions had a direct impact on Libei's war efforts for the year. If Wei Huaigu was indeed purposely delaying this report, there had to have been a slip-up somewhere for which he didn't dare shoulder responsibility.

This sweltering heat was unseasonable. It was only the beginning of the fifth month, yet it felt like the height of summer. The sun was scorching at midday; by the afternoon, the weather had turned overcast and windy, the air thick with the humidity of an approaching rainstorm.

Wei Huaigu sat in his chair for a full hour holding that relay report, the back of his robe soaked through with sweat. He felt dizzy. Several times, he opened his mouth to speak, but couldn't say a word. At last he steeled himself and jolted to his feet. "Prepare my sedan! We're going into the palace!"

Xiao Chiye, returning from the drill grounds at Mount Feng, was still riding toward the city when fat raindrops began pelting down on him. Meng swooped to perch on his shoulder. As he reached the gates, he saw Qiao Tianya galloping toward him.

Before Qiao Tianya could close the distance, Ding Tao came spurring over from the other direction. He tumbled out of his saddle and reported in a quavering voice, "Your Lordship! It's bad news! There's been an urgent military dispatch: the Hanma tribe trespassed into our territory the day before yesterday and encountered Shizi on the eastern mountain range. Shizi—" Ding Tao's tearful voice rose. "Shizi has been severely wounded. Our cavalry lost!"

Qiao Tianya yanked his horse to a skidding halt. Thunder exploded in the sky above, blasting apart the darkness cast by the billows of grim clouds. Rain crashed down in torrents. Xiao Chiye was still astride his horse. For the first time, his face revealed a dazed expression, as if he didn't understand Ding Tao's words.

In the nearly thirty years since Xiao Fangxu established the Libei Armored Cavalry, Libei had never suffered such a defeat. Even when Xiao Jiming had led his light cavalry to pursue the Hanma tribe for several hundred li in the past, he had returned from the desert unharmed.

Xiao Chiye had never thought his eldest brother would lose.

Never.

VETERAN GENERAL

HEAVY RAIN CHURNED UP the puddles at the palace entrance, where Xiao Chiye's horse had just reached the palace gates. Red silk umbrellas emerged one after the other from a line of sedans, all of them sheltering important ministers of the third rank and above.

The Minister of War, Chen Zhen, deliberately slowed his pace to wait for Xiao Chiye at the foot of the vermilion steps leading up to the palace hall. When he saw Xiao Chiye striding over in the rain, he began, "Ce'an, listen to me. No army in the world is invincible. A defeat is a lesson that will guide one toward future victory. Jiming has been fighting with the Biansha's Hanma tribe for years. He's only human."

Chen Zhen had known Xiao Fangxu for many years. He spoke bluntly, but Xiao Chiye understood he meant well. Xiao Chiye nodded, his face devoid of expression. Together, they ascended the stairs and waited before Mingli Hall to be summoned. As the rain soaked his shoulders, even the faint light of the lanterns seemed to shrink back from him.

An umbrella suddenly moved overhead to shelter Xiao Chiye. Shen Zechuan had come up beside him, holding the umbrella aloft to shield him from the deluge. Standing shoulder to shoulder, the two figures in drenched red robes brought to mind a pair of wicked gods emerging from a rainy night.

A moment later, Fuman lifted the curtain, made his obeisance to the court officials waiting outside, and began to summon them in one at a time. Hai Liangyi was called first, followed by the various ministers from the Grand Secretariat, and finally, Xiao Chiye. Not even Shen Zechuan was allowed to enter unless invited.

Xiao Chiye hung back, his gaze on Shen Zechuan laden with too many emotions. In an instant, he'd turned from a valiant, vicious hound into a lone wolf that had strayed from its pack.

Shen Zechuan suppressed the urge to stroke Xiao Chiye's cheek; he couldn't, not here. They stood for what seemed a long time in the shadows of the palace walls, weighed down by shackles invisible to the eye.

Xiao Jiming was severely wounded, and there were no other capable generals in Libei. The war was ongoing; Qudu must appoint a new general to Libei to take over Xiao Jiming's command. But this person couldn't be Xiao Chiye.

It seemed Qi Zhuyin's remark a year ago had been prophetic: she had warned Xiao Jiming that the Libei Armored Cavalry needed a new general. Too much military power was concentrated in their family's hands. If the Libei Armored Cavalry could only follow a general with the surname Xiao, then once the banner of the Xiao Clan fell, the Libei Armored Cavalry would weaken, unable to sustain its former glory.

The grandson-heir, Xiao Xun, was only six years old. If Xiao Jiming was out of the equation, Xiao Chiye was the only feasible successor to the Libei Armored Cavalry. Yet he was in Qudu, and Qudu would never release him unless the heir consort, Lu Yizhi, entered the capital with the young Xiao Xun to replace him as hostages.

Xiao Chiye's willfulness had always been a bluff, and now he'd once again been plunged into a chasm with no way out. His heart howled with longing for home, but all he could do was gaze at Shen Zechuan in silence. Other than Shen Zechuan, no one else would understand.

"Your Lordship?" Fuman prompted in a whisper.

Xiao Chiye went in.

"The Ministry of Revenue assigned officials to check the military provisions before they were dispatched via the Northeast Provisions Trail. If there was a problem with the provisions, why didn't the Ministry of Revenue report it then?"

Cen Yu was first to step forth and condemn Wei Huaigu without even taking time to pen a formal memorial. "The express relay report was delayed four whole hours after arriving in Qudu! If we issue the order to recall the provisions now, we'll have to brave the rain and treacherous conditions on what's already a difficult route. It will take four days to reach Libei! Wei Huaigu, you're going to get people killed!"

Wei Huaigu said nothing. He knelt on the floor like a statue and didn't dispute a word of Cen Yu's tirade.

The moment Xiao Chiye entered, the hall fell silent. Some ministers stared at the ground, while others pressed a hand to their foreheads, stricken. The crash of the rain outside was deafening, but the suffocating heat of the hall was worse.

"Ce'an." Li Jianheng began, then hesitated. "Take a seat."

Xiao Chiye bowed but didn't sit. "This humble subject has only just dismounted and has heard no details. What's happened in Libei?"

"What the hell? Has no one told the marquis about such a serious matter?!" Li Jianheng flung the report to the ground below the throne. "Wei Huaigu, tell him yourself!"

Wei Huaigu lowered his head, not looking at Xiao Chiye. "Something went wrong with the military provisions transported to Libei last month. According to the relay report from Yang Cheng, the Assistant Administration Commissioner of Juexi, there was mold in this shipment of rice, yet it was still distributed after arrival at Libei. Thousands of soldiers fell ill the night before the battle."

Who in the hall would dare look Xiao Chiye in the eye?

The Xiao Clan, who guarded the nation's frontier, had rendered tremendous meritorious service five years ago when they came to the emperor's aid after the fall of Zhongbo. Among the Biansha tribes, the Hanma was the toughest to fight, and it was Xiao Jiming alone who defended the entirety of the northeast against their incursions. Yet, as their reward, two emperors and their governments had imprisoned the Xiao Clan's youngest son in Qudu and let his eldest brother, who selflessly shed his sweat and blood in their defense, eat moldy and rotten grain! How would anyone have the guts to meet Xiao Chiye's gaze?

"The military provisions were prepared by the Provincial Administration Commission of Juexi," Xiao Chiye said without moving a muscle. "If Yang Cheng knew of this, why did he wait until the provisions arrived in Libei to report it? He's the Assistant Administration Commissioner of the southwest; I know of no grudge nor enmity he could have with Libei. Why would he risk his head to do this? The officials from the Ministry of Revenue triple-checked the provisions, and the official documents all reported new grain from last year's harvest. But now, it's turned old and moldy. These are all minor officials of low rank—so again, why would they do such a thing? The supplies arrived in Libei via the Northeast Provisions Trail, and the supervisor in charge of the granary from the Libei Armored Cavalry also had to inspect them before distributing them to the troops. For such a large shipment of moldy grain to make its way into the mouths of the officers and soldiers at the frontier pass, these layers of painstaking arrangements can only be described as methodical."

His voice gained more gravity with every word. "The Libei Armored Cavalry has guarded the pass for thirty years. A loss on the field merits punishment, but let me say this before everyone here: a minor defeat for Libei is a blow to our Xiao Clan, but a major defeat is a crisis for our Great Zhou. For several years, the Hanma tribe has been lurking on the eastern side of the Hongyan mountain range, waiting for their opportunity. Five years ago, after defeating Zhongbo's troops, the Hanma led the men and horses of the rest of the eleven tribes to the very gates of Qudu without hesitation. It has been a mere five years, yet the page on the tragic massacre of the six prefectures of Zhongbo has somehow already been turned. We have yet to redress our nation's humiliation, and now we're going to allow one of our own to add another strike?"

Color drained from the faces of everyone present. Xiao Chiye held nothing back; he had come tonight to raise hell. Someone was playing games with soldiers' lives, and they wanted to dismiss him with that same old bureaucratic nonsense? Not a chance. He was out for blood, and would pursue this case to the end. All the rest be damned; he was done playing nice.

The Minister of Justice, Kong Qiu, was first to find his voice. "The adulteration of military provisions can no doubt be traced to those at the bottom rung who resell grain at a profit. Many merchants with full granaries made a fortune during the famine in Zhongbo a few years back. But the laws in place nowadays are strictly enforced; I never expected officials and merchants were still colluding to commit such unconscionable crimes. We owe our generals in Libei a thorough investigation. This humble subject requests a joint trial by the Three Judicial Offices, supplemented by an investigation in both Baimazhou and Qudu, to be conducted by the Embroidered Uniform Guard. We must get to the bottom of this travesty!"

"That's not all. Another urgent matter requires our attention." The Minister of War, Chen Zhen, cast a glance at Xiao Chiye. "The military provisions for the five commanderies of Qidong also come from Baimazhou. We must dispatch an urgent report to Marshal Qi. This grain cannot be distributed any further!"

"And how shall we make up for the shortage?" Xiao Chiye's tone was icy. "Those two shipments of provisions represent the bulk of the harvest amassed in the three major granaries of Juexi last year. Now that you're recalling them, what will you send in their place? Where will you find the grain? If these provisions aren't replenished within five days, Libei and Qidong will be fighting a war on empty stomachs. This is a question of feeding hundreds of thousands of soldiers."

"We'll borrow from Huaizhou, Hezhou, and Cizhou," Hai Liangyi said decisively. "The debt from these loans shall be borne by the imperial court. This is an emergency—the state treasury can't withdraw so much money on short notice to purchase the grain outright, so we can only promise to exempt these three prefectures from taxes for the next two years."

"Baimazhou gathered all the grain reserves from the thirteen cities into these two shipments of provisions. The three prefectures the Grand Secretary mentioned cannot compare to that. Not to mention, these three prefectures are distant from one another, scattered all across the empire. Preparing and coordinating the shipments alone will take several days."

"Tell Qi Zhuyin that Qidong's military provisions will be halved this year," Hai Liangyi instructed. "They have military fields to sustain them; they won't starve. Hezhou is right beside Qidong, but the grain from Cizhou and Huaizhou must be shipped out tonight." Although he was sick, he remained clear-headed. "Heir Xiao is wounded; he oughtn't remain long at the front line. The Prince of Libei is ill and is similarly unable to lead. Chen Zhen, draw up a list of our generals and hand it to me in an hour. Within three days, Qudu must deploy a capable officer to Libei to assume command."

In minutes, Hai Liangyi had taken charge of the situation and given the final word. It was clear Wei Huaigu wouldn't get away this time. Xiao Chiye didn't intend to let him off; the only reason he wasn't at his throat right now was that the deployment of a commanding general was far more important.

Yet Wei Huaigu's behavior was peculiar. He knelt right where he was, as all the while the ministers were speaking and plans were being made, and said not one word in his own defense.

After retreating from the court, the officials gathered in Mingli Hall's brightly lit side room. Hai Liangyi couldn't bear the cool nights, so Kong Qiu draped an overcoat over him. He gathered the folds of it around himself and gestured for everyone to take a seat.

"The impeachment memorial will be on the Grand Secretariat's desks tomorrow," Cen Yu said. "How many times is this for the Wei Clan? His Majesty is mindful about showing mercy; the incident with Wei Huaixing over the assassination case didn't implicate Wei Huaigu, and Wei Huaigu never admitted fault for what happened with the public ditches either. But what about these military provisions? He can't escape punishment for negligence and dereliction of duty!"

"One's duties as an official in the imperial court have nothing to do with one's family background and standing," said Hai Liangyi.

"We mustn't find fault with others on the basis of their surname. If a man makes a mistake, then impeach him." Hai Liangyi had yet to drink a single drop of water that night, but he seemed tireless as he looked at Xiao Chiye. "Heir Xiao has been leading the troops for several years. If he was able to fight his way out of the Hanma tribe's siege and return to Libei, his life is not in danger. Your Lordship needn't be so anxious. Qudu will work through the night to get Libei anything it lacks."

Xiao Chiye understood. To maintain the status quo amid the current tensions, Hai Liangyi could never let Xiao Chiye return to Libei; there was no question of this. Xiao Jiming was defeated, but he wasn't dead—and even if Xiao Jiming died, Xiao Chiye still couldn't return home, because there was still Xiao Fangxu.

He sat facing an entire room of veteran ministers, yet Xiao Chiye was terribly calm. "There are many decent generals in Qudu, but those who can adapt to the battlefields of Libei are few and far between. The eastern Hongyan Mountains border the desert, and we're nearing the hottest days of the year. The heat on the frontier is brutal. I'm afraid any officer born in the southwest will be unsuitable."

He had reacted quickly to the situation, so quickly he appeared unassailable. In the hall, he had preemptively laid out the case regarding the military provisions, and now he was telling Hai Liangyi that the new general deployed to Libei had to be someone from Libei or Qidong; he didn't want an armchair strategist who was all talk and no action.

Hai Liangyi nodded approvingly at Xiao Chiye. At a moment like this, one should not be swayed by emotion or act impulsively for personal gain. That Libei lacked a commander was an indisputable fact. Skilled deputy generals like Zhao Hui were formidable, but they were all men whom Xiao Fangxu had personally taught. These deputies were meant to take on the tasks of coordinating and assisting a commander. They could lead a squadron of soldiers to outflank the enemy, but they couldn't convince their fellows that they were fit to lead all of Libei.

Yet since the reign of Xiande, the Zhou empire had faced a dearth of able generals. Of the Four Great Generals, one was injured, and other than Zuo Qianqiu, the remaining two had their own important duties to attend to. The talents that emerged later were all high-ranking military officers from Qidong—core members of Qi Zhuyin's army that she had trained from scratch. It was Qidong's military affairs they were familiar with. To lend any of them to Libei was easier said than done. Besides, the Qi Clan was about to enter a marriage alliance with the Hua Clan. If a general from Qidong took command in Libei, even temporarily, this would break the careful balance again and make it difficult for the emperor to hold Qidong in check.

Who should be assigned?

Even Hai Liangyi's head hurt thinking about it.

As they sat burning with anxiety inside the hall, Fuman hurried in from outside. "Your Excellencies, look who's here!"

Xiao Chiye turned his head and sprang to his feet. The entire hall followed suit, rising one after another. Hai Liangyi stepped forward to welcome the new arrival personally.

The man who garnered such respect peeled off his hooded overcoat, revealing white hair; he greeted Hai Liangyi, then looked at Xiao Chiye. "This humble one raced through the night to reach Qudu and seek an audience with His Majesty regarding the crucial matter of Libei."

There was a lump in Xiao Chiye's throat as he cried, "Shifu!"

Zuo Qianqiu didn't stop to make conversation with him. Instead, he greeted Hai Liangyi with a smile. "It's been many years since I last saw the Grand Secretary. I hope you are still in good health?"

Hai Liangyi gripped Zuo Qianqiu's wrists. "As old as Commander Zuo may be, can you still serve your country?"[4]

Zuo Qianqiu sighed. "Although my face has aged and my hair has grayed, I have yet the strength to draw a bow. There's no need for the Grand Secretary to worry. I came for two reasons: first, to stand in temporarily for Jiming and take command of the troops in Libei; and second, to deliver a message from Xiao Fangxu."

The entire room listened with rapt attention.

Something stirred in Zuo Qianqiu's eyes as he looked at Xiao Chiye. "The might of the Prince of Libei has reverberated like a tiger's roar through the Hongyan Mountains for so many years. His son has suffered a loss, and as his old man, he wishes to personally reclaim victory from Amur of the Hanma tribe."

The rain thundered down. A gyrfalcon let out a long cry as he swooped among the dark clouds of Qudu.

At the farthest edge of the world, the banner of Libei flapped in the wind. In that rain like heavy ink, Xiao Fangxu, who hadn't set foot on the battlefield for decades, donned his armor and strapped on his blade to lead the troops into battle.

The wind tore at Xiao Fangxu's cape, and he swept off his incongruous bamboo hat to look up at the sky.

"Amur." Xiao Fangxu's voice was deep. He raised an arm in the rain to release his Libei gyrfalcon and laughed into the wind.

---

4   Adapted from "Old as Lian Po Is, Can He Still Eat," from Joy of Eternal Union: Reminiscing the Past at the Beigu Pavilion at Jingkou by Xin Qiji, a poet and military leader during the Southern Song dynasty.

"Libei has drawn a border in the east; why are you trespassing? I told you decades ago, the Hongyan Mountains are the stomping ground of my Libei Armored Cavalry!"

His voice reverberated through the pelting rain. The armored cavalry behind him, cloaked under black armor, drew out their blades as one; in that moment of unified motion, their oppressive might called to mind a crouching behemoth suddenly opening its eyes.

91

LIBEI

ZUO QIANQIU HAD ARRIVED in the nick of time, leaving no chance for Qudu to select a general of their own. Thunder on Jade Terraces, Zuo Qianqiu, was known far and wide for his military achievements. He was the great general taught by Silver Spear of Snowy Pass, Feng Yisheng, and the senior of Xiao Jiming, Qi Zhuyin, and Lu Guangbai. It had been years since he had walked away from Tianfei Watchtower, and few had seen him since. He had no private troops; he was a child from a humble background who had been adopted by Ji Wufan, the chief commander of the Embroidered Uniform Guard during the reign of Yongyi; he had no family background to create conflicts of interest. His willingness to come out of obscurity and lead the troops was something Hai Liangyi couldn't have dared to hope for.

As Zuo Qianqiu waited for Li Jianheng to summon him, he stood with Xiao Chiye under the eaves, watching the rain.

"I had to make haste, so I didn't bring any message for you." Zuo Qianqiu's overcoat was half-soaked; he hadn't stopped once on the entire journey except to change horses. He spoke deliberately. "Jiming has returned to the camp, and the military medics are taking good care of him. Don't worry."

He was silent on the extent of Xiao Jiming's injuries. Xiao Chiye looked down; after a pause, he asked, "How was he injured?"

Zuo Qianqiu gazed out into the rainy night. "There are some words I will only say to you while standing here. Someone tampered with Jiming's food; they got Zhao Hui too. The squadron dragged their sick bodies to the battlefield and just happened to encounter Amur, the toughest of the lot. Jiming received three great gashes. It was Zhao Hui who tumbled off his horse and, with the ten or so remaining soldiers, carried his general from the battlefield on his back and broke through the siege."

Xiao Chiye clenched his fists.

There was darkness in Zuo Qianqiu's eyes, but his voice remained level. "Jiming has fought battles in the past while in ill health. After so many years pushing himself on the battlefield, he may seem fit on the surface, but in truth he's plagued by old ailments. This time, he has badly damaged his constitution. We should see it as an opportunity: let him recuperate for half a year and build up his strength again."

Zuo Qianqiu had taught both brothers, and he couldn't be any clearer about their temperaments. Xiao Jiming was soft on the out-side but tough inside; he didn't inherit Xiao Fangxu's preternaturally strong and healthy physique, nor his father's uncompromising, hard-nosed approach. And whatever he lacked, Xiao Chiye possessed. Perhaps a lesser man would have been jealous, but Xiao Jiming cher-ished his family. He had inherited the compassion and benevolence of his mother, the Princess Consort of Libei; it was so ingrained in his nature that he had never harbored a single ill thought toward his younger brother. He saw himself as a sanctuary for the family and did all he could to heal his wounds himself. All these years, he had never uttered a cry of pain. Lu Guangbai had repeatedly said that he was only human, but though Xiao Jiming indeed had mortal desires, he had forced himself to become the indestructible guardian of Libei.

This battlefield defeat had destroyed half of Xiao Jiming's lifetime of honor and glory. At this moment, Xiao Chiye abhorred his cage with every bone in his body. He chafed against his shackles, opening new and old wounds, raw and bloody. His gaze followed the raindrops to the ground, where the pooling water bore the weight of his silent agony.

He held himself together and said calmly, "The meals in the camps are all prepared by our own people. Dage eats the same food as the common soldiers. Harming him means harming thousands of men in the camp. We can't let this go. Whoever did this will pay with their lives!"

"The mess cooks who prepared the food have already been executed." Zuo Qianqiu looked at Xiao Chiye. "It was Jiming's idea."

Libei had to bear such a grave trespass against them, yet they had reported it as a matter of military provisions adulterated with mold rather than a pointed attempt at murder. Xiao Jiming had only broken out of the enemy siege after sustaining deep wounds. He'd hung onto consciousness long enough to give the order to execute those mess cooks, all to prevent an investigation into such a conspiracy. A deliberate attempt to kill him suggested a power struggle, and bringing that out into the open would only muddy the waters— it was too easy for Libei to be used as someone else's weapon. With Xiao Jiming incapacitated, appointing a new general would fall to Qudu. Even if Qudu investigated, who could guarantee that the person who put the poison in his bowl was the true murderer? Killing by proxy wasn't unheard of. Assuming the food tampering was just the first step in a larger plan, if Libei reported the attempt and the imperial court couldn't find the perpetrator, the noble clans, in their conniving attacks, might distort the facts and accuse Libei of using Xiao Jiming's injuries as a ploy to deceive the court and get Xiao Chiye back.

"You did well too. You didn't tell them you wanted to return to Libei to rally the forces and avenge your brother." Zuo Qianqiu's expression was solemn. "If you had spoken frankly and fought for command of Libei before the emperor, then their guilt tonight would've turned into defensive calculations. It would plant suspicion in His Majesty's mind and set the stage for future troubles."

"I expected the Grand Secretary wouldn't set me free." Xiao Chiye slowly pulled himself together. "It's as Shifu says. Grasping at military power will only make His Majesty afraid of me, and I still have twenty thousand men of the Imperial Army in my hands. That would be a major taboo. Making a scene right now will only delay aid to Libei. Shifu coming here has helped me out of my predicament."

"When I have my audience with His Majesty later, I'll discuss the issue of the military provisions with the Ministry of Revenue and Grand Secretary in detail. I need to head back at dawn tomorrow at the very latest. Your father has already declared war with Amur at the edge of the eastern mountain range. He's launching a frontal assault as we speak. No matter what, we have to arrest their momentum."

This wasn't an appropriate place to talk, so Zuo Qianqiu turned the conversation back to military affairs. "It's been a long time since I last led troops. I'll have to familiarize myself with the situation once I get back to camp. The Libei Armored Cavalry's strength lies in offensive strikes, while I specialized in defensive warfare back at Tianfei Watchtower. I need to discuss this with your father properly. There's one more thing—Zhao Hui was also seriously injured in the battle. His only remaining family is a younger sister who married into Qudu. Remember to send Chen Yang to the Ministry of Rites later to let them know that all is well."

Just as Fuman came out to summon Zuo Qianqiu inside, Xiao Chiye nodded in acknowledgment. Zuo Qianqiu took one final look at him. "You're alone in Qudu. Take care of yourself."

Xiao Chiye made a formal disciple's bow, and Zuo Qianqiu strode forward, lifted the curtain, and vanished from sight.

Fei Sheng had gotten his wish; these days, he was working by Jiang Qingshan's side. Something had gone wrong with Juexi's military provisions, and Jiang Qingshan, who still held the post of Provincial Administration Commissioner of Juexi, was summoned to Mingli Hall to discuss the matter. He was sure to be there for a few hours at least. Fei Sheng's old habits of laziness reared their head again; hoping to rest for a moment in the office, he sent a junior eunuch to fetch him some food.

He was sitting on the chair waiting with one leg casually crossed over the other when he heard a sound from the doorway. He looked up; when the candlelight revealed his guest to be Han Cheng, he scrambled up to pay his respects.

Han Cheng, who had braved the rain to get there, motioned for him to rise. As Fei Sheng stepped forward to remove his superior's overcoat, Han Cheng asked, "Has His Majesty summoned anyone for a meeting?"

Fei Sheng knew what he wanted to ask. He replied deferentially, "Marshal Zuo is here."

"Zuo Qianqiu?" Taken aback, Han Cheng blinked. "The Prince of Libei certainly lives up to his name—his reactions are so swift he leaves no opening to exploit. No other candidate in Qudu can surpass Marshal Zuo. It seems the Libei Armored Cavalry is still the *Libei* Armored Cavalry after all."

Fei Sheng concurred but didn't pursue the topic. These were matters he'd best not involve himself in, and he preferred to stay as far away as he could.

Han Cheng saw straight through him; it was for exactly this reason he held Fei Sheng in contempt. These common sons born to concubines were all like this. No guts and no spirit. They eyed the carrot dangling before them all day long, but made no attempt to snatch it.

Outwardly, he showed Fei Sheng an amiable countenance. "Although this matter involves Jiang Qingshan's subordinates, it's not a job he personally handled. The higher-ups won't blame him for this. Working under him is a good move; it will open many doors for you," he said. "He's set to head for Zhongbo next month. When the Embroidered Uniform Guard travels there for work in the future, they'll be relying on you to pave the way. Xiao-Sheng, work hard and do your best."

Fei Sheng murmured his agreement and saw Han Cheng out. As he lowered his head to lift the hem of Han Cheng's robe across the threshold, he spotted a corner stained greyish black. He hurried to brush it away for Han Cheng and fawned on him, saying, "Did Your Excellency come over on foot? How—"

Unexpectedly, Han Cheng yanked the corner of his robe away. Fei Sheng's flattery promptly dried up.

The heavy downpour outside cast Fei Sheng's face into flickering darkness. The office fell so silent one could hear a pin drop. After a beat, Fei Sheng raised his head and forced a smile, as if nothing had happened. "I've wiped off that bit of mud for you," he said, obsequiously. "Your Excellency, please be careful on your way out."

Han Cheng stared at him and slowly released his grip on his robe. He smiled back, and after a moment said, "You may go about your business."

The moment Han Cheng had gone, Fei Sheng's face turned icy. Under the candlelight, he lifted his hand and looked carefully at what remained of the mud on his fingertips. There was wood ash mixed in, which the rainwater had turned into sludge. It was hard to make out the color, but he caught a hint of red.

The Xi manor had burned down. Fei Sheng had been all over it looking for Shen Zechuan's missing men, and he remembered—the dye used in the estate was a red clay imported from overseas, very valuable and difficult to obtain. Not even a manor belonging to a prince or the other nobility could match the Xi Clan for money and resources. Other than them, no one else in Qudu would use it.

What was Han Cheng doing at the Xi manor on a night like this?

Fei Sheng wiped away the mud on his fingers. The cold sweat that had broken out on his back when his eyes met Han Cheng's had yet to dry. He watched the candle flicker. His mind was awhirl, but he was sure of one thing—within that brief exchange, Han Cheng had already decided to kill him.

The next day, Zuo Qianqiu mounted his horse again to ride for Libei. Xiao Chiye accompanied Hai Liangyi to see him out of the city. He couldn't return home, but he could at least send Chen Yang and Gu Jin out; they would follow the grain distribution officials to Huaizhou and Cizhou to supervise the preparation of the military provisions. Nothing could go wrong with the shipment this time. Xiao Chiye couldn't trust the men from the Six Ministries, but he had planted Wang Xian in Cizhou long ago, and had also convinced Pan Lin to send Liang Cuishan to Huaizhou. With these men as his eyes on the ground, he wouldn't miss a single detail.

Xiao Chiye hadn't slept all night. He wiped sweat from his face with a cold handkerchief and climbed into his carriage. "When Liang Cuishan returns," he said, "I'll have to thank him properly."

Shen Zechuan was waiting inside. He hadn't slept last night either, having stood guard at Mingli Hall throughout all the discussions. "I've already made arrangements to settle his family in a manor in Huaizhou. Someone will be on night patrol to watch over them, so he can focus on his job with peace of mind. Unlike Cizhou, the officials in Huaizhou have no dealings with us, and now we're asking them to prepare military provisions on such short notice. The Huaizhou prefect can't be pleased."

"Huaizhou has been exempted from providing military provisions for eight years. Hai Liangyi named them because they can afford this." Xiao Chiye covered his eyes with his handkerchief and slouched back in his seat. After a moment, he continued, "Wei Huaigu must be arrested today. We can't let the Ministry of Justice get to him first."

They were friendly with the Minister of Justice, Kong Qiu, and had spent a pleasant evening drinking together previously. This bit of friendship, however, couldn't compare to the influence of Hai Liangyi. Xiao Chiye had already given up the idea of playing by their rules. If he wanted to cut off any path of retreat for Wei Huaigu, this case had to bypass the joint trial by the Three Judicial Offices and land in the hands of the Embroidered Uniform Guard—in Shen Zechuan's hands.

"Wei Huaigu." Shen Zechuan fiddled with the authority token he had set on the little table and considered this solemnly for a moment. "He'd already intercepted the express relay report—he didn't want it to reach the emperor. Yet he changed his mind at the last minute. Why?"

Xiao Chiye recalled the sight of Wei Huaigu kneeling in Mingli Hall last night. "Actually, he *was* acting strange. Knowing him, he should be trying to pass the buck or pick some scapegoat from the Ministry of Revenue to take the blame. But not only did he not try to wriggle his way out, he even answered obediently."

Shen Zechuan set the token back down with a sharp *click*. "Baimazhou had a bumper harvest last year. If the military provisions have been adulterated with old and substandard grain, where did all the fresh grain go?"

Xiao Chiye pulled the handkerchief off his face and clutched it in his hands. "Greed is the motive for injury. If this grain set out from Baimazhou via Hezhou's waterways, it could bypass Qudu and head directly into Zhongbo, where they can slap a merchant's label on it and sell it at a high price as food for the common folk."

"The rumors that Jiang Qingshan was going to Zhongbo to assume the position of its Provincial Administration Commissioner were going around before the new year. If someone took advantage of this, then it's clear what's going on." Shen Zechuan looked up and met Xiao Chiye's eyes. "Someone in the Provincial Administration Commission of Juexi has been colluding with merchants to resell military grain at a profit. In past years, Jiang Qingshan oversaw the entire operation and strictly checked the provisions, so they carried out this operation on a small scale. But this year, Jiang Qingshan is due to be transferred out of Juexi. He entered the capital after the new year to report for duty and has remained here undergoing the judicial process of vetting and waiting for a review. Without him supervising Juexi's preparation of the military provisions, he left an opening for them to exploit. It's just that no one expected them to be so audacious as to swap the provisions with moldy grain."

"There can't be many with the capacity to move so much grain." The look in Xiao Chiye's eyes was deep and unfathomable. "No one would touch this transaction without a caravan of traveling merchants to handle the goods."

"Xi Hongxuan," Shen Zechuan said slowly.

"Xi Hongxuan." Xiao Chiye said the name with certainty. "He died not because of you or me, but because he'd already become a sacrificial pawn, too capable of implicating others with what he knew. Wei Huaigu tried every means possible to shove the blame in the Ouhua Pavilion case onto Xi Hongxuan. Was it because the two of them were already privately reselling military provisions for profit? Wei Huaigu was worried Xi Hongxuan would be subjected to a thorough investigation, so he wanted him dead?"

Shen Zechuan contemplated this. "It makes sense. Xi Hongxuan said before that Wei Huaigu was too money-minded. Why did he agree to Wei Huaigu's demands so quickly? He knew Wei Huaigu well, and easily assumed he would blackmail him. But if that's the case, with Xi Hongxuan dead, Wei Huaigu had no need to take the significant risk of continuing their operation. I suspect Wei Huaigu isn't responsible this time. Someone knew about the earlier deals and held it over him as leverage. He must have known as soon as he saw the relay report that he'd been set up. There's no escape for him now. And considering that he didn't attempt to exonerate himself, I'd say it's very likely he knows who the other party is. He's trying to imitate Hua Siqian now—using his own life to prevent the Wei Clan from falling further."

Listening to the drumming of the rain outside as they unraveled the deceptions and schemes, Xiao Chiye felt exhaustion wash over him. Xiao Jiming had done what was necessary. Libei's timely execution of the mess cooks had prevented Libei from becoming a pawn others used to eradicate dissidents.

No. Maybe they weren't just a pawn. The perpetrators wanted to use Xiao Jiming's defeat to reduce Libei's military power. They wanted to break up the Libei Armored Cavalry, which had ever been in the hands of the Xiao Clan, and hand it over to Qudu to command and control. Even if they couldn't topple Libei entirely, this could put them under Qudu's supervision, thereby holding the Xiao Clan in check.

"If Commander Zuo hadn't arrived in time last night..." There in the cramped carriage, Shen Zechuan held Xiao Chiye's hand and looked at him. "Then Qudu would have appointed a new general by the morning, and the Libei Armored Cavalry would no longer be the Libei Armored Cavalry."

Xiao Chiye's fingers were ice-cold. After a long moment, he lifted his hand to stroke Shen Zechuan's hair. "The Libei Armored Cavalry is the army of our Great Zhou," he rasped. "Father built it with his own hands; it's far more important than my brother and me. All these many years, Qudu has never understood us: we are the impenetrable fortress in Libei, not traitors."

92

ANXIETY

THE SKY WAS DARK by the time the rain stopped, only a few thin rays of light piercing the thick clouds. The coming and going of black boots kicked up fallen water, sending drops splashing across puddles that reflected the fractured dome of heaven. It was the beginning of summer, yet Qudu seemed still stuck in the rainy season; it had been days since the capital last saw clear skies. Hai Liangyi, finally given a minute for himself, sat on a wooden chair drinking strong tea. He was old, and it was hard to keep his spirits up. He was already feeling fatigued, but there were officials bustling around him attending to their duties, and documents exchanging hands that required his perusal and approval. He was not at liberty to rest.

"Secretariat Elder." Kong Qiu left the cases on his desk long enough to take a chair below Hai Liangyi and said respectfully, "We must hold the Ministry of Revenue responsible for the disaster with the military provisions. This pupil submitted a request to His Majesty yesterday for a joint trial conducted by the Three Judicial Offices. This matter can't be delayed. Perhaps this pupil should make the arrests tonight."

Hai Liangyi was slow to answer, brushing the tea foam in his cup aside. He looked out the window, and only after a long time had passed did he say, "Sitting for so long has made me tired. His Majesty is still having his meal; come with me for a walk outside."

Kong Qiu took Hai Liangyi's overcoat from a junior eunuch and draped it over the older man's shoulders. The two walked together out of the office. The light outside had faded; lantern in hand, Kong Qiu followed Hai Liangyi along the paths of the small garden within the secretariat compound.

"You want to arrest Wei Huaigu, and there's nothing wrong with that." Surprisingly, bathing in the night wind made Hai Liangyi more comfortable. He took a few more deliberate steps. "This incident concerns the stability of the frontier. Certainly, you mustn't be too lenient with Wei Huaigu. Handle it by the book."

Kong Qiu lit the way for him. He guessed Hai Liangyi still had something to say; dropping into more familiar tones, he said, "I shall do as Teacher says. This pupil thinks the same. He was unbelievably brazen this time—even if the empress dowager wishes to shield him, it'll do no good. This pupil has seen how he's acted increasingly out of line this year. Someone should've checked him a long time ago. Military affairs are not like other governmental business. Malfeasance on this scale must never be tolerated or condoned."

"That the Prince of Libei has donned his armor to ride onto the battlefield once again is an admonition to Qudu." Hai Liangyi stopped and stood in silence for a long while; night was falling, and he could no longer see the glow between the sky and the earth. "Xiao Fangxu is the king wolf. In all the years of the power struggle between Libei and the Hua Clan, he has stayed behind the lines due to ill health. He has watched as Xiao Jiming exhausted himself, and Xiao Chiye remained trapped in the imperial city. He placed both his sons in dangerous circumstances. Why do you think he did this?"

Affected by Hai Liangyi's tone, Kong Qiu's heart grew heavy. "Concessions. The Prince of Libei is making concessions to Qudu via his sons. The longstanding noble clans have established themselves as a fortress in the capital, and he has bucked their rule from the frontier. Perhaps he once had the opportunity to advance, but he retreated."

"He retreated, yet the empress dowager didn't understand." Physically and mentally drained, Hai Liangyi continued, "The empress dowager didn't understand, and neither did Wei Huaigu or the noble clans. Xiao Fangxu broke through their antiquated hegemony. His retreat was not out of fear, but because he was willing to accept the sovereign-subject relationship between our Zhou empire and Libei. But as they say, that which waxes will wane. Chasing after the Xiao Clan like this to beat them down is as good as daring Xiao Fangxu to retaliate. Power struggles have always been unavoidable, but when they start encroaching on our defenses, it's an ominous sign that preludes collapse. Zhongbo fell during the reign of Xiande. Back then, the imperial court was crawling with corrupt officials who disregarded governance and made a mess of our court. We may try these days to pick up the pieces, but we face trouble within and without."

Hai Liangyi coughed in the cool wind but refused Kong Qiu's attempt to take his arm. "It's only this year that the state treasury has recovered sufficiently to bear the expenses for regional aid. Juexi did well in providing the military provisions for the two major armies. With Libei and the Bianjun Commandery stable at our borders, and with a capable minister like Jiang Qingshan soon to be transferred to Zhongbo, there's hope for Zhongbo's revival. The Imperial College is growing, and counts more and more scholars from common households among its number. The Chief Surveillance Bureau has Cen Yu to lead it, and of the up-and-coming talents, Yu Xiaozai is particularly promising. His Majesty is also no longer distracted by vice and indulgence." Sorrow washed over Hai Liangyi. "I have recently thought that a new dawn was beginning in our Great Zhou, yet I now find increasingly that though my spirit is willing, my flesh is weak."

Alarmed, Kong Qiu grasped Hai Liangyi by the arm to support him, the rims of his eyes reddening. "Why does Teacher speak such demoralizing words? The Prince of Libei is not that kind of person. This pupil will preside over the trial personally; I will not let Libei suffer this injustice. There's still a chance to turn the tide!"

But Hai Liangyi seemed to sag in his grip. How far could his emaciated body walk while holding up the Zhou empire? He was just one man. He couldn't save the situation on his own, no more than a single log could prop up an entire palace. He couldn't act recklessly and unscrupulously like the noble clans, nor could he put complete faith in Libei. He was the Grand Secretary of the Grand Secretariat, and the palace he supported was Li Jianheng. He was the fulcrum that must maintain the balance in any given situation. Even if the decision he made led to his complete annihilation, he still must make it.

"Libei's fury has been ignited. Xiao Fangxu is leading his troops to the eastern side of the Hongyan mountain range, but once the Biansha threat subsides, he will no doubt turn back to settle the score with Qudu." Hai Liangyi paused for a moment amid a bout of coughing. "No matter how he rages when the time comes, we mustn't release Xiao Chiye, even if Libei is willing to exchange the heir consort, Lu Yizhi, and grandson-heir, Xiao Xun, for him. The Prince of Libei placed both his sons in dangerous situations with the intent to strengthen them, precisely for this day. Xiao Jiming is severely wounded; this is the perfect time for him to lie low. Xiao Chiye made a name for himself in his youth, and Xiao Fangxu let him remain a hostage in Qudu for six years to temper him into steel. Now that this blade is forged and his name is known, allowing his return will sow the seeds of future disaster. We'd be releasing a tiger back into the mountain.

"I am an old man, Boran, I can't hold out for much longer! We must treat Libei with respect, but we cannot release the rope we tether them with. Many will lambaste me after I die for being age-fogged and muddleheaded. But Boran, who dares say to my face that Libei will never rebel? That Qidong will never rebel? Even if the Xiao Fangxu of today can endure it, can the Xiao Chiye of tomorrow tolerate it when he is commander in Libei? This is not a risk our Great Zhou can afford to take! I will shoulder responsibility for deciding what justice Libei should have; they will get all they're due. Wei Huaigu had the audacity to resell military provisions for profit. Go ahead and behead him in accordance with the law! I will remonstrate and impeach whomever pleads for mercy!"

Kong Qiu murmured his acknowledgment.

Hai Liangyi paused to brace himself before he continued, "I will send a letter to the Prince of Libei assuring him that there will be no military inspector. The imperial court will not assign a eunuch to stir up trouble. All major and minor military affairs in Libei will continue to be managed by the Prince of Libei himself."

Kong Qiu hesitated. "I'm afraid the empress dowager won't agree."

"Is there no emperor in our Great Zhou? It's been the rule for a hundred years that the harem should not interfere with government affairs. This matter is not up to her to decide. Besides, fighting a war is serious business. What's the use of sending a few castrated bureaucrats who know nothing but how to fawn over others? They're a waste of rations." Hai Liangyi took a few more steps and continued, "The eunuchs are all personal attendants of the Son of Heaven. There's a reason the Twenty-Four Yamen are called the 'inner court'—they've long resided deep in the palace, and neither understand the suffering of the common folk nor the ways of the sages. Pan Rugui attended the Eunuch School, but everything he did was to frame loyal, upright men and undermine the state. A wise man foresees risks and mitigates them. The eunuch faction has just been eliminated; we mustn't hand them power again so readily. I'll have Chen Zhen draft the memorial when we return. Submit it to His Majesty tonight."

Fuman had come looking for them with a lantern in hand. He didn't dare encroach on their conversation and merely made his obeisance solemnly from afar. "Secretariat Elder and Minister Kong, this way, please. You've been summoned to the hall."

Hai Liangyi grunted; he didn't look kindly upon Fuman either. Kong Qiu supported Hai Liangyi by the arm as they returned along the path. Only when he was right beside the Grand Secretary like this did he realize just how thin the man had become. Grief stabbed at his heart, although his expression betrayed nothing in the twilit darkness.

Xiao Chiye tidied his robes and crown and entered Mingli Hall once again. This time, he spotted Xue Xiuzhuo in his place at the end of the hall.

Having smoked his pipe outside to steady himself, Cen Yu made his argument: "This case involving the military provisions is of grave importance. It involves collusion between officials of our court and merchants for illegal gains. What kind of example is this for the local officials? If we do not deal with it promptly and severely, those scum will think they can get away with it and never have any regard for the law." After an impatient breath, he continued, "Your Majesty, I request we start the investigation and prosecution tonight.

We must apprehend Wei Huaigu, commit him to prison, and send someone to keep an eye on the Wei Clan's account books and manors. We can't let them take advantage of the chaos to transfer their ill-gotten gains who knows where."

Li Jianheng had also been without rest for a day and a night, and was now so tired he could barely keep his eyes open. He nodded with some difficulty. "The military provisions are indeed a major issue. Wei Huaigu has made a mess of matters. Whether he should be executed or have his properties seized, it is for the Grand Secretariat to decide. Deal with him as you deem fit."

"The reach of this case is such that even Jiang Qingshan will have to remain in his post pending the trial." Xiao Chiye spoke next. "The Wei Clan is large, with land and power strewn all over the empire. I'm afraid any investigation of their dealings can't be done in under a fortnight if the Ministry of Justice acts alone." Xiao Chiye rubbed at the webbing between his thumb and index finger, slowly rotating his thumb ring. "Likewise, the joint trial by the Three Judicial Offices regarding the epidemic case is still pending. If we are to nip any similar cases of official-merchant collusion elsewhere in the bud, the Chief Surveillance Bureau will also need to free up personnel to leave the capital and check the accounts of the various outer regions. It seems to me that every office has its own difficulties and is similarly short on manpower."

"Your Lordship has a point," Xue Xiuzhuo concurred softly, "but everything has its priority. Libei is fighting a war as we speak; the matter of military provisions is of utmost importance. The Ministry of Justice and the Chief Surveillance Bureau naturally must put this matter first, there's no question."

That blockhead Li Jianheng could tell Xiao Chiye was trying to hint at something to him. But after Xue Xiuzhuo's interruption, he didn't know how to continue. Anxious, he looked to Hai Liangyi. "What does the secretariat elder say?"

Hai Liangyi didn't look at any of them. After a moment's pause, he said, "Is Your Lordship worried that the joint trial by the Three Judicial Offices will take too long?"

"The processes of the joint trial are complex," Xiao Chiye explained. "Wei Huaigu has been at the top for too long; his thinking and methods are far detached from those of the common man—who knows what he may try? I worry that detaining him for the considerable length of the trial will cause further complications."

"That's right," Li Jianheng hastily cut in. "The Wei Clan has always shown filial respect to the empress dowager. If this case drags on too long, we fear the empress dowager will be overwhelmed with worry and her health will suffer."

"But without the joint trial by the Three Judicial Offices, we can't thoroughly investigate the various loose ends under him," Kong Qiu countered. "These profiteers are only so audacious because they've had Wei Huaigu to shield them. Letting them all run free would be a disaster."

"I'm not saying we shouldn't investigate. I'm merely worried about the time it will take." Xiao Chiye looked at Li Jianheng. "Surely this is not the only course for Qudu to take?"

Something seemed to click in Li Jianheng's mind, and he slapped his thigh in understanding. "If we want this investigation done quickly, we should let the Embroidered Uniform Guard handle it! Shen Zechuan was pretty fast when he handled the matter of Xi Hongxuan and those bandits he assembled, no? Why not put him in charge of this too?"

"But this is such a major case," Xue Xiuzhuo objected. "It simply won't do to hand it over to the vice commander of the Embroidered

Uniform Guard. Shen Zechuan is limited by his rank. It'd be more appropriate to hand it to the chief commander, Han Cheng."

Xiao Chiye shifted his gaze to Xue Xiuzhuo and hooked his lips into a smile. "You're right. Shen Zechuan is not suitable to take charge of this case. He's young and lacks experience, and he has a longstanding grudge against me. I won't sleep easy if we hand it over to him."

His quick retreat from his position convinced Hai Liangyi of his course. Hai Liangyi knew Han Cheng was on good terms with Xiao Chiye. There was a chance Xiao Chiye might use this connection to push Han Cheng too far in his handling of the case; it would be more balanced to hand the responsibility over to the man who had been always at odds with Xiao Chiye: Shen Zechuan. With the two of them standing in opposition and monitoring one another, neither would be able to tamper with the case.

"Your Lordship," Hai Liangyi began, "this is your prejudice speaking. Shen Zechuan is young indeed, but it was by imperial decree that he was promoted to his current position, where he's dealt with one difficult case after another. Letting him gain more experience is also a good thing." He turned to Li Jianheng. "Appointing the Embroidered Uniform Guard to take the lead as the chief investigators on this case means it will be handled by the Imperial Prison, and it just so happens that Shen Zechuan is the northern judge. Given his official duties and job responsibilities, that he should handle this case is reasonable. Even so, we oughtn't insist on reckless speed. Although we are bypassing joint trial, the Three Judicial Offices should still supervise. Does Your Majesty agree?"

Li Jianheng knew Hai Liangyi was making a concession by doing this. Not daring to appear overly partial toward Xiao Chiye, he instantly concurred. "We'll issue the edict right away; he can start the investigation tonight."

With this, two consecutive days of official discussions in Mingli Hall finally reached a momentary conclusion. Everyone would return home and rest for a night. As they exited the hall, Li Jianheng personally instructed the eunuchs to carry Hai Liangyi in a sedan to the palace gates where his carriage waited, while Kong Qiu and the rest walked out after him. Xiao Chiye nodded farewell to them and left alone.

Watching Xiao Chiye's retreating back, Kong Qiu sighed. "He's too upset to trust the Ministry of Justice with this case. He wants to investigate with Han Cheng."

Cen Yu descended the steps. "And why wouldn't he—just look at who Han Cheng is. The secretariat elder was right to choose Shen Zechuan. Yanqing, are you heading straight back to your residence?"

Xue Xiuzhuo walked a few steps behind them, a smile on his face. "Yes. I've been sleeping in the office these last two days. I should go back tonight and prepare. There are still other cases to handle in days to come."

Cen Yu was the type to look after his juniors and often supported their careers. He had personally guided Yu Xiaozai of the Chief Surveillance Bureau, whose career had blossomed under his mentorship. He had also occasionally given Shen Zechuan advice out of genuine concern. He valued Xue Xiuzhuo's talents as well, so when he heard these words, he found it only natural to speak a few words of encouragement.

The three men stepped into their carriages at the palace entrance and went their separate ways.

It was deep in the night when a steward of the Xue manor heard a knock at the door; he threw on his clothes and came out for a look. Standing at the threshold was a solemn-looking contingent of the

Embroidered Uniform Guard, sabers at their waists. Before the startled man could ask any questions, Qiao Tianya, in the lead, leisurely pushed the man aside and squeezed his way through the door.

"Have you eaten? It's so early; you probably haven't yet. Go tell the kitchen to prepare meals for the Embroidered Uniform Guard too. And while you're at it, wake everyone up. We're here to search the estate."

Lifting his lantern high, the steward stepped forward to block his path. "Your Excellency, how can you do this?! You haven't produced any search warrant—"

"Any who obstruct official business will be arrested and taken to the Imperial Prison." Shen Zechuan stood at the entrance, his eyes cold and ruthless. "Tell Xue Xiuzhuo I'm looking for him."

93

GENERAL

THE EMBROIDERED UNIFORM GUARD swarmed through the Xue manor, storming along the verandas and surging inside; in every corner, the household was startled awake. The women huddled in fear as they were herded out of their rooms to assemble in the central courtyard. The Embroidered Uniform Guard had a reputation for clandestine arrests, and in their eyes, Shen Zechuan was a man-eating predator.

Xue Xiuyi swiftly dressed and stepped into the courtyard. Seeing Xue Xiuzhuo already standing under the eaves, he lunged forward and grabbed him, hissing resentfully, "What did you do to bring the Embroidered Uniform Guard to our door?! If you've gotten us into trouble, I'll have you disowned by the clan!"

Xue Xiuzhuo turned his head to look at his snarling eldest brother, allowing himself to be manhandled. Eyes filled with pity and indifference, he said, "The whole family shares in fame and fortune, but when misfortune beckons, one person alone bears it all. Dage, have no fear. It's still far from your turn to lead this clan."

He pushed Xue Xiuyi away and walked along the steps toward Shen Zechuan.

This was the second time Shen Zechuan and Xue Xiuzhuo had met face to face. When the Embroidered Uniform Guard arrived, Xue Xiuzhuo hadn't yet gone to bed; he'd been in the study going through case files and had promptly walked out draped in an azure, wide-sleeved robe. This man had a calm and steady aura, and his scholarly elegance was not something that could be donned in a day. He was genuinely capable—something Shen Zechuan had never denied.

"To what do I owe the pleasure of the vice commander's presence at this late hour?" Xue Xiuzhuo was of a similar height to Shen Zechuan, and he stood firm as he greeted him. "Had I known, I would've prepared refreshments and welcomed you at once."

"I received the imperial edict just this evening. His Majesty has ordered me to take charge of the military provisions case. The Embroidered Uniform Guard wouldn't dare be sloppy with such a major case; we have already arrested Wei Huaigu." Shen Zechuan scrutinized the calligraphed couplets hanging in the main hall, not meeting Xue Xiuzhuo's eyes as he continued, nonchalant, "Wei Huaigu has always been friendly with Assistant Minister Xue. For the sake of clearing Your Excellency of any conflict of interest, the Xue manor will be searched tonight."

"I'm aware that the Court of Judicial Review is assisting the Embroidered Uniform Guard with the case. But I am an appointed official of the imperial court. If the Embroidered Uniform Guard wishes to search my estate, you'll need a warrant issued by the Ministry of Justice." Xue Xiuzhuo looked around the courtyard and saw panic and confusion everywhere. "However—I can see this case is urgent, and the vice commander has the special prerogative to act first and report later. Uncle Xue, hand the keys to the inner courtyard to the Embroidered Uniform Guard. Wherever they wish to search, lead them there."

Shen Zechuan cocked his head. "You're certainly something. You've even prepared for an imperial edict issued on a whim."

Xue Xiuzhuo smiled. "Of course I must act with caution when encountering a character like the vice commander. It's late, and chilly out. If the vice commander doesn't find it beneath you, perhaps you'd like to have a cup of tea with me inside. The grounds of the manor are large. By the time you're done searching, it will be time for morning court."

"I'll skip it." Shen Zechuan turned slowly. "How could I accept tea from such a prominent clan—I'm not worthy of the honor. Does this mean I can expect to return empty-handed again today?"

"That will no doubt depend on what the vice commander is looking for. If you're looking to investigate the case, then I regret to say you will. Wei Huaigu and I are mere acquaintances; we share no personal connections."

Shen Zechuan fell silent. As he stared at Xue Xiuzhuo, that subtle feeling of being toyed with surfaced again.

Qiao Tianya returned only after a long while. From across the courtyard, Shen Zechuan saw him shake his head—Shifu and Xiansheng were not here.

"As they say, the wily hare has three burrows," Shen Zechuan said softly.

"Just the fish at the bottom of the cookpot getting a momentary reprieve, that's all," Xue Xiuzhuo said deferentially.

"You have one chance with me." Shen Zechuan stepped closer to Xue Xiuzhuo. "Where are they?"

It was a moonless night, and the damp chill that came after rain pervaded the air. The men and women herded into the courtyard had covered their faces to weep. Xue Xiuyi didn't know the details, but fearing Xue Xiuzhuo would infuriate Shen Zechuan, he took a quick step forward and bowed with his hands clasped before him, asking with trepidation, "Who is Your Excellency looking for?

We're harboring no fugitives from the military provisions case! All the people of the manor are here. Your Excellency, please interrogate them as you will. We'll tell you everything we know; we won't hold anything back!"

Xue Xiuzhuo said nothing.

Seeing he couldn't be swayed, Shen Zechuan said to Xue Xiuyi, "I'm looking for wanted criminals of the imperial court. I've heard there's a group of prostitutes kept in Assistant Minister Xue's manor. Is that right?"

Xue Xiuzhuo's gaze flickered. Xue Xiuyi cried, "Yes, yes, there is! Soliciting and consorting with prostitutes are all activities impeachable by the Chief Surveillance Bureau. He's been careful to hide them, so the grandmasters of remonstrance have no idea. Your Excellency, Your Excellency, please take a look. Those youths are right here. They're nothing but trivial playthings. How could they be wanted criminals of the imperial court?"

Noting the minute change in Xue Xiuzhuo's expression, Shen Zechuan shifted his gaze to the boys and girls. "Do you not know the significance of Xiangyun Villa in the recent assassination case? Everyone there is a wanted criminal. Assistant Minister Xue bought these young men and women from such an establishment without so much as a word. Why wasn't the Ministry of Justice notified?"

Xue Xiuzhuo pushed Xue Xiuyi aside. "These people all have proof of household registration. Although they came from a brothel, they're all decent, innocent people. The vice commander is investigating the matter of the military provisions tonight. This has nothing to do with them, so why are you so insistent?"

"Their innocence will be determined after a trip to the Imperial Prison." Shen Zechuan glanced over his shoulder. "Take them."

The young people all hugged themselves and started crying. Qiao Tianya took the lead and dragged them all away. Under Xie Xiuzhuo's tutelage, the boys had been taught to carry themselves like the sons of distinguished clans; they were no match for the stern Embroidered Uniform Guard. They wept and wailed as they were apprehended. Xue Xiuyi was so frightened his knees knocked together. Still wanting to say a few words to ease the tension, his thoughts landed on Xiao Chiye.

"Y-Your Excellency!" Bracing himself, Xue Xiuyi choked out, "Since this matter concerns Libei, then why not a-ask what His Lordship thinks? If something really is wrong, then by all means, go ahead and take Xue Xiuzhuo away!"

Xue Xiuzhuo suddenly took a few steps forward to block Qiao Tianya's way, bellowing, "Even on a case, the Embroidered Uniform Guard still must follow proper procedures! Vice Commander Shen, before you detain my people, I want to see an arrest warrant from the Ministry of Justice!"

"Take them away!" Hand on his hilt, Shen Zechuan forced Xue Xiuzhuo to take a step back. "If you want an arrest warrant, I'll give you as many as you want tomorrow morning!"

"Shen Zechuan!" Xue Xiuzhuo flung his sleeves back. "I'll impeach you for abusing the power of public office to settle private grudges!"

"Go ahead. Submit the memorial for impeachment tonight!" Shen Zechuan's tone turned frosty. "These people are now in my hands. I'll kill one for every day I don't see Xiansheng! Take a guess: how long will it take before I reach your precious pupil?"

"You wouldn't dare!" Xue Xiuzhuo flew into a rage. Qiao Tianya was already dragging the prisoners away, their cries increasing in urgency. He grabbed Qiao Tianya's arm to hold him back.

"By arresting innocent commoners, all of you are accessories to crime. What the hell kind of case are you investigating?! Stop!"

"Get in my way again and I'll start right now." Shen Zechuan's thumb pushed his blade out of its sheath to reveal the cold glint of steel.

The moment he saw Shen Zechuan reach for his blade, Xue Xiuyi was so seized with terror that he fainted where he stood. Cries of "Eldest Master!" rose from the surrounding servants as they hurried to help him up. Xue Xiuzhuo, who was being hauled backward by several guards, watched helplessly as the Embroidered Uniform Guard shoved all the students up onto the wagons.

"Shen Zechuan!" Xue Xiuzhuo gripped the arm blocking his way, his composure all but gone. Eyes bloodshot, he spat resentfully, "You dare to kill him. You dare kill him?! You bloody-minded tyrant! You aren't worthy of being Xiansheng's student!"

Shen Zechuan leapt atop his horse and rode away, leaving Xue Xiuzhuo's shouts of abuse behind.

Far south of the beleaguered Libei frontier, the Bianjun front was heating up as well.

Lu Guangbai had returned to his camp for a rest, yet hadn't even dismounted when he saw his deputy general hastening toward him. "What's the matter?"

The deputy general's expression was ugly. "General," he whispered, "Qudu has dispatched a military inspector eunuch here. He came escorting this year's provisions."

After a moment of silence, Lu Guangbai slid out of the saddle, removed his helmet, and lifted the curtain to enter the tent. A eunuch was seated in the very center, dressed in a python-patterned robe that showed off his status and a wide-brimmed official's hat. When he saw Lu Guangbai enter, he made no move to rise and pay obeisance.

Lu Guangbai set aside his long spear. "Gonggong has certainly traveled a long way. Surely you're in need of a rest; I've ordered the men to tidy up a tent."

Yingxi was a recently promoted eunuch, but he had connections within the palace. He knew his masters had never looked kindly on the Lu Clan of the Bianjun Commandery, and thus he also looked down on Lu Guangbai. When he deigned to reply, he said, "This place is remote and barren, and staffed by clumsy oafs. How would they know how to serve their betters? The general needn't go to such trouble. I've already taken a look around, and that tent is so dark and filthy as to be uninhabitable. I sent some men off to Cangjun to buy some timber. I plan to build a residence here—I have to stay for half a year!"

Lu Guangbai wasn't good with words. He knew military inspector eunuchs were always this pretentious, and couldn't be bothered to make any more conversation. He unfastened his arm guard; with the removal of that iron skin, pus and blood dripped onto the ground.

Yingxi covered his nose in horror at the sight of it. "How did it fester like that?!"

The deputy general had dragged a medical chest over to dress Lu Guangbai's wounds, but when he saw his arm, he exclaimed, "General, it's rubbed raw! We have to get the army medic to take a look."

Lu Guangbai motioned for him to shut up and felt for the dagger strapped to the side of his thigh. He sat and poured alcohol onto his wound, then held the dagger in the candle flame until it was searing hot. The deputy general rushed to hold back his sleeve for him. Yingxi had never seen someone so ruthless with their own body, and his hands and feet went cold as he listened to the sound of festering flesh gouged out. Lu Guangbai sprinkled medicine over the wound and held his arm out for the deputy general to bandage it up for him.

"The Horsemen are tricky," he said as the deputy worked. "Without a deployment order from on high, we can't pursue them beyond a certain range, and we're too busy fighting to bother with flesh wounds when we're locked in attrition battles." Lu Guangbai braced his hands on his knees and looked back at Yingxi. "Did Gonggong come with the military provisions?"

Yingxi swallowed his nausea and nodded.

Lu Guangbai rose. "I'll go take a look."

Without another word, he stepped out of the tent with his deputy general and strode toward the provisions. The rest of the men who had escorted them had already left. Lu Guangbai made his way into the granary and opened one of the bulging burlap sacks. When he saw the provisions within, he frowned. He reached out to grab a handful—it was all damp and moldy rice.

"General," the deputy general said, "It's not just poor quality this time; the quantity is pathetic too. We have twenty thousand men in the Bianjun Commandery, and our troops are deployed every day to engage in constant small skirmishes. We're more mobile, and therefore eat a lot as well—the amount we need to fill our bellies is far greater than the stationary garrison troops of Qidong's other four commanderies. This bit of rotten grain won't even last until autumn!"

Lu Guangbai let the rice stream out of his scar-covered palm. "Secretariat Elder Hai has always looked out for us. Last year's provisions were all allocated in a timely fashion. Why short us this time?"

The deputy general's chest heaved. He opened his mouth several times to say something but pressed his lips shut over his words.

"If you have something to say, say it," Lu Guangbai said. "What's this? Spit it out."

"General!" The deputy general was indignant. He stepped forward and grasped a handful of the rice, his voice breaking with emotion. "They gave us less! Why? Obviously because they were in a hurry to ship to Libei! Fucking hell! So the Libei Armored Cavalry are all good men and loyal soldiers, while the garrison troops of our Bianjun Commandery are undeserving bastards?! Those court officials have always fawned over those at the top and bullied those at the bottom; they step on you at every opportunity! But we're fighting a war out here! We're putting lives on the line—how could they play favorites?! What issue have they taken with our Bianjun Commandery?! We're dirt poor, yet they skimp everywhere they can! I asked the men who escorted the supplies what we're supposed to do in autumn, and they said the imperial court told us to play it by ear and figure it out ourselves! Play it by ear? Fuck them to hell and back!"

The deputy general clenched his fists. "Qidong's military provisions were reduced by half and supplied to Libei. But the other commanderies aren't actively fighting! And they have military fields to eat off of, while we've got nothing but air and hot sand! Once autumn arrives, the horses of the Twelve Tribes of Biansha will be fat off the grass of the steppe, and it will be even harder for us to fight them! With this meager supply of grain, we—"

"Not a word more!" Lu Guangbai bellowed, cutting off the deputy general's tirade. Lu Guangbai stood for a long time in the darkness; eventually, he peered at the starry sky outside the granary and rasped, "I'll...think of a way."

The beacon towers of the Bianjun Commandery stood in silence above the rolling terrain; the night sealed off the light of the sky like muddy water obstructed a drain. Lu Guangbai didn't enjoy the prestigious reputation accorded to the other three great generals. He was like a stubborn rock stationed at the edge of this vast desert, enduring the weight of oppressive pressure from three directions until it had chipped all his natural smoothness into sharp, jagged edges. The members of their Lu clan had died one after another, leaving only Lu Guangbai to inherit Lu Pingyan's spear.

Lu Guangbai was not a particularly clever man. He was unlikable. He came late to his fame and had none of the natural talents granted to Xiao Jiming and Qi Zhuyin. He was Lu Pingyan's youngest and stupidest son. And yet, with these meager qualities, he had held the Bianjun Commandery aloft after Lu Pingyan's retirement. He maintained a tight grip on the strategic passage through which the Biansha Horsemen repeatedly attempted to advance and overwhelm them. He had no shifu; he was a general who had learned his craft by following in the footprints of Lu Pingyan, tumbling through the desert sands. He treated others with sincerity and was riddled with scars.

All that night, Lu Guangbai didn't sleep. He sat on the dirt slope before the camp, hugging his spear, wracking his brain for a way to resolve the military provisions shortage. Qi Zhuyin had jurisdiction over the five commanderies, but she had long emptied her own private savings coming to their aid over the years; he couldn't ask her for help this time. His old man at home was still ill, and he couldn't very well ask Lu Pingyan to drag his sick body from door to door begging for a loan.

When the deputy general got up in the middle of the night to relieve himself, he saw the lonely silhouette of Lu Guangbai's back.

He thought to go over and tell the general to rest, but before he could approach, he saw Lu Guangbai bend over and reach out to touch the earth at his feet. His head, thus lowered, stayed down for a long, long time.

RAGING WAVES

HEN ZECHUAN moved quickly.

Wei Huaigu was sent to prison and placed on trial, while Yang Cheng from the Provincial Administration Commission of Juexi was also apprehended by the Embroidered Uniform Guard. This was a major case in the first year of Tianchen, and the entire court of civil and military officials watched with rapt attention. It didn't take long for the Imperial Prison to wring a confession out of Yang Cheng: Wei Huaigu had been reselling military provisions since the fourth year of Xiande.

Using his position as the Minister of Revenue, Wei Huaigu would buy provisions from Yang Cheng each time they were dispatched. He then sold them at a higher price to Xi Hongxuan, who transported the stolen military grain via a number of land and sea routes to the six prefectures of Zhongbo and even across the Sea of Xuhai, making an enormous profit off the harvest while letting the common folk of Juexi bear the land tax for the fields.

Shen Zechuan looked through Yang Cheng's confession. "You've been running this operation of yours for a long time. Did your conscience suddenly awaken that you decided to expose Wei Huaigu through the relay report?"

Yang Cheng, who had already spent several days in the Imperial Prison, hung his head. "They filled the gap with moldy grain this time;

it's not just a matter of money anymore. Libei is fighting a war. Once sent, this grain would become the poison that kills our soldiers at the frontier. I was afraid something bad would really happen to the Heir of Libei."

Only Yang Cheng, Shen Zechuan, and Xiao Chiye sat at the table. Cloaked in shadow, Xiao Chiye spoke up: "You were so certain this grain would reach the Heir of Libei's mouth?"

Yang Cheng shifted uneasily; his lips were pale. "I was just afraid. I may be greedy, but I'm no murderer."

"Don't be afraid." Shen Zechuan cast a glance at Xiao Chiye and softened his tone. "You may be in the Imperial Prison, but this case is being personally overseen by His Majesty. If you have anything to say, you can feel safe telling us."

The contrast between these men was stark. Yang Cheng gulped; he was still dazed from the interrogation he'd endured last night. "I didn't know," he muttered. "I didn't think—"

"What didn't you know?" Shen Zechuan asked gently.

"I didn't think something would actually happen to the Heir of Libei." Yang Cheng began to sob weakly. "I didn't know! I was worried the Libei Armored Cavalry would be defeated because of this and let the Biansha Horsemen in again."

Xiao Chiye leaned forward, his shadow like a ferocious beast that loomed over Yang Cheng. In a voice like ice, he said, "So you knew these military provisions could cause the Libei Armored Cavalry's defeat, yet you still sealed them up and loaded them into the wagons. You deserve to die."

Yang Cheng shivered under Xiao Chiye's gaze. He cried incoherently, "Your Lordship—I confess. I-I deserve to die!"

"You won't die." Shen Zechuan turned his peerless face to him, those expressive, upturned eyes brimming with compassion.

"The main perpetrator in this case is Wei Huaigu. He used his position to coerce you; there was nothing you could do. I understand how difficult it must have been—surely His Lordship understands as well. Yang Cheng, you entered civil service in the era of Yongyi. You've been an official in Juexi half your life, and you climbed your way up to the post of Assistant Administration Commissioner. You're a capable man; all your past reviews prove this. Now that Jiang Qingshan has left Juexi to take charge in Zhongbo, the position of the Provincial Administration Commissioner will be vacant. Based on age and experience, you would've been the first candidate considered by the Ministry of Personnel. Your future should have been bright, yet you forfeited everything for a few coins. Was it worth it?"

Hunched over the table, Yang Cheng's shoulders shook.

"I heard you grew up in Baimazhou. Your family was poor, and you lost your father when you were just six. Your mother raised you and your siblings all on her own. She spent more than half of her life working herself to the bone to send you and your brothers to school. She lived to see you become an official and set up your own manor, yet you went and committed such a grave mistake." Shen Zechuan's tone was gentle as he said, "From today onward, she'll be left alone, forsaken. I hardly dare mention the scorn and curses she'll endure following this case. How could you be so heartless?"

Yang Cheng burst into helpless tears. He was a scholar at his core; the social virtues of propriety, justice, integrity, and honor were deeply ingrained in him. He was a filial child, attending to his mother's every need when he was home. Burying his face in his hands, he cried, "I've made such an unpardonable mistake; I'm worse than swine. I'm too ashamed to see her again!"

"This case is not yet closed. Whether or not you'll be executed remains up for debate." Xiao Chiye tossed the confession down and looked sidelong at him. "Since you still know shame, you must have a shred of conscience left. The questions I'll ask you next will be off the record. Answer truthfully, and I'll find a way to preserve your life so your old mother can live her remaining years in peace. If you dare make excuses and conceal the truth, I'll have you beheaded tomorrow at Duancheng Gate for all to see. With one relay report, you sold out Wei Huaigu and upset quite a number of people's golden rice bowl. You're on the inside of this operation; you should understand best what fate awaits the widows and orphans your co-conspirators will leave behind. Without me to vouch for you, the lives of everyone in your family are in danger."

Yang Cheng wept for a long time. When he'd finally cried himself out, Shen Zechuan brought him a cup of hot tea. Hastily wiping his tears, Yang Cheng thanked him twice over. He was silent a long while, holding the tea in both hands, then said, "Your Lordship's willingness to protect me is a life-saving kindness. I wouldn't dare ask to re-enter civil service as an official again; a sentence of exile is lenience enough. This case implicates too many. It's a long story, so I will tell it to Your Lordship slowly.

"Since the first year of Xiande, the state treasury has been horribly depleted. The Ministry of Revenue's account books are a mess. During his time as the Grand Secretary of the Grand Secretariat, Hua Siqian colluded with Pan Rugui to approve many construction projects that squandered public funds. Most of them weren't actually built—like the Linlang Garden in Qinzhou. These gardens were merely a pretext to pass the Grand Secretariat's scrutiny and get approval to draw money from the state treasury. Everyone involved knew of this illegal collusion between officials and merchants; money flowed into their pockets like water.

"Wei Huaigu approached me in the fourth year of Xiande. I'll be honest, Your Lordship. I knew I shouldn't touch this money, but I felt I had no choice. When provincial officials like us entered Qudu, the Pan and Hua factions took turns calling on us and asking for ice respects—I'm sure you know that former practice of buying a promotion with bribes. The noble clans have the inherent dignity of their status to help them along. The ones truly held back by these 'ice respect' and 'coal respect' bribes were officials like me from common households. Without money, we couldn't enter the central administration. Without money, we couldn't get anything done at all.

"That year, Juexi faced a plague of locusts, and not a single grain was harvested from any of the thirteen cities. It was Jiang Qingshan who shouldered this burden and saved our lives. He opened the commercial granaries by force to offer aid to commoners and prevented hunger from deteriorating into famine. But this made Jiang Qingshan a thorn in the side of the business tycoons of Juexi—the capital was all too aware of this. Debtors waited outside the doors of his home, and his elderly mother had to work the loom to help pay off his debt. But what debt was this? We all knew he was repaying the debt on behalf of Qudu. Yet there's one thing no one else knew save for the officials in the Provincial Administration Commission of Juexi: just how timely Zhongbo's defeat was.

"The state treasury was empty then, and Juexi was in crisis. Libei and the Bianjun Commandery still had to fight the Biansha Horsemen. Even the harvest down in Hezhou was dismal. Common people across these regions had been starving to death since the beginning of the year. The Ministry of Revenue was backed into a corner, yet they had no way to provide aid to anyone because the state treasury had been drained dry. Hua Siqian owed every region an explanation, and Hai Liangyi was already digging into the accounts. Hua Siqian was in a terrible fix. When the Hua Clan in Dicheng sold some of their manors, the Xi Clan snapped them up—we all knew that Hua Siqian was selling assets to fill the hole in the state treasury, but there was no way he could replenish a pit of that size alone. Thus Hua Siqian began to collect on his debts.

"Whether Hua Siqian got his money back I don't know, but this was the moment the Biansha Horsemen launched their assault at Chashi River. The garrison troops in Duanzhou suffered a crushing defeat, and Shen Wei fled from the enemy and holed himself up like a tortoise, leading Zhongbo's prefectures to fall one after another. Thanks to the Libei Armored Cavalry and Qidong Garrison Troops providing reinforcements from the north and south, our forces stopped the Biansha Horsemen at the gates of Qudu. But although the land was reclaimed, the massacred cities had become hollowed-out shells. The relief grain Juexi received that year was precisely the grain that belonged to the dead of the six prefectures of Zhongbo."

Shen Zechuan shot to his feet. He stood in the darkness without saying a word.

Xiao Chiye's heart chilled as well. He and Shen Zechuan had made many guesses in the past, but it had never occurred to them that the defeat of Zhongbo had been orchestrated for the purpose of filling the empty granaries across the empire—thereby saving Hua Siqian and the other officials whose positions were at risk because of the investigation into the state treasury.

"More than a hundred thousand people died in Zhongbo." Stupefied, Shen Zechuan gripped the edge of the table. His gaze seemed to lose focus as he spoke, his voice growing hoarse. "More than…more than thirty thousand soldiers. Do you know what you're saying?"

This revelation had blindsided him. He had spent six years convincing himself that all those people had died because of a struggle for power. Those bright and spirited people, those young faces—all of them had been alive once, just as Ji Mu had. Duanzhou had been first to fall. They'd all died tragic deaths. The singing that reverberated in the Chashi Sinkhole would remain Shen Zechuan's nightmare for a lifetime.

The defeat of Zhongbo had left countless victims. No one had collected the bodies of the soldiers who fell in battle. The dreams of the survivors drowned in blood.

Under the weight of this oppressive atmosphere, Yang Cheng wrapped his arms around his head. "The substitution of the military grain terrified me this time. Zhongbo had troops to come to its rescue, but Libei's only reinforcements must come from Luoxia Pass. If the Biansha Horsemen were to breach Libei, I'd become a sinner condemned through the ages!"

"The arrival of the Biansha Horsemen and the fall of Zhongbo were too well-timed." Xiao Chiye's voice was cold. "It was no coincidence that the Hanma tribe shifted their troops south to the Chashi River crossing; it was because they received information."

If that was true, the Hanma tribe's recent encounter with Xiao Jiming at the eastern side of the Hongyan mountain range was no coincidence either. There were people everywhere in the empire relaying information to the Twelve Tribes of Biansha: in Qudu, in Zhongbo, in Libei, even in Qidong, these people kept the Twelve Tribes of Biansha as their own tame beast, like raising a jackal so famished it would tear into anything you tossed at it. And when necessary, they would let it through the border to gobble up traces of any filth they couldn't wipe clean.

"I can't say if anyone else in the central administration is still selling provisions," Yang Cheng said fearfully, "but it was such a close call this time! There are reserves in the state treasury now, and the Grand Secretariat is carrying out stringent audits on the Ministry of Revenue's accounts. It'd be treason to allow the Biansha Horsemen to invade our nation again. I don't know—I didn't dare take the chance. There are people monitoring my private correspondence, so I could only inform Qudu through the relay report!"

Shen Zechuan suddenly grabbed Yang Cheng and lifted him out of his seat. "If you wanted to report Wei Huaigu, why did you affix the Ministry of Revenue's tag when you sent the missive? The instant that report entered Qudu, it landed in Wei Huaigu's hands!"

The teacup slipped from Yang Cheng's fingers. Amid the sound of porcelain shattering, he said in a trembling voice, "What? No! I affixed it with the tag of the Ministry of Justice!"

Shen Zechuan was stunned. Shaking with fear, Yang Cheng said in disbelief, "I'd be dead if this report landed in Wei Huaigu's hands! I've heard the Minister of Justice, Kong Qiu, is a man of courage. He isn't from a noble clan, so he wouldn't delay things or cover for Wei Huaigu. I checked it over and over before dispatching it to make sure—it was the Ministry of Justice I tagged!"

"We've been had." Xiao Chiye held a hand out to steady Shen Zechuan, his eyes flinty. "Wei Huaigu isn't the culprit this time. When Wei Huaigu received that relay report, he knew someone had already read its contents. It was blackmail—he *had* to turn himself in."

THE STATE

W EI HUAIGU, a man over fifty, had been stripped of his official's robes and treated as a common prisoner. He stood shackled on the other side of the iron bars from Xiao Chiye. No one had maltreated him in the days since he'd been put on trial. His hair, which had been tied up in a topknot, was tidy, and his face was clean. Yet he seemed to have aged several years in a few short days; he looked haggard.

"The trial ended last night." Wei Huaigu sank down into the chair in his cell. "My confession has been submitted, and I'm awaiting my sentence. What more do you two wish to ask?"

"Embezzlement of state treasury funds, resale of military provisions for private profit, the poisoning of frontier generals—all three are capital offenses." Xiao Chiye looked closely at Wei Huaigu. "Wei Huaixing has also been stripped of his position and thrown in prison pending impeachment. The Wei Clan has fallen and knocked out two court ministers with it. You've made no attempt to refute it. What, did you find your conscience this time?"

"This matter concerns Libei. Who would dare bend the rules or play favorites? No one would speak up for me." Wei Huaigu leaned back in his chair as if he were still sitting in his seat at the Ministry of Revenue's office. He looked at Xiao Chiye. "Even your father has come out of retirement to take up command in this crisis; I'm sure

His Majesty hasn't slept a wink the past few days. The Prince of Libei is the same tough nut he used to be. He knows how best to execute a rap on the knuckles."

"You knew those provisions would be delivered to Libei when you were filling wagons up with moldy grain. But you still did it, didn't you? You weren't the slightest bit afraid that no one would speak for you then." Xiao Chiye took a step toward the bars. "To send that rot into my Dage's mouth, adulterating the supplies was only the first step. When the grain arrived in Libei, you bribed the officials in charge of the granary to close one eye and send it to the camps. This was the second step. You then bribed the mess cooks of the Libei Armored Cavalry and mixed this poison into the dishes before they were served to the soldiers at the frontier pass—this was the third step."

Xiao Chiye stopped and slanted a look at Wei Huaigu. "These arrangements required time and effort. The moment the whole scheme came to light, you would never be able to deny your involvement. Now, not only will you not get away with it, you'll be subjected to an interrogation by the Ministry of Justice, which will expose your history of reselling military provisions for profit. You must have considered this."

Wei Huaigu didn't respond immediately. He glanced at Shen Zechuan, who had been sitting behind Xiao Chiye all this time, and laughed. "Er-gongzi has made progress during these six years in Qudu. Back when you first entered the capital, you spent your days picking fights and baying for blood." He pointed at Shen Zechuan. "Vice Commander Shen knows this all too well, right? That's why I said Xiao Fangxu has an iron fist, to dare polish his son against the edge of a blade. You have your father to thank for the man you are now."

Xiao Chiye looked at Wei Huaigu with indifference; it was Shen Zechuan who pushed aside the confession statement and sat forward. With both hands clasped lightly on the table, he said without a hint of emotion, "That's right. You look upon today's Xiao Ce'an and find it unfair. During the reign of Xiande, your son frittered away his days mixing with the brothel crowd. By the time the Grand Secretariat was seeking new personnel in the current reign of Tianchen, entering officialdom through the imperial examinations would've been an insurmountable challenge for him, even if he wanted to. You're growing old, yet the Wei Clan has no lawful son capable of upholding the clan's name. You pinned your hopes on a marriage alliance, but unfortunately, the Fei Clan saw the writing on the wall—Commandery Princess Zhaoyue married into the Pan Clan instead. As the Minister of Revenue, you repeatedly demoted and relegated newly appointed officials to remote regions because you feared being replaced by up-and-coming talents. Today, the Wei Clan appears to sit at the height of power, but in reality, it's a lovely vase full of water that's about to spill. With your death, you will have sealed the Wei Clan's fate."

Touching his shackles, Wei Huaigu said, "The influence of any clan is like the tide: its rise and fall are merely facts of the world. They who thrive one moment may decline the next. All this is pre-destined. There's nothing I'll regret when the time comes for the Wei Clan. For as long as our Great Zhou has existed, it has gone through changes with every generation; only the Eight Great Clans have abided unchanged. My death will ensure the Wei Clan's survival."

"Will the Eight Great Clans truly remain unchanged?" Xiao Chiye said. "The internal strife between the Xi brothers led to the end of their bloodline—they have no descendants from either the principal wife or any concubines. From now on the Xi Clan will be a shadow of itself. It's only a matter of time before they are squeezed out of the political arena."

Wei Huaigu laughed. "As long as the Xi Clan exists, they're still in the game. Today you kill Xi Hongxuan, hoping to cut apart the Xi Clan's family fortune—yet you can't bear to give up the Xi Clan's businesses. You'll have to continue relying on their people to keep things running. So tell me, is the Xi Clan really dead? They've merely lost a helmsman. This is a temporary predicament; as long as their lady of the house still controls the businesses under the Xi Clan's name, then when she finds someone she fancies in the future, all he has to do is marry into the family and change his surname. Their child will bear the name Xi. These will be the new lawful sons that will continue the Xi Clan's legacy."

Candle wax dripped like tears onto the table. The night was coming to an end. It was deathly quiet outside. Wei Huaigu stood up, like a teacher leading a discussion.

"There's a question I've always wanted to ask Xiao Fangxu in person. It seems I won't have a chance now, so I can only ask you. Xiao Chiye, your father came from humble roots. He experienced his share of hardship on the frontier before he finally surmounted the sea of suffering to gain his own lands and title. You all claim to have broken the shackles of the noble clans. But it's been thirty years now, and Libei and the Xiao Clan have become a single, inseparable entity. He came to have sons too. You and Xiao Jiming are both lawful sons born to the principal wife. To avoid disputes between sons of lawful and common birth, he refused to take a concubine or remarry when his wife died. He turned you and Xiao Jiming into the only choices for leadership over the Libei Armored Cavalry. Is this any different from the impenetrable fortress built at the inception of a noble clan? You walk the very same path as us."

After a moment of silence, Xiao Chiye answered him. "You think this way because you can't comprehend that there are people in this world willing to be bound by love. My father never remarried or took a concubine because my mother was the only one in this life with whom he was willing to exchange vows. He established the tactics and arms of the Libei Armored Cavalry; he understands this force better than anyone else. This cavalry is his third son, one that's even more important than my brother and me. All along, the only ones who have seen us as the only choices for the Libei Armored Cavalry are people like you. My presence in Qudu does not put a collar around the Libei Armored Cavalry—only around Xiao Fangxu and Xiao Jiming. There's one thing you still don't understand: my father has indeed set up an impenetrable fortress around the position of the Libei Armored Cavalry's commander. But this isn't a barrier of iron meant to safeguard the status of a noble clan. Rather, it's a hurdle to be cleared—a test of whether one can truly lead the Libei Armored Cavalry against the ceaseless incursions of Biansha, can bear the ravages of fire and ice. Thirty years ago, Xiao Fangxu was the man who overcame this hurdle and bore the weight of this responsibility. Ten years ago, Xiao Jiming did the same. Someday, if someone else is able to break through, has no fear of hardship and suffering, and is willing to be forged and tempered in the same way, then that man shall be the new commander of the Libei Armored Cavalry."

"How honorable and dignified you make Xiao Fangxu out to be. But in reality, the Xiao Clan has monopolized military power in Libei for three decades." The look in Wei Huaigu's eyes was mocking.

"That's simply because the two men who have consecutively borne this weight happen to be surnamed Xiao." Xiao Chiye's eyes seemed to blaze with an almost blinding brilliance. In the dim light of the prison, it was as if he was both Xiao Fangxu and Xiao Jiming, as well as the fiery pride all three men of the Xiao Clan kept hidden beneath their armor. "You call my father a king wolf, but there is no hierarchy of blood lineage in a wolf pack. As long as you can defeat us, you can lead us. Everything the Libei Armored Cavalry has today, it has earned. And someday—"

Xiao Chiye's voice came to a stop.

But Shen Zechuan knew what he wanted to say. He wanted to say that someday, when *he* returned to Libei, he would also partake in a fight among wolves. As long as he could defeat his challengers, he would become the third king wolf. The pride and willfulness of the Xiao Clan sustained itself fearlessly against opposition. This was Xiao Fangxu's soul, and he had instilled this spirit in both of his sons, as well as the Libei Armored Cavalry.

"Do you know why the Qi Clan, who similarly guards our frontier and holds military power firmly in their family hands, has never faced the same hostility from the noble clans?" Wei Huaigu met Xiao Chiye's eyes and said mildly, "Because the Xiao Clan were all born with a rebellious streak. This pride of yours is precisely the cause of Qudu's distrust of Libei. And do you know why the noble clans will never truly fall? Because we know when to bend instead of break; we seize the opportunities presented to us. The Li Clan is the root—the foundation—of Great Zhou. We surround it, see it bud, and let it grow. We take turns, and we give to one another. *We* are the soil that sustains Great Zhou. The land that supports you under your feet, the sky you look at when you raise your head—all the stability you enjoy comes from the noble clans holding our nation together. Those who threaten this stability are our enemies. Twenty-six years ago, the crown prince of the Li Clan led the Eastern Palace in an attempt to destroy the status quo. How naive. The crown prince didn't understand that once the noble clans collapsed, the Li Clan would wither too—that was why he was doomed to die.

"Hua Siqian may die, as may Xi Hongxuan. And so can I. But it's merely our bodies that perish. The noble clan behind us is that sky and earth—it can't be overthrown by human hands alone. Nobody— *nobody*—can defeat us. How many years has it been, yet the only scholar from a common household to have ever broken through our ranks in the imperial court and posed a risk is Hai Liangyi. He laid low for close to thirty years, patiently waiting. He's at the top now, but does he dare to turn the world upside down without careful consideration? He revitalized the Imperial College and promoted scholars from common households. Every step he takes is cautious, because he knows using brute force to knock us aside will be the ruin of the empire. But he's already old—how much longer will he live? After his death, this little plank bridge he constructed will crumble and fall apart. He can't possibly succeed."

Wei Huaigu burst out laughing. He gripped the bars and looked at Shen Zechuan. "Qi Huilian led the Eastern Palace, charging forward like a sharp blade and refusing to compromise with us. He thought he could change the world, but he ended up causing the death of the crown prince. These so-called geniuses should reflect on their shortcomings. His is a cautionary tale of radicalism."

"Stop him!" Shen Zechuan jumped to his feet.

Xiao Chiye lunged forward, but it was too late. Wei Huaigu had begun to cough violently. He doubled over, his cupped hands full of blood, and lifted his eyes to look at the two of them. Enduring the excruciating pain, he gasped through bloody teeth, "You can't win! You're doomed...doomed to fail!"

Xiao Chiye kicked the cell door open, hauled Wei Huaigu up, and pried his jaw open. Foul blood trickled down his chin as Wei Huaigu's life guttered out. His convulsing limbs gradually stiffened, his eyes still open in a final glare.

The flame of the candle died. Only the whine of the wind could be heard inside the prison.

"The imperial heir!" Xiao Chiye dropped the corpse and raced out with Shen Zechuan at his heels.

The sky was brightening outside, but the city was still shrouded in dense, dark clouds. The passing rainstorm threatened to resume at any moment. A heaviness hung in the air, cut by the chaotic patter of running footsteps.

Xiao Chiye pushed open the door of the prison and saw the panic-stricken girls inside. The stench of blood assailed his nostrils. Every one of the boys had been killed, their bodies strewn over the ground. Sweat beaded on Xiao Chiye's temples. He clutched Wolfsfang's hilt as his eyes swept across the terrified faces of the living and the dead.

He and Shen Zechuan hadn't made any move yet—so who had killed the imperial heir?

Cool wind blew against Xiao Chiye's drenched back as he and Shen Zechuan stepped out into the courtyard. He was still staring when he heard galloping hoofbeats behind them. His voice breaking from the jolting stride, Fuman shouted in a fluster, "Y-Your Lordship! Please come to the palace quickly! His Majesty is in terrible danger!"

Xiao Chiye started forward, but Shen Zechuan took hold of Xiao Chiye's arm and held him back. He was so calm his gaze made Fuman shiver. "What do you mean by danger? Make yourself clear."

"His Majesty is critically ill," Fuman cried, snot and tears running down his face. "He urgently summons His Lordship for an audience. There is an important matter he wishes to entrust to His Lordship!"

96

THE FALL

THE IRON GRAY sky presaged the inevitable storm.

Xiao Chiye removed Wolfsfang at the entrance of the palace and stepped into the long, dark hallway. Eunuchs knelt on either side, heads bowed. It was silent both inside and outside Mingli Hall.

With scuttling steps, Fuman led Xiao Chiye to the door and lifted the curtains. The drapes within the bedchamber hung low, the air in the room thick with a suffocating heat mixed with the stench of blood.

"Your Majesty, look," Fuman whispered between sobs, "His Lordship is here!"

From behind the drapes, Li Jianheng grunted. "Send everyone else away. We wish to have a chat with the marquis. No one is to disturb us before the secretariat elder arrives."

Fuman shuffled quietly out with the other servants.

"Ce'an." Li Jianheng shifted on the sheets. "Open the curtains."

Xiao Chiye lifted the hanging drapery away from the bed. The sheets were mottled with blood; Li Jianheng looked as if he was soaking in a pool of filthy crimson. His chest heaved as he struggled for breath.

"Brother." Tears and sweat covered Li Jianheng's pale face. He wiped at his brow with a trembling hand, smearing his entire face with blood. "Where the hell have you been? The anxiety was killing me."

Mu Ru was lying on her side next to Li Jianheng. Already dead.

Xiao Chiye suddenly felt a little lonely. He had known this must be a trap, yet he had come anyway, all to earn this one last *Brother* from Li Jianheng. The friendship of their reckless youth had been crushed to dust beneath the unforgiving wheels of power; yet in this moment, it seemed to have been glued back together—he felt transported to the past. He pinned back the curtains and rasped, "It was windy on the way here, and there were too many people on Shenwu Street. I couldn't ride as fast as I liked."

Li Jianheng lifted the hand on his stomach and looked at the seeping stab wound there. "You've been so good to me. You knew the danger in coming here, yet you still came. It wasn't in vain that I called you my brother."

Xiao Chiye dragged over a chair to sit and looked at Li Jianheng, his throat bobbing several times before he could speak. "I told you a long time ago she wasn't a good match for you."

"But I liked her so much." Li Jianheng dazedly rubbed the blood between his fingers. "And I thought she liked me too. Fuck...so this is how much it hurts to be stabbed."

Xiao Chiye scrubbed his hands over his face and propped his elbows on his knees. "Did you call me here to tell me something?"

Li Jianheng's eyes found him, and he chuckled at Xiao Chiye through his tears before his face crumpled again. Voice breaking, he choked out, "I called for you, and so you came. What the fuck is wrong with you, Xiao Ce'an? Don't you know this place is surrounded...that they're waiting for you out there with swords in their hands?"

Just as Xiao Chiye had done when resolving tough situations for Prince Chu in the past, he calmly nodded. "I know."

Li Jianheng swallowed another sob. "If you hadn't come, I wouldn't have to apologize."

Xiao Chiye's eyes were bloodshot. "You're the emperor. The emperor doesn't need to apologize."

Li Jianheng pressed a hand to his wound and shook his head, tears coursing down his face. "I... Brother. I really...wanted to be a good emperor. Just a few days ago I was memorizing classics. Tell this to the secretariat elder on my behalf when you head out."

"You're the emperor. Tell him yourself."

"That won't do." Gasping and hoarse, Li Jianheng said, "I'm the emperor; I can't go myself. It's too humiliating. He's a loyal subject. Tell me, why am I so...so stupid? I...I really did want to call him my second father. And I'm scared—scared that after I die, both of you will be stabbed too."

"How can you leave this life behind when you're such a scaredy-cat?" Xiao Chiye croaked.

Li Jianheng gestured weakly. "Imperial Brother is waiting for me. I'm afraid he's going to scold me again. I've let him down."

Xiao Chiye snorted a laugh. "That's all you've got?"

"I..." Li Jianheng's breathing was shallow. He pursed parched lips again and again. "I've let you down too. I didn't stick by you. We were both in situations we had no control over. I really...really regret it. You should go, Ce'an. After you leave here, just go. Get on your horse and go home. My hands are empty, but it would be embarrassing if I didn't give you something."

Xiao Chiye rubbed his face again.

Li Jianheng raised a finger and pointed toward the wall. He muttered, beginning to slur, "That...that bow. It's the one you helped me obtain from Imperial Brother. But, fuck, I-I can't draw it.

Take it with you. The wolf pup should stay in the grass—grasslands. Your thumb ring must have gone rusty by now."

"I don't want it." Xiao Chiye rejected him heartlessly. "That's your family's Conqueror Bow."

"But you are a conqueror..." Li Jianheng's voice had thinned to a whisper. He gazed at the bow. "In my next life...don't...don't bring me here again...I want to be a swallow of our Great Zhou...nesting under the eaves of abundance..."

He fixed his eyes quietly on the Conqueror Bow and didn't move again.

The wind shook the drapes in the bedchamber. Seated on that chair, Xiao Chiye listened as muffled thunder crashed outside and torrential rain roared down.

Han Cheng finished his last mouthful of tea, holding the cup in his hands as he walked out the door to look over the soldiers of the Eight Great Battalions, standing by for battle. He flung the teacup to the ground and boomed at the top of his lungs, "The Imperial Army has a scant eight thousand men in Qudu. The men at the drill grounds at Mount Feng can't provide reinforcements if no word reaches them. Xiao Chiye is already a caged beast. Today, we must take him down!"

Rain pounded the ground. The thunder of densely clustered footsteps wrapped around the imperial palace. Sheaths scraped against armor as the Eight Great Battalions laid siege to the imperial bedchamber. Fuman's legs went weak as he listened. All the eunuchs cowered in the corners, lest they be sacrificed to these swords.

Xiao Chiye finally stood. Under the hatching of light and shadow, he drew down the bed curtains for Li Jianheng; only then did he turn around to take down the Conqueror Bow that weighed a hundred catties.

The doors had been thrown open. Xiao Chiye pushed aside layer upon layer of fluttering drapery and walked out into the sluicing rain without a backward glance.

Han Cheng raised a hand, and his men drew their blades. There was nothing for him to shout because they had already won. In this heavy downpour, they wanted to reverse the tide and make Xiao Chiye kneel once more.

Xiao Chiye looked out at that sea of dark heads. He stepped out from under the palace eaves and walked down the long steps. He had no blade. By the time the rainwater wiped away his indifference, he'd collided with the crowd. He held the Conqueror Bow out before him to block those blades, pushing the wall of soldiers back with an unrelenting, indomitable aura that drowned even the roar of the torrential rain.

Outside the palace, Shen Zechuan spurred his horse forward, the Embroidered Uniform Guard and Imperial Army behind him like a scarlet serpent as they crashed through the palace gates amid the flash of blades, surging toward Mingli Hall.

The entire palace had been locked down, the heavily armored soldiers prepared for siege. Everywhere was pandemonium; the din of battle filled the air, and the rearing horses turned the fighting into a frenzy. Ignoring the sea of people, Snowcrest charged straight for Xiao Chiye, who used the momentary opening to swing into the saddle and catch Wolfsfang as Shen Zechuan tossed it over.

Xiao Chiye drew the blade. "Qudu is not the home I dream of. I'm going home today. Whoever dares stand in my way—I'll kill him!"

With that, he tightened his grip on the reins and drew blood with the first brandish of his blade.

The rain battered their faces as Xiao Chiye carved a bloody path through the crowd. The battlefield spilled from the interior of the palace out onto the streets. Realizing he'd lost his advantage, Han Cheng shouted, "Guard the city gate to the death. We can't let this treasonous spawn who has slain his own sovereign escape!"

But the Eight Great Battalions were no match for the Imperial Army. Even if they bested them in numbers, they feared death, and so the fearless troops of the Imperial Army forced them back and back again. By the time they arrived, the city gate had fallen. Blade in hand, Shen Zechuan climbed up the city wall first, dispatching anyone who stood in his path. He called for his men to open the gate, and that tightly shut door lifted with a rumble. Beyond the curtain of rain was the home Xiao Chiye had spent six years longing for.

Han Cheng turned back and shouted, "Bring him! Hurry!"

Xiao Chiye's horse had already shot through the open gate. He raised a hand, motioning for Ding Tao to lead the men toward the drill grounds at Mount Feng; they had to take the twenty thousand men from the Imperial Army with them. In that crush of soldiers, he wheeled his horse around and spread his arms wide toward Shen Zechuan atop the city wall. In a deep, ringing voice, he called out, "Lanzhou, come with me!"

But the Embroidered Uniform Guard stood tall and still. In the heavy rain, Shen Zechuan held firmly to the battlement. He gazed at Xiao Chiye on the other side, as if to take in the whole sight of him.

The Eight Great Battalions had regrouped to pursue the Imperial Army out of the city gate. At that moment, the suspended city gate let out a muffled groan, as if straining under its own weight; the iron chains swiftly recoiled, and it came rushing down with a thunderous *clang*.

"Ce'an." Shen Zechuan raised his voice, the words gentle even through the hissing rain. "Go home."

Xiao Chiye felt as though his heart had plunged into icy water. He gripped the reins hard, already spurring his horse back toward the city as the city gate slammed into the ground with a resounding shake. Its bulk trapped the pursuing soldiers from the Eight Great Battalions within the city and shut Xiao Chiye out.

Like a beast enraged, Xiao Chiye howled, "Shen Lanzhou!"

Shen Zechuan didn't look at Xiao Chiye again. He turned to regard Han Cheng and the densely packed soldiers from the Eight Great Battalions.

Han Cheng looked away and spat. "Shen Zechuan," he snapped, "you've ruined my plans!"

"Do you think you deserve to call yourself a member of the Embroidered Uniform Guard?" Shen Zechuan looked down on him, his voice frosty. "Since Ji Wufan, the Embroidered Uniform Guard have been heroes of indomitable spirit and clear conscience. Yet today, you laid a trap and conspired to murder the Son of Heaven. Han Cheng, it's only right that I kill you!"

Han Cheng threw his head back and laughed. "Who do you think you are? The last descendant of the Shen Clan! I treated you well—I guided and supported you over and over, and this is how you repay me? Here! Bring that man over and show him to Vice Commander Shen!"

Two soldiers at last appeared, driving a disheveled Qi Huilian before them. He collapsed in the rainwater and cursed, "Treacherous vermin!"

Han Cheng reached down and yanked at his chains, spurring his horse forward and dragging Qi Huilian through the street. He pointed at Qi Huilian and called up, "Haven't you been looking for him all this time? Here he is! Shen Zechuan, come and get him!"

"Traitor! Scum!" Qi Huilian was boiling with fury as mud smeared his face.

Taking in the paleness of Shen Zechuan's face and the darkness in his eyes, Han Cheng sneered. "Your eldest brother was the Heir of Jianxing; I remember the Biansha Horsemen dragged him to his death just like this. But there was no love lost between you, so it didn't hurt you then. Does it hurt today, now that it's your teacher's turn?"

"Han Cheng!" Shen Zechuan spat Han Cheng's name through clenched teeth. "You went to such trouble to hide Xiansheng from me. What do you want?"

"He was initially of great use!" Han Cheng called back, then turned hostile. "But you let Xiao Chiye go and ruined my trap. You're no longer useful to me, and neither is he! If you want to save him, kneel down and kowtow to me; admit your mistakes! If you kneel and address me as *Father* thrice, I'll spare the both of you!"

Shen Zechuan took a step forward. "Deal."

"Bullshit!" Qi Huilian lifted his head from the muddy water. He scraped off the filth and staggered to his feet. Eyes fixed on Shen Zechuan, he cried, "I didn't teach you the scroll for you to accept humiliation! I, Qi Huilian, refuse to bow even to heaven and earth; how can my student kneel to this odious scum?!"

His shackles clanked and clattered. Kicking up muddy water, Qi Huilian stumbled forward and shouted at the top of his lungs. "A hundred years passed like a dream,[5] and still I come and go as I wish! I've lived a life of wealth and glory, fame and fortune, and I—" He laughed maniacally as he tugged at the chains around his neck.

---

5   "A Hundred Years Have Passed as If I Were Dreaming I Was a Butterfly" from Double Tune: Traveling by Boat in the Night; Autumn Thoughts by Ma Zhiyuan, a poet and celebrated playwright from the Yuan dynasty.

"I have laughed at all the heroic figures throughout the land—no other talent surpasses me in the world! Who could compare to me, Qi Huilian? I am the renowned top scholar from Yuzhou, first in all three levels of the civil exams! When I declaimed before the throne and counseled the emperor—Han Cheng, where were you? You were just a rat in a ditch!"

Qi Huilian swayed as if intoxicated as he stood in the rain. "Vermin like you are unworthy of carrying my shoes! The noble clans are the rotten boils on this land. Tell Hai Liangyi that the Zhou empire is already beyond remedy. Neither he nor I have the ability to turn the tide!" Qi Huilian laughed as he turned around haughtily and spat at Han Cheng. "But I won't admit defeat. In this life, I will only teach the throne; I will only serve as Imperial Preceptor! Lanzhou! The cage is broken, and the world will surely plunge into turbulence. I've taught you all I could. Why not..."

With his back to Shen Zechuan, Qi Huilian choked with silent sobs. The downpour drenched him to the skin, but it couldn't douse the fervor that had blazed all his life. For twenty years he had called for the crown prince, yet in this moment, it was Shen Zechuan he couldn't bear to face.

"Why not overturn this rotten sky and earth and create a world you can call your own? Lanzhou, go. Don't look back. Xiansheng will shoulder the burden of those thirty thousand wrongfully perished souls on your behalf. Don't be afraid. Have—"

Han Cheng's blade sank into flesh, and Qi Huilian's blood spattered in the rain. He toppled onto his back; gazing at the steely clouds overheard, he murmured, "Have no fear."

Thunder shook the skies. Shen Zechuan fell to his knees. He sat dazed, allowing the torrential rain to batter him. As the silence stretched, his mask shredded to pieces. He let out the first howl of

despair in these six long years. No sanity was left in his reddened eyes as his hand found Avalanche's hilt and drew the blade.

"Han Cheng—!"

He hated this sky and earth to death; he loathed these faces to death. Shen Zechuan pushed himself up off the ground. Avalanche flashed through droplets of rain, flinging blood into the crush of soldiers rushing toward him. He killed one man, then another. He strode over those bodies without hesitation, like a beast abandoned. His blade opened throats so fluidly it appeared as a stream of quicksilver, leaving blood sprayed across half Shen Zechuan's face.

He stumbled forward, as if lost. Blood ran like tears across his cheeks.

Retreating again and again, Han Cheng bellowed, "Kill him!"

Raindrops burst apart in the wind. In a flash, a long arrow buried itself in the ground before Han Cheng.

Xiao Chiye swung down from the city wall on a length of iron chain, kicked a man down, and ran him through with a flip of his hand. Leaving the corpse skewered before him, he swiftly used it to block the flashes of fresh blades. When he extracted Wolfsfang from the corpse, the man's blood had soaked both his palms.

Xiao Chiye dragged Shen Zechuan back with one arm and whistled.

Meng spread his wings and dropped. In the chaos, the falcon fell upon Han Cheng's right eye. Han Cheng scrabbled his hands across his face in panic. He heard the thunder of hooves beyond the walls; Ding Tao had led the men charging back toward the city.

"Break down the gate!" Ding Tao yelled.

The Imperial Army swept forward, but before they could make a move, a dull *boom* rang out again as the gate was slowly hoisted up.

Dragging the iron chain, Fei Sheng wheezed and led the Embroidered Uniform Guard to heave with him. "Fuck them and their ancestors! This son of a bitch is so heavy, dammit! Your Lordship, get on your horse and go!"

Snowcrest streaked in through the gap as Qudu was engulfed in the sounds of slaughter.

Across the empire, those same sounds echoed through the Bianjun Commandery as the men fought for their lives. Lu Guangbai could barely lift his spear now. He shouted as they withdrew, "Where are the reinforcements?!"

The deputy general, wounded himself, answered, "They...they didn't come."

The rain drummed against the sand. Lu Guangbai looked back in the direction of the camp.

Xiao Chiye had pulled Shen Zechuan up onto his horse. He pressed him to his chest as they broke through the heavy rain toward the city gate.

Lightning flashed and thunder boomed. A rift seemed to have been torn in the sky as the rain poured down mercilessly onto the desert sand. Lu Guangbai ripped off his tattered cloak and nailed his spear into the ground at his feet. He said over the blowing storm, "We can't fight anymore."

Lying at the side of a sandy slope, the deputy general looked at him.

"Fate wants to bind me here for life, but this is not the path I choose." Piece by piece, Lu Guangbai stripped off his armor, engraved with the Zhou empire's emblem. He wiped the wind and water from his face, his eyes filled with world-weariness and his words with self-mockery. "The desert sand has buried my brothers. I no longer wish to submit myself to a meaningless fate. The imperial edict can't save my men, and the imperial court can't feed my mounts."

Xiao Chiye galloped out of Qudu, countless soldiers of the Eight Great Battalions in pursuit behind him. They charged ahead, tearing through the dark and rainy night.

"I'm no longer willing to lay down my life for this cause." Lu Guangbai closed his eyes. Blood trickled down his fingers and soaked into the yellow sand. His throat bobbed. When he opened his eyes, they were dim and heavy.

Rain had washed the blood on Shen Zechuan's cheeks away. Sobs of grief escaped his throat. In this sorry escape, he'd forsaken all his past obedience to those who held power over his life. Like a sharp sword, the company pierced through the downpour.

Lu Guangbai washed his hands clean in the rainwater and once again picked up his long spear.

They were all prisoners on the run from fate. They had once been willing to stay shackled. But the rainstorm had toppled the great edifice of the state, and its collapsed debris rushed toward them like floodwater.

Onward, onward!

Lu Guangbai's voice rang over the desert: "I want to scale that mountain. I'm going to fight for myself!"

97

IN PAIN

THE RAIN that had fallen without cease for several days subsided at last into a drizzle, leaving the public roads a river of mud.

Qudu fell into a state of mourning. The sudden death of the young Tianchen Emperor shocked the city, and rumors spread like wildfire behind closed doors: the Marquis of Dingdu, Xiao Chiye, had colluded with the vice commander and northern judge of the Embroidered Uniform Guard, Shen Zechuan, to assassinate the emperor and seize the throne.

As the Tianchen Emperor had no imperial heir, the ministers presented a memorial requesting the empress dowager preside over pressing matters of state in place of the emperor. She repeatedly excused herself on the grounds that the harem must not interfere with state affairs. It was only after the chief commander of the Embroidered Uniform Guard, Han Cheng, kowtowed thrice in remonstration that she was convinced to step in.

With the Eight Great Battalions reassuming control over Qudu's patrols and defenses, the streets crawled with soldiers at all hours. The common folk didn't dare venture outside, and the taverns and brothels shut their doors. The old, bustling Qudu was a thing of the past. Even the vermilion walls and glazed tiles appeared washed out in the misty drizzle.

Hai Liangyi had collapsed several times as he wept before the imperial coffin. He now lay at home, unable to swallow even a drop of medicine. His hair seemed to have paled to white overnight, and the spirited eyes that once gleamed with brilliance had dimmed. After all the tears he had shed, they appeared muddled and cloudy.

"Teacher." Kong Qiu sat at the foot of the bed with his head bowed. "You must take the medicine. The world is in turmoil, and everyone is waiting for you to take the helm and steer the state toward stability once more. You must have a care for your health!"

The tear tracks at the corners of Hai Liangyi's eyes had yet to be wiped clean. His gaze drifted, and it was only after a long time that he said, "Take the helm and steer the state back toward stability? Boran, what can I do? The situation can no longer be saved."

The bamboo tube in the courtyard tapped gently against the rock in the stream, exposing the cracks spidering across its surface. Rain whispered down, but it couldn't cover those scars. Hai Liangyi was simply too old. His vitality had been eroded by the ups and downs of his post, and now, there were signs he might never recover from his illness.

Grief overwhelmed Kong Qiu. He sat where he was, weeping with his face in his hands. "How...how did it come to this?!"

"Han Cheng is a hypocrite. He speaks honeyed words while possessing the heart of a viper; he is petty and narrow-minded. Now that he's in power, the entire imperial court of civil and military officials will be walking on eggshells. Even worse, he chased Xiao Chiye out, leaving Libei without a shackle. From now on..." Hai Liangyi burst into a fit of coughing, then propped himself up and vomited blood. In his weakness, he couldn't hold back his sorrow and cried hoarsely as he gripped the edge of the bed. "From now on, our territory will be torn asunder, and our nation will descend into chaos. The century-old empire of the Li Clan will fall into ruins! I've sinned. I'm a sinner! I, Hai Renshi, have spent all my life shamelessly navigating official circles to advance my own agenda. Yet all of it was vain toil for the benefit of these villains! I...oh, I..."

Hai Liangyi hung his ash-white head and wailed, his voice so hoarse and hopeless that it drove Kong Qiu to despair.

"Teacher, Teacher!" Kong Qiu rushed to help him up, then looked back and shouted, "Help!"

The curtain lifted, but it was Yao Wenyu who entered. When he saw Hai Liangyi, he knelt at once on the footrest with no regard for the filth and took his handkerchief to wipe away the tears and blood for his teacher. He instructed the attendant to draw water and rinse the handkerchief, then helped Hai Liangyi lie down. After speaking a few soothing words, he said softly to Kong Qiu, "Your Excellency, may I ask you to wait outside, please?"

Hastily, Kong Qiu retreated.

At long last, Hai Liangyi's cries subsided. With the bowl in his hand, Yao Wenyu personally fed his teacher medicine. It was only after Hai Liangyi was asleep that he lifted the curtain and stepped out.

Kong Qiu looked as if he wanted to speak, but Yao Wenyu motioned for him to follow the attendant to the main hall while he made his way along the veranda to a back room for a change of clothes.

When Yao Wenyu reappeared, he asked the attendant to serve tea and sat in the lower position to Kong Qiu's right. "My apologies for keeping you waiting, Your Excellency."

For a moment Kong Qiu held the teacup in silence. "Teacher has no son. It's a comfort to have you here taking care of him. I shouldn't have said so much to upset him."

"Although Teacher is ill at home, he's still concerned about state affairs. Even if Your Excellency hadn't brought it up, it's difficult for him to dismiss them from his mind. Crying is better than bottling it up in his heart." Yao Wenyu held the teacup and stirred it a few times before saying, "The situation as it stands is volatile. Teacher won't have long to rest, anyway."

Kong Qiu sighed. He knew Hai Liangyi treated this young man as his own son, so he didn't hold back. "His Majesty passed so suddenly. We were already in a disadvantageous position. The Han Clan has established control of the military in Qudu, and the empress dowager has established control of the government. After this incident—what will become of Libei?"

Yao Wenyu was fair by nature and looked no different from the porcelain teacup in his hand. "At this point, we must begin to discuss countermeasures. Han Cheng is the chief commander of the Embroidered Uniform Guard. If he wishes to overstep his authority and take the reins of government from within the Grand Secretariat, his only recourse is to request that the empress dowager issue an imperial edict. Wei Huaigu ingested poison and committed suicide over the military provisions case—the vacancy he left in the Grand Secretariat will need to be filled. Even so, all the important affairs of the imperial court must still be deliberated over and endorsed by the various ministers under Teacher."

Setting down the teacup, Kong Qiu asked humbly, "But the empress dowager is presiding over state affairs, and any changes in the Grand Secretariat are subject to her approval—if she issues a change of personnel and allows Han Cheng to enter, what should we do?"

Yao Wenyu smiled. "Putting the empress dowager in charge of state affairs is a desperate measure to begin with. Her surname isn't Li; how long can she convince the masses she's acting on behalf of the Son of Heaven? Set aside everyone else for now; what's crucial today is the Qi Clan. Although Qi Zhuyin cares little for government affairs, the Qi Clan's reputation for loyalty rests firmly on her shoulders. She will never allow the empress dowager and Han Cheng to commit outrage in Qudu. The empress dowager will want to win her over; she won't cross the line just yet. Rather than worry about the empress dowager's attempts to stuff the Grand Secretariat, Your Excellency ought to worry more about Han Cheng's next steps."

"Han Cheng has made every effort to ingratiate himself with the empress dowager," Kong Qiu said. "He has succeeded."

"In my humble opinion, it's just the opposite." Yao Wenyu looked out toward the misty rain outside. "Right now, it does seem Han Cheng has gained the favor of the empress dowager. But if we consider the bigger picture, I'd say it's instead the empress dowager who's thrown her lot in with Han Cheng. She's only risen to power again currently because the emperor has no heir. The imperial court cannot be without a master, and because of the paucity of options, everyone has compromised and made concessions. But the Zhou empire must have a new Son of Heaven, and thus her grip on power is temporary. In contrast, the military power Han Cheng holds in his hands is the real deal. The fact that he dared lay a trap for Xiao Chiye in Mingli Hall shows clearly that he has another card up his sleeve. He has little to fear."

"You mean..." Kong Qiu was shocked. "Han Cheng has an imperial heir?"

Yao Wenyu sipped his tea. "The Guangcheng Emperor often stayed nights outside the palace. Perhaps another imperial heir exists, perhaps not. But the way things stand, even if Han Cheng doesn't have a true imperial heir to put on the throne, he will use every means possible to create one."

Kong Qiu's heart went cold. "Han Cheng has men and horses in the Eight Great Battalions, and the Embroidered Uniform Guard answers to him as well. The officials in the capital all have their families to think of; they might not be willing to clash with him if it really comes to it. If he shoves someone up on the dragon throne to rule the imperial court, we..." He trailed off.

Yao Wenyu changed the topic. "Has the Imperial Army already passed through Dancheng?"

The Imperial Army had indeed passed through Dancheng, but they had yet to reach Zhongbo. Xiao Chiye raced the entire way, but the soldiers and horses needed rest; eventually, they had to make camp.

Shen Zechuan had fallen gravely ill, plagued by both his old ailments and fresh despair. He seemed to be conscious, yet out of reach. It was as if he was trapped in a mire of nightmares, engulfed once more by rainwater and filthy blood.

Since the pox, Xiao Chiye had privately suspected that Shen Zechuan had never fully regained his health. The medicine he had consumed in his younger years had turned into latent poison that sickened his already weak body. Xiao Chiye didn't dare take chances; as soon as they stopped, he went looking for a physician.

Shen Zechuan's thoughts were thick and slow, and there was a dreadful roaring in his ears. He heard Xiao Chiye's voice as he lay on the pillow, yet he also seemed to hear his teacher's final shouts. In his brief moments of wakefulness, he imagined he was still in Duanzhou. He smelled familiar dishes, as if the person hovering just outside the door was his shiniang, Hua Pingting.

But he dared neither move nor look.

He had seemed to possess everything, yet he still had nothing to his name. He thought he had killed that weakest part of himself, that this mortal flesh would shed no more tears. But he had been too naive, too full of youthful arrogance—it had only seemed so because he had yet to experience such immeasurable pain. He had come this far, only to feel as if he was being skinned alive.

Xiao Chiye drew Shen Zechuan into his arms.

The nape of his neck, which once radiated seduction, had turned deathly pale. Face ashen amid dark hair, he looked like a cloud in the night. Xiao Chiye stayed at his side, holding him so tight it hurt.

"Are you cold?" Xiao Chiye whispered.

After a sluggish pause, Shen Zechuan nodded. He turned his head, pressing his cheek against Xiao Chiye's. The heat of it breathed the warmth of the living into him. He reached out in the darkness to stroke Xiao Chiye's arm around him, feeble and slow.

Xiao Chiye flipped his palm and found Shen Zechuan's hand, interlacing their fingers. All the warmth in him, he gave to Shen Zechuan. His chest was the most searing; it pressed against Shen Zechuan's back, as if he could dissolve Shen Zechuan with its heat. He sheltered Shen Zechuan in the circle of his arms, permitting no one else to get close. He clumsily licked at Shen Zechuan's wounds; this was his way of healing. He didn't want this person to be in pain ever again.

"Qiao Tianya has gone to look for Shifu." Shen Zechuan's eyes were dark and bruised. "When will he be back?"

"Soon." Xiao Chiye squeezed Shen Zechuan's hand. "Soon."

"I can't wipe the blood clean," Shen Zechuan said.

"We've embarked on a path of carnage; we don't need to be clean anymore. As long as we're together."

Shen Zechuan pressed his thin lips together. "I—"

He paused, as if he had forgotten what he wanted to say. Listening to the sound of the rain outside, he closed his mouth again.

Xiao Chiye pinched his cheeks to open that tightly pursed mouth and asked, "What did you want to say?"

Shen Zechuan tried to turn his face aside, refusing to let Xiao Chiye look at him, but Xiao Chiye's grip was iron as he asked once again, low, "What did you want to say?"

Shen Zechuan's face was pale under his gaze. His lips parted several times, but couldn't bring himself to speak. Xiao Chiye gazed at him steadily. It seemed an endless time later when he finally heard Shen Zechuan sob, "It hurts."

Xiao Chiye cupped Shen Zechuan's cheeks. Shen Zechuan looked as if he had slipped backward into childhood. Tears streamed down his face as he repeated "It hurts, it hurts" over and over, lips quivering.

Stroking Shen Zechuan's hair, Xiao Chiye wiped his tears with his thumbs. "Where does it hurt? Tell me."

Shen Zechuan broke down and wept, his shoulders trembling. He was overwhelmed by his grief, as though venting all these years of anguish in one night. Yet he was so foolish; he didn't even know where he was hurting—only that he couldn't endure the pain any longer. He numbly let Xiao Chiye wipe his cheeks as fresh tears brimmed in his eyes. There was nothing left of the machinations that had suggested a maturity beyond his years, only raw pain.

Xiao Chiye rolled over and pulled Shen Zechuan into his chest, giving Shen Zechuan a haven to shed his mask without being seen. They clasped each other tightly, and Xiao Chiye listened as Shen Zechuan cried himself hoarse. He was like a small, abandoned animal; like a battered child left broken and bleeding. The fabric at Xiao Chiye's chest was gradually soaked through. He caressed Shen Zechuan's hair, answering again and again:

"It won't hurt anymore. I promise. Lanzhou will never hurt again."

98

ON THE RUN

THE RAIN STOPPED at the first light of dawn, and the world appeared as a vast, murky expanse under the interplay of light and darkness behind the clouds. Qi Zhuyin trod through the mud as she stepped off the drill grounds. She secured her arm guards and watched her deputy general—a man named Qi Wei—ride into the camp. Strong and sturdy, but cautious by nature, he could hoist an axe on the battlefield and hold a needle off it. He was held in high esteem among the troops.

Qi Wei dismounted and nodded to the soldiers along the road as they greeted him. He headed straight to Qi Zhuyin's side. "Marshal, we've received news!"

"Qudu or Bianjun?" Qi Zhuyin asked.

"Both." Qi Wei wasn't a tall man. He looked around, then reported, "Qudu was caught in a sudden storm and was entirely cleaned out. The second young master of the Xiao Clan fled in a hurry with twenty thousand soldiers from the Imperial Army. They have already arrived at the border of Zhongbo—looks like he's headed for Cizhou."

Unruffled, Qi Zhuyin tightened her arm guard; a hint of a smile tugged her lips as she bit down on the rope. "That lad sure runs fast."

"First there was the adulteration of the military provisions, and now this hunt for Xiao Chiye. The Prince of Libei will surely lose his temper this time." Keeping pace with Qi Zhuyin as she walked,

Qi Wei said, "If Libei revolts, we'll have to station additional garrison troops in the six prefectures of Zhongbo, and the Zhongbo troops will fall under the marshal's command."

Qi Zhuyin tugged on her outer robe. "Zhongbo is a big place. Even if all the soldiers there could be transferred to my command, I don't have the nerve to accept. What's happening in Qudu isn't urgent. First, tell me what happened to the garrison troops of the Bianjun Commandery? Lu Guangbai fought an ambush all the way into Biansha territory?"

A hesitance crossed Qi Wei's rugged face. "Marshal, General Lu disregarded military orders and chased the Biansha Horsemen across the border. I suspect—"

He fell silent, unwilling to speak the words.

"The military provisions were reduced by half this year. Bianjun's in for a tough time holding out with just that," Qi Zhuyin said. "I've already signed a memorandum of debt with the Yan Clan of Hezhou under my father's name. The money was meant to buy grains for the Bianjun Garrison Troops. So what is it that you suspect? I won't hear it without proof."

Qi Wei knew Qi Zhuyin valued her generals and had always been evenhanded in meting out reward and punishment. She would never punish them for simply voicing their suspicions. But he had noticed something odd when he went to Bianjun to scout, and now his misgivings were roused. Not daring to conceal anything, he truthfully replied, "Marshal, I wouldn't dare speak without proof. I went to Bianjun to learn what had happened after the ambush. Not only did General Lu not return to camp, he even took the garrison troops from the beacon towers."

Qi Zhuyin stopped in her tracks and looked at Qi Wei. "He took the garrison troops from the beacon towers?"

Qi Wei nodded. But before he could go into more detail, they heard a commotion close by. Both turned and saw the guards stopping a sedan with intricately carved borders from entering the camp. When the guards refused them entry, Yingxi yanked aside the curtain personally and announced in a shrill voice, "Don't you know who I am? Why are you stopping my sedan! I'm the military inspector dispatched by His Majesty himself in Qudu! Go announce my arrival, quick. Tell Marshal Qi that I have something important to speak to her about!"

Watching this from afar, Qi Zhuyin murmured to Qi Wei, "Tell him I'm busy and don't have time to see him. Every one of these eunuchs from Qudu is the same. Just offer him good food and wine; tell him to keep his mouth shut and not to cause trouble. I'm going to the Bianjun Commandery. Lu Guangbai is not a deserter. If any from Qudu ask, tell them I'm not around, no more than that. It's all troubled waters over in the capital. Keep an eye on my father too. If he tries to send a message to Qudu, intercept it and tell him to behave himself."

Qi Wei had more to say, but Qi Zhuyin had already swung herself effortlessly atop the horse.

Before she left, she turned back to Qi Wei. "Things in Qudu will take at least half a month to settle. No doubt the wedding next month will be delayed. Remove all that red silk at home and store it for now. That stuff costs money."

After saying her piece, she led her men to skirt around Yingxi's sedan and rode straight for the Bianjun Commandery.

Shen Zechuan drank the medicine, and his illness gradually showed signs of improvement. The Imperial Army continued marching northeast. The pair of them would have to think of a way to convince Cizhou's prefect, Zhou Gui, to let them pass through—but before that, they had to shake off the pesky and persistent Eight Great Battalion troops pursuing them.

"It's Han Jin who's hounding us." Tantai Hu held his blade as he sat huddled on the rock. "If we can't send him packing before we arrive in Cizhou, he'll use a deployment order from Qudu to force Zhou Gui to seal off the city. We'll be trapped in Zhongbo without a path of retreat."

Xiao Chiye folded his arms and said nothing. A rudimentary map was laid out before him. Xiao Chiye wasn't afraid of facing Han Jin, but he had to consider the timing as well. The longer this dragged on, the worse it would be for the Imperial Army. It was only because Qudu was in a state of chaos that Qi Zhuyin hadn't deployed troops to hunt him down. Once the waters calmed and the capital had a hand free to order Qi Zhuyin to pursue them, these twenty thousand soldiers of the Imperial Army would be on a collision course with a wall of Qidong armor.

"The difficulty isn't in the fighting, but how quickly we can do it." Shen Zechuan's pale face had yet to regain its color. He picked up a stone and drew a few lines in the dirt on the ground. "Han Jin dared chase us this far because he has Dancheng at his back. To the Eight Great Battalions, the door to the granary of Dancheng is wide open; they're not worried about food and clothing. Our twenty thousand men ran all the way here without stopping for breath, and we have no provisions to sustain us. If we want to reach Libei via Cizhou, this is our most pressing issue."

Tantai Hu still wasn't used to looking at Shen Zechuan straight-on. He fell silent for a moment, then glanced at Xiao Chiye.

Without glancing at him, Xiao Chiye said, "If you have something to say, say it."

Tantai Hu shifted on the rock. Pointing at Shen Zechuan's scratches on the ground, he said, "We're old acquaintances with Cizhou. Can't we ask Zhou Gui to lend us some provisions under the pretext that they hadn't yet received the news from Qudu?"

"No," said Shen Zechuan, dropping the stone. "At this juncture, any action will be seen as taking sides. Zhou Gui may not intend to, but no matter why he does it, in Qudu's eyes he will be a traitor who provided aid to rebel forces. Once we pass through Cizhou, he will be taken into custody in Qudu to be impeached and punished. Zhou Gui has a family; he'll never agree to this."

Ding Tao looked up from his book. "Chen-ge went to prepare the military provisions some time ago, didn't he? He must be rushing back to us now."

"The military provisions he prepared have already been dispatched to Libei. It's the Libei Armored Cavalry's food at the front line. There's nothing left to fill the stomachs of the Imperial Army." Xiao Chiye squatted and examined the map. "Even if he and Gu Jin come, they won't be able to bring much in the way of food."

As the saying went, food and fodder should go before troops and horses. Six years ago, Libei and Qidong had so swiftly beaten back the Biansha Horsemen because their enemies had no reserve supplies and couldn't afford to fight a war of attrition. Now, the Imperial Army, caught in a similar dilemma, likewise couldn't afford to fight a war of any length. Overtaking Cizhou might be an option, but it was certainly a bad one. They had spent close to a hundred thousand taels of silver fostering their relationship with Zhou Gui, all as a safeguard for the future.

"Turn back and attack Dancheng." Tantai Hu pondered the situation. "They have a granary. We won't linger in the city. Just get in, take the grain, and leave. We can negotiate everything else with Zhou Gui when we arrive at Cizhou."

"No." Shen Zechuan sighed softly. "Direct military routes connect Dancheng to both Chuancheng and Qudu. Turning back now will give Qudu time to deploy the rest of the Eight Great Battalions. The march back will waste our time and sap our energy, and we may not be able to take the city with the necessary speed."

Tantai Hu burned with humiliation at having both his proposals vetoed by Shen Zechuan. He rubbed his hands together and said nothing more. His elder brother, Tantai Long, had been a brave man and a general, but Tantai Hu had had no one to teach him this kind of strategy. Yet though he was embarrassed and awkward, Shen Zechuan's logic had already won him over; he wasn't an unreasonable man. At the very least, he was willing to admit he was a boor.

Xiao Chiye seemed to sense his thoughts. He lifted a hand to pat Tantai Hu on the back and said nonchalantly, "We can't attack Dancheng because of the time constraint, but it *is* a solid idea. In the past, you only ever fought against the Eight Great Battalions on the streets of Qudu. Now that we've left, if there's something you don't know, just ask. There will be plenty of moments in the future where you'll need to lead troops and make decisions, and you won't have Lord Shen around every time to give you pointers. Lao-Hu, the sea of learning knows no shore. If you're willing to take the plunge and have fun in spite of this, you'll have a bright future ahead of you."

Shen Zechuan left the muddy soil scrawled into a mess and looked up at the sun. "Han Jin is from Qudu. He was only accustomed to riding horses on the hunting grounds; he won't have the stamina to catch up to us quickly."

"We can lay an ambush here and plunder Han Jin's provisions." Xiao Chiye surveyed their surroundings. "We won't need twenty thousand men for that."

"He's afraid of you." Shen Zechuan's fingertips were stained with mud. "He's been timid in his pursuit all this while. If we want him to fall for an ambush, we'll need bait."

"I'll keep five hundred men and wait here for him. There's the Silt River to the east, and it's backed by mountains on two sides and close to the forest on one. Lao-Hu will lead two thousand men to lay in ambush there." Xiao Chiye wiped the mud off Shen Zechuan's fingertip. "Tonight, Ding Tao will bring some men to the town along the way for food and wine. Say that the Imperial Army has fled here, and that everyone is demoralized because I'm too poor to feed them and can't get out of Zhongbo. Many of the soldiers are deserting."

Han Jin was young, and he had last interacted with Xiao Chiye when the public ditches were clogged. Shen Zechuan was right—he was afraid of Xiao Chiye. In fact, there were very few among the noble young masters in Qudu who weren't. Xiao Chiye's physique and personality had made him a local tyrant long before the Autumn Hunt. But the coup at the Nanlin Hunting Grounds had been a watershed moment. For lawful sons like Han Jin who weren't the eldest in their family, it should have been a breeze to become officials with their fathers and elder brothers looking out for them. They seemed, on the surface, no different from Xiao Chiye, yet they had never stood out the way Xiao Chiye did. Han Jin would pursue Xiao Chiye with caution, but he wouldn't pass up the opportunity to defeat him if he could.

As long as Xiao Chiye revealed a weakness.

"Other than that..." Shen Zechuan considered before he said to Ding Tao, "You also have to say that I don't get along with the marquis and have had so many disputes with him on the road that we're going our separate ways."

"We're in a difficult position both internally and externally." Xiao Chiye agreed, baring his teeth. "Make it as tragic as possible."

Ding Tao scribbled it all down in his little book.

Tantai Hu wasn't convinced. "Can Tao-zi act? Say it for us here first."

Ding Tao rubbed his eyes and held up the book to read. "Oh, woe is me! Misfortune has befallen my master, who is pursued relentlessly by the Eight Great Battalions yet has nary a copper in his pockets for porridge. We fled Qudu in such haste we didn't shutter the shops nor take money from the manors. Our pockets are as empty as our bellies, and to think my master still owes the jewelry shop on Shenwu Street several thousand taels of silver... Guess there's no way he's paying *that* back."

He continued with great feeling. "Lord Shen has fallen severely ill after getting chilled in the rain, yet we have no money even to call for a physician! Alack, when poverty comes to the door, love flies out the win—uh, anyway, Lord Shen has forsaken my master. Our soldiers and horses are on the run with hollow bellies. I'm so hungry—so hungry my stomach aches with it! I couldn't take it a moment longer, so I took a few brothers with me to rob some houses and cobble together enough money for a meal. Look, we were all good men from decent families, yet we've been forced to this extremity. We're just padding our bellies a little before we go seek refuge with Han Jin in Dancheng! Oh, but Han Jin is *wonderful*. He has money and grain aplenty. Only by throwing in with him will we have any hope of a future! The future is—"

"Your master thinks that was pretty well said," Xiao Chiye cut in. "Lao-Hu, strip off his little robe and smear his face with mud.

Give him three strings of copper coins and send him on his way. No need to eat and drink in a tavern anymore, you can beg for alms along the streets in town—why are you looking so pitifully at Lanzhou?"

99

THANK-YOU GIFT

HAN JIN CAPTURED several deserters from the Imperial Army one after another. All of them were filthy, and so famished they looked sallow and emaciated. After making some inquiries, he learned of the Imperial Army's desperate predicament. Still, he didn't dare advance without careful consideration— twenty thousand Imperial Army soldiers wasn't a small number. At every moment he was weighing his chances of winning against Xiao Chiye in a head-on battle.

He sat inside the tent and stared down the deserters. "The Imperial Army's performance at the Nanlin Hunting Grounds was extraordinary. And they killed so many of our people when they were vying with us for the city gate patrol back then. You followed Xiao Chiye into defecting from the capital and marched with him until now. How could you simply turn your backs on him at the drop of a hat?"

"Your Excellency, there's nowhere to go," said the deserter kneeling at Han Jin's feet. "We fled all the way here, just to be left stranded far from civilization with no villages or shops in sight. We have neither food nor shelter. Cizhou stands in front of us, and the Qidong Garrison Troops wait to the south. It's only a matter of time before we're surrounded and caught."

Han Jin thought carefully for a moment. "Are there many deserters?"

"When I fled, there were a few hundred others," the man answered. "The Imperial Army is duckweed in a muddy ditch; it will scatter at the first strike. A single blow would end them!"

"Xiao Chiye has no plan for this?" Han Jin wondered. "I heard he's strict about military discipline; the soldiers under his command are all very afraid of him."

"Your Excellency doesn't know this, but..." The deserter, who had been speaking a while, swallowed thickly and continued, "Can you give me something to eat first? I ran the entire fucking way; my stomach's growling so loud I can't hear myself speak!"

Han Jin motioned for his men to hand him some rations, and the deserter began to gobble them down on the spot. Chewing, he said, "They're *so* afraid of him! In the past, we brothers had nowhere to go in Qudu; we didn't have much choice but to do as he said. We ended up offending all the masters of the Eight Great Battalions. But now he's gone and become a traitor, how could we dare to keep following him?"

These deserters really did appear to be down and out. Moreover, they were all fugitives his own men had captured. Han Jin didn't think they were faking it. After making some careful mental calculations, he instructed his men to lead the deserters out, then invited his advisors into his tent to deliberate on strategy.

Among the advisors was Gao Zhongxiong, the man who had taken the lead back when the Imperial College had rebuked the Xiande Emperor over Shen Zechuan's release from the Temple of Guilt. The demonstration had offended Pan Rugui, and Gao Zhongxiong had been thrown in prison with no one to vouch for him. He had since given up the idea of becoming a court official and thrown in his lot with Han Jin. He was a passionate scholar, full of patriotic fervor, and had always abhorred traitors to the state.

Shen Wei, Pan Rugui, and their ilk were all men he held in contempt. And now, upon hearing that Xiao Chiye had fled Qudu after assassinating the emperor himself, he was even more furious and unable to stand by.

Gao Zhongxiong pointed to the map. "Xiao Chiye is already at the end of his rope. We cannot tolerate him running loose in Zhongbo. My lord has an army of strong men and sturdy horses, as well as the city of Dancheng to fall back on. In my opinion, there's no time to lose. We should deploy troops at once to pursue and engage the Imperial Army. If we can capture Xiao Chiye before he enters Cizhou, it would be a major accomplishment."

Han Jin hesitated. "But even with the desertions, Xiao Chiye still has more than ten thousand men—and they're all real soldiers, battle-tested in the Autumn Hunt. If this is a trap..."

"But the soldiers of the Imperial Army are demoralized; they're not of one mind," Gao Zhongxiong countered. "If Xiao Chiye can't command them, there's no difference between ten thousand men and one man. They're just a motley crew of fugitives; they're nothing to worry about. The military commissioner has already pursued him all the way here. If we can't capture him quickly and bring him to justice, how will we explain to Qudu?"

Halfway convinced, Han Jin asked, "But what should I do if he's allied with Cizhou's prefect, Zhou Gui, against me?"

"My lord," Gao Zhongxiong said urgently, "Zhou Gui is a man with a family. Would he cast aside a decent official position to plot a revolt with the traitor Xiao Chiye? He wouldn't dare. Dispatch troops now, and we can catch Xiao Chiye by surprise. If we press our advantage and seize victory, we'll return to Qudu in triumph."

By this point, Han Jin had been sleeping in a tent for days and was covered in bug bites. His mind was on Qudu, where his eldest brother,

Han Cheng, had aided the empress dowager in taking control of the government. The glorious rise of the Han Clan was within arm's reach. It was the perfect time for him to return and call up his friends for a lavish celebration. The longer he had to stay here, the more irritable he became. After hearing Gao Zhongxiong's argument, he weighed the pros and cons and promptly agreed.

The next day, Han Jin woke early and led the troops out while there was still dew on the leaves. Based on information provided by the captured deserters, he followed the Imperial Army's trail to the forested area beside the Silt River. Fire pits were dug all over the forest, but he didn't see nearly enough to feed twenty thousand people.

Any doubts Han Jin had about those deserters' story evaporated. His spirits soared; sitting astride his horse, he drew his blade and brandished it. "Those traitors are rats in a trap. Search the forest. We're sure to find their trail!"

The soldiers of the Eight Great Battalions surged forward.

Xiao Chiye was squatting by the stream, washing his face. When he heard the rumbling of hoofbeats, he looked back just in time to see Han Jin spurring his horse over.

The moment Han Jin caught sight of him, he bellowed, "The traitor's here! Catch him!"

Xiao Chiye whistled to summon Snowcrest. The five hundred men from the Imperial Army who were scattered among the trees ran about in a panicked fluster, hollering as they were chased through the forest. Han Jin couldn't help but grow excited. He laughed aloud, then shouted, "Your Lordship, who would have thought you'd find yourself at my mercy today!"

Abandoning his own men, Xiao Chiye fled alone on his horse. Han Jin, afraid he would slip away, led his men in hot pursuit.

The Eight Great Battalions charged through the forest, following Han Jin northeast at breakneck speed. The farther Han Jin galloped, the more anxious he became. He shouted ahead, "Xiao Chiye! You have nowhere to run! Surrender yourself!"

Casting a glance behind him, Xiao Chiye tried to rally his men to mount some resistance, but they were no match for the Eight Great Battalions' ferocity. The sight of five hundred men running for their lives was a sorry sight. In no time at all, they'd fled to the edges of the forest. They made a beeline for the Silt River, where the Eight Great Battalions' soldiers finally boxed them in.

"Xiao Chiye!" Han Jin reined his horse to a halt and waved his sleeve at the horizon. "Look around you. These are all soldiers from my Eight Great Battalions! You're besieged on all sides. What are you still struggling for? Beg for mercy now, and I'll spare your life!"

Snowcrest wheeled to face them, stamping in place. Xiao Chiye said frostily, "You want to kill me? Sure. I just want to ask one question first. Why didn't Han Cheng come himself today?"

"My eldest brother is currently the noble regent, attending to weighty official duties. Why would he come all the way out here to deal with *you*?" Han Jin leveled his sword at Xiao Chiye. "Dismount your horse now and surrender, and your Xiao Clan still has a slim chance of survival. You alone made this heinous mistake—are you willing to let your entire family pay with their lives?"

"I've made many mistakes." Xiao Chiye looked down his nose at Han Jin. "But it's hardly the Han Clan's place to discuss that with me."

The moment the words left his mouth, several hundred people on either side of him surged to their feet, completely surrounding Han Jin. Tantai Hu led the soldiers forward, slashing at everyone in his path and throwing both men and horses off their feet in the confusion. The men around Han Jin were all mounted members of the

Embroidered Uniform Guard Han Cheng had assigned to protect him. They realized immediately that they had fallen for a trap and raised their whips to strike Han Jin's horse, attempting to drive him out of the pincer movement through the edge of the forest.

When had Han Jin ever seen such a battle formation before? He was knowledgeable enough when it came to the military exercises held at the Qudu drill grounds, but he had never fought a real battle. He was frightened entirely out of his wits. The sting of the whips jerked his horse into action, and it broke into a mad gallop toward the periphery of the forest, the Embroidered Uniform Guard forming a protective circle around its rider.

Shen Zechuan stood in the shadow of a tree at the edge of the forest, blade in hand, and watched Han Jin approach.

Han Jin would have charged straight through, but a sharp-eyed guard deftly reined in the horse. Under their sheen of cold sweat and fresh blood, the guards exchanged glances. Eventually, the man in the lead spoke up. "Vice Commander! It's fate that has led us to encounter each other today. Why not let us go for the sake of our past comradeship?"

Shen Zechuan had thinned alarmingly in the past few days. The bones of his wrist as he held the blade resembled the snow-white arc of a crescent moon peeking out from the opening of his unadorned white sleeve. His eyes seemed to reflect glacial ice, even as a smile as warm as springtime gradually spread over his face. "I understand my fellow brothers were entrusted with this mission by another and had no choice but to obey."

This soldier knew Shen Zechuan was a malicious, ruthless character. When he saw that particular smile, he stepped before Han Jin and shuffled a few paces back. The sounds of fighting and killing filled the air behind him. He knew Xiao Chiye was closing in on them as well, one step at a time. Sweat trickled down the man's temples. "Your Excellency has a bright future ahead of you—why follow a traitor and suffer untold hardships out here in the wilderness? If you are willing to release Commander Han now, the chief commander of the Embroidered Uniform Guard will forget any past grudges and welcome you back to the capital with open arms!"

Unexpectedly, Shen Zechuan chuckled. His laugh was clear and languid, pleasant to the ears. His pale skin appeared extraordinarily delicate under the dappled sunlight between the leaves. He drew his sword with a terrible slowness, scraping Avalanche's slender blade against its sheath.

"I'm very grateful to Han Cheng." Shen Zechuan gripped the hilt and paused. "Words cannot express the extent of my gratitude toward him. When you return to the capital, please bring him a thank-you gift on my behalf."

A chill jolted up Han Jin's spine and he nearly tumbled off his horse.

Xiao Chiye knelt by the water and rinsed away the blood on his blade. Crouching nearby, Shen Zechuan buried both palms in the stream, not removing them even after Xiao Chiye had finished washing Wolfsfang. Xiao Chiye squatted opposite Shen Zechuan. He was much taller than him, but like this, he could still lean his forehead against Shen Zechuan's. Their palms met in the water, and Xiao Chiye grasped his fingertips.

Shen Zechuan's sobs of a few days ago seemed to be a forgotten dream; he was clean and composed under the sunlight. Very slowly, his index finger stroked along Xiao Chiye's hand and slid through the space between Xiao Chiye's fingers. His palm fit into Xiao Chiye's palm, bringing along with it the icy softness of the current.

Tantai Hu was a short distance away leading the men to clean up the battlefield. They still had to stay overnight in this forest. There were soldiers everywhere nearby, but Shen Zechuan's hand clung to his—as if he was nonchalantly playing with it, yet also like a seduction long premeditated.

The stench of blood was still on him.

Xiao Chiye let him do as he wished. "You left only one soldier alive and sent him back home. What if he doesn't bring the message back to them?"

Shen Zechuan looked at the shimmering surface of the stream. "He's a member of the Embroidered Uniform Guard. As long as he's alive, he has to complete his mission. Han Jin has fallen into our hands. If he doesn't bring this news back, then he has failed in his duty. He's sure to die anyway, so he might as well die with a little dignity. Not to mention, the heads in that burlap sack all belong to on-duty members of the Embroidered Uniform Guard with their authority tokens. He has to bring his brothers home."

Xiao Chiye's fingers itched to wipe away the droplets of blood on Shen Zechuan's wrists, but there were eyes all around. The pair gazed at each other for a moment. He suddenly grasped Shen Zechuan's hand, then leaned forward and said, "You left your earrings back in Qudu. I'll have some new ones made for you once we arrive in Libei."

"You have an outstanding bill of several thousand taels of silver." Shen Zechuan looked at him. "Tighten your belt and make some money first, Er-gongzi."

"I can marry into a rich family. Pledge my body for money." Xiao Chiye's voice was low.

Pressing their joined hands against the soft sediment of the stream bed, Shen Zechuan whispered into Xiao Chiye's ear, "Five hundred taels for one night…"

That flicker of sensuality hung in the air between them. Before it could shift the atmosphere, Shen Zechuan looked back with a serious countenance at Tantai Hu, who was hovering, unsure of his approach. "Han Jin intended to return to Qudu as soon as possible and had Dancheng supplying him with whatever he needed; he probably didn't bring much in the way of provisions. Tell everyone to eat their fill tonight. Tomorrow morning, we—"

Shen Zechuan stopped. He cast a swift sidelong glance at Xiao Chiye before he continued, "...will continue northeast."

Xiao Chiye said nothing and earnestly set to washing his handkerchief, all the while caressing Shen Zechuan's hand beneath it until even his palm blushed red.

LATENT THREAT

>>> ——— ✦ ❀ ✦ ——— <<<

NEWS OF HAN JIN'S rash attack made its way quickly back to Qudu, where it caused quite a stir. The only surviving member of the Embroidered Uniform Guard had stumbled into the city carrying a sack of human heads and a clear message: Shen Zechuan and Xiao Chiye had split completely from Qudu. There was no possibility they would sit down to negotiate.

Han Jin's capture sent Han Cheng into a rage. The Embroidered Uniform Guard had been falling apart since Shen Zechuan left Qudu. The men under Ge Qingqing were still in Juexi looking after the Xi Clan, and Fei Sheng had gone to ground with his own trusted subordinates. Han Cheng hadn't many men left with him.

Under Ji Wufan's command, the Embroidered Uniform Guard had been at the height of power and peak of glory. By the time Ji Lei took up the mantle, it was already on the decline. Now, in Han Cheng's hands, it had become no more than a fractured squad of ceremonial guards. The men under Fei Sheng's command were capable, but the moment Han Cheng had exposed his intent to kill him, he'd lost any chance of winning Fei Sheng over to his side.

"Once the immediate situation has stabilized, the Twelve Offices of the Embroidered Uniform Guard will have to be reorganized. Our current lack of manpower is disgraceful; we can't get anything done with so few people." Sitting a step below the empress dowager,

Han Cheng continued steadily, "I have noticed lately that too many sons of noble clans are in positions with practically no obligations. Why not recruit them? Giving them something to do will prevent them from stirring up trouble at this sensitive juncture."

The empress dowager wore a crown of jade, her hair pulled back into a tidy bun. Pendant earrings inlaid with gold and gems dangled from her ears. She was well suited to this elegant and poised manner of dress, in the same way a peony ought to be grown within the vermilion gates of the affluent. Only gold and jade in their glorious splendor were worthy of adorning a divine beauty like her. Though the bloom of her youth had faded, her graceful demeanor was undiminished. At present, she held a wooden spoon, teasing a parrot. Without turning, she said, "The Embroidered Uniform Guard is a place where serious work is done. It's already providing for many sons of noble clans. Continue stuffing unqualified men into the ranks, and sooner or later it will be rendered useless. The Eight Great Battalions were routed outside Dancheng. If you ask me, both forces not only need an infusion of new blood but a dismissal of some old-timers as well."

Han Cheng had only been thinking of finding decent posts for the young masters of noble clans at the behest of their families. He concurred at once. "I have the same intent. I'll discuss it with the Ministry of War tomorrow and submit a memorial to the Grand Secretariat. Your Majesty, Hai Liangyi is so ill he can hardly stand up straight. He's been toiling for the state all his life. At the very least, we mustn't let him ruin his health beyond repair. We should come up with some arrangement for him."

By this, he of course meant that Hai Liangyi ought to be relieved of his post and sent back to his hometown. Smiling amiably, the empress dowager tapped the wooden spoon once more and handed it to Aunt Liuxiang, who stood nearby to serve. "He suffers from an affliction of the heart and simply has yet to regain his footing. He understands the Six Ministries best. How could we rashly dismiss him at such a crucial time? Let's wait a few more days."

Having been tactfully rebuffed, Han Cheng inwardly gnashed his teeth, though his expression remained unchanged. "Your Majesty leads the administration now, so naturally it is for Your Majesty to decide. Since the Eight Great Battalions have been defeated outside Dancheng and Xiao Chiye has fled to Zhongbo, the Ministry of War ought to deploy the Qidong Garrison Troops to stop him as soon as possible. Otherwise, the Libei Armored Cavalry will gain twenty thousand more men as reinforcements when he returns!"

The empress dowager wiped her hands clean. "If you had stopped him in Qudu, we would not have these pressing worries now. Zhou Gui, the prefect of Cizhou, knows his job, and he's also caught in a tight spot. He must still deal with Libei in the future, so he cannot afford to offend them. Xiao Chiye's return to Libei is a foregone conclusion. If we mobilize Qi Zhuyin now, she'd be fighting the Libei Armored Cavalry head-on. It's easy for us to talk of deploying troops, but where are the provisions to sustain the army as they march north? Hezhou can't bear the additional burden."

"Are we just going to let Xiao Chiye return to Libei?" Han Cheng leapt to his feet in astonishment. "This will make Libei even more formidable!"

The empress dowager allowed Aunt Liuxiang to support her with an arm as she stood at the entrance of the courtyard and gazed out at the vividly colored blossoms. "Han Cheng, do you imagine Xiao Chiye will be of assistance when he returns to Libei?"

Han Cheng, leaning forward attentively, said deferentially, "I don't understand. Please enlighten me."

"Since Xiao Jiming took command of the Libei Armored Cavalry from Xiao Fangxu, it has taken him ten years to get to where he is today. He is the heart of Libei's military forces, the one the soldiers look up to." Spotting Hua Xiangyi pouncing on butterflies in the garden with the maidservants, the empress dowager couldn't help but smile. She watched for a moment longer before she continued, "Xiao Chiye has been away from Libei for six years. His return now makes him look like a wolf pup intruding into someone else's territory. He said Qudu is not the home of which he dreams, but he's too young to understand the phrase *time changes everything*. With his twenty thousand men of his Imperial Army, he will find himself out of his element in Libei. Xiao Fangxu has always been rigid in organizing the Libei Armored Cavalry under a single command. This is the reason he's still standing today, but it will also make it hard for Xiao Chiye to find his place. Amid such a pack of wolves, Xiao Chiye—if he wishes to break through and become the king wolf—must first possess the determination to bite the former king of wolves to death."

The empress dowager looked back and smiled at Han Cheng. "The Xiao Clan can't stomach the sight of internal strife among other clans, but sometimes, strife is inevitable. The Xiao Clan has always been a paragon of brotherly love and harmony, but how long can brotherhood last in the face of competing military power? The battlefield is cruel; millions of battered soldiers shed their blood there. But the battle for power is more brutal still, and a change of hands often means infighting and fratricide."

Han Cheng shrank a little under the empress dowager's gaze and lowered his head in agreement. "Your Majesty is wise. But now that Xiao Jiming is so injured, it's entirely reasonable for Xiao Chiye to stand in for him."

"Did Xiao Jiming die?"

Han Cheng shook his head.

"No. Xiao Jiming did not die," the empress dowager said. "He can still coordinate military affairs from behind the troops, while Xiao Fangxu, who has come out of retirement, commands the soldiers at the front. This father and son control the Libei Armored Cavalry together, something that requires strong mutual understanding and consideration for each other. But Xiao Chiye possesses both the ability to coordinate military affairs and the ability to charge into battle and slaughter the enemy. If he barges into this homogenous army and upsets the equilibrium, he'll be the unforeseen variable that unbalances the Libei Armored Cavalry. Perhaps he doesn't intend to take his father or elder brother's place. But very soon, he will understand that Libei isn't as indivisible as we perceive it to be. His return is the latent threat that will fracture Libei."

The trajectory of this situation was not something anyone could have directed; it was something that took shape based on the opportunities presented. The seed had been sown the day Xiao Fangxu founded the Libei Armored Cavalry, its strength powerful enough to stand against the imperial capital of Qudu. As for what fruit it would eventually bear, no one knew.

"In this world, the common man endures the worries of common men, while the talented must endure the agony of genius," the empress dowager said calmly. "There is already a Xiao Jiming—why beget a Xiao Chiye? Six years is neither a particularly long nor short time, but it's enough to change many things. Xiao Chiye's agony in Qudu springs from the fact that he isn't a man content with carefree mediocrity—yet when he returns to Libei, he will continue to be tormented by the selfsame suffering. Once these models of brotherhood realize that killing each other is the only way forward, his anguish will intensify. Whether Xiao Jiming cedes his position to Xiao Chiye or Xiao Chiye excuses himself to avoid conflict, these brothers who were once loyal and devoted to each other will grow estranged."

Even in the warmth of the fifth month, Han Cheng felt himself prickle with goosebumps, followed by a tingling thrill.

"The former emperor has been formally interred. There ought to be some progress on the preparation of a new ruler," the empress dowager said, changing the subject. "You say you've found a true imperial heir. When are you planning to produce him for me to have a look?"

Han Cheng bowed slightly. "I've dispatched men to bring the imperial heir to Qudu with all speed. Your Majesty can expect to see the heir in five days at the latest."

The empress dowager watched him. "If you're so sure he's the imperial heir, you must have credible proof. The concerns of the civil officials under Hai Liangyi won't be easy to dismiss. Han Cheng, you should make all necessary preparations."

Han Cheng kept her company a while longer, then said his fare-wells and left. The moment he had gone, Hua Xiangyi approached the empress dowager with a bouquet of flowering branches in her arms.

"The Han Clan has never climbed so high before. Give him an inch, and he loses all sense of propriety." The empress dowager looked in the direction of Han Cheng's departure and pulled Hua Xiangyi along to stroll for a few steps. "Han Jin was defeated in Dancheng. The man's a fool. He had timing, geography, and numbers all in his favor, yet he was still taken captive. How can such a person be trusted with heavy responsibilities? Han Cheng entered the palace today to hint that I should dispatch men to save him.

He cannot fathom that they've only kept Han Jin alive this long to threaten him."

"I've noticed the chief commander looks awfully well lately. He doesn't even address himself as 'this subject' when he enters the palace to pay his respects." Hua Xiangyi leaned against the empress dowager. "Auntie, he has lofty goals. Considering how quick he was to prepare this so-called imperial heir, I fear he's already unsatisfied with being the chief commander of the Embroidered Uniform Guard."

"He wants to be prince regent." The empress dowager picked a blossom from the branches in Hua Xiangyi's arms. "I've already looked into the child. How could he claim that's an orphan of the late Guangcheng Emperor? It's merely a child of some distant relative he found in his hometown. Rather delusional for such a lowly thing to dream of ruling the Li Clan's empire, don't you agree?"

The empress dowager thought for a moment. "Still, there really is no one else at present."

They spoke a few more words before Fuman hurried over. Bowing low, he announced, "Assistant Minister Xue requests an audience."

Tantai Hu distributed the rations that night. It was as Shen Zechuan expected: Han Jin had traveled light when he led the troops after them and brought little in the way of provisions. The Imperial Army, however, had gone hungry for several days; at least tonight they could eat their fill.

Shen Zechuan had grown terribly thin after his teacher's passing, but this forest had long been cleared of game; there wasn't even a rabbit to be had. Xiao Chiye gave Shen Zechuan the steamed bun and meat jerky he had set aside and settled down to eat dry biscuits and rice gruel like everyone else.

Tantai Hu crouched down next to the fire. "I've carried out Master's instructions and sent someone to notify Zhou Gui so he can prepare. Once we make our way past Cizhou the day after tomorrow, you'll be home!"

Xiao Chiye threw more wood into the bonfire. "That notice to Zhou Gui is so he can put on a show with us. With Han Jin in our hands, he'll have no choice but to give way."

"Han Jin really appeared at the most opportune time." Tantai Hu grinned. "Just yesterday we were worrying about how to get past Cizhou, and now he's delivered himself right to our doorstep!"

Shen Zechuan warmed his hands by the fire and said nothing, his eyes on the flames.

Tantai Hu soaked his biscuit in his soup. "I ate rations like this when I served in Dengzhou's garrison troops years ago. The Zhongbo of today is entirely different from the Zhongbo back then. I barely recognize it now."

Ding Tao poured a bit of rice from his bowl to feed the sparrow in his sleeve. "It's not so bad here near Cizhou. If you go further east, you'll see what it really means to be unrecognizable."

With his perfect recall, Ding Tao could still vividly see the tragic scenes he had witnessed in Duanzhou and Dunzhou six years ago when he followed Xiao Chiye with the army to clean up the aftermath of the Biansha massacre. He'd been barely ten then, and had only just procured a little notebook to take notes like his father did. After what he saw, he had nightmares the rest of the journey.

"You came after the battle. You've never seen what Zhongbo looked like before." Tantai Hu lowered his eyes to the soup in the bowl. "My parents took me to see Dunzhou when I was a child. It was a big city, almost as bustling as Qudu. The fireworks and lanterns during the new year holidays were beautiful, and so was the turtle mountain display—they built a shell of lanterns as tall as two men for the Lantern Festival. People crowded and jostled with one another to see it... There were so many people."

Shen Wei had been the Prince of Jianxing, and his manor had been in Dunzhou. For a moment, everyone looked at the ground. No one dared glance at Shen Zechuan, and they equally feared offending Xiao Chiye. During these days on the road, the Imperial Army had gradually discovered the subtle and delicate relationship between the two of them. Seeing the evidence before their eyes was entirely different from merely hearing rumors, as they'd done in the past.

How should they treat Shen Zechuan? Should they regard him as their madam—the wife of their commander? But which lady of the house could command the Embroidered Uniform Guard in three separate raids? When he'd hacked off the heads of his former subordinates who were protecting Han Jin, not one of the officers from the Imperial Army could bring themselves to watch.

Shen Zechuan was too different from Xiao Chiye. He didn't look or behave like the supreme commander the Imperial Army was familiar with. He appeared gentle and modest, yet he rarely changed his mind during official discussions. He would overrule even Tantai Hu to his face. And compared to Xiao Chiye, he was far more cold-blooded. In the past, they had all privately considered Shen Zechuan merely a beauty—a delicate vine clinging to the stronghold of power. But after Shen Zechuan had donned the scarlet python robe of the Embroidered Uniform Guard, everything he had once concealed was exposed, shifting their perception of this last descendant of the Shen Clan. His beauty was no longer a vision anyone could wantonly admire—it was an unrivaled allure that bespoke a ruthless strength.

Other than the perpetually clueless Ding Tao, there were very few in the Imperial Army willing to look Shen Zechuan in the eye. Even Tantai Hu could sense a certain strain. The soldiers took their orders from Xiao Chiye, and they didn't mind if Xiao Chiye preferred men—but they had to determine where Shen Zechuan stood as soon as possible. Shen Zechuan had the ability to vie with Xiao Chiye for power and authority. This was what had thrown them off balance these last few days: a subtle wariness of the unknown.

Xiao Chiye rubbed his thumb ring. He was about to speak when Shen Zechuan turned his palms toward the fire and said, "The wild herbs and vegetables in Duanzhou are delicious."

The tense atmosphere eased a little. Ding Tao raised his head. "I heard the others back in Libei say a handful of wild vegetables from Duanzhou in the winter are as costly as gold. I want to try them! Gongzi, did you eat them often?"

"When the ice and snow melted in spring, my shiniang always made dumplings with the most tender wild vegetables," Shen Zechuan replied. His fingertips were clean and fresh-scrubbed, as if they had never been tainted with blood. He smiled. "I rarely ate them. That's why I remember it so clearly."

Ding Tao, his mouth watering, wrote carefully in his notebook with the bit of ink he had. "I want to eat it. We'll definitely get a chance to in the future. As long as I write it down, I won't forget."

Tantai Hu rubbed the back of Ding Tao's head with a smile and chided, "Grow up! What delicacy haven't you tasted in Qudu? To think you're still coveting wild vegetables!"

Everyone laughed, and the topic of Zhongbo was thus diverted. Shen Zechuan warmed his hands and said nothing more.

That night, Xiao Chiye rested his head on a stone. He had yet to fall asleep when he felt a piece of warm oilpaper pressed to his cheek.

He sat up, took a sniff at the packet in Shen Zechuan's hands, and smiled. "Where did you get this bun from?"

"Ding Tao brought it back from town. He told me to keep it for later." Shen Zechuan settled down next to Xiao Chiye.

They sat side by side, with their backs to the sleeping forest and the boundless starry sky before them. Xiao Chiye opened the oilpaper and pushed it toward Shen Zechuan. "Eat. It'll get cold if you keep it any longer."

"I'm full," Shen Zechuan said. "You can have it."

Knowing Shen Zechuan had saved it especially for him, Xiao Chiye accepted the bun but broke it into two—half in one hand for himself, half in the other for Shen Zechuan. Shen Zechuan took a few token bites and let Xiao Chiye finish the rest.

"You still have to decide whether to take my bride price of two million taels to Libei or leave it in Cizhou." Xiao Chiye drank from the waterskin. "You already sent Ge Qingqing a message; he'll surely keep an eye on the Xi Clan's businesses for you. Once we reach Libei, Qiao Tianya and Chen Yang won't be far behind. When the time comes, we'll build a new courtyard..."

Xiao Chiye stopped, sensing something off in Shen Zechuan's abnormal silence. He fell quiet. "Is there something you want to tell me?"

Gripping that little bamboo fan that never left his side, Shen Zechuan looked at Xiao Chiye from of the corner of his eye. "Ce'an, I can't go to Libei with you."

The way he spoke was so gentle—just like days ago, when he had stood at the battlements atop the city gate and said with the same tenderness, *Ce'an, go home.*

101

TREASURE

S HEN ZECHUAN HAD, back at the Temple of Guilt, received Qi Huilian's entire lifetime of knowledge. When he had knelt at Qi Huilian's feet six years ago, he already knew the path he would take. It was in pain and anxiety that he tempered his body and spirit. He had entertained the naive thought that he could throw off the constraints of the noble clans by relying on political strategizing alone.

But he had failed.

Shen Zechuan looked ahead. The murmuring waters of the river flowed past like a life that had plunged into darkness, unable to change direction, twinkling only with the borrowed light of the starry sky reflected in it. He nudged the little bamboo fan open, then eased it closed again. "I left Qudu, but I am still caged," he said. "This is my punishment for taking my chances. I need to find a new way out. Xiansheng entrusted his entire lifetime of convictions to me. I promised I'd fight to the end of this battle for him. We endured everything in the past because Qudu hadn't seemed to have reached a point of no return. But now I understand that its decline has long been irreversible; it's already the sun setting beyond the western hills."

In that heavy downpour, Qi Huilian had shouted about the rotten sky and earth, yet even then, his raised arms had seemed a futile attempt to hold up the collapsing state. He'd taken an entirely different path from Hai Liangyi, yet both had lit the same torch. In the last moments of his life that had blazed always for the Li Clan, he had cast aside the crown prince, that imperial son he had never been able to let go of, and chosen Shen Zechuan, who came from nothing.

To any bystander, Qi Huilian's two students would have seemed worlds apart, as unalike as clouds and mud. The crown prince was a lawful son of the Li Clan, born to become a wise sovereign. Qi Huilian had thought that, with this undisputed descendant of direct lineage, they could create a new world.

But he had failed.

He had found Shen Zechuan in the mire. Shen Zechuan, whose mother was of lowly birth and whose father was a traitor who fled from battle. Shen Zechuan, who was no son of lawful birth. Yet Qi Huilian chose such a Shen Zechuan. His lifelong conviction had changed, and he no longer bowed to the determination of lineage. He hoped for Shen Zechuan to pierce through this wretched, decaying empire.

"I've given up enduring in silence." Shen Zechuan rested his fan on his knee and turned slightly to gaze at Xiao Chiye. "I'm choosing another way to fight. I want to remain in Zhongbo. You once said to Tantai Hu, 'The wrongs suffered by our families have yet to be avenged, and the humiliation of our nation has yet to be redressed.' You were right, Ce'an; the humiliation Zhongbo has suffered should be redressed in Zhongbo. This is what I want to do. One day, we will gallop together under the skies of Libei, and that will be when I've become strong and powerful. Two million isn't enough to take away the wolf pup of the Prince of Libei. Such a betrothal gift is not worthy of my Xiao Ce'an. If I'm in Zhongbo, I will one day become your indestructible shield."

The waterskin fell, splashing water across the ground and soaking the corner of Xiao Chiye's robe. Under the soft veil of moonlight, Xiao Chiye grasped Shen Zechuan's hand and pulled him into a fierce embrace.

After a long time, Xiao Chiye's hoarse voice rumbled beside Shen Zechuan's ear, clinging close. "I'll leave my back to you, and you'll leave your chest to me. We cannot do without each other. I'll choose the best horse in Libei for you. We'll build a house on the demarcation line between Zhongbo and Libei and meet there—every month. If you want to marry me, two million silver isn't enough; I want Lanzhou's priceless smile, far dearer than a thousand gold."

Shen Zechuan wrapped his arms around Xiao Chiye, embracing this captivating scent. Xiao Chiye was the wind sweeping over the meadow to assail the turbulent river of Shen Zechuan's heart, offering him a taste of the sweetness of love. After losing Duanzhou, and now his teacher, he had little left. He could only stride across that ravine of unfathomable depth to build a fortress for whatever was left of his heart's treasures.

The prefect of Cizhou, Zhou Gui, had been particularly busy with his official duties in recent days. Since word came that the Imperial Army had passed Dancheng and was on their way to Cizhou, he'd tossed and turned in bed, unable to sleep at night.

Kong Ling, Zhou Gui's chief advisor, was a man from the prefecture of Dengzhou in Zhongbo who had come up with the prefect as fellow students. Earlier today, he had prepared wine and instructed the chef to prepare several refreshing cold delicacies. He now sat cross-legged on the veranda across a small table from Zhou Gui, conversing over drinks. Tiny white blossoms fell from the pagoda tree in the courtyard, filling the air with their fresh, sweet fragrance.

"I've hardly slept the past few days," Zhou Gui said, reaching for his wine cup.

Sitting casually, Kong Ling sampled one of the dishes and swallowed a mouthful of strong wine. "I know. The bandits in Dunzhou have converged into a sizable group; they can't be underestimated. We have no soldiers or horses—we can't afford to provoke them. But of course we just happened to have a bumper harvest last year. That bandit chief Lei Changming is eyeing Cizhou's granary."

"All the grain has been sent to the Libei Armored Cavalry as military provisions. The granary in Cizhou is practically empty. I wrote a letter to Dunzhou's prefect, but you know he's a puppet propped up by Lei Changming; would he dare reason with Lei Changming on our behalf? What can I do but suffer in silence." Zhou Gui couldn't even manage a sip of wine. "And then there's that second young master of Libei who rebelled and fled the capital. Twenty thousand Imperial Army soldiers are due to arrive at the city gate any day now. Chengfeng, I'm in a dilemma. I can't let them pass, but I can't *not* let them pass either!"

Kong Ling set down his chopsticks. "If Libei rebels, Cizhou will be caught right in the middle. We won't be able to sit on the fence for long. You'll have to make a decision as soon as possible."

"It's not up to me." Zhou Gui sighed miserably. "We're genuinely cornered: wolves before us and tigers behind. We can afford to offend neither Libei nor Qudu, and we have Lei Changming staring us down like a beast eyeing its prey."

Kong Ling plucked some flowers off the pagoda tree and tossed them into the wine. "Lei Changming is a bandit. He'll be hunted down and annihilated sooner or later. But the governments of the six prefectures all have their own problems to attend to and can't join forces to suppress the bandits. We don't know when the imperial court will send men over either. We watch Lei Changming growing bolder by the day; he's already become the local tyrant of Zhongbo. But there's no use fretting now."

"When the Biansha Horsemen breached our territory six years ago, Duanzhou and Dunzhou bore the brunt of the attack and became barren wastelands where bones of the dead lay exposed in the wild, and nary a rooster crowed for thousands of miles.[6] The war turned all those acres of fertile farmland into abandoned fields. Who would be willing to serve as a soldier in the garrison troops now?" Zhou Gui looked out over the courtyard and gestured around them. "We in Cizhou were able to conserve our strength and resources only thanks to the Libei Armored Cavalry's swift rescue. I've always kept in mind the goodwill they showed us; I have no complaints whatsoever about providing them with military provisions. But the accusation of regicide is a heinous one—I couldn't feign ignorance even if I wanted to. In less than a month, I expect Lei Changming will come to ask for grain and money, and Xiao Chiye will arrive in Cizhou at the same time. When these two tyrants cross paths, who knows what disaster they'll bring down on us?! This is truly what it means when they say that when it rains, it pours!"

After another sip of wine, Kong Ling had an idea. "If Xiao Chiye is bringing twenty thousand well-trained soldiers from the Imperial Army to Cizhou, doesn't that make them *our* soldiers? With Xiao Chiye here to personally assume command, even Lei Changming will think twice!"

"The Imperial Army remains in Qudu year-round. When have they ever seen a real battlefield? Lei Changming trounced the garrison battalions in Duanzhou and Dunzhou, and he doesn't fear the Biansha Horsemen either. What he counts on is the solidarity of

---

6   Lines from "Graveyard Song" by Cao Cao.

those under his command. Moreover, he's familiar with Zhongbo's terrain. Even if they come to blows, Xiao Chiye might not necessarily come out on top." Zhou Gui flapped his hand. "Besides, Second Young Master Xiao is young. He hasn't fought many battles, and he has his father and elder brother watching over him. If something happens to him in Cizhou, how will I answer to Libei?"

Kong Ling stroked his goatee. "Xiao Chiye made a name for himself helping the Tianchen Emperor ascend the throne. The fact that the Imperial Army was willing to follow him after he rebelled and fled from Qudu shows he's capable and has his men's loyalty. Why else would they be willing to risk their heads and flee this far with him? But seeing is believing. We can take his measure when he arrives."

"I've heard he's difficult to get along with." This was what Zhou Gui was most worried about. "And he's been in Qudu a long time. If he puts on airs like a rich young master, I'll have to hurry and figure out how to send him away. We can't afford to have him stirring up trouble!"

A few days later, the Imperial Army arrived at the foot of Cizhou's city walls. Zhou Gui didn't dare let them into the city immediately and merely opened the gate to admit Xiao Chiye and Shen Zechuan. He had given instructions to prepare a banquet to welcome their guests, but Xiao Chiye turned it down, explaining that they were exhausted from their journey. Instead, he asked Zhou Gui to prepare a table of simple home-cooked dishes over which they might reminisce about the past.

They had never met before, only corresponded through letters—what past was there to reminisce about? Xiao Chiye was clearly looking for an opportunity to speak with Zhou Gui without distraction.

Shen Zechuan changed his clothes and remained behind the screen, looking at the courtyard from the window.

Xiao Chiye had come in late. He was still undressing himself; after unfastening half of his clothes, he leaned over the top of the screen to look at Shen Zechuan behind it. "Can you see clearly through this thing?"

Seeing him peer so easily over the screen, Shen Zechuan marveled once again at this man's excessive height. "There are some things that will only move one's heart when seen through a dream or an illusion. It wouldn't be an enchanting sight if I could see clearly."

Xiao Chiye's open robe exposed half his chest. His last piece of clothing hung unabashedly on him, the firm muscle of his torso faintly visible through the sheer screen. He was still leaning over the top of it, watching Shen Zechuan. After fleeing Qudu, he no longer wore a neat crown, yet his messy hair did nothing to diminish his dashing good looks. He seemed to display more of his carefree side the closer he got to Libei.

"What a frivolous fellow." Shen Zechuan stepped up to the screen and cupped the back of Xiao Chiye's head before tilting his face up to kiss him.

Xiao Chiye pinched Shen Zechuan's chin and, taking full advantage of his height, raised it high, exposing Shen Zechuan's smooth and fair neck.

The kiss sent electricity racing up Shen Zechuan's spine.

"Take a good look." Xiao Chiye rubbed at the wet sheen on Shen Zechuan's radiant lips. "Are you not enchanted?"

Shen Zechuan licked the remnants of the kiss off his lips, deepening their rosy hue. "There's still a little something missing."

"Five hundred taels for tonight." Xiao Chiye bent down closer and whispered, "Satisfaction guaranteed."

"I'm afraid my frail body couldn't take it." Shen Zechuan leaned back slightly. With the flimsy fabric of the screen separating them, his fingertips longingly slid their way down the shadow of Xiao Chiye's chest.

The expression in Xiao Chiye's eyes was dangerous. "Don't think so little of yourself," he murmured. "Lanzhou."

Shen Zechuan withdrew his hand. "When we came in earlier, I saw another person beside Zhou Gui. Who is he?"

"I didn't recognize him." Xiao Chiye changed his clothes with nimble fingers. "He should be Zhou Gui's chief advisor. We'll know once we ask during dinner later."

"Since he didn't let us through immediately, he must have some reservations." Shen Zechuan watched as Xiao Chiye stepped out from behind the screen, then turned back to the window. "When we're discussing tonight, you mustn't—"

Xiao Chiye picked Shen Zechuan up by the waist and turned to press him against the wall beside the window. Hands sliding down to cup his rear, he held Shen Zechuan tightly against him and kissed him hard. Shen Zechuan lifted his arms to hook them around Xiao Chiye's neck. The sudden kisses disoriented him and threw his breathing into disarray.

"I mustn't leverage my power to bully them." Xiao Chiye's expression was serious. "I know. I'll do as my wife says."

While Shen Zechuan was still catching his breath, Xiao Chiye fastened his high collar for him, then brushed aside his ink-black hair to pinch his right ear.

"I want to hang an earring here as soon as possible. I'll engrave my name, Xiao Ce'an, on it."

102

CIZHOU

>>>———————◆———❖———◆———————<<<

ZHOU GUI ACCEDED to Xiao Chiye's wishes and set up a table of home-cooked dishes in his own courtyard. When Shen Zechuan stepped through the entrance, he found the little courtyard tasteful despite its simplicity. It had a natural beauty, absent any valuable wares of gold and jade.

Zhou Gui welcomed Xiao Chiye and invited him to take the seat of honor. It was presently the sweltering sixth month, but a clear stream ran beside the table with hanging branches brushing against the water, so it was pleasantly cool and cheery. Zhou Gui had dismissed all the servants; only Kong Ling remained standing in attendance to pour wine.

Xiao Chiye cleaned his hands and watched as his cup was gradually filled to the brim. "Prefect Zhou has truly gone to quite a bit of trouble. Even the wine prepared is On Horseback from Libei. I've been away from home so many years; it's been a long time since I enjoyed it."

This was a grain wine from the Libei Armored Cavalry, bold and intense in flavor. A few sips in the snowy winter could warm the body. There was a story behind its name, On Horseback: more than thirty years ago on his wedding night, the Prince of Libei, Xiao Fangxu, received an urgent report regarding an incursion by the Biansha Horsemen. With no time to change out of his wedding finery, he mounted his horse and rode onto the battlefield. Before he set off, the Princess Consort of Libei—herself still in her red wedding robes—lifted a jug to pour and exchanged a nuptial toast with Xiao Fangxu on horseback. This sight was common enough at the frontiers, but as the groom was the celebrated Prince of Libei, the onlookers couldn't help but lament. From then on, "for most of three hundred and sixty days in a year, on horseback he rides, weapon in hand"[7] came to be the reputation of the Libei Armored Cavalry.

When Zhou Gui saw Xiao Chiye's serene expression, his anxiety eased. "We are close to the Northeast Provisions Trail. When the military provisions were delivered last month, the army sent quite a few jars of wine over. Your Lordship is about to return home, but Cizhou has no fine things to entertain you with. I can only offer you a gift of something already given."

Xiao Chiye laughed. "It's local dishes made from the bounty of the land that are the most flavorful. Compared to the fussy delicacies of Qudu, the spread on this table is a greater show of sincerity. There's no need for Your Excellency to be modest. The arrangements for the military provisions are complex, and it's all thanks to Your Excellency's valuable assistance that Cizhou could finish sealing and loading the grain in just a few short days. It's only fitting that I offer you a toast to show my appreciation."

Zhou Gui couldn't accept the toast sitting down and hurriedly rose to his feet. He held the cup in both hands for a toast, then drank with Xiao Chiye, only taking his seat after the cup was empty. "The Libei Armored Cavalry is fighting the Hanma tribe at the front line, and military provisions are crucial to the battlefield. What I did was

---

7   "Now Then, Three Hundred Sixty Days Out of Each Year, I'm Riding, Spear in Hand, My Trusted War Horse Dear" from Composed on Horseback by Jiguang, a general and writer of the Ming dynasty. Refers to his military dedication.

only my duty. How can it be worthy of a special thanks from Your Lordship? I really don't deserve it."

"It's true Cizhou had a bumper harvest last year, but it's been continuously providing aid to Duanzhou and Libei since the start of spring. That's all grain saved up by the commoners of Cizhou. Of course I must show my gratitude." As he spoke, Xiao Chiye raised a hand to stop Kong Ling, who had moved to pour more wine. "This is a private feast; there's no need to stand on ceremony. Sir, please take a seat with us."

Kong Ling was quick to react. He promptly bowed where he stood and sat down.

"Where does the good sir hail from?" Shen Zechuan asked with a smile.

The wheels in Kong Ling's mind turned faster. Seeing Xiao Chiye starting to dig into his meal, he could tell the main negotiator tonight was Vice Commander Shen. He inclined his head and answered, "Please, I don't deserve such an address; I'm merely a commoner from the countryside of Dengzhou."

"Dengzhou has no lack of talents. How should I address you?"

"My name is Kong Ling, and my humble courtesy name is Chengfeng." Kong Ling sat upright and kept his eyes on Shen Zechuan as he said, "Tantai Hu of the Imperial Army is the blood brother of a dear friend of mine, the late Tantai Long."

"To think one would run into an old friend in a foreign land." Shen Zechuan turned and threw Xiao Chiye a smile. "Ce'an, let's bring Lao-Hu to meet with Mister Chengfeng someday. Encountering a friend in turbulent times isn't something to take for granted."

He addressed Xiao Chiye as *Ce'an*; that alone was enough for Kong Ling to reevaluate his opinion of this orphan of Shen Wei. Shen Zechuan had been rather inconspicuous when he entered Cizhou, save for his conspicuously good looks. Kong Ling knew he was Shen Zechuan, the vice commander of the Embroidered Uniform Guard, whom the Tianchen Emperor had personally made an exception to promote. But after leaving Qudu, Shen Zechuan had lost that authority. As far as Kong Ling was concerned, he had no soldiers and no men; he was merely a vassal who had fled with Xiao Chiye. A vassal, however, could never sit as equals at the same table and address Xiao Chiye by his courtesy name.

Xiao Chiye poured wine for himself. "I'll leave it up to you."

Zhou Gui cast a glance at Kong Ling, then looked back at Shen Zechuan. Kong Ling rose to offer him a toast. "I've heard much about the vice commander."

"You're too kind," Shen Zechuan demurred. "Please, sit. Let's talk over drinks."

"I'm just a minor clerk under His Excellency's command," Kong Ling responded. "I wouldn't dare discuss official affairs with Vice Commander Shen. It's already a blessing for me to sit here with my cup of wine and listen to your counsel."

The corners of Shen Zechuan's lips lifted. "The good sir is truly too modest. I heard you used to be Tantai Long's advisor in Duanzhou. When the Biansha Horsemen breached our borders, Tantai Long was in favor of fighting them head-on, and you were the one who devised all his battle strategies."

These two had entered Cizhou scant hours ago, yet they'd already dug up everything about their hosts. Kong Ling's heart sank. "I was merely an armchair strategist, dreaming on paper."

"It's a pity Tantai Long died at Shen Wei's hands." Shen Zechuan drank his wine. "And Duanzhou fell without a fight."

Shen Zechuan said it so lightly, as if Duanzhou's fall was a house of cards that had collapsed—nothing worth hating, nothing worth resenting.

Kong Ling's expression gradually grew glum. It was several moments before he forced a smile. "The vice commander has lived a life of luxury in Qudu. What would you know of the people's suffering after Duanzhou fell? White bones left out in the sun, stretching for thousands of li from the Chashi River to Dunzhou. It wasn't only that Shen Wei was a rat who shrank from battle; he set up a banquet with Shen Zhouji to strangle Tantai Long to death. The Zhongbo troops were defeated, and while I, Kong Chengfeng, was fortunate enough to find a new master and live on, most of Tantai Long's men were completely wiped out. You're right. It's a pity Tantai Long died at Shen Wei's hands. He was a good man of Zhongbo."

"You had a narrow escape," Shen Zechuan said. "With your talents and learning, you'd certainly come across a master who recognized your worth if you went to Qudu. Yet you remained in Cizhou. I don't understand."

Kong Ling wanted to stand up, but knew it would be rude; he could only raise his head and look at Shen Zechuan. "The vice commander doesn't understand. How could you understand? The calamity of war struck like a bolt from the blue and turned Zhongbo into a scene of utter devastation. There is neither fame nor fortune to be found here. In the vice commander's eyes, perhaps Zhongbo is like willow catkins scattered in the breeze, but to us, Zhongbo still has hope of getting back on its feet."

Shen Zechuan smiled. "Duanzhou lost its garrison troops, and a band of outlaws has proclaimed themselves king of the land. The fields there sit unplowed, and there's no sign of human life beyond half a mile outside the city. Does this hope of getting Zhongbo back on its feet extend to all six prefectures, or just Cizhou? On one side, Cizhou drags out an ignoble existence subservient to Qudu, but on the other, it accedes to every one of Libei's requests. To be such a fence-sitter... Indeed, I don't understand."

Now Kong Ling jolted to his feet. "What would you know of Cizhou's difficulties? Qudu was so preoccupied with infighting after the fall of Zhongbo that we never received a response despite numerous memorials asking for help. It was His Excellency here who personally handled the reclamation of the fallow fields. This bumper harvest comes after three years of backbreaking work. You're right— Cizhou *is* stuck between Qudu and Libei, but we have always done our utmost to help each time Libei has faced difficulty. Vice Commander, isn't it a bit too harsh to say that Cizhou is a fence-sitter?!"

"It's as you've said." Shen Zechuan's expression shifted. He spoke unflinchingly. "I know Cizhou has its own difficulties, so we've come for the specific purpose of discussing them with both of you. We'll come straight to the point: Your Excellency isn't willing to let the Imperial Army pass for fear of Qudu's censure. But considering how the situation has deteriorated, clinging to Qudu isn't the wisest strategy. Han Cheng conspired to murder the Son of Heaven. Ce'an and I didn't leave Qudu to spare our necks, but to pick up the pieces. The empress dowager now controls the imperial court, and the noble clans have once again sealed off the main gate of Qudu. How long can the Imperial College thrive under these conditions? Wasn't it precisely due to Hua Siqian's dismissive attitude back then—when Your Excellency and Mister Chengfeng submitted repeated memorials after Zhongbo's troops were defeated—that Zhongbo was robbed of any chance at recovery? Even in Qudu, I've heard about the bandits plaguing Zhongbo for years. Zhongbo will never stabilize as long as those bandits run free. How do you intend to advance your plans to restore Zhongbo to its former glory? The beginning of any undertaking is full of hardships, like a lone figure in rags driving a wooden cart, blazing a new trail through the mountains and forests.[8] Gentlemen, I admire your determination. But the road ahead is arduous—so why not change course, and let Zhongbo handle its own affairs?"

Holding his wine in one hand, Zhou Gui held Kong Ling back with the other. "Since the vice commander is speaking frankly, I won't beat around the bush either. It's indeed the case that I'm not willing to let His Lordship pass—I worry Qudu will hold us responsible and punish Cizhou by increasing our taxes. If Cizhou disregards Qudu's orders and acts on its own, we will lose their support, and it will be that much harder for us to accomplish anything in the future. We have no military force, no wealthy merchants, and nowhere near the same level of confidence as Libei. The vice commander can be as persuasive as you like, but I cannot gamble with the lives of the common folk of Cizhou."

"On the contrary," Xiao Chiye said, motioning for Kong Ling to sit, "Lanzhou isn't trying to persuade Your Excellency to fight alone. Cizhou is close to the Northeast Provisions Trail, and hasn't yet established a fully operational garrison. As long as Your Excellency is willing to allow my troops to come and go without obstruction, then, until the Cizhou Garrison Troops are re-formed, my Imperial Army of twenty thousand men will stand in for them and protect the city."

Zhou Gui contemplated this in silence, but Kong Ling spoke up. "I don't doubt that Your Lordship will keep your promise, but I have to ask you this: now that Libei has revolted, the Northeast Provisions

---

8   From Zuozhuan, or The Commentary of Zuo. An adage that refers to enduring great hardships for the sake of pioneering work.

Trail will become obsolete. Where will military provisions for the Libei Armored Cavalry come from in the future? Cizhou?"

"The Northeast Provisions Trail is a key route opened for the specific purpose of transporting goods for the Libei Armored Cavalry. Wouldn't it be an awful pity for it to go to waste?" Shen Zechuan fiddled with the wine cup, his eyes placid. "The Libei Armored Cavalry and the Imperial Army together have one hundred and forty thousand soldiers and horses. Military provisions must still pass through the Northeast Provisions Trail."

Kong Ling exchanged a glance with Zhou Gui and blurted in astonishment, "The marquis has been charged with regicide. How would the thirteen cities of Juexi dare prepare military provisions for the Libei Armored Cavalry now?"

Shen Zechuan smiled. "Juexi is Juexi. Qudu is Qudu. Mister Chengfeng, since I dare to say such a thing, naturally I have the means to do it. How about it? As long as Lord Zhou agrees to let the Imperial Army pass through tonight, Cizhou will never fight alone again."

Zhou Gui hesitated, but held his voice steady when he replied. "I trust in His Lordship's good word, but I don't trust the situation not to change. My lords keep saying the Imperial Army will suppress the bandits after passing through, but if you renege on your promise, Cizhou will truly have nowhere to turn!"

"There's no hurry." Shen Zechuan set down his wine cup. "I shall remain in Cizhou until the Imperial Army quashes the bandits. If Your Excellency needs more assurances, we can hand over our captive, Han Jin, to you. If we go back on our word, Your Excellency may use Han Jin's life to appease Qudu."

Li Jianheng was dead, and there was no news from Qudu about a new ruler. The various regions were already beginning to show signs of restlessness. It was only out of fear of the Qi Clan in Qidong that no one dared follow in the footsteps of Libei and raise their own banner. But Cizhou was different. It was in such close proximity to the Libei Armored Cavalry that if it could really obtain their military support, Cizhou could throw off the yoke of the noble clans.

"It won't be long before news of my entry into the city today makes it to Qudu," Xiao Chiye continued, in no hurry. "Whether Your Excellency lets me pass or not, the empress dowager will be wary of Cizhou after tonight."

The color drained from Zhou Gui's face. "Your Lordship, Your Excellency—you—!"

"Besides," Shen Zechuan added mildly, right on Xiao Chiye's heels, "if the gentlemen wish to establish an operational Cizhou Garrison Troops, then the most pressing tasks are recruiting soldiers and purchasing horses. Cizhou relies on its cropland to make a living, and none of the businesses in or around Cizhou trade through Juexi and its ports. It'll likely take you several years to amass the necessary funds with tax money alone. It just so happens I have some savings— and I'm willing to contribute what little I have. How about it, Prefect Zhou? Can the Imperial Army pass now?"

103

BEAUTY

HOW COULD ZHOU GUI refuse when the cards had been laid out so plainly? Xiao Chiye and Shen Zechuan had zeroed in on their weakness, using both carrot and stick. Everything they said struck at Cizhou's most pressing issues. They could only end the private dinner here.

Zhou Gui personally saw the pair to their courtyard, then walked back with Kong Ling, lantern in hand. He asked with a worried frown, "What do you think?"

"Difficult." Kong Ling answered as he strolled. "They're both tough to deal with, but everything they said was true. At present, the empress dowager rules the imperial court, and the secretariat elder is old and ill. There is dissent within the Grand Secretariat; Jiang Qingshan's transfer to the post of the Provincial Administration Commissioner of Zhongbo is no longer certain. If they arbitrarily appoint some official from the noble clans, Cizhou's good days will be numbered."

"I think so too." Basking in the watery moonlight, Zhou Gui contemplated a moment. "I fear if we agree too quickly, they will see Cizhou as easy to manipulate. But if we take too long, they may run out of patience, and Cizhou will lose this chance to get back on its feet. It'll be difficult to get the timing right."

"Playing hard-to-get may not work on Xiao Chiye." Kong Ling looked back at Zhou Gui. "We should make up our minds as soon as possible. Dragging it out will only be to our disadvantage."

Kong Ling was right. As things stood, Xiao Chiye was in a hurry to pass through Cizhou, which gave them leverage. Cizhou also had some influence over the Northeast Provisions Trail, which Shen Zechuan claimed they still planned to use. Xiao Chiye and Shen Zechuan couldn't brute force their way through, and they couldn't afford to fall out with Cizhou either; thus, at this hour, Cizhou held the upper hand. But the longer they hesitated, the more the scale would tip. This was not least because of the immediate threat from Lei Changming and his group of bandits. If Lei Changming came to plunder Cizhou, Zhou Gui would have no choice but to ask the Imperial Army for help. At that point, Xiao Chiye would become the one with the upper hand.

But Zhou Gui was still hesitating. "Xiao Chiye isn't a petty man; I can't imagine he would simply sit back and watch from the sidelines. Let's...let's wait for Qudu to make a move."

"How rare of you to be so short-sighted." Kong Ling heaved a long sigh. "Risking all the lives in the prefecture on the assumption that he isn't a petty man. We may know a person's face, but not his heart! If they raise their price then, it'll be more difficult to negotiate than it was today."

"I hesitate precisely because this matter concerns the lives of an entire prefecture." Zhou Gui took a few steps to catch up with Kong Ling. He shook back his sleeves to gesture broadly. "Chengfeng, is it really so easy to declare independence and crown yourself king? Think of the former crown prince and his precipitous fall from grace. Libei has revolted, but if you consider all the angles, you'll see this battle won't be an easy one to fight. Independence is not entirely beneficial to Libei. Not only do they need to repel the Biansha Horsemen, they must also guard against Qidong's advances. If the Northeast Provisions Trail is cut off too, won't they become a beast trapped in a cage? They won't survive long! When the time comes, Libei will scarcely be able to fend for themselves. What will our Cizhou do then? Won't we be meat on the chopping block? And we'll have to live with the infamy of being traitors!"

"Now that it's come to this, it's impossible for us to escape completely unscathed," Kong Ling advised, earnest. "Think it over carefully again tonight."

The moment Xiao Chiye stepped into the room, a graceful, delicate figure came forward. The fair-skinned maidservant knelt daintily before Xiao Chiye; her jet-black hair was pulled up in a bun, exposing a large portion of creamy nape and chest above her carefully arranged neckline. Smoothing a lock of hair at her temple, she called out, lashes lowered, "Your Lordship..."

Xiao Chiye didn't spare her a glance as he moved to shrug off his outer garment. Hearing the rustle of cloth, the maidservant hurriedly rose to help him.

Shen Zechuan bumped Xiao Chiye's shoulder as he walked in, and Xiao Chiye took gentle hold of him. Letting Xiao Chiye support him, Shen Zechuan lifted his chin a fraction and lightly kicked off his shoes.

"Go prepare some hot water," Xiao Chiye said. "The vice commander is drunk."

The maidservant had gathered her clothes closer around her and bent to pick up Shen Zechuan's shoes when he lowered his little bamboo fan to lift her face. Frozen, she could do nothing but look up along the fan at Shen Zechuan. His brows were faintly knit, yet his eyes looked as if peach blossoms unfurled their petals at the corners of his lids, accentuating his sparkling eyes. She was overwhelmed by a sense of inferiority and hastily averted her gaze, too abashed to look at Shen Zechuan again.

Shen Zechuan said nothing. After studying her, he moved his fan away. The maidservant deferentially arranged his shoes, then retreated with her head lowered. Xiao Chiye waited for the door to close behind her before he pulled Shen Zechuan to him and asked, "Pretty?"

Fingers wrapped around the bamboo fan, Shen Zechuan didn't answer as he stepped on Xiao Chiye's feet with his socks. He tugged at the outer garment Xiao Chiye had yet to take off and leaned closer. As Xiao Chiye walked him across the room, he saw the indolent expression on Shen Zechuan's face, that relaxation that often came after drinking wine. He lowered his head to kiss him, but Shen Zechuan leaned back coyly, just out of reach.

Their breath carried the sweet intensity of On Horseback. All the weariness of their journey had fallen away during these few days of rest. Shen Zechuan had looked pale since fleeing Qudu, but with Xiao Chiye's care and affection, he had begun to look like a jade stone warmed by careful hands. Under Xiao Chiye's palms, his body was firm and hot.

"Kong Ling is Tantai Long's old subordinate. Until Lei Changming is eliminated, he won't rest easy." Xiao Chiye helped Shen Zechuan undress, pulling off his clothes and caressing his lower back. "Lei Changming is anxious to get his hands on a large quantity of grain. Sooner or later, he'll come for Cizhou. As long as we can convey the stakes to Kong Ling, he'll think of a way to persuade Zhou Gui."

"Hm..." On Horseback was too strong a wine for Shen Zechuan. He was gazing at Xiao Chiye and listening to him seriously, but his cheeks were too flushed, and the expression in his eyes revealed another kind of seriousness.

"Letting the Imperial Army step in to patrol Cizhou feels a little like holding them hostage. It's fine as a temporary measure, but if it goes on too long, Zhou Gui won't stand for it. We'll have to thank Ding Tao for finding out so quickly that Kong Ling was Tantai Long's old subordinate." As if Xiao Chiye couldn't read the intention in Shen Zechuan's gaze, he hummed a question. "Hm?"

Shen Zechuan went up on his toes, then dropped back down. The more placid his expression, the more intense the scarlet bloomed on his skin. The potency of the wine made him sweat.

"Give me a kiss," Xiao Chiye murmured, voice deep. "I did as you said and didn't bully them at all."

Gripping Xiao Chiye's clothes tight enough to wrinkle them, Shen Zechuan endured it for a moment, then said, "I can't reach."

Xiao Chiye's heart thumped, and he lowered his head once more. When Shen Zechuan reached up to kiss him, Xiao Chiye pulled back again. "Let's bathe first."

Shen Zechuan raised his chin high and his lips, red and glistening from the wine, parted slightly. His tongue flicked out to wet the corner of his parched lips. All he was doing was gazing at Xiao Chiye, but the manner of it set Xiao Chiye's entire body aflame, seducing Xiao Chiye until he stopped teasing him and acted instead.

In the past, Shen Zechuan hadn't understood the beguiling allure he possessed. But within their new and heady intimacy, he seemed to have learned how to fan the flames of lust without saying a word.

Zhou Gui had just woken the next day when he saw Kong Ling leading the maidservant in. Stunned, he stopped mopping his brow with his handkerchief and asked, "What's this? Didn't I tell you to stay by the marquis's side and serve him well?"

The maidservant turned aside and covered her face with her handkerchief. "Your Excellency, shouldn't one look at things clearly before taking action? Who do you think the man standing beside His Lordship is? I didn't dare to touch the hem of his robe! They're so besotted with each other, neither would even look me in the eye!"

It took Zhou Gui a moment to understand. When he did, the color drained from his face, and the handkerchief fell from his hand. He was a scholar over forty who had never frequented brothels. His household was very much in order, and his only concubine was a woman he had taken at his mother's behest. In the past, he'd only heard a little about men who had a penchant for other men. He'd never expected the relationship between Xiao Chiye and Shen Zechuan to be like that.

"This...this!" Zhou Gui wiped his face and groused to Kong Ling, "Why didn't you remind me about this? Now we've thoroughly offended him!"

Kong Ling looked slightly unwell. "How would I have known?"

They looked at each other and sighed in unison. Amid this stalemate, a young servant knelt outside the door and reported, "Your Excellency, an urgent report from last night. Lei Changming of Dunzhou has gathered forty thousand bandits and is heading right for Cizhou!"

"How are there so many?" Zhou Gui's heart went cold. "Half a year ago, he only had ten thousand or so..."

"It's truly the case that what you fear will come upon you!" Kong Ling cried. "Quick, invite the marquis here. Tell him we agree to last night's offer of alliance!"

ELDER BROTHER

L EI CHANGMING was a native of Chazhou. In his early years, he had served as an armed escort. He'd spent his life doing manual labor, as he never studied or attended school. During the reign of Yongyi, the commander of the Duanzhou Garrison Troops took his younger sister as a concubine, and she rose to favor in the commander's manor. Because of this, Lei Changming enjoyed a comfortable life for a few years and spent his days at the gambling dens. It was a pity the good times didn't last; the Duanzhou commander was a fickle man, and within a few years, he spurned Lei Changming's sister. With no one to repay the debts he owed, Lei Changming had little choice but to set out once more to work as an armed escort.

Near the end of the reign of Yongyi, Lei Changming accepted a job from the Yan Clan of Hezhou. During the journey, he risked his life fighting off robbers to protect the youngest master of the Yan Clan, Yan Heru, and, as a result, got into the Yan Clan's good books. After the fall of Zhongbo in the reign of Xiande, he borrowed money from the Yan Clan to recruit men and buy horses. He then led a revolt against the Duanzhou Garrison battalion and slew the commander the imperial court had appointed in an act that firmly established him as an outlaw of Duanzhou. He had initially recruited a scant few thousand men, but thanks to the

316   BALLAD OF SWORD AND WINE

imperial court's apathy after the Biansha incursion, Zhongbo never recovered from that heavy blow. Desperate commoners increasingly turned to banditry, and Lei Changming gradually became a warlord in Duanzhou. At present, the men under his command far exceeded the number of soldiers in the garrison troops throughout the various prefectures of Zhongbo.

"Half a year ago, Lei Changming had a total of fourteen thousand men between the prefectures of Duanzhou and Dunzhou." Zhou Gui held back his sleeve and pointed at the map for Xiao Chiye. "He established his base on Mount Luo, located between Duanzhou and Dunzhou—he's set up his own nest of brigands there. When the imperial court rebuilt the garrison troops of Dengzhou, they tried to besiege Mount Luo, but met with no success. They gave up after a few attempts, and no one bothered with it after that."

Xiao Chiye secured his arm guards, leaning against the table to look at the map. "He's bringing forty thousand men to Cizhou. He'll definitely have left a portion of his forces to guard Mount Luo. He likely has at least sixty thousand men and horses, double the Qidong Garrison Troops."

Although Xiao Chiye's words weren't accusatory, they were enough to make Zhou Gui sweat. The six prefectures of Zhongbo fell under the jurisdiction of legitimately appointed prefects, and yet they had simply watched for six years as the bandits grew in dominance until they rivaled a regular army.

"His Excellency has no dealings with Duanzhou and Dunzhou, but we usually send field officials there to assist with the military garrisons' affairs," Kong Ling said from his seat. "Yet somehow he assembled so many men in just half a year, and we never caught wind of it."

"Your Lordship," Zhou Gui said earnestly. "I originally thought Lei Changming had merely ten thousand or so men, and annihilating him would be the work of a month or two. But now he's charging towards Cizhou with forty thousand troops, and we have only your twenty thousand men from the Imperial Army. We're at a huge disadvantage! Why not..."

Why not send someone to Libei and ask Xiao Fangxu to transfer the soldiers guarding the Northeast Provisions Trail south to provide reinforcements?

Xiao Chiye finished securing his arm guards but didn't speak. Zhou Gui took a breath to try to persuade him, but Kong Ling sensed something else in Xiao Chiye's silence. Using the motion of serving tea, he surreptitiously pressed down on Zhou Gui's arm, and Zhou Gui swallowed back his words.

"There's no need for Your Excellency and Mister Chengfeng to panic." Shen Zechuan was seated nearby, looking at the courier report. "Lei Changming's forty thousand men have to eat too. He can't travel at speed, and his supply squadron will have to carry sufficient rations to sustain them across hundreds and thousands of li to fight this battle with us in Cizhou. Besides..." A peculiar expression crept over Shen Zechuan's face. "This report may not be entirely accurate."

"Why does the vice commander say so?" Zhou Gui flicked up the hem of his robe and stepped closer to peer at the report from the relay station. "This is an urgent report personally sent by the official deployed to Dunzhou to handle the bandit case. How can it be inaccurate?"

"Did he see Lei Changming's forty thousand soldiers and horses with his own eyes?" Shen Zechuan mulled it over. "Believing Lei Changming's claims based only on some traces of fire pits is jumping to conclusions. I suspect Lei Changming already knows the Imperial Army has arrived in Cizhou. That's why he put up the banner of his forty thousand men, to throw us into disarray."

"That's right." Eyes still on the map, Xiao Chiye added, "If he really has forty thousand men, the battle would be easier to fight. We could draw him into a war of attrition and watch him deplete his resources feeding all those mouths. He would be in more dire straits than we are."

"But he still has the support of the Yan Clan of Hezhou," Zhou Gui said, anxious. "He was able to grow his numbers precisely because of the Yan Clan's financial assistance. There's a waterway in Hezhou that leads right to the granaries in Juexi. It's easy for them to supply him with additional rations via water."

"Your Excellency, you must be mistaken." Shen Zechuan laughed. "If the Yan Clan is still backing Lei Changming, why would he be rushing to Cizhou? Have you forgotten that he's coming to Cizhou for grain?"

"He came to Cizhou once before the new year, and came again a few months later," Xiao Chiye reasoned. "From this, we can not only guess that he might have fallen out with the Yan Clan, but also that his assets back on Mount Luo are no longer enough to sustain him. He's got the Chashi River to his east, and the Biansha Horsemen are even better at pillaging than he is. He has no one to turn to, so the only thing he can do is return and demand grain from Cizhou."

"But then why did he wait until the Imperial Army arrived to make another trip?" Kong Ling circled the table slowly as he pondered. "Your Lordship's arrival in Cizhou will obviously hinder him."

"Because Han Jin is in the Imperial Army's hands." Shen Zechuan closed the report and stood up. "It's only with the Yan Clan's assistance that he has survived this long. Now that they've parted ways, he needs a new patron if he wishes to continue lording over the land from his mountain stronghold. He's a bandit. The more men he has under his command, the harder it will be for him to keep them in line. Those elsewhere can live off the land, but Zhongbo is poor and barren. Even if he digs out the entire mountain, all he can eat is rocks. He's good at seizing opportunities; he managed to gain fame and fortune because he made the right choices at three turning points in his life. Now he has soldiers, which Zhongbo lacks. But he has no connections—and Ce'an just happens to be leading the Imperial Army through Cizhou. If he can defeat the Imperial Army and rescue Han Jin, he can report his meritorious service to Qudu, and the Han Clan's connections will get him a military official post in Zhongbo."

"A brilliant plan—leave behind banditry and reinvent himself as a genuine official of the imperial court." Zhou Gui stomped his foot in indignation. "He has no regard for the commoners of Cizhou at all!"

"This is all just conjecture. We'll have to trade blows with the man before we can get a better feel for him." Xiao Chiye hung Wolfsfang on his belt and said to Zhou Gui, "Libei lies beyond Cizhou; Lei Changming can't come at the city from the north. If he can't sneak through the city itself, he won't be able to surround Cizhou and trap us. Your Excellency should seal the city gate immediately—even the dog holes must be covered up. Those under his command are a ragtag bunch who aren't even listed in the household register; they would try anything to get in."

"Is Your Lordship thinking to fortify the city and face them head-on?" Kong Ling's brows knit with concern. "The city walls of Cizhou are old. I'm afraid they won't withstand Lei Changming's assault."

"The Imperial Army will not defend the city from inside the walls." Hand on the hilt of his blade, Xiao Chiye bared his teeth. "But I'll make a bet with you. Lei Changming won't dare face my soldiers head-on. That is what he's most afraid of."

At dusk, Xiao Chiye and Shen Zechuan made an inspection tour of the city's perimeter; armed with their blades, they walked side by side atop the city wall.

"This wall was last repaired during the reign of Yongyi." Shen Zechuan gave the earthen walls of the battlement a push, and bits of clay, eroded by the wind and rain, crumbled to the ground.

"Zhou Gui is poor. The issue of food has been his most urgent priority the last few years. It's no surprise he's been too preoccupied to pay any attention to the city's military defenses." Xiao Chiye squatted, picked up a chunk of earth, and rubbed it into pieces in his hand. "The Imperial Army can stand before Cizhou, but it cannot retreat into the city."

Xiao Chiye was conscious that Zhou Gui wanted to seek assistance from Libei, but he wasn't willing to ask for help. He would be returning to Libei soon, but arrangements for the twenty thousand Imperial Army men he had brought with him had not yet been discussed with his father and brother. Xiao Chiye understood the Libei Armored Cavalry. A complete army like that wouldn't accept the Imperial Army quickly—the two forces would have to go through an arduous bonding process before they could learn to get along. And if he opened his mouth now to ask for help, and Xiao Fangxu came, Xiao Chiye would never have the chance to shine on his own merits again once he returned to Libei. Cizhou would be his first battle upon returning home. He had to win it. He had to win it on his own.

Clouds stretched across the horizon as sunset painted half the sky red. They saw rows upon rows of houses, smoke curling from stoves within, and heard the clamor of human voices. Shen Zechuan laid his hand on the top of Xiao Chiye's head. The two of them—one standing and one squatting—looked out at the scene spread beneath them.

"Lei Changming is capable," Shen Zechuan said, "but you are the one who decides if he's an overreaching bandit or a brilliant villain."

"Brilliant villains are born of troubled times." Xiao Chiye put his hands on his knees and rose to his feet. "I'll take the Conqueror Bow with me."

He stood like a lush tree bathed in the dimming light of dusk, like a mountain looming before the city wall. Shen Zechuan watched his shackles gradually fall away. Xiao Chiye had built up real momentum, and now was the time for him to show his mettle.

Shen Zechuan gazed at him. "When you return to Libei, His Lordship will see that you've grown taller again."

"I was already taller than him the last time I saw him." Xiao Chiye laughed. "As a child, I thought my father was like a towering tree. He put me on his shoulders and lied that I'd be able to touch the clouds. Dage wanted to sit on my father's shoulders too, but he was already attending school by then; he felt he had to maintain his dignity as the older brother. He never said a word to my father but was happy just watching him carry me around."

Shen Zechuan laughed too and gazed back at the sunset. "Everyone says Shizi looks like the Princess Consort of Libei."

"Somewhat." Xiao Chiye's eyes reflected the rose-tinted clouds. "I resemble Father more, that's all. Actually, there was a time when my brother was miserable. When my father fell sick and retired to his manor, my brother was only in his teens." Xiao Chiye's profile was calm and serene. "All of a sudden, he had to fight for respect from those ferocious men. It was tough. He was mocked most often for being unlike our father—he didn't have father's strong and robust physique. He once said to Zhao Hui—"

A wave of sadness inexplicably washed over him. He turned his head and took Shen Zechuan's hands in his own, his throat bobbing. "We two brothers are truly strange. I envy my brother's steadiness, and I also envy his composure. I used to think, *If only I had been born a few years earlier.* Then I would be the eldest brother, the heir. I could've gone galloping through the mountains to my heart's content. I wouldn't have had to take a single step out of Libei. But one day, my brother came home wounded and saw me shooting arrows in the courtyard. And he said to Zhao Hui, 'I really envy A-Ye.'

"I thought my father and brother would never feel pain and would never fall. They would shed blood but never tears. But on the day my brother got married, he drank himself drunk. Such a steady person gingerly took my sister-in-law's hands and gazed at her with tears in his eyes, as if already anticipating the future. He treasures his family, and so he feels fear too.

"There is nothing about me that is superior to Dage. If I had to choose something, it would be the good luck of inheriting a fine physique from our father." Xiao Chiye gripped Shen Zechuan's fingers tightly. "Before, I never really understood why he got teary looking at my sister-in-law. But now, I do."

CUNNING

>>>———————◆———❁———◆———————<<<

W HEN LEI CHANGMING arrived at the mountain
foothills a hundred li from Cizhou, it was starting to
drizzle. Instead of rashly marching onward, he stopped
and made camp.

"They mean to fight a protracted battle." Tantai Hu crouched
in the grass, looking down at the bandit camp. "He's organized
his troops in such a long column; it's impossible to tell how many
soldiers and horses there are."

"But their fire pits are densely clustered. Just looking at it gives
me goosebumps." Ding Tao drew a circle around the spot where Lei
Changming had stationed his troops. "I made some inquiries in the
towns along the way. Every one of them confirmed that he brought
more than forty thousand men this time. On the way here, they took
in all the stray bandits in this part of Cizhou."

"Mixing truth with falsehood makes it impossible for others to
distinguish the actual situation." Xiao Chiye rose and brushed aside
an overhanging branch, leaves heavy with water droplets. "If he has
so many men, why recruit deserters and traitors? There's nothing
an army fears more this close to a battle than last-minute additions.
Green troops will throw his men's rapport into disarray and turn a
ferocious army into a disorderly mob."

"I had the same thought." Tantai Hu followed Xiao Chiye out of the forest. "The louder he is about his forty thousand men, the hollower his words. Master, he's afraid of us."

Heedless of the drizzle, Xiao Chiye took off his cloak and tossed it to Ding Tao behind him. As he fastened his blade on his belt, he looked at Tantai Hu. "If he was that afraid, he wouldn't have come. He's seizing his opportunity to intimidate us. He saw that we hail from the capital and wants to give us a scare."

True battle had been avoided at the Nanlin Hunting Grounds because Qi Zhuyin had led the Qidong Garrison Troops to suppress the coup. On the surface, Xiao Chiye hadn't been involved. The Eight Great Battalions had always belittled the Imperial Army in Qudu and treated them as obsolete. Though the Imperial Army had taken over Qudu's patrols these last few years, the substitution only happened because authority changed hands with the new emperor. The Imperial Army had never fought a proper battle, and thus Lei Changming had deemed them, along with their leader Xiao Chiye, a bunch of untested lads still wet behind the ears.

"It's to our advantage if he underestimates us, but if we do the same for him, we deserve to be beaten. Lei Changming is no ordinary man. Look how he's come to dominate the southeast of Zhongbo; he must have his strengths." Xiao Chiye swung atop Snowcrest, took up the reins, and continued, "Tantai Hu, six years ago, you escaped from Dengzhou to Qudu. Now you've returned. Let me ask you, do you still remember what I said when you led your troops to join the Imperial Army?"

The rain dripped into Tantai Hu's eyes as he looked up at Xiao Chiye. "This humble subordinate wouldn't dare forget a word. Master said that the wrongs suffered by our families have yet to be avenged, and the humiliation of our nation has yet to be redressed!"

"That's right." Xiao Chiye reined in the prancing horse and lifted his eyes to the dense mass of bodies huddled in the rain—his army. He said quietly, "The Biansha Horsemen razed numerous cities in Zhongbo. The Libei Armored Cavalry and Qidong Garrison Troops may have fought them off, but was this trespass avenged? To the Biansha Horsemen, this was as good as riding their horses to and fro for a jaunt! What was that saying circulating in Qudu? 'Rather a dog than a man of Zhongbo.' How can we let someone else redress the humiliation Zhongbo suffered under those scimitars? In our dreams we gallop all night without stopping, and now Lei Changming is the obstacle that stands in our way. The opportunity to battle with the Biansha Horsemen again is right before our eyes—do we lose?"

Victory and defeat were both inevitable in the military, but no army was willing to keep losing forever. In the past six years, the Imperial Army had transformed from an unorganized rabble into a well-trained, combat-ready force. It was as if the Imperial Army was a part of Xiao Chiye. They had been buried together in the golden sand, disappearing like insignificant ants into the crevices of the Zhou empire's mighty armies. It didn't matter how others had described them in the past. It didn't matter if they were always labeled good-for-nothings. They were finally ready to emerge from the ground and reveal their true mettle.

A sharp gust of wind unfurled the banner over their heads. Tantai Hu compressed his lips and declared, "We *must* win."

The pounding of rain grew urgent around them. Tantai Hu wiped roughly at his eyes; as the shouts of his comrades behind him swelled into a wave, he called hoarsely, "We must win!"

We must win!

From this moment until the moment of death in battle, *We must win* had to become the Imperial Army's one and only creed.

Up against a seasoned fighter who had long made a name for himself in these lands, they had to draw their blades; they had to spur their horses swiftly onward, they had to defeat every obstacle in their path, one by one—they could only win. The Libei Armored Cavalry could lose, and so could the Qidong Garrison Troops. Even Lei Changming's forces could withstand a defeat. But the Imperial Army and Xiao Chiye could not. When they had broken free of their shackles, they had also abandoned their supports. If they couldn't win here, they could only die.

Xiao Chiye brought his horse around and swiped rainwater off his chin. He was like a wolf who had caught a whiff of blood on the wind. He drew Wolfsfang, that blade that symbolized ruthless avarice, and called to the pack behind him, "Time for us to dine!"

The rain hammered down, breaking the surface of the puddles at their feet.

As soon as Lei Changming heard the special envoys from Cizhou had arrived, he went to receive them in his tent.

"Mister Chengfeng." Cloak still wrapped around him, Lei Changming sat high in his seat and scrutinized Kong Ling. "It's been a while."

Kong Ling bowed in greeting. "Previously, the chief came to Cizhou often. We're old acquaintances. Why take up arms and create such an uproar this time?"

Despite being a bandit chief, Lei Changming was not a boorish fellow. No ornaments adorned his scarred arms, and his clothes were plain and practical. The broadsword he carried showed signs of wear. At a glance, he might be mistaken for one of the industrious commoners of Zhongbo who toiled in the fields. He'd received no formal education and had the blithe air of a bandit who lumbered his way through the wide world year-round—yet that seemed to be only a disguise, for he was in fact keenly perceptive.

Lei Changming didn't feign civility with Kong Ling. He fixed his eyes on Shen Zechuan behind him and grinned. "It's true we're old acquaintances who can share a drink and chat. So why did Mister Chengfeng bring an officer of the Embroidered Uniform Guard along?"

"Didn't the chief descend upon our city with your large army so you could meet with the marquis and Vice Commander Shen?" Kong Ling responded with no loss of composure. "Allow me to introduce the two of you. Vice Commander Shen, meet Chief Lei— Lei Changming, renowned across the six prefectures of Zhongbo. He is the highest power in the two prefectures of Dunzhou and Duanzhou. Chief, meet Vice Commander Shen—Shen Zechuan, an official in the Son of Heaven's inner ministerial circle, promoted with a special exception from Qudu."

"I've heard your name," Lei Changming said, showing interest. "Shen Zechuan, huh. So you're Shen Zechuan. I heard Han Cheng schemed to seal the city and surround you, and you killed what remained of his elite troops on your own. Every strike of your blade was lethal, the blows so fast they were barely visible to the naked eye. If you're following Xiao Chiye, why are you wasting time with Zhou Gui instead of riding for Libei? A law-abiding prefect like him can't accommodate a god of carnage like you, can he?"

"I'm also a law-abiding person." Shen Zechuan lifted his right hand slightly to reveal his unarmed waist. "I didn't even bring my blade, Chief Lei."

Lei Changming raised a hand to forestall the guards who had pressed close when Shen Zechuan began to move. He pointed at Shen Zechuan. "You don't even remove your blade before the Son of Heaven, yet you did so to see me." He boomed a laugh. "Could it be that I'm more esteemed than the Son of Heaven?"

"The empress dowager rules now, and court discipline is lax. There has not been a true Son of Heaven on that throne for a long time." Shen Zechuan smiled. "The chief is a hero without peer. Of course I must observe etiquette."

"Everyone who stays long in Qudu learns to say such pleasing words." Lei Changming leaned back in his seat, pried apart a sweet potato on his plate, and took a few bites. "Speak. What do you want from me?"

"My purpose in coming to the chief's tent today is twofold: first, to pay my respects, and second, to express my desire to discuss our future." Shen Zechuan scrutinized the tent as he spoke. "You've pitched camp here, but now what? If the Imperial Army doesn't come, how long does the chief plan to wait?"

"You ought to understand Xiao Chiye better than me." Lei Changming finished his sweet potato. "His father and elder brother are renowned generals. I imagine he's not too bad himself. I'll wait for him to approach me for a parley. Cizhou is only so big; it won't take me long to figure out where he's hiding. But if he occupies Cizhou and refuses to leave, I can't enter. This has to be resolved, doesn't it? I'll wait. I'm in no hurry."

"His twenty thousand Imperial Army soldiers are skilled in horsemanship and archery. Their combat prowess on horseback is equal to that of the Libei Armored Cavalry. Fighting him now would be a mistake." Seeing those guards shifting again, Shen Zechuan smiled preemptively. "He's in the city, feeding his troops from Cizhou's granary. The chief is outside and must rely on army rations and supply lines to sustain your forces. The amount of money required to feed and clothe forty thousand men is appalling. The longer this stalemate drags on, the more you have to lose. I'm sure the chief understands this better than I do."

"So what? I can afford to dawdle, but can the Imperial Army? Xiao Chiye can't live off Cizhou's grain forever. The Prince of Libei is fighting a war; Xiao Chiye is in a hurry to go home to him. The only thing I'll lose waiting him out is money, but for Xiao Chiye, it's lives that hang in the balance. He rebelled, but the Qidong Garrison Troops didn't. Qi Zhuyin can lead her troops here in half a month. If the Libei Armored Cavalry comes south to provide the Imperial Army with reinforcements, Libei'll have a headache on two fronts. Qi Zhuyin is no easier an opponent than the Biansha Horsemen. If you'd dealt with this woman before, you would know what she's capable of. She even dared set the Biansha tribes on fire. It would be easy for her to fight Cizhou, but does Xiao Chiye dare to fight her?" Lei Changming wiped his mouth. His smile was casual, his expression cool and collected. "Is Xiao Chiye even worthy?"

Shen Zechuan's expression turned regretful. "If the chief's supplies are truly adequate, then I won't say any more on it. Truth be told, it's precisely because I worry Marshal Qi could arrive at any moment that I wanted to discuss a deal with you today."

Kong Ling turned slightly pale and shuffled closer to Shen Zechuan. "Vice Commander, we didn't—"

"What kind of deal?" Lei Changming asked.

"If Xiao Chiye can pass through Cizhou without a hitch, then that's all well and good," Shen Zechuan said. "But now that the chief has come forth with your own formidable force, his twenty thousand men are no longer my only—or best—option. The deal I wish to discuss concerns exactly this question of supplies. I happen to still be in possession of some two million silver taels, which I'm willing to let you spend on rations for this battle. But in exchange, you must agree to vouch for me before Han Cheng and preserve my life when you become an official in the imperial court."

"Shen Zechuan!" Kong Ling blurted, stricken. "How could you dupe us?! Did we not agree that this two million would be given to Cizhou to rebuild the garrison troops?!"

"I only said I was willing." Shen Zechuan turned his head a fraction and said sincerely, "I didn't say I *would*."

Kong Ling grabbed Shen Zechuan's sleeve. "You lied to us! You treacherous bastard!"

Lei Changming laughed again. Hands braced on his knees, he wondered aloud, "Are you for real? Shen Zechuan, if you had so much silver, why would you let the Imperial Army gnaw on mud the entire way here as they fled for their lives? Don't try to fool me."

Shock had muffled Kong Ling's ears; those words didn't register. His face flushed with anger and his goatee trembled as he said to Shen Zechuan in disbelief, "Was that impassioned speech of yours a lie, too? You! You used Zhongbo's calamity to mislead us and lay your own trap. Are you even human?!"

"Every man has his own ambition." Shen Zechuan smiled lazily. "Cizhou and the Imperial Army have reached a dead end. Isn't it natural that I should seek a new master? Mister Chengfeng, you of all people should understand this."

Without moving a muscle, Lei Changming said, "If you can really produce two million silver and help me save Han Jin, I'll take care of things with Han Cheng for you."

"I've already brought some silver with me," Shen Zechuan said. "Is this proof enough of my sincerity, Chief?"

CRUDE

SHEN ZECHUAN COULDN'T bring two million, but he'd
brought enough to show his intent. Lei Changming looked
at the chests all filled to the top with genuine silver ingots
stacked neatly in order. He grabbed a handful and weighed them in
his palm. "Is this all? The brothers under my command who make
a living selling sugar-filled pancakes can produce this much. Vice
Commander, aren't you looking down on me a bit too much?"

"If I'd really brought two million right away, the chief might not
dare accept it." Shen Zechuan had taken his seat. "Good deals are
worth discussing slowly. The only ones who should be anxious at
present are Cizhou and Xiao Chiye."

Lei Changming waved a hand for his men to drag Kong Ling out
of the tent, leaving only his own guards and Shen Zechuan within.
All this while, he had remained seated, maintaining his distance
with Shen Zechuan. "You and Xiao Chiye broke out of the siege
in Qudu. You could be considered sworn friends who have faced
death together. How is it that you've suddenly fallen out with him
and come to plead with me instead?"

"If the chief knows my name, then you must also know that Shen
Wei is my father. He let the enemy into Dunzhou and birthed the last-
ing grudge between Libei and me. Xiao Chiye and I may have buried
the hatchet, but Xiao Jiming won't necessarily agree." Shen Zechuan

looked troubled. "All men aspire to make a name for themselves. Xiao Chiye is like a clay Buddha crossing the river—he can't even save himself, so how can he carry me? There've been some misunderstandings between Lord Han and myself, but they are all minor issues; they don't warrant a death sentence. As long as someone vouches for me, I can still return to Qudu and serve the imperial court."

"So you still want to be an official, huh?" With both hands propped on his knees, Lei Changming said, "My young friend, to tell you the truth, I want to be an official too. We used to laze away in the mountains and wilderness. Our days were carefree, but it wasn't a proper living. Every move we make is scrutinized by the Qidong Garrison Troops."

"So we have a common goal." Shen Zechuan lifted his little bamboo fan slightly. "Isn't that perfect?"

"But I've been deceived before by scholarly types like you, and that makes me leery." Lei Changming put on a look of dread. "The two million silver you're offering remains in Cizhou. How do you plan to bring it to me? And Han Jin, too. How are you going to help me save him? Make yourself clear today, so I know where we stand. Only then can I take you under my wing."

"The silver is no issue. The chief can send a trusted man to Cizhou and ask Zhou Gui for the money. He knows where the silver is kept. As long as you can move it, you can have the money today."

"You think he'll simply give it to me if I ask?" Lei Changming rubbed his palms together, as if remembering the feeling of the silver.

"Do you not have Kong Ling in your hands?" Shen Zechuan asked with a smile. "That's Zhou Gui's trusted aide. And you have forty thousand men and horses. Zhou Gui won't dare refuse. He's always striven to be a good official who cares for his people as his own children. He won't risk provoking you when he has so much to lose."

Lei Changming looked at Shen Zechuan, as if getting the measure of him. The tent fell quiet. Lei Changming's guards stood on all sides. Shen Zechuan touched the teacup, but didn't drink. At last, Lei Changming laughed. "I have ample supplies, so I'm in no hurry. It won't hurt for the two million to sit there a few more days. Men, pour more tea for Young Master Shen. Our top priority is discussing how to save Han Jin. After all, whether or not we meet Han Cheng in Qudu hinges on him."

Kong Ling had been locked up in the stables. He lay across the hay, securely bound with coarse hemp ropes, and panted heavily. The horse standing in front of him lifted its tail and discharged a pile of steaming dung. Dizzy with the stench, Kong Ling turned his head away to gasp for breath. The group of bandits watching outside roared with laughter.

"That traitor deceived me!" Kong Ling shouted indignantly. "Bah! A gentleman would rather die than be humiliated. Don't even dream of using me to threaten Cizhou!"

Horsewhips promptly jabbed at Kong Ling's face. His clothes were covered in mud and horse dung, and the circle of bandits gawking at him made his head spin. He fumed with shame and hatred. "You're all in cahoots! You! Lei Changming! What good can come out of conspiring with such an unrighteous person?!"

But no matter how Kong Ling cursed and spat, there were only roars of laughter around him. Kong Ling was a well-read and erudite man, and everyone from the seasoned soldier Tantai Long to the scholar-official Zhou Gui had treated him with courtesy. Who wouldn't address him respectfully as Mister Chengfeng everywhere he went? But now, not only was he tied up in a stable, he was openly ridiculed by the lowest kind of criminals. The memory of the snowy night he fled Dunzhou rose before him. The faces of these bandits overlapped with the faces of the Biansha Horsemen, and the garbled sounds of laughter filled his ears. Unable to restrain himself, Kong Ling began to shake with sobs.

"Get back to your patrols!" An officer appeared from deeper in the camp and bellowed, "What are you all gathering here for? Is this old fart more important than your tasks? If the patrol is delayed, I'll see you all skinned! Move it, disperse!"

Kong Ling's assailants broke up noisily. Finally alone, Kong Ling inched over to the edge of the stable and put his head against the railing to let the dripping rainwater wash away the filth. He gulped in fresh air, his goatee so dirty it had become a cake of mud.

In the distance, men entered and exited the chief's tent. When they lifted the flap, Kong Ling could see Lei Changming preparing to host a feast for Shen Zechuan. He spat into the mud and closed his eyes.

Some time later, he felt a light pat on his cheek.

Kong Ling opened his eyes. It was the officer he'd seen earlier, a man in his early thirties. His face was tanned, and he had a hard-bitten air to him. "Mister Chengfeng!"

Kong Ling was alarmed.

"Don't be afraid. I'm General Tantai Long's old subordinate. I used to hold a post in the Dunzhou Garrison Troops. I met you once." This man forced a smile, then sighed. "Mister... You really don't deserve this kind of treatment."

"If you were Tantai Long's subordinate, how can you follow a brigand like Lei Changming and wreak such havoc?" Kong Ling asked woodenly. "When Tantai Long was alive, there was nothing he hated more than criminals like these."

"What else could I do?" the man replied with a bitter smile. "After Dunzhou was recovered, the imperial court took the grain away and used it to feed Juexi. Those of us who survived were so starved we were gnawing on tree bark. The chief might be a bandit, but he's a righteous man, and generous. It's only by following him that we have enough food to fill our bellies. We have no choice."

Kong Ling knew he was telling the truth, but words failed him. He could only remain silent.

The man helped Kong Ling up. "I heard about the chief's plan at the banquet table earlier. He's prepared to use you as a bargaining chip to negotiate with the prefect of Cizhou. I remembered you're a strong-willed man; I was worried you couldn't bear the humiliation, so I found a chance to step out. Sir, I'll take you away on horseback this minute!"

Kong Ling looked at his sincere expression. "If you let me go, Lei Changming won't let you off lightly."

This man untied the rope around Kong Ling's wrists. "I'll take you to Cizhou and come back to beg forgiveness. I used to be a loyal and righteous soldier under General Tantai's command, but I've been reduced to a bandit in order to fill my stomach. I can hardly live with myself some days. But the chief has treated me well too; I can't turn my back on him. Sir, let me help you on the horse!"

When he was seated in the saddle, Kong Ling gripped the man's arm and said, voice thick with emotion, "You are a good man."

The man climbed atop his own horse and draped a cloak over Kong Ling. With a flick of the reins, he brought Kong Ling around to the main entrance of the camp. There were still men patrolling in the rain. When they saw him, they all offered respects. He flashed his token without a word and led Kong Ling out of the camp.

They had only been riding a few minutes when they heard furious shouting behind them—the bandits were in hot pursuit.

"We're still many miles away from Cizhou, sir!" The man braved the rain to guide the way. "We'll ride through the night if we have to!"

Kong Ling swayed from the jolts and bumps, clutching the reins tightly as they fled the camp. They couldn't seem to outrun the pounding of hooves behind them. Branches lashed at his face in the dark, but he didn't dare look anywhere but ahead. He endured the pain, determined to hurry back to Cizhou and alert Zhou Gui as soon as possible.

Shen Zechuan ate very little. He ignored the singing and dancing in the tent and sat in his seat, drinking wine.

Lei Changming had brought quite a number of concubines along with him on this march; many were women he'd grabbed in broad daylight back in Duanzhou. He sent one over to pour wine for Shen Zechuan, then urged him with gusto, "Drink up, my young friend! I've brought no shortage of excellent wine. Drink all you want tonight."

The bandit chief was already flushed in the face. His voice gradually grew louder, and he didn't hold back as he teased his companions, pinching and groping the woman in his arms until her neck and shoulders were purpling with bruises. Shen Zechuan raised his cup and downed the wine without saying a word.

"You're the son of the Prince of Jianxing, Shen Wei," Lei Changming continued between bites of meat. "You grew up in luxury, so you don't know the value of rice and wheat. But you certainly have the brass of someone who has traveled through the land—offering two million at the drop of a hat! My young friend, not that I'm bragging, but I think you chose well throwing in your lot with me! Xiao Chiye is just a brat. He might have some influence in Qudu, but now that he's returning to Libei, what prospects does he have? He's dragging along twenty thousand stray dogs that the Libei Armored Cavalry certainly won't take! Don't tell me the Prince of Libei is going to let him command the Cavalry? Not a chance. Xiao Jiming is the real deal!"

Before those women could touch his wine jar, Shen Zechuan poured for himself and agreed with a smile, "Yeah."

Lei Changming gobbled down more pork shoulder and wiped grease from his lips. "Though, out of all those generals, I fear only Qidong's grand marshal, Qi Zhuyin. She's the only woman among the four great generals of the realm. I saw her once when I worked as an armed escort in Hezhou. What the fuck. Such a pretty thing, yet she wields an executioner's blade—an executioner's blade! Doesn't Xiao Chiye use an executioner's blade too? One straight slash, and it'll cleave flesh and bone. It takes real physical strength. You know, another reason I came to Cizhou is to do the marshal a favor. I'll capture Xiao Chiye for her and send him back to Qudu; then Qidong can cut ties with Libei without her wading into it. Say, with a merit like this, could I become a general under her command?"

"I've heard Marshal Qi has five great generals under her command. They're all skilled in combat, men she single-handedly trained in the Qidong Garrison Troops," Shen Zechuan said. "But if you really joined them, I'm sure you'd come out on top and be the big brother of them all."

Lei Changming roared with laughter. He scooped up the woman in his arms and covered her with slobbery kisses despite her cries, then wiped his greasy hands clean on her silk robes. "I made my mark on these mountains. I've been all over, and I've fought my share of battles. If you mention Lei Changming, who in Zhongbo won't tell you I can fight? My young friend, you know Lu Guangbai of the Bianjun Commandery, right? The Lu Clan is poor as dirt, but he seems like an unyielding man. It's only by virtue of his stubbornness that he's kept up the desperate fight at Bianjun; he has no other capabilities. If you ask me, Lu Guangbai is the most incompetent among the four great generals. He's called—what is it—Beacon-Smoke and Rising Sand? Bianjun lights those beacon towers every year; what's so special about that? Might as well vacate his post and let me take over. I guarantee I'd do a far better job!"

Seeing that he was drunk and starting to boast, Shen Zechuan reached out and gently righted the chopsticks on the table. "He's indeed rather unimpressive," he concurred with a smile.

"Men like Marshal Zuo are the real heroes." Lei Changming poured wine into his open mouth, spilling half down his chest. Not bothering to wipe the spillage, he tossed the cup away. "That's the man who took the enemies' heads from a thousand li away, who struck fear into his enemies' hearts with one arrow! When I was down in Hezhou in those early days, he was all the storyteller in the teahouse there spoke of. They say he killed his wife to protect the city and that his hair turned white after that. I ask you, how can you hear his story and not shed a tear?! It's a pity his hero's spirit was snuffed out too early and he ended up retiring. Otherwise, he and I might even've been sworn brothers!"

The whole tent was pandemonium, as if a host of demons caroused wildly within. Those so-called guards and deputy generals all showed their true colors as they dragged prostitutes over to them to drink and make merry, whether they were standing or sprawled on the ground. An army like this had no discipline. They were just like Lei Changming—bandits who depended on the sharpness of their blades to plunder and pillage.

Sitting among them, Shen Zechuan began to subtly sense that something was off.

Lei Changming shouldn't be such a man. This short-sighted, careless man who enjoyed life as it came—how could he have risen to the top of this crowd of bandits? What Shen Zechuan saw of this man was entirely different from what the rumors suggested.

Hands chasing after a prostitute, Lei Changming pulled her into his lap to fondle and grope. As he poured more wine and sang some obscure folk song from Dengzhou, he danced and gesticulated crudely, like a bull that had rashly crashed onto the chessboard. He enjoyed himself without restraint and drank himself sloppy.

Suddenly, he smacked his forehead and pointed at Shen Zechuan. "Wait! Your mother was a dancer from Duanzhou! Quick my young friend—get up and dance for us!"

107

ODD

THE SOUND OF RAIN outside the tent sank to a whisper, and the tent flap opened, dissipating the heat within. Lecherous howls of drunk men rang out from the camp in the deep of the night, while bandits with arms slung over each other's shoulders played guessing games. Lei Changming was too warm; he unfastened his clothes and laid his chest bare. He was tanned, with plenty of scars and tufts of chest hair that grew like weeds beneath his clothes. Drunkenly embracing the woman in his arms, he sang and danced, and even called out to Shen Zechuan, "My young friend, get up!"

At this moment, the flap twitched, and several bandits entered, heads lowered, to place down food.

Shen Zechuan opened the little bamboo fan a few inches and stood up. The light of the candles in the tent was dim. He raised the fan at an angle to block the side of his face, then looked at Lei Changming and asked softly, "What dance would the chief like to see?"

Lei Changming found Shen Zechuan exceedingly alluring. He was heart-wrenchingly beautiful when seen this way, his beauty so stunning he outshone everything else in the room. Lei Changming took a gulp of wine to embolden himself, then shoved the woman out of his lap and pounced toward Shen Zechuan. He tripped instantly over a discarded wine jar, cutting a sorry figure as he crashed forward at Shen Zechuan's feet. Sprawled on the ground,

Lei Changming wheezed, his hot breath reeking of wine. He reached for the hem of Shen Zechuan's robe, but grasped nothing but empty air. He chuckled and began to laugh.

"Smells nice." Lei Changming stretched his neck and sniffed the air. "You really smell so good. Come now, my young friend. Help me up. I'll dance with you. We can dance whatever you'd like! Damn, so this is what they mean by the fragrance of a beauty!"

Shen Zechuan looked sidelong at him as he crawled on the ground like a hairy, pot-bellied spider, chasing the hem of Shen Zechuan's plain white robes. In this absurd, comical moment, Shen Zechuan felt a sudden wave of abhorrence wash over him. His hatred, freed of its dam, was like magma—so scalding his fingers gripping the fan went white.

His teacher had told him to leave Qudu and return to Zhongbo. Yet the Duanzhou he pined for had fallen into the hands of men like this. Lei Changming and his bandits were malice incarnate, fiends who had occupied the mountains and rivers.

Resting his bamboo fan lightly at the edge of his lips, Shen Zechuan smiled and took a slow step back. Amid the rowdy din filled with flickering, monstrous shadows, he bent forward and said, "Come here."

Lei Changming had been trying to climb to his feet, but now, he abandoned the effort and crawled on hands and knees toward Shen Zechuan. In his stupor, he felt that what he saw was no human being, but an untouchable demon of the night. Salivating, he swallowed heavily, his unfocused eyes coming to rest on the tiny white jade stone dangling from Shen Zechuan's right ear. Someone had carefully polished that jade into a perfect sphere, and its luster looked exceedingly gentle against Shen Zechuan's earlobe under the light of the lamps. Other than his bamboo fan, it was the only adornment he had.

"My young friend," Lei Changming said with new urgency. "Quick, help me up."

The bandits attending them set down their plates without looking up. Trays in hand, they stepped aside as if to leave. The shouts and laughter of men and women blended with the rainy drizzle, the hallucination of another world in Lei Changming's ears, at once both near and far. He was like a drooling, chained jackal, dragged toward Shen Zechuan by an invisible force. The tent was upside down; Lei Changming felt dizzy from too much drink.

My young friend.

Lei Changming chanted with an almost religious reverence.

Shen Zechuan. Beauty. My young friend.

He carelessly tore at his own open tunic, feeling as though the scars on his chest were on fire. He had never felt like this before. His eyes were wide open, yet he seemed to be caught in a dream. Scrabbling on hands and knees, he finally reached Shen Zechuan's feet, where he tilted his head up and barked a laugh, trying to tug at the hem of Shen Zechuan's cloud-white robe.

"Such a temptress." Lei Changming reached out a trembling hand and murmured ingratiatingly, "What a ravishing sight you are..."

In Zhongbo, Lei Changming had killed men like flies and abducted countless women and children. He loved beautiful creatures by nature—loved to tear the delicate, the untainted, and even the ignorant, into a bloody mess. He had committed all manner of foul deeds, and he thought even ghosts would veer away when they saw him. He had no fear of karma. People like him had done wrong, yet they still slept soundly, dreaming dreams of limitless wealth and glory. They didn't remember the bodies they had trampled to pieces. They too had been like the clouds—far away and impossible to reach.

Lei Changming's vision blurred, and Shen Zechuan's face became more and more indistinct. In contrast, that round little jade stone seemed to get sharper and sharper in his vision, until it became something he recognized.

My young friend.

He had once tricked a child this way; he had pinned down their limbs and violated them in the pitch-dark tent. He remembered drinking that day, and that the scars on his chest had burned the same way. Those limbs he'd gripped were so slender; in his frenzied state, Lei Changming had entertained the thought of breaking them. He'd bent and twisted them in his grip, watching as that rosiness turned pale, then into a sea of bruised flesh on a body that would never struggle again.

Panting, Lei Changming pounced at Shen Zechuan again and again, attempting to grab him, but failed each time. He shook his head hard. The cacophony of human voices was making his head ache. He crawled forward and crashed into a small table; wine and dishes slid off and splattered all over him. Half-naked, he shouted, "My—!"

The tent reflected in Lei Changming's eyes suddenly righted itself as blood sprayed over his cheeks and across his gaping mouth. His body was still frozen in place, but his head had already rolled to the floor. It knocked against the wooden leg of the table, its expression so vivid it turned one's stomach.

The laughter in the tent came to an abrupt halt, though the candle flame still flickered. Everyone froze where they were, looking like stiff corpses. Wind blew through the tent flap, open to reveal the drizzling gloom outside. Night pressed in like the creeping silence, and the gust extinguished the last of the candle flame.

Shen Zechuan pressed Avalanche, which he had pulled out from under his cushion, against the tablecloth and wiped it in silence.

Fresh blood, shed from the blade, left a long red scar on the pale cotton. He took his time. No one had seen him draw the blade, yet now they marveled at the sight of him wiping it patiently.

Inexplicably, Shen Zechuan started to laugh; it was the most unbridled mirth he had let out in years. He sheathed his blade and picked up his folding fan, stepping on Lei Changming's head to nudge it upright.

"Dance, huh?" Shen Zechuan lowered his lashes and said to Lei Changming, "Are *you* even worthy?"

The bandit had just pushed down his pants to relieve himself when a pair of hands sliced his throat and dragged him into the undergrowth. The patrols in the camp were slack. Small groups of Lei Changming's men had gathered at the foot of the watchtower nearby to play dice, unaware that their own men were quietly dwindling in number.

"Tell the mess cook to save some meat and serve us a plate. This rain keeps pissing down. It's unbearable. We won't last out here if we don't drink a little wine!" The squad commander tossed the dice and raised his head to yell at the man behind him, "You go. Yes, you. You're in the way standing there!"

He lowered his head and returned to his game, joining the men as they chewed on meat jerky. They fished into their waistbands and tossed the copper coins they had left into the betting pool, hoping to get lucky.

"If this hand ain't cursed!" One of them slapped his palm as if he was swatting away bad luck, then rubbed it on his thigh. "I'm not playing anymore!"

"No!" His companion elbowed him. "That's no fun! Aren't we entering the city tomorrow? You need money to visit the brothels and get on the pleasure boats, you know. Give it another go! Every dog has his day!"

"Bah!" The quitter spat in the other man's face. "With our chief's reputation, what do we need money for at the brothels? Whores don't get to ask for money. We're doing them enough favors by patronizing them! What if they spread some filthy disease to me?! I'm done playing! The chief seems like he's going to be up all night. Look how drunk they are in the tent; none of them'll be ready to fight a battle tomorrow. I'm gonna sleep for a few hours."

As soon as the man turned around, he bumped into someone else; his head struck their armor with a loud *thwack*. The collision stunned him, and he started to shove the other person. "The fuck you blocking—"

There was a wet sound of a blade sliding into flesh. The man's words died in his throat as he slumped forward with an empty stare. His assailant held the body up and pushed it back into the dice-playing crowd. Dice tumbled to the ground. The men were already in a foul mood at having to take the night watch; they grabbed the man's collar to give him a beating. Yet when they turned him over, they saw his eyes bulging—he was dead.

The Imperial Army swiftly drew their blades. Before the bandits could react, they charged out of the darkness and cut them down. Blood splattered onto their armor. Tantai Hu wiped his face and shouted, "Kill them!"

They'd had no warning from the patrol squad; the bandits that had gone to rest in the camp were caught entirely off-guard by the Imperial Army. Tantai Hu led the charge into the tents; his men covered the bandits' mouths and noses, then stabbed them one at a time, leaving behind mattresses soaked in crimson. The surviving bandits fled the camp in a panic, but without orders, they ran around like headless

chickens in the rainy night. The Imperial Army had completely surrounded the encampment. The moment the wily old veterans among
the brigands saw those drawn blades, they surrendered without a fight
and crowded together, wading across the muddy ground to kneel and
beg for mercy.

Xiao Chiye spurred his horse into the camp. Snowcrest stamped
its hooves before the crowd as Meng descended from the sky and
landed on Xiao Chiye's shoulder, bringing a gust of bitter wind as he
folded his wings. Xiao Chiye's broad and muscular silhouette was an
ebony cloud in the rainy night, blotting out all light. His back was
to that faint and flickering candlelight in the tent, his gaze a blade
so cutting any prying glances vanished in a panic.

Tantai Hu was doing a headcount.

Xiao Chiye reined his horse around, his shoulders drenched.
Meng tilted his head at that deathly still military tent, as if he knew
that there was fresh meat inside for him to eat.

Shen Zechuan wasn't in the tent. He was standing outside,
a closed umbrella in his hand, looking down at his own bloodstained
boots.

Xiao Chiye leaned down, and Meng hopped onto Shen Zechuan's
shoulder. Shen Zechuan raised his head and met Xiao Chiye's eyes.

"What is a young master like you doing here"—Xiao Chiye lifted
a finger and ran it lightly across the tip of Shen Zechuan's nose—"all
alone in the rain?"

Shen Zechuan spread his little bamboo fan to show it to Xiao
Chiye. He sounded a little sulky as he said, "My fan's dirty."

A few splotches of blood marred the open fan, like red plum
blossoms spilling over the inked words, their blooms feeble. It was
unsightly no matter how he looked at it. On top of that, those words
had been written by Xiao Chiye himself. Ever since this fan had

been gifted to him, it had never left Shen Zechuan's side, just like that blue handkerchief.

"These splashes are rather well-placed." Xiao Chiye's gaze never left Shen Zechuan's face. "Give this fan to me. I'll make you another one."

Shen Zechuan slid the closed fan into Xiao Chiye's back collar at an angle and nodded his head. Xiao Chiye smiled at him. "Did you enjoy the feast?"

Shaking the umbrella open to shield both of them, Shen Zechuan answered, "Passable. Too noisy."

Xiao Chiye dismounted and took the umbrella; he only covered Shen Zechuan, leaving half his body exposed in the rain. He reached a hand out to lift the tent flap and surveyed the interior. After a little silence, he said, "There's something odd about this camp."

Shen Zechuan raised his hand to stop Meng from flying inside. "I don't believe he's the same Lei Changming who subdued the two prefectures of Duanzhou and Dunzhou."

They were still talking when Tantai Hu hurried over. He was still covered in blood, and he looked uneasy as he paid his respects. "Master," he reported, "the numbers don't tally. I asked some bandit squad commanders, and they couldn't even say how many men they have under them. It was only after I pressed them that I learned they're all stray bandits Lei Changming has just taken in. These are not the men he brought from Mount Luo!"

108

SILVER

NO WONDER *everything had gone so smoothly tonight!*

In an instant, Shen Zechuan understood many things. He whipped his head around to blurt it out, then stopped and looked at Xiao Chiye.

"Lao-Hu," Xiao Chiye said, swiftly mounting his horse. "Leave two thousand men to guard this place. Ding Tao, get your horse and ride around to the northeast side of Cizhou. Tell the men lying in ambush to head south immediately; block the road on the southern side. The rest of you, follow me back to the city."

This strategy of luring the Imperial Army away from their base had likely been long planned—perhaps it had been in the works before Lei Changming had even left Mount Luo. This entire time, the reports Cizhou had received were all vague, the most frequent being sightings of fire pits in the bandits' abandoned camps. The precise number of Lei Changming's men had become a matter of opinion, and this mix of truth and falsehood, reality and pretense, had lured them into guessing that the reported forty thousand men were just a front. They had assumed Lei Changming wouldn't have the guts to launch a surprise attack. None of them expected he had no intentions of fighting Xiao Chiye head-on at all.

"There's no way Kong Ling wouldn't recognize Lei Changming," Shen Zechuan said as Xiao Chiye pulled him up into the saddle. "At this point, I suspect everything we've ever heard about Lei Changming is false. 'Lei Changming' is someone else's puppet."

Xiao Chiye tossed the umbrella to Tantai Hu, covered Shen Zechuan with his own cloak, and reined his horse around. "Even under duress, Kong Ling doesn't have the authority to make any promises. The man who took him most likely wants to use Kong Ling to open Cizhou's gates. Then he'll be the one inside, and we'll be the ones without."

Xiao Chiye could afford to fight Lei Changming's rumored forty thousand men because he still had Cizhou's granary to back him up. His well-fed army could swiftly cut down a mob of bandits already weary from their long march. But his enemy, knowing his own shortcomings, had decided not to fight Xiao Chiye directly. Instead, he had drawn on their foes' strength to bolster his own deficiencies and turned Xiao Chiye into a stray dog in the wilderness. Now their positions were reversed: the Imperial Army was stranded outside the walls, cut off from Cizhou's provisions.

"All this time, he's been watching from the shadows." Shen Zechuan pulled his cloak closer around him in the wind. "He knows every step we've taken."

"Cizhou is not our territory, after all. He must have an informant in the city. But we know nothing about him." Xiao Chiye burst out laughing and tightened his arms around Shen Zechuan. "This man sure is something!"

The rain had subsided, though the night breeze still carried with it a few scattered drops. Hooves splashed through the mud as they galloped toward Cizhou. Yet no matter how fast they rode, they couldn't hope to catch up. Kong Ling had crossed into Cizhou's territory some hours ago.

Kong Ling had been a sedentary scholar since coming out of obscurity to take up an official post, and he was nearly forty-five. His bones almost shook apart from the impact of the ride, and he panted for breath as he slid off the horse to the ground. He let his companion prop him up, then cupped his hands toward him. "I was saved thanks to you, brave friend. I can't imagine what would have happened to me."

"You're too courteous, sir." Though this man seemed taciturn, he had looked after Kong Ling the entire journey. "I'm afraid the men behind us will overtake us any minute. Sir, drink some water and we'll move on. Once we reach the city gate, have them open it as soon as possible!"

They had stopped midway at an inn that still had its lanterns hung up; they weren't there to stay the night, but to allow Kong Ling—whose legs were still trembling—to drink some hot tea and catch his breath. The tender insides of his legs were badly chafed, making it difficult for him to sit. He stood in the main hall and gulped down his cup of tea.

The sound of hooves rang on the road outside. Kong Ling's companion didn't stand, but his hand quietly slid to the blade at his waist as he angled his face into the darkness and glanced sidelong at the door.

A group of road-worn travelers strode over the threshold, led by two men of similar stature. Oddly, the entire group was tall and muscular; despite the rough clothes they wore, they possessed an imposing aura.

The man in the lead removed his bamboo hat to reveal a stubbled jaw and a lock of hair hanging over his forehead. He swept a seemingly nonchalant glance at the two men in the hall drinking tea. Grinning, he set down a bag of money and said to the innkeeper, "Staying for the night. One fine room and three rooms with pallets. Any hot food left? Give us some steamed buns and sliced beef with shaojiu."

"We have the money; why are you being cheap?" The man beside him removed his bamboo hat as well. He was powerfully built. He grabbed the money pouch and opened it, calling to the innkeeper, "Fine rooms for each of us!"

A muffled cough rose from the center of the group of men. An old man who had kept his cloak on all this while said softly, "Silver doesn't fall from the sky. We have yet to reach our destination. Let's endure it one more day. Tianya, make sure everyone rests after eating their fill. Don't goof around."

Qiao Tianya blew at the stray lock of hair and plucked the money bag out of Fei Sheng's hands. He tossed it to the innkeeper. "Do as I said earlier. Quick as you can on the food and wine; don't drag your feet. Shifu, you've braved the elements with us the entire way. How can we let you squeeze in with us now that we're here? You are our elder; this is our duty. Anyway, if my master finds out, he'll have my head. Getting a good rest is the kindest favor you could do us."

Not to be outdone, Fei Sheng spoke up too. "I wasn't thinking earlier. Shifu, let me bring you to the room to rest. Once the food arrives, I'll bring it up to you."

Ji Gang's physical strength wasn't what it had been. He didn't protest and allowed Fei Sheng to lead him upstairs.

Although Kong Ling didn't know who these travelers were, he could sense they shouldn't be trifled with. They were all armed with blades, and he worried they were also bandits. After thinking a moment, he set down his teacup and said to the man beside him, "My brave friend, I've had enough rest. Let's continue on our way!"

They had hardly moved when those strange travelers took their seats beside them. The inn wasn't large, and the group of strangers had filled all four square tables. Either by intention or coincidence, Qiao Tianya planted his ass down right beside Kong Ling and cut off Kong Ling's way out.

"Hey there." Qiao Tianya poured himself tea and asked, "Are you two on the road too?"

Kong Ling's companion let his toughness fall away, transforming into an ordinary farmer. He rubbed his hands and smiled shyly, as if unaccustomed to dealing with inquiries like this. "Aye, I'm traveling with my eldest brother."

Qiao Tianya clearly didn't have the ounce of self-awareness it would take to move out of their way. He drank the tea and narrowed his eyes as if he'd burned his tongue. "Where are you headed? Mayhap we're going the same way. I'll tell you, we haven't had an easy time of it on this journey. Didn't some marquis in Qudu rebel? The local authorities are all over the roads, all of them old hands at fishing for bribes; we were forced to take a detour. Sorry about this chatty mouth of mine; I've gotten carried away. Where are you going?"

Kong Ling could neither sit nor walk out. His inner thighs burned with pain. Striving to maintain his composure, his goatee quivered as he replied in a Dengzhou dialect, "Malian Town. Ya know of Malian Town, buddy?"

"Near Cizhou, huh? Then we are going the same way. We're heading for the city of Cizhou, right before Malian Town." Qiao Tianya propped an elbow on the table and stared at the other man. "Buddy, you look familiar."

At this point, Kong Ling's companion had sensed he was being watched. He glanced at the other travelers from the corner of his eye. Gears turned in his mind, and he made some rough guesses— these travelers, he surmised, must be members of the Embroidered Uniform Guard disguising themselves to hunt down Xiao Chiye and Shen Zechuan. They were only suspicious because he was carrying a blade. He relaxed, leaning into the simple and honest act as he answered, "I'm a farmer from Dengzhou."

As he spoke, he fumbled around his lapels and fished out a crumpled travel permit and a hand-copied household register with the official seal of Dengzhou. He opened it to show Qiao Tianya. "We're going to Malian Town to visit our elder sister who married over. She just had a baby and they're h-hosting a banquet."

"Oh, a joyous event!" Qiao Tianya seemed even happier than the purported uncle. "I love kids—and my favorite drink is the kind you toast with at one-month celebrations!"

Seeing Qiao Tianya prattling on again, Kong Ling forced a smile. "The rain has stopped. We should be on our way; we can't spare the money to stay overnight."

On the other end of the hall, Fei Sheng had come down the stairs. He hadn't thought much of this man at first, but noting Qiao Tianya hadn't moved an inch, he also started to size him up. In a flash, he slid over and took a seat behind the man, boxing him in from the front and back with Qiao Tianya.

"What are you guys chatting about?" Fei Sheng picked up a steamed bun from the plate the waiter had set down and took a big bite. He looked around at them. "Seems like you've all hit it off."

"Chatting about sons." Qiao Tianya nudged his chopsticks toward them and said warmly, "Have you two eaten? You haven't, have you? Come, let's have our meals together! Waiter! Two more sets of chopsticks!"

Even Kong Ling had sensed something off by now. He thought to sit back down and speak when a teacup on the table suddenly overturned, splashing tea across his companion. The man jumped to his feet. He hastily wiped himself with his sleeves as he apologized to Fei Sheng. "Sorry, sorry!"

Taking advantage of the opportunity, he squeezed past Fei Sheng and took two a few steps toward the waiter, pleading, "Buddy, lend me a towel to wipe myself."

Fei Sheng stood as well and exchanged a glance with Qiao Tianya. At every table in the room, their astute brothers grasped their blades. Fei Sheng strode out aggressively and bumped into the man's right shoulder. The impact sent the man crashing into the table and chairs in front of him, teetering to catch his balance.

He pulled the man up by his clothes. "You did it on purpose, didn't you?"

The man's temples were drenched in sweat, and he was so anxious he didn't know where to put his hands. He bowed to Fei Sheng again and again. "Sorry, so sorry..."

That reaction—this man didn't know martial arts.

Fei Sheng cast another glance at Qiao Tianya and shoved the man again. "Just my fucking luck!"

The man collapsed backward, clumsily knocking over the table and chairs and striking the back of his head on the corner of the table.

"Why did you hit him?" Kong Ling exclaimed in surprise. "He's bleeding!"

Only then did Qiao Tianya pretend to stop Fei Sheng. "Forget it, forget it. We're all travelers. Leave these men alone."

Fei Sheng let loose a torrent of expletives as Qiao Tianya persuaded him to come back and sit. He glared at the man several more times. As their party started digging into their food, Fei Sheng stood up again. "I got so pissed off I forgot to deliver the meal to Shifu!"

Kong Ling had already helped support his companion to the entrance. The man touched the back of his head and came away with a palmful of blood. He glanced timidly over his shoulder at Qiao Tianya and the rest, then shrank back, fearful of attracting more notice. He untied the horses and walked off into the night with Kong Ling.

Fei Sheng finally dropped his blowhard act. "Why are you provoking them? We're on the wanted list too. Better to lie low now that we're right on the border of Cizhou; don't stir up trouble."

"I just had a feeling about that guy..." Qiao Tianya swallowed two mouthfuls of shaojiu and frowned in thought. "Was there really no reaction when you bumped into him?"

"Nope." Fei Sheng took a bite of the beef. "Anyone can put on an act, but the body doesn't lie—when you're accustomed to reacting swiftly, it's difficult to hold back from parrying a surprise blow. There was something weird about him for sure, but he indeed doesn't seem to be a fighter."

"What if he *can* control himself?" Qiao Tianya suddenly asked.

"Then he's formidable." Fei Sheng gestured with his chopsticks for emphasis. "He'd have to be of the same caliber as Ji Gang-shifu. Think about the marquis. With a body like His Lordship, there would be no way to hide it—his naturally endowed physique has blessed him with explosive strength. Before you so much as think of touching him, you have to be careful, especially if you're approaching him while he's asleep. Otherwise, with his reactions, you'd be risking your life. The kind of self-control it takes to endure can only be built up through decades of practice. That man didn't seem that old. I doubt he can do it."

Qiao Tianya applied himself to his meal and let the subject drop. They ate and drank their fill, and the innkeeper worked out the bill for Qiao Tianya. When he returned the change, Fei Sheng, who had little better to do, fiddled with the ingots—and realized something unusual. The weight and relative purity of this silver were subtly different from the silver they had brought from Qudu, which had been minted and issued by the Ministry of Revenue.

Fei Sheng was usually a competitive man who sucked up to others when it benefitted him, but in truth, the skills he possessed were unrivaled. Suspicions aroused, he held the silver up to the light and scrutinized it before asking Qiao Tianya, "Zhongbo has had dealings with Juexi for many years. Most of the silver in circulation here comes from Juexi, right?"

"That's what they say." Qiao Tianya propped his elbows on the counter and turned to look at those silver taels. "New silver like this is something you don't see every day. A lot of the transactions in Zhongbo these days are shady scalping deals; most people typically won't dare use silver from Juexi directly. Everyone exchanges them for copper coins, or uses silver issued from other regions. But with the state treasury empty during the reign of Xiande, there's been very little new-minted silver from anywhere. The only clan who could still have very new silver is the Xi—"

The Xi Clan, who mined silver.

If this silver hadn't come out of Shen Zechuan's coffers, it came from the people who had schemed to empty out the Xi Clan's vaults. Whether it was the former or the latter; both had enormous implications.

Qiao Tianya straightened up in a flash. "Leave half the men here to keep watch and take care of Shifu. The rest of you, follow me. Old Fei, you were fucking wrong! Get after him!"

109

JINGZHE

Q IAO TIANYA SCRAMBLED out of the inn with his men, but there were no longer any traces of their quarry on the road. Fei Sheng leapt astride his horse and pointed west. "Since he's been alerted, he knows he can't stay here. He can't escape our eyes in town, so he'll most likely take a detour to hurry toward Cizhou."

According to Qiao Tianya's information, Shen Zechuan was still in the city of Cizhou. He stuffed the silver ingot back into his lapels, but before he could speak, he heard Ji Gang's voice behind him.

Ji Gang gathered his cloak and downed the bowl of medicine in his hand in one draft. "Don't stop for my sake. Let's ride for Cizhou now. We have to inform Chuan-er about this before anything else."

This concerned Shen Zechuan's safety. Qiao Tianya knew Ji Gang wouldn't be persuaded to rest tonight, so he motioned for the Embroidered Uniform Guard members at the back to lead the horse over. Ji Gang got on and straightened his back. With a jerk of the reins, he led the men in a charge toward the town gate.

Kong Ling was miserable beyond description. Both his thighs had been chafed raw until they burned. He didn't say a word as he followed, grimacing, behind his companion's horse. Just as Fei Sheng had predicted, they didn't linger in the town—they left quickly, his companion leading the way off the main roads.

"Sir, please bear with it for a few more hours." As the man spurred his horse on, he looked back to shout, "We'll reach Cizhou's city gate before daybreak!"

Nodding his head, Kong Ling panted, "The roads around here are full of forking paths. I don't think they can catch us even if they wanted to."

"But the rain has stopped." The man's stamina was exceptional; he hadn't gasped for breath once the entire journey. "There's no way to cover our trail now. They're bound to follow faster!"

Kong Ling gripped the robe over his knees and gritted his teeth. "Keep going! My brave friend, we'll continue on our way! As long as we can reach Cizhou's gate, we will be safe."

But the path they had been taking grew boggy after diverging from the public road. The mud sucked at their horses' hooves, and they couldn't maintain their original speed; it was only with difficulty that they pushed forward. Looking at his companion's back, Kong Ling sighed and said with emotion, "It's really all thanks to your help. If you insist on returning to Lei Changming after we arrive at Cizhou, I'll pick out the best horse for you."

The man let out a hearty laugh. "There's no need to stand on ceremony, sir. I'm just doing what I ought. I'm a soldier who only knows how to fight and kill; I can't do what lofty scholars like you do. I hold you in great esteem, and I'm already content to have been able to travel with you tonight."

Kong Ling was taken aback at this man's integrity. He felt a lump in his throat. When he remembered Shen Zechuan, that turncoat who switched his allegiance to the enemy in their hour of need, he couldn't help but wipe his eyes with his sleeve. "To think there are still good men like you in Zhongbo. There's hope yet for our land's rejuvenation! My friend, how should I address you?"

The man looked back. "My name is Piaopo, *heavy rain*. A crude and inelegant name like this isn't fit for the good sir's ears. My parents are both honest people who make a living on the few acres of fields they have. There was a drought the year I was born, so my father named me after the downpour, hoping to call down their salvation."

"Brother Piaopo is a righteous man," Kong Ling said. "A name is but a word. It sounds good to me!"

It was too dark for Kong Ling to see the path ahead of them. Perhaps the route Piaopo picked was too well-hidden; no one had found them yet. Kong Ling pounded his thighs. After glancing up at the horizon several times, he finally spied the first rays of dawn, illuminating the city walls of Cizhou at the far end of their road.

"Sir!" Piaopo made a grab for Kong Ling's reins and led his horse alongside his own. "Tell the city officer to open the gate. We'll pay our respects to Lord Zhou now!"

They pushed their horses to a gallop along the last of the path, splashing through puddles. They had arrived at the foot of Cizhou's city walls.

Kong Ling hugged the neck of his horse, entirely spent. He smoothed his goatee, then lifted his head to shout hoarsely, "It's me!"

Heads popped out over the battlement above. Shocked at what he saw, one officer couldn't help but blurt out, "Mister Chengfeng!"

"Quick! Go get His Excellency!" Kong Ling dismounted the horse with trembling legs and handed the reins to Piaopo. "Tell him I'm back!"

"Open the city gate first," Piaopo said. "Sir—"

Kong Ling nodded, gasping for air. He bent over, hands braced on his knees, and smiled bitterly. "Let me catch my breath. We'll enter the city soon. We need to meet His Excellency first to clear up any suspicions about you. Otherwise, we'll be delayed by the city officer's interrogation."

Very soon, Zhou Gui hurried over. When he saw Kong Ling from above, he blurted, "Chengfeng, what's going on? Quick, open the gate!"

The city gate groaned as several soldiers from within lifted the bar and pulled the city gates open, letting the first rays of morning sun through the gap. Kong Ling wiped sweat from his brow and strode in first. A stretch of bridle path lay just beyond the gate. Zhou Gui hurriedly descended the wall and led his men to the head of the bridle path to receive Kong Ling and his companion.

But Kong Ling, who had been walking in front, abruptly furrowed his brow and bellowed, "Shut the gates!"

The soldiers behind him who had slipped around the door to push it open froze at once. In that instant, Piaopo burst forth. He grabbed the back of Kong Ling's collar and yanked him backward in a swift retreat. To his surprise, Kong Ling stumbled and dropped to his knees, deliberately dragging his weight. Waving his hands, he shouted at Zhou Gui, "This man is a liar! Zhou Gui, tell the men to loose the arrows! You mustn't let him go free!"

Zhou Gui stepped forward. "Take him down!"

That originally docile horse beside Piaopo whinnied, rearing up to trample the soldiers manning the gate. Piaopo swung up atop the horse, and the steed crashed back through the city gate. He hauled Kong Ling behind him with just one hand; Kong Ling's body was suspended at one side of the saddle, his legs and feet scraping across the ground as he was dragged along.

Unnatural strength!

This man's strength was by no means inferior to Xiao Chiye's.

Kong Ling was unable to break free as he was pulled along at high speed. His back slammed against the iron buckle of the horse's saddle, knocking the wind out of him as if the strikes might perforate the lungs in his frail chest. All he could see was the sky as he flailed his arms and kicked with both legs against the grip tightening on him. "Zhou Gui! Release—release the arrows! This man has reinforcements!"

An irritated *tsk* escaped Piaopo's lips. He lifted Kong Ling up by the neck and hollered at the soldiers surging out of the city gates, "Go ahead! Zhou Gui, shoot! We'll see who dies first—me or Mister Chengfeng!"

Zhou Gui was a mere civil official. He pushed away the guards and, stricken, shouted, "Stop!"

Red-faced from strangulation, Kong Ling clawed at his collar. Piaopo leaned in closer to him and said with a grin, "How very astute of you, sir. Didn't you still regard me as a righteous man on our way here? Why have you turned against me?"

"Tantai—Tantai Long's soldiers!" Kong Ling gasped. "Th-they were all from the th-three prefectures in the east. None of them would be familiar w-with the backroads of Cizhou!"

Piaopo threw his head back and laughed as he sat steady on the horse. "So I see. Sir, you are truly formidable. You were even acting with such sincerity earlier. But I've already arrived at Cizhou. Did you think you could settle the matter by tricking me into the city and killing me?" He turned his head and spat. "It's too late!"

At once, those pursuing bandits who had vanished earlier thundered up from behind them. Although they hadn't the uniform armor expected of a regular army, their numbers were terrifying. They were dressed in various styles and colors, holding their weapons aloft as they urged their horses through the woods and grasses in a headlong charge. Kong Ling could see no end to them.

"A few months ago, I instructed Lei Changming to tell you we wanted grain. Instead, you let the Imperial Army into Cizhou and handed our granary to Xiao Chiye." Casting off his disguise at Piaopo, Lei Jingzhe flung Kong Ling to the dirt. Reining his horse around toward the city, he called out to Zhou Gui, "You think Xiao Chiye's twenty thousand soldiers will scare me off? I sent men repeatedly to persuade you to pledge allegiance to me, but you put me off again and again! Zhou Gui, you're now a traitor aiding a rebel army. By razing Cizhou today, I'll be ridding the people of a scourge!"

Looking at the more than ten thousand men before him, Zhou Gui's heart sank. He felt dizzy and hastily grabbed onto the guard beside him for support as he squeezed the words through gritted teeth. "I will open the granary and give you the grain, but you mustn't hurt the commoners of Cizhou!"

Lei Jingzhe cracked his whip, and the bandits behind him roared with laughter. The hooves of his horse stomped around Kong Ling, and foot soldiers surrounded him to prevent his escape, forcing him to roll and crawl to dodge the sharp hooves. Lei Jingzhe pointed his horsewhip at Kong Ling on the ground. "Now I'm the host, and you're the guest. Whether or not you open it, the granary is mine. I'm taking my men home to eat—the fucking gall of you to negotiate with *me*."

Zhou Gui staggered a few steps. "We emptied half a granary for your Mount Luo bandits last year, when Cizhou was in the middle of a famine," he fumed. "Had we not, how many of your men on Mount Luo would have starved?! Can't you spare the commoners of Cizhou on account of this favor?"

"What nonsense." Lei Jingzhe's expression went flat, and he responded coldly, "Lei Changming bought that grain with money at my behest."

He was right. Lei Changming had indeed paid for the grain—but he'd bought half a granary of fine rice in Cizhou at the dirt-cheap price of unpolished rice. The sum he'd offered was so meager it couldn't have chased away a beggar in the city's streets.

Zhou Gui was so stunned by this brazen claim he could scarcely breathe. Thumping his chest and stamping his foot in anger, he cried, "You! Are you people still human?! Don't even think about entering the city today!"

Lei Jingzhe had run out of patience. He knew Lei Changming wouldn't be able to keep up the façade for long. The Imperial Army was most likely already on its way. He lowered his voice to a growl. "Zhou Gui, I just want to enter the city and play for a few days. Must you insist on fighting me when you stand no chance of winning?! It's the same as throwing eggs against a rock!"

Hunched over trembling in the mud, Kong Ling sneered. His sleeve flapped up as he pointed at Lei Jingzhe and cried, "Play for a few days? When have you ever kept your men under control when they enter the city? Each time Lei Changming comes, a dozen women in Cizhou meet their end! Bah! You're degenerates, every one of you; what benevolent and righteous act are you putting on?! Everyone will die if we let you enter the city today, so us folks of Cizhou may as well fight to the death out here!"

The horsewhip struck Kong Ling so hard it split open the flesh on his back. Kong Ling had initially thought they could take this man down at the city gate. He had never expected the bandits' main force to be so close on their heels. He was painfully aware that his gullibility had brought a catastrophe upon Cizhou. Overwhelmed with grief and sorrow, he bent over on the ground and retched.

Lei Jingzhe turned and led his men in a charge straight toward Zhou Gui. "We'll slaughter our way into the city," he called. "Once Qudu issues an appointment order, we'll become the garrison troops of Cizhou who eliminated the rebels for the imperial court!"

Zhou Gui saw the fierce horses racing toward him, the sea of blades reflecting the light of dawn. With an unexpected burst of strength—even knowing it was useless—he spread his arms between the gap in the gates and bellowed, "Even if I die here today, you shall not enter the city!"

Sunlight speared through the clouds on the horizon, and a wave of golden light broke through the darkness like the raging tide. Eyes wide, Zhou Gui watched as those blades came rushing toward him. In that moment, the ear-piercing twang of a bow rang out, reverberating low over the ground and high through the air as an arrow streaked toward Lei Jingzhe's head, whipping up a gale in its wake.

The Conqueror Bow was firm and steady in the wind. Under the shocked gazes of everyone around him, Xiao Chiye maintained his draw stance, arm pulled perfectly back. A notch on the bone ring on his thumb shifted, revealing the eyes behind the bowstring, forbidding and unblinking.

110

SON OF A CONCUBINE

L EI JINGZHE REACTED on instinct. Unable to dodge, he brandished his broadsword to ward off the blow. The arrow struck the blade with a *clang*, the impact numbing Lei Jingzhe's entire arm. Making a quick decision, he spurred his horse past Zhou Gui in an attempt to lead his charging men into the city.

"Shut the gates—!" Zhou Gui was swept off his feet and thrown to the ground. Paying no heed to the sorry sight he presented, he lifted the hem of his robe and shouted at the city guard.

Pressing their shoulders to the city gates, the guards shouted in unison and heaved the gates toward the center in a rush to shut it. But Lei Jingzhe's horse was faster. His blade arrived with his steed, cutting down the men pushing at the gates. Just as he pressed his knees to his horse's flank to charge into the city, Lei Jingzhe felt a chill at the back of his neck and lurched forward. A split second later, the back of his horse sank as a youth of sixteen or seventeen sprang onto it.

Ding Tao slashed his palm, knifelike, toward Lei Jingzhe's neck. Lei Jingzhe turned aside to dodge and flung his sword arm back toward Ding Tao. Clinging to the saddle, the boy slid down the horse's hindquarters to evade the blade. His feet touched the ground, and he raced along with the madly galloping horse for a breathless moment before he hoisted himself up and clambered onto the horse again.

"Hey!" Ding Tao gripped Lei Jingzhe's arm; when the man turned, he raised his hand and flung a brushful of ink onto Lei Jingzhe's face.

For all Lei Jingzhe's plotting, he had never expected such a move from this heroic youth. The ink in his eyes blinded him, but he possessed a keen sense of hearing. He had sensed Ding Tao's movements instants before his attack, and now he unerringly found Ding Tao's collar and flung him off the horse.

Ding Tao crashed heavily on the ground and felt a jolt of pain go up his back. He cried out, but before he was done yelling, another horse came straight for him. Ding Tao hastily rolled to dodge its hooves, leaving his back exposed to Lei Jingzhe's eyes.

It was now or never!

Lei Jingzhe hurled his steel blade.

The bandit who had caught up with them had grabbed hold of Ding Tao's ankle, leaving him sprawled flat in the muddy water—he couldn't dodge. He braced both arms against the ground but was dragged back down again. The steel was singing right behind him. Face smeared with mud, Ding Tao gritted his teeth and raised his torso to shout at the city guards with his last breath, "Open the south gates! Reinforcements are here!"

Lei Jingzhe swore furiously at the same moment his steel blade was intercepted midair by a narrow sheath. The impact of the collision sent the blade spinning away, stabbing into the ground at a sharp angle.

Ding Tao turned back for a look, badly shaken. The bandit who had yanked his ankle was dead, his head several feet away from his body. Ding Tao scrambled to his feet, hopped several times to reach safety, then poked his head out from behind Shen Zechuan atop Snowcrest and said to Lei Jingzhe, "You're dead meat now!"

One side of the city gate had been shut. Lei Jingzhe had led his men to crowd the head of the bridle path and squeeze through, but now someone stood in their way. He recognized this man. The color of the robes peeking out from under his cloak, an unbroken white, was the same he'd worn every day since leaving Qudu. Lei Jingzhe pulled his horse back a few steps, but in the next instant, he brandished his whip and spurred his horse forward. Shen Zechuan swept off his cloak and tossed it to Ding Tao; beneath him, Snowcrest pawed at the air and charged. As the wind rose, Avalanche burst from its sheath.

In the moment before he was on Shen Zechuan, he reached for the broadsword of a nearby subordinate. The horses' screams were like the call of war horns. The two powers collided as the edges of their blades met and shrieked in unison, a sound so piercing listeners quaked with fear.

Lei Jingzhe had encountered an opponent unlike any other. The terrifying strength the bandit possessed seemed to have plunged into an icy lake. No matter how forceful and fierce he was in wielding his blade, it was neutralized by a force as gentle as water, dissolving to nothingness. The harder he fought, the more he felt Shen Zechuan was leading him by the nose. Gradually, he found himself trapped in a vicious cycle, unable to escape.

But Lei Jingzhe was a shrewd man. He held up his broadsword and pushed back against Shen Zechuan's blade, feinting a strike; yet in the next instant, he turned on his heel and fled.

The earlier opportunity had already slipped him by. He had already been thinking of retreating when Ding Tao shouted that the reinforcements had arrived; it was evident by now that Xiao Chiye had his men surrounded. If he didn't withdraw posthaste, and insisted on staying to attack the city instead, he would soon be besieged on all sides. At that point, he wouldn't be able to hold out for long.

"Retreat!" Lei Jingzhe called, turning his horse's head southeast.

Shen Zechuan didn't give chase. Xiao Chiye, still on the east side of the city, swung up onto his horse and led his men in hot pursuit of Lei Jingzhe. Lei Jingzhe whipped his horse's flank and tore off at great speed. Amid the jolts and bumps, he looked back and pointed at Xiao Chiye, then at Shen Zechuan, and bellowed, "We'll meet again!"

The bandits wore little armor, so they moved quickly. They had plenty of practice fleeing; the whole army dashed back to the mountain forest with no regard for formation. In the blink of an eye, they had fled helter-skelter, hollering to each other as they disappeared into the undergrowth.

Once again, Xiao Chiye lifted the Conqueror Bow. The sound of the string being drawn on that hundred-catty bow was bone-chilling. Xiao Chiye's eyes fixed on Lei Jingzhe's back. The bandit chief was about to dart into the trees, yet Xiao Chiye seemed to have no intention of releasing the arrow.

With a cry, Meng wheeled in the air and stooped at Lei Jingzhe with sharp talons, aiming for Lei Jingzhe's eyes. Overcome with dread, he was forced to slow down as he flung up an arm to cover his face and twisted to dodge the gyrfalcon's attack. At this instant, Xiao Chiye released the bowstring. The arrow burst forth like a golden ray shooting from the blazing sun, faster than eyes or wind could trace. In the moment it took for him to gasp for breath, the arrow was flying toward Lei Jingzhe's eyes.

In that perilous second between life and death, Lei Jingzhe grabbed the bandit riding beside him. Leaning back as far as he could, he exerted all his strength to shove the man in front of his own body.

The arrow pierced the chest of the bandit so hard the impact sent Lei Jingzhe tumbling off his horse. He rolled on the ground, clambered to his feet and tossed away the body, then mounted his panicked horse and fled.

Zhou Gui met Shen Zechuan at the foot of the city gates. Unsure whether he should laugh or cry, he wiped his face. "What timing! You came not a moment too soon!"

Shen Zechuan dismounted and helped Kong Ling up personally. "I'm sorry to have made Mister Chengfeng suffer," he said remorsefully.

In the face of his impeccable etiquette, Kong Ling waved a hand. He straightened and looked out at the Imperial Army. "The vice commander needn't take it to heart. I'm willing to suffer anything to take down these bandits."

"But when all's said and done, I put you in a terrible spot without warning you." Shen Zechuan turned his head to call out to Ding Tao, "Go get a clean robe for Mister Chengfeng, and call the physician over too."

For Cizhou's sake, Kong Ling wouldn't hold a grudge against Shen Zechuan. It would be asking too much for him to feel no resentment, but he understood there had been a reason for Shen Zechuan's actions, so he let Ding Tao support him as he bowed to Shen Zechuan. Xiao Chiye, who had also dismounted his horse, walked swiftly toward them.

"I never thought there was another man hiding behind Lei Changming." Kong Ling looked up into the forest covering the mountain slopes. He had just survived a great ordeal, yet he was still plagued by worry and anxiety. "This man is heartless and skilled in disguise, and cautious to boot. Now that we've let him escape, we're sure to face more trouble in the future."

"If His Lordship and the vice commander hadn't arrived when you did, Cizhou would not have escaped this calamity today." Zhou Gui shook out his sleeves and bent in a long, deep bow.

"It was only because Your Excellency showed no fear in the face of danger and bought us time." Xiao Chiye turned his head aside to wipe the dust off his face. "The Imperial Army still has troops lying in ambush near the public road south of Cizhou. We also left troops to stand guard at the encampment Lei Changming left behind in the east. The Imperial Army has him surrounded. He won't find it easy to escape."

"Thank goodness for Your Lordship's reinforcements from the south, or he wouldn't have retreated so quickly." Kong Ling sighed heavily. "Your Lordship is wise. We'll send someone to open the south gate right away."

Xiao Chiye laughed and looked at Shen Zechuan, but didn't say a word.

"There's no need for Your Excellency and the good sir to rush," Shen Zechuan explained, "The Imperial Army's reinforcements are still more than ten li away on the public road."

Stunned, Zhou Gui looked at Ding Tao. "But then—"

Ding Tao's back still ached. When he saw everyone looking at him, he nodded solemnly. "They're still on the public road, not headed this way. On our way here, Gongzi told me to yell that phrase if I was in dire straits; he said it was a magical weapon that would bring us victory. Sure enough, that bandit fled right after I yelled it!"

Kong Ling turned to Shen Zechuan and moved to bow again. "Vice Commander, please accept this bow of mine."

Lei Jingzhe had obviously attempted to lure the Imperial Army away and charge straight into Cizhou because he feared a head-on confrontation with Xiao Chiye. This man was sharp—he didn't know the extent of Xiao Chiye's capabilities, and he wasn't willing to stake his troops on a gamble. Shen Zechuan had been certain he would flee as soon as he thought he would have to face Xiao Chiye's reinforcements. If any of the adults among them had tried this ploy, Lei Jingzhe would have suspected some trick. Only the young Ding Tao, who yelled it at the most critical moment with his life hanging by a thread, could make Lei Jingzhe believe it without a doubt.

"My good lad." Zhou Gui felt such warmth toward Ding Tao then that he would have been happy to take the boy as his own son. He thumped Ding Tao on the back as he marveled, "You were so convincing even I believed it!"

Ding Tao's back was screaming, but he didn't dare complain. He had no choice but to nod vigorously through the pain.

Kong Ling walked into the city with them. "I initially thought he was a mere bandit who had taken to the wild, but he'd spoken eloquently throughout our journey here. Although he claimed to be from poor and humble origins, I don't think that's the case. He could control Lei Changming, yet he looks to be a generation younger. I've been trying to guess who he might be, but I can't figure it out."

"He let Lei Changming be the chief, yet he could freely deploy these bandit-soldiers. This man is someone who moves around Lei Changming year in and year out. From an outsider's perspective, he's likely a trusted subordinate or equivalent." Xiao Chiye took the reins to lead Snowcrest.

"Not only that," added Shen Zechuan, who had given it some thought last night. "Lei Changming was a headstrong character. He wouldn't willingly lower himself to become someone else's chess piece. That this man has such influence among the bandits shows

Lei Changming had no suspicions about him; he believed in him completely. It would be much easier for blood kin to achieve this level of trust. Mister Chengfeng, has Lei Changming any relatives?"

Kong Ling thought for a moment. "Lei Changming's family is poor. I heard he had a younger sister who married the commander of the Duanzhou Garrison Troops as a concubine. Later, when the Biansha Horsemen invaded, both of them were killed." He sucked in a breath. "Ah, but his younger sister did bear the commander a son."

"The son of a concubine from the Zhu Clan in Duanzhou," Zhou Gui picked up the thread. "I remember now. When I was still a tax circuit intendant during the reign of Yongyi, I followed my superior to participate in the child's one-month celebration banquet. Although the child was a son of common birth born to a concubine, the boy was the eldest son—the first son of Zhu Jie, the commander in Duanzhou at that time."

"If he's really that child, I'm not surprised he's so shrewd." Kong Ling turned to explain to Shen Zechuan and Xiao Chiye. "The prospect of the mother depends on her son, and both mother and son lived well in the Zhu manor for a time. But after Zhu Jie's principal wife gave birth to a lawful son, they were spurned by Zhu Jie."

Just as Shen Zechuan was about to ask the name of this boy, Zhou Gui stared blankly at Shen Zechuan's face and suddenly exclaimed, "Ah—the vice commander's mother was also present at that celebration banquet!"

MOTHER

THE MOMENT THE WORDS left Zhou Gui's mouth, he felt he had said too much.

Shen Zechuan's birth mother was a woman named Bai Cha, but she was not a lady of the Bai Clan from the Qidong Cejun Commandery. Her name, meaning *white tea*, came from her moniker in the pleasure house, where someone had once praised her thus: "pure as white jade, fine as porcelain; her delicate beauty needs no paint, she was the finest ware in the house." At the time, Duanzhou was still well-known in Zhongbo for its pleasure houses and evening entertainments, and it was there that the beauties of the land gathered. The literati vied to organize banquets, at which they critiqued these night-blooming flowers and came out with a ranking list; every season, they would deliberate and adjust the ranking of Duanzhou's beauties.

Bai Cha was the most celebrated flower during the reign of Yongyi, and for five years, no other beauty dethroned her from her spot. Each time she listened to the ranking of the courtesans through the screen, everyone in Duanzhou would turn out en masse. When she danced for the Prince of Jianxing, Shen Wei, teeming crowds would flood the street outside. Countless people climbed onto the ridges of roofs or stepped on the shoulders of their fellows, all to catch a glimpse of her slight figure through diaphanous layers of hanging drapes. Her beauty grew more and more legendary as singers fell over themselves to compose odes to the flowers. Even the Guangcheng Emperor, who resided deep in the imperial palace, had heard her name. Hoping to take advantage of the imperial inspection tour to catch a glimpse of this beauty in person, he had repeatedly asked Hai Liangyi, who was still the Deputy Grand Secretary of the Grand Secretariat at the time, when the tour would be scheduled.

Zhou Gui had indeed seen Bai Cha at the Zhu Clan's newborn son's one-month celebration banquet, though he had only managed a glimpse of that legendary beauty through a gap in the screen. Lei Changming's younger sister had come up in the same pleasure house as Bai Cha. Before the Duanzhou garrison commander had taken her as a concubine, she was an old hand, a veteran who coached the fledglings. Bai Cha had attended the banquet on behalf of the girls of the establishment.

All this had happened many years ago, and Zhou Gui's memory of it was rather a blur. But when he'd looked at Shen Zechuan earlier, he'd realized Shen Zechuan's side profile was reminiscent of the lovely Bai Cha's, and, in a moment of excitement, blurted it out.

With no change in expression, Shen Zechuan replied, "What a remarkable coincidence."

He was neither intrigued nor worked up. His impression of his birth mother was as of a blank piece of paper. Though he had heard hundreds of rumors about her, there was no trace of her in his mind worth remembering. In his life, the role of his mother belonged to his shiniang, Hua Pingting, just as the role of his father belonged only to his shifu, Ji Gang. It was for this reason he had gone to such great lengths to destroy Ji Lei for harming Hua Pingting. The two people who had given him his life were never actually involved in it. Bai Cha had died early and left nary a word for Shen Zechuan,

while Shen Wei had openly detested him. The Princess Consort of
Jianxing had ruled over all domestic affairs of the manor. Before the
age of seven, Shen Zechuan and Shen Wei had met a grand total of
seven times, during the family's yearly Spring Festival celebration.
They had never had a single exchange of words one might expect
between a father and son.

Shen Wei's loathing of him, however, had been evident none-
theless.

They weren't like father and son; they were mortal enemies born
to abhor one another. Shen Zechuan's life in the Prince of Jianxing's
manor in Dunzhou had been confined to a corner of an eave in the
inner courtyard; he couldn't leave without permission. His daily
leisure consisted of sitting on the veranda and counting the white
clouds that drifted past that small corner of the blue sky. By the time
he was seven, he could recognize many words, but he'd learned all of
them on the sly, by crawling through the dog hole in the courtyard
month after month to eavesdrop under the windows of the school
Shen Zhouji and his other elder brothers attended.

In those years, the power struggle between his elder brothers
who had come of age had been intense. Even his father's concubines
schemed against one another. The entire inner courtyard was in
pandemonium, to the point that Shen Wei was reluctant to spend
any time at home. He kept a mistress outside the manor and lived
with her for several months out of the year, turning a blind eye to the
strife under his own roof. Later, Shen Zhouji, a lawful son born to
the principal wife, emerged victorious and sent all his common-born
brothers of age away to the various prefectures to take up respectable
sinecures. Yet the princess consort worried even the common sons
who were still children would cause trouble in the future. She elected
to send them away, too, ostensibly to complete their education with

a teacher she'd hired in Shen Wei's ancestral home in Chazhou. In truth, this move eliminated the possibility that any son of a concubine could compete with her own son for power again.

Shen Zechuan was the only son whom Shen Wei personally instructed be sent to the old manor in Duanzhou. The prince refused to hire a teacher or allow his son to attend school. He was originally cared for by a deaf and mute old woman with poor eyesight, but upon reaching the old manor, the job was handed over to a maidservant his mother had left there. The woman was greedy for money. Every month, she pocketed the majority of the silver meant for Shen Zechuan's care and fed Shen Zechuan out of the meager share that remained. Three meals a day gradually became two, before eventually becoming only one—and all of them were cold leftovers.

He still felt gnawing hunger when he thought of it. He loosened his grip on Avalanche and said, "Ding Tao, help Mister Chengfeng inside for a change of clothes. Ce'an and I will play host today and invite both gentlemen to a meal. Let's save our conversation for the feast."

Zhou Gui was no smooth talker. Kong Ling, afraid the prefect might say something else to incur Shen Zechuan's displeasure, grabbed Zhou Gui by the arm and pulled him away, letting Zhou Gui support him into the city.

Kong Ling had finished changing, but Zhou Gui was still anxiously pacing in circles. "Say, why did I have to go and mention that?"

"Really," Kong Ling chided, "of all the things to bring up. Doesn't this make it seem like you suspect him of being involved with those ruffians? Fortunately they aren't suspicious by nature, or we would really be in a bind."

"It was a slip of the tongue. I'll have to apologize to the vice commander at the feast later." Zhou Gui sighed. "He came to help Cizhou out of a fix. I can't squander his goodwill like this."

"Don't go out of your way to bring it up." Kong Ling sat and thought for a moment. "If Shen Zechuan were a narrow-minded person, he wouldn't have come. If you dwell on it and insist on apologizing, it'll seem like we're bothered about it. Besides, he might really not care. It's not his mother but Shen Wei who's abominable."

It wouldn't do to let Shen Zechuan and Xiao Chiye wait for long, so they merely tidied themselves before setting off for the feast.

Despite calling it a feast, it was a rather simple lunch. Everyone had been rushing about last night, culminating in the confrontation with the bandits at the city gate at dawn. Mindful of Kong Ling's age, Shen Zechuan didn't keep them for idle conversation. Once they finished their meals, he suggested Kong Ling head back early to rest.

Xiao Chiye had to make arrangements for the Imperial Army's patrol and dispatch someone to the bandits' old camp to contact Tantai Hu. It was nearly dusk by the time he was done busying about. After a search, he found Shen Zechuan standing atop the city walls.

"There's still work to be done after tonight." Xiao Chiye climbed up to stand beside him on the battlements. "I thought you were resting inside."

"I slept for an hour." Shen Zechuan turned back to gaze at Xiao Chiye. "With everything that's on my mind, I won't be able to sleep even if I try."

Xiao Chiye tilted his head and patted Meng, who was perched on his shoulder, to tell him to go play by himself. He had never found the time to change his clothes and was still coated in dust and dirt as he stood beside Shen Zechuan. "What can you see from here?"

Shen Zechuan gazed out at the undulating terrain of the forest. The impending darkness ready to blanket the sky was still huddled in the shade of the trees, while a warm, bloody sunset shone across half the horizon. Meng soared overhead like a pebble tumbling amid a sea of rosy silk-tree flowers, stirring up waves of clouds.

"The future," Shen Zechuan answered calmly. "In the future, Cizhou will be the node that connects Libei's trade routes. We'll establish a trail in the southwest that leads straight to Hezhou, and it'll end at the ports of the waterways there. That way, going from the wagons to the boats, all trade goods can arrive at the Port of Yongyi in half a month. The Xi Clan's fleets will open up new trading opportunities, exporting local specialties and importing exotic rarities. The silver vaults that were cleaned out can one day be filled again. I don't begrudge that money, wherever it's gone; we'll have even more in the future. Cizhou sits behind Dunzhou and Duanzhou, the gates of Zhongbo. If these two prefectures want access to grain and commodities in the future, they will have to live in harmony with Cizhou."

"You'll need to strengthen your defenses after we reclaim Dunzhou and Duanzhou. The rebuilding of the garrison troops is the first priority. You'll have to be careful in your choices. Those whom you can trust and who are up to the task can attend to garrison duties, but the capable ones might not necessarily be willing to submit to another's lead. When the time comes..." Xiao Chiye turned around and pointed in the direction of Libei. "I'll build armored cavalry barracks on the southeast side of the Northeast Provisions Trail. If anyone dares mess around, just whistle and I'll lead my men right over."

Shen Zechuan laughed and said softly, "Cizhou is too important to you and me. We can't afford to cede this city to anyone else.

Zhou Gui is a good official, but he isn't suited to governing an entire prefecture. He can't save anyone with zeal alone, not when he's surrounded by a pack of wolves on all sides."

"We're short people." Xiao Chiye had been mulling this over since he'd left Lei Changming's camp. If Cizhou was to be their starting point, then they would be stretched increasingly thin as their territory expanded. They were also constrained by a lack of capable, trustworthy men to administer official affairs. If Qiao Tianya or Chen Yang had been here, they would doubtless have prevented the worst of Cizhou's current predicament. Then again, amid so many moving pieces, it was impossible to say how any one move might unbalance the board and give away their position prematurely.

"Zhou Gui is suited to be the tax circuit intendant of the six prefectures. His love for the people is his guiding light. A man like that would never allow officials and merchants to collude on his watch. But he's also too benevolent. He has neither the will nor the gall to enforce severe punishments—that's why he can't suppress the local bandits. It's precisely because Kong Ling understands this feature of Zhou Gui's character that he came to help him remove the obstacles in his path and handle matters more efficiently." Shen Zechuan spoke thoughtfully. "If the two of them can continue to work as one, there's much they can achieve in the future."

"And Lei Jingzhe," Xiao Chiye asked. "What do you think of him?"

"This man will no doubt fail." Shen Zechuan took a few steps forward along the battlements. "I thought he was a man to be reckoned with when we left the camp, but after seeing him this morning, I've changed my mind."

"As expected, you and I are of the same mind." The light was beginning to fade; Xiao Chiye stepped up next to Shen Zechuan and kept pace with him. "Lei Changming was his uncle by blood.

In order to get a head start in Cizhou, he abandoned Lei Changming at the encampment to die. After a move like that, he may not be able to win over his men—not to mention when he dodged my arrow, he used his own man as a shield. He's shrewd all right, but not benevolent. If he wants to pledge allegiance to Qudu and obtain an official position, he'll have to turn the bandits under his command into a regular army. He has yet to understand that being a bandit is different from being a general. One cannot accumulate prestige and trust with brutality alone. And he changes his orders over and over on the battlefield. A general does not retract an order he has given; he must be impartial in meting out reward and punishment; and he must remain steadfast and unwavering—only then is he able to command his soldiers.[9] Lei Jingzhe is simply not cut out to lead an army."

"I worry more about Qi Zhuyin." Shen Zechuan hesitated before the stairs. "The marriage alliance between Qidong and the Hua Clan is as good as sealed. Now that Libei has rebelled, Qidong is the last crutch Qudu has left to rely on. No doubt Qi Zhuyin will receive a promotion and noble rank in the coming days. The empress dowager already had great admiration for her to begin with. Once her title is conferred, she'll deploy troops north. No matter what, I must turn Cizhou into an impregnable fortress before Qi Zhuyin arrives."

"The grand marshal is a tough opponent. Dage is the heavy cavalry, Lu Guangbai is the guerrilla, and Qi Zhuyin is cavalry and infantry combined. She's resided in the Cangjun Commandery for a long time. She doesn't deploy troops rashly, but when she does, she prefers to launch sudden assaults to storm the enemy. When she penetrated deep into the desert to save Qi Shiyu, she was like a sudden downpour that overwhelmed her opponents. She's known to cut her foes down with a single blow to strike terror into the

---

9   From The Three Strategies of Huang Shigong, *a classic treatise on military strategy.*

enemies' hearts. When they face her in battle, they quiver in fear."
Xiao Chiye mulled over it for a moment. "I want to fight her."

Shen Zechuan looked at him.

"It's not like I want to fight her right now." Xiao Chiye patted his
shoulder. "Look at you, glaring at me so fiercely."

Shen Zechuan took a step down the stairs. As if it had just
occurred to him, he looked back and asked, "Where's my fan?"

Xiao Chiye pinched Shen Zechuan's chin, then cleared three
steps in one stride and crouched down before him to offer his back.
"Come on up and I'll give it to you."

CHASING THE STARS

T HE GLOW of the setting sun had faded, leaving a scattering
of stars that adorned the sky and peeked through the
branches. The Imperial Army's patrol squad made their
rounds through Cizhou's streets and alleys. With Shen Zechuan on
his back, Xiao Chiye walked along the street shrouded in a cloak
of soft shadow. It was a warm summer night, and Xiao Chiye had
unfastened the high collar of his short jacket as he strolled.

Shen Zechuan lifted his chin and rested it atop Xiao Chiye's
head. Xiao Chiye was too tall, exposing Shen Zechuan's shoulders
to the moonlight. He had only to turn his head, and he would be
able to look over the walls into other people's courtyards.

"I'll head for Lei Changming's old encampment tomorrow morning and cut off Lei Jingzhe's escape route from the east. He won't dare
head north, and there are still troops lying in ambush to the south.
I'll be back in three days at the latest." Shifting Shen Zechuan on his
back, Xiao Chiye said, "It's been a long time since we had any news
of Qudu. We need to send someone to find out what's going on as
soon as possible. Until then, we can't guess Qi Zhuyin's movements."

"The marriage between Hua and Qi has been delayed again and
again. Qudu needs Qidong; the empress dowager won't let Qi Shiyu
wait any longer." Shen Zechuan considered. "The wedding won't be
delayed past the eighth month."

"Hua Xiangyi can get married all she wants," Xiao Chiye said. "As long as she produces no heir, Qi Zhuyin will have the final say in Qidong. She's going there to be a second principal wife, even if she's younger than Qi Zhuyin. Any son she bears will be Qi Shiyu's lawful son. Once Qi Shiyu croaks, mother and son will become the obstacle that stands in the way of Qi Zhuyin's uncontested grip on military power."

"The marshal's prestige among her troops cannot be underestimated. Will she really fear a lawful brother so much younger than herself?" Shen Zechuan wondered. "If she chooses peace and lives in harmony with Hua Xiangyi, she could save herself a lot of trouble."

"It hasn't been easy for Qi Zhuyin to be conferred a title. Just look at the setbacks she faced when she took over the five commanderies of Qidong. Qudu's not the only one deeply uneasy because of her gender; even the internal military administration officials of Qidong have been muttering to themselves." At this point, Xiao Chiye paused. "Besides, I handed Qi Zhuyin the genealogy records I got someone to copy quite a while ago. Knowing what she knows, she'll never let Hua Xiangyi give birth to a child."

As long as Hua Xiangyi's standing in Qidong remained uncertain, the empress dowager couldn't turn the Qidong Garrison Troops into her own personal force. Yet all of this was dependent on the premise that Qudu still had no real emperor. If Qudu were to crown a new Son of Heaven before winter, then Qi Zhuyin would be back under the throne's command and on a path to confront Libei.

"I'm worried about Lu Guangbai." Xiao Chiye knit his brows faintly. "At the end of autumn, the Biansha Horsemen will cross the border to plunder food. Their horses will be plump and well-fed then, so they'll take risks in order to better survive the winter. The Bianjun Commandery relies on the imperial court for their military provisions. The Twelve Tribes of Biansha know how poor Bianjun is, and they know the location of their granary. It's close to the camps, so they go after Lu Guangbai every time. Qidong's military provisions were halved this year. He's already struggling to survive, much less defend the border. Me leaving Qudu will have only made things worse for him."

This was something not even Shen Zechuan could help with. If Bianjun wasn't so far east, and if Tianfei Watchtower and Suotian Pass weren't stationed on either side, perhaps they could have sent a message to Ge Qingqing, who was still in Juexi's Port of Yongyi. He might get Xi Dan to think of ways to purchase enough grain from Juexi, then route it to Qidong through Hezhou, to mitigate Lu Guangbai's immediate crisis. But Cangjun stood between Hezhou and Bianjun. With obstacles left and right, there was no other passage unless they transported the grains right under Qi Zhuyin's nose. And Qidong wasn't like sheltered Juexi; Qi Zhuyin had established layers upon layers of impenetrable defenses there. Passing through it without raising any alarms was simply an impossible task.

Bianjun was the night watchman standing at the edge of a cliff, facing a desperate and hopeless situation.

Finding that the atmosphere had gotten heavy, Xiao Chiye turned a circle with Shen Zechuan on his back. "Our first priority now is to dispatch Lei Jingzhe. Once we secure Zhongbo, it'll be easier to help Bianjun. We can travel there directly if we can cross Tianfei Watchtower. Don't I reek of sweat? Why are you still sniffing me?"

Shen Zechuan wiped at the sweat on the side of Xiao Chiye's neck with his fingers, then snuggled against his cheek. "Start running."

Hitching him up on his back, Xiao Chiye answered, "Too tired to run."

"If Er-gongzi can't do it," Shen Zechuan pinched Xiao Chiye's cheek and teased, "I'll take the lead tonight."

Xiao Chiye pretended to put him down. "Sure. Hop off. Er-gongzi will see how you plan to carry me back from here."

Shen Zechuan tightened his arms around his neck. As he lifted his legs higher along Xiao Chiye's ribs, he said with mock solemnity, "Why get so fired up over such a small thing? Go on, I believe in you."

Xiao Chiye hoisted him up again.

Clinging to his back, Shen Zechuan edged his fingertips down along the lapels of his jacket, peeling them apart as he whispered into his ear, "What can't Er-lang do? Er-lang can do anything."

Xiao Chiye turned his head, surprisingly calm as he asked, "Where to?"

"To—"

Xiao Chiye strode forward with his long legs and broke into a run. Carrying Shen Zechuan on his back, he ran past the cover of the trees, stepping on summer moonlight as he darted into an alley where the lamps had been extinguished. The patrol squad came and went without noticing them. Xiao Chiye easily leapt over the small steps, the dappled shadows of leaves falling upon his hair. There was a clatter as their silhouettes collided with the starlight on the ground and broke it to pieces, like the free and reckless wind gusting across heaven and earth.

The young servant boy guarding the door to their small courtyard yawned. When he heard the knock, he thought the marquis and vice commander had returned. Clothes gathered around him and lantern in hand, he went to open the door with a smile but found the street empty.

"A ghost?" the boy blurted softly. He poked his head out but didn't see anyone to his left or right; confounded, he trotted quickly back to his room with his outer robe wrapped tightly around him.

The corridor was dark without the lantern light. Shen Zechuan's footsteps were in such disarray he almost tripped Xiao Chiye. Xiao Chiye pressed Shen Zechuan against the door. As they kissed, he pulled at the ribbon Shen Zechuan used to secure his hair. The kisses left Shen Zechuan gasping for breath, and he reached behind him to feel for the lock.

"No key." Xiao Chiye lifted Shen Zechuan against him slightly. His face pressed in close, and he looked hungrily at Shen Zechuan. "We can't get in."

Shen Zechuan's heels slid down along the back of Xiao Chiye's waist, but he raised his hand and pressed a palm against Xiao Chiye's approaching lips to stop them in place. He whispered, his breath hot in Xiao Chiye's ear, "Well, I suppose if we can't get inside, *you* can't get inside."

Xiao Chiye pried Shen Zechuan's lips apart and lowered his head to swallow that teasing tongue. All of last night's exhaustion from their manic journey seemed to have been swept clean. Shen Zechuan swallowed thickly; the door behind him creaked every time Xiao Chiye rocked against him. Trying to dampen the sound, he pulled Xiao Chiye closer until there was no room for breath between them.

"Let's build a home." Grinding against Shen Zechuan's soft flesh, Xiao Chiye's throat tightened as he spoke between escaped sighs. "Here. Anywhere."

Shen Zechuan was sweating as he raised his head, his vision gone misty with tears. He made not a sound. They hadn't satisfied each other for a long time, and the stimulation was so intense he

was trembling slightly. Just a few moments, and he was already on the cliff's edge. His chest heaved violently, and he clutched at the clothes on Xiao Chiye's shoulder, crumpling his robes. It was only after a turn that he managed under his breath, "No. Don't. I-inside the room."

But Xiao Chiye took this *no* as a reply to his question and thrust forward, almost making Shen Zechuan cry out on instinct.

"What can't Er-lang do?" Xiao Chiye held Shen Zechuan firmly in his arms and lifted Shen Zechuan's chin so they were eye to eye. Ruthless and wicked, he said, "Er-lang can do anything."

The corners of Shen Zechuan's eyes quickly reddened, and even his partially exposed neck had flushed pink. He opened his mouth several times in an attempt to speak, but only wordless sounds escaped. Sweat drenched his clothes, and Shen Zechuan gradually grew breathless. He pressed his forehead to Xiao Chiye's chest, dizzy, as the waves of ecstasy crashed over him. It hadn't been an hour, yet he'd already surrendered twice.

By the time Xiao Chiye had finished his bath, Shen Zechuan was asleep. Seeing the first glimmer of dawn outside the window, he didn't rest; he merely drank a cup of strong tea and crouched by the bedside to watch Shen Zechuan slumber.

He fell asleep after all.

Xiao Chiye raised his hand to caress Shen Zechuan's cheek.

Once he returned to Libei, he would have to invite the Venerable Master Yideng here. After turning it over in his mind these past weeks, he'd concluded that Shen Zechuan's frequent illnesses— whether the cold or the pox—definitely had something to do with the medicine he'd taken in his youth.

Too thin.

Xiao Chiye gazed down at Shen Zechuan in the soft silence of their room. He had also found Shen Zechuan thin when they were in Qudu, but he had been much better than now. Shen Zechuan's bout of illness after Qi Huilian's death had come and gone quickly, but he had yet to be fed back to health. There had been nothing wholesome for him the entire journey here. Xiao Chiye held him, watched him, protected his growing reliance on him in every way he could.

Shen Wei and Bai Cha didn't matter.

Xiao Chiye lowered his head and pressed his cheek to Shen Zechuan's as he stared with deep hostility at the sunlight attempting to creep across the sheets toward Shen Zechuan.

Shen Lanzhou belonged to him—Xiao Ce'an.

When Xiao Chiye spurred his horse out of the city, Zhou Gui and Kong Ling came to see him off. Pulling at the reins, he said, "I'll return in three days, regardless of success or failure. The Imperial Army stationed here will stay put for now. The instant they sniff out Lei Jingzhe's trail, send someone to inform me. Although Cizhou's city walls are old and worn, you can't just leave them be. Lanzhou will explain some specific arrangements for reinforcing them to you both later."

"Be assured, Your Lordship," Zhou Gui said. "All our men in Cizhou will heed the vice commander's advice."

"As for the reconstruction of Cizhou's garrison troops..." Xiao Chiye paused. "I won't meddle in it. These are military affairs Lanzhou will deliberate over with both of you. The Imperial Army is only standing in as manpower on patrols; beyond this, I'd be overstepping. If there are any issues, please talk them over with Lanzhou. I'm not at liberty to decide."

The warm buzz that had begun in Kong Ling's heart went cold again. They had originally feared Xiao Chiye would use the patrols he'd volunteered as an excuse to interfere with the reconstruction of Cizhou's garrison troops. He was briefly relieved to hear Xiao Chiye reject the idea, but worry overtook him immediately after. Xiao Chiye didn't want Cizhou's military power. He wouldn't accept Cizhou's remuneration, nor would he take Cizhou's grain. In that case, why had he gone to the trouble of running all over after Lei Jingzhe? Why not head north and return home to live a free and unfettered life?

Kong Ling deliberated over his response, but before he could speak, Xiao Chiye continued, "Since I've agreed to suppress the bandits for you gentlemen, I'll not renege on my promise. Lord Zhou is willing to risk his head to let the Imperial Army pass through Cizhou, so naturally I must reciprocate his friendly sentiment. What's more, for the past few days, the Imperial Army's rations have been borne by the common folks of Cizhou. We have eaten your rice, so we will surely fight your battles."

Zhou Gui bowed in farewell. "Then we shall wait here for Your Lordship to return in triumph."

"There's another matter I want to discuss with you while we're here." Xiao Chiye's horse took a few restless steps as its rider looked at Zhou Gui and Kong Ling. "I have no intention of taking a concubine in this life. While I'm residing in Lord Zhou's manor, there's no need to send anyone else to my room. Man or woman—I don't want any of them. We've got plenty on our plates, and I don't have the energy to beat around the bush, so I'm taking the opportunity to make this clear to both of you today."

Kong Ling knew he was referring to the maidservant last time and couldn't help his look of embarrassment. Whether he smiled or tried to reply, there was no appropriate response.

CHASING THE STARS   397

"Lanzhou lived in Zhongbo for a long time, and it's inevitable people will bring up old affairs. But he, Shen Zechuan"—Xiao Chiye raised the horsewhip and pointed in the direction of Qudu—"is the student of Qi Huilian, the grand mentor of the crown prince in the Eastern Palace; the last disciple of Ji Gang of Duanzhou; the former northern judge and vice commander of the Embroidered Uniform Guard, and the head of household of my—Xiao Ce'an's—future residence. As for any other names, he has nothing to do with them."

This time, it was Zhou Gui who didn't know how to answer. He wasn't a man adept at perfunctory words to begin with, and Xiao Chiye's declaration had rendered him dumbstruck. His mouth opened and closed. "Uh. Uh..."

Xiao Chiye turned his horse and rode away with his gyrfalcon wheeling above him.

It was a long moment before Zhou Gui returned to his senses. Clutching his sleeves, he asked Kong Ling, "Wh-what did His Lordship mean by this? Then the Prince of Libei—"

Kong Ling calmly wiped his sweat. "He has laid his cards out plainly on the table. He doesn't give a hoot about the troops in Cizhou, but whatever you do," he warned, "don't mention Shen Wei or Bai Cha again."

THE STORY CONTINUES IN
Ballad of Sword and Wine
VOLUME 4

CHARACTER
&
NAME
GUIDE

CHARACTERS

MAIN CHARACTERS

Shen Zechuan
沈泽川 SURNAME SHEN; GIVEN NAME ZECHUAN, "TO NOURISH THE RIVERS"

COURTESY NAME: Lanzhou (兰舟 / orchid; boat)

TITLE: Vice Commander of the Embroidered Uniform Guard

WEAPON: Avalanche (仰山雪 / Yang Shan Xue): A straight, single-edged saber longer than normal swords. It used to belong to Ji Gang's adoptive father.

The eighth son of common birth to Shen Wei, the Prince of Jianxing. Due to his father's alleged collusion with the enemy during the invasion of Zhongbo that led to the slaughter of thirty thousand soldiers in the Chashi Sinkhole, he was sentenced to imprisonment and was obligated to pay his father's debt as the last surviving member of the Shen Clan.

Xiao Chiye
萧驰野 SURNAME XIAO; GIVEN NAME CHIYE, "TO RIDE ACROSS THE WILD"

COURTESY NAME: Ce'an (策安 / spur; peace)

TITLE: Supreme Commander of the Imperial Army and Marquis of Dingdu

WEAPON: Wolfsfang (狼戾 / Langli): A single-edged executioner's blade forged by the best craftsman in Qidong.

The second and youngest son of lawful birth to Xiao Fangxu, the Prince of Libei. Sometimes called Xiao Er, or Second Young Master Xiao.

QUDU

CEN YU 岑愈: Courtesy name Xunyi. The Left Censor-in-Chief of the Chief Surveillance Bureau.

CHEN YANG 晨阳 ("MORNING SUN"): Leader of Xiao Chiye's guards.

DING TAO 丁桃: Young guard to Xiao Chiye. He carries a little notebook everywhere he goes.

FEI SHENG 费盛 ("FLOURISHING"): Son of common birth in the Fei Clan. An assistant commander in the Embroidered Uniform Guard.

FEI SHI 费适: Lawful son of Fei Kun, the Helian Marquis.

FENGQUAN 风泉: A junior eunuch, Pan Rugui's "grand-godson" and Mu Ru's younger brother. Promoted to Director of the Seal at the Directorate of Ceremonial Affairs.

FU LINYE 傅林叶: The Right Censor-in-Chief of the Chief Surveillance Bureau.

FUMAN 福满: A eunuch of the inner palace.

GE QINGQING 葛青青: Judge of the Embroidered Uniform Guard who served under Ji Gang when the latter was still the vice commander.

GU JIN 骨津: Guard to Xiao Chiye. He has excellent hearing.

HAI LIANGYI 海良宜 ("VIRTUOUS AND PROPER"): Courtesy name Renshi. Deputy Grand Secretary of the Grand Secretariat and teacher to Yao Wenyu.

HAN CHENG 韩丞: Chief Commander of the Embroidered Uniform Guard after Ji Lei's death.

HAN JIN 韩靳: Military Commissioner of the Eight Great Battalions.

HUA HEWEI 花鹤娓: The empress dowager, widow of the Guangcheng Emperor.

HUA XIANGYI 花香漪 ("RIPPLES OF FRAGRANCE"): The third lady of the Hua Clan, adored niece of the empress dowager. Betrothed to Qi Shiyu.

JI GANG 纪纲: Shen Zechuan's shifu. Once the vice commander of the Embroidered Uniform Guard, he is one of the three adopted sons of Ji Wufan, the former chief commander of the Embroidered Uniform Guard.

KONG QIU 孔湫: Courtesy name Boran. Minister of Justice.

LI JIANHENG 李建恒: The Tianchen Emperor. As the final survivor of the Li Clan, he ascended the throne after the death of the Xiande Emperor.

LI JIANYUN 李建云: The Xiande Emperor. Son of the Guangcheng Emperor and elder brother to Li Jianheng.

LIANG CUISHAN 梁淮山: A clerk in the Ministry of Revenue. After his audits of the Imperial Army's accounts, he received a series of promotions that led him to work directly under Pan Lin.

MU RU 慕如: Imperial Concubine Mu. The daughter of a common family and sister to Fengquan. Adored by Li Jianheng, she was officially appointed as an imperial concubine after his ascension.

PAN LIN 潘蔺: Courtesy name Chengzhi. Vice Minister of the Ministry of Revenue and lawful son of Pan Xiangjie.

PAN XIANGJIE 潘祥杰: Minister of Works. Head of the Pan Clan of the Eight Great Clans.

QI HUILIAN 齐惠连: Grand mentor to the deceased Crown Prince of Yongyi, and later, Shen Zechuan's teacher.

QIAO TIANYA 乔天涯: Previously named Qiao Songyue. The former judge of the Embroidered Uniform Guard, he now takes Shen Zechuan as his master.

TANTAI HU 澹台虎 ("TIGER"): Member of the Imperial Army.

WEI HUAIGU 魏怀古: Minister of Revenue.

WEI HUAIXING 魏怀兴: Vice Minister of the Court of Judicial Review.

XI DAN 奚丹: Steward of the Xi Clan.

XI HONGXUAN 奚鸿轩: Secretary of the Bureau of Evaluations in the Ministry of Personnel. Xi Gu'an's brother and the second son of lawful birth in the Xi Clan.

XUE XIUYI 薛修易: Xue Xiuzhuo's elder brother of lawful birth.

XUE XIUZHUO 薛修卓: Courtesy name Yanqing. Assistant Minister in the Court of Judicial Review. A capable young official and son of common birth in the Xue Clan.

YAO WENYU 姚温玉 ("GENTLE JADE"): Courtesy name Yuanzhuo. Hai Liangyi's only acknowledged pupil, said to be an extraordinary talent.

YU XIAOZAI 余小再: Courtesy name Youjing. Investigating Censor in the Chief Surveillance Bureau.

JUEXI

JIANG QINGSHAN 江青山 ("GREEN HILLS"): Provincial Administration Commissioner of Juexi.

YANG CHENG 杨诚: Assistant Administration Commissioner of Juexi.

LIBEI

XIAO FANGXU 萧方旭 ("RISING SUN"): Prince of Libei. Father to Xiao Chiye and Xiao Jiming, and one of the past Four Great Generals of the empire of Zhou.

XIAO JIMING 萧既明 ("APPROACHING BRIGHTNESS"): Heir of Libei and commander of the Libei Armored Cavalry. Xiao Chiye's elder brother; he is married to Lu Yizhi, Lu Guangbai's sister. One of the current Four Great Generals, he's known as "Iron Horse on River Ice."

XIAO XUN 萧洵: Grandson-Heir of Libei. Lawful son of Xiao Jiming and Lu Yizhi.

LU YIZHI 陆亦栀: Heir Consort of Libei. Xiao Jiming's wife and Lu Guangbai's sister.

ZHAO HUI 朝晖 ("MORNING SUN"): Xiao Jiming's dependable deputy general.

ZUO QIANQIU 左千秋: Xiao Chiye's shifu and one of the current Four Great Generals, he's known as "Thunder on Jade Terraces."

QIDONG

QI ZHUYIN 戚竹音 ("SOUND OF BAMBOO"): Grand marshal of the Qidong Garrison Troops. One of the current Four Great Generals, Qi Zhuyin is known as "Windstorm through the Scorching Plains" and commands all five garrisons in the commanderies of Qidong.

QI SHIYU 戚时雨 ("TIMELY RAIN"): Qi Zhuyin's father and one of the past Four Great Generals of the empire of Zhou.

LU GUANGBAI 陆广白 ("EMPTY EXPANSE"): Commanding general of the Bianjun Commandery in Qidong. Brother to Lu Yizhi and one of the current Four Great Generals, known as "Beacon-Smoke and Rising Sand."

LU PINGYAN 陆平烟 ("PACIFY BEACON SMOKE"): Lu Guangbai's father and one of the past Four Great Generals of the Zhou empire.

ZHONGBO

KONG LING 孔岭: Courtesy name Chengfeng. Chief advisor to Zhou Gui, prefect of Cizhou.

LEI CHANGMING 雷常鸣: A bandit chief in Zhongbo. His base is Mount Luo.

LEI JINGZHE 雷惊蛰: A bandit of Mount Luo. The eldest common son of Lei Changming's sister and Zhu Jie, the commander of

Duanzhou during the reign of Yongyi.

ZHOU GUI 周桂: Prefect of Cizhou.

PAST

BAI CHA 白茶 ("WHITE TEA"): Shen Zechuan's mother. A dancer from Duanzhou.

SHEN WEI 沈卫 ("DEFENSE"): Prince of Jianxing and Shen Zechuan's father. Found guilty of colluding with the Biansha Horsemen to invade Zhongbo, he allegedly self-immolated to evade justice.

JI MU 纪暮: The only son of Ji Gang and Hua Pingting, and Shen Zechuan's adoptive elder brother.

HUA PINGTING 花婷婷: Wife of Ji Gang and mother of Ji Mu; Shen Zechuan's shiniang. She was born in the Hua Clan.

INSTITUTIONS

The Embroidered Uniform Guard 锦衣卫

The Embroidered Uniform Guard, sometimes referred to as the Scarlet Cavalry, are the elite bodyguards who report directly to the emperor. They are a non-military secret police and investigative force. The Embroidered Uniform Guard is organized into the Twelve Offices, which include the Carriage Office, Umbrella Office, Elephant-Training Office, and Horse-Training Office, among others. The Xiuchun saber, a single-edged blade, is their signature weapon.

The Imperial Army 禁军

The Imperial Army of Qudu was once the Imperial Guard of the eight cities and the impregnable fortress of the imperial palace in Qudu. However, with the rise to power of the Eight Great Battalions, their duties were reduced significantly, and the Imperial Army became a dumping ground for sons from old military households. They are one of the two major military powers in Qudu.

The Eight Great Battalions 八大营

Led by a member of the Eight Great Clans, the Eight Great Battalions are one of the two major military powers in Qudu, tasked with patrolling and defending Qudu against external forces. Responsible for defending Qudu, the capital city and heart of the Zhou empire, the Eight Great Battalions hold the empire's life in their hands.

The Eight Great Clans 八大家

The Eight Great Clans originated from the Eight Cities of Qudu. One clan holds sway in each city—the Xue Clan of Quancheng, Pan Clan of Dancheng, Xi Clan of Chuncheng, Fei Clan of Chuancheng, Hua Clan of Dicheng, Yao Clan of Jincheng, Han Clan of Wucheng, and Wei Clan of Cuocheng.

The Grand Secretariat 内阁

The most distinguished and influential body in the central government, it is staffed with Grand Secretaries who are responsible for handling the emperor's paperwork, recommending decisions in response to memorials received from the officials, and drafting and issuing imperial pronouncements.

The Six Ministries 六部

The Six Ministries comprise the primary administrative structure of the Zhou empire's central government and include the Ministry of Works, Ministry of Justice, Ministry of Personnel, Ministry of Rites, Ministry of Revenue, and Ministry of War. Coordinated by the Grand Secretary of the Grand Secretariat, the heads of these ministries report directly to the emperor.

The Six Offices of Scrutiny is an independent agency set up to inspect and supervise the Six Ministries. It includes the Office of Scrutiny for Revenue.

Chief Surveillance Bureau 都察院

Also known as the Censorate. One of the major agencies of the central government, responsible for maintaining disciplinary surveillance, auditing fiscal accounts, checking judicial records, carrying out inspections, impeaching officials for misconduct, recommending new policies and changes in old policies, and other duties involved in regulating government actions.

The Court of Judicial Review 大理寺

An important central government agency responsible for reviewing reports of judicial proceedings, making recommendations for retrials, and participating in important judicial proceedings at court alongside the Chief Surveillance Bureau and the Ministry of Justice, which are collectively known as the Three Judicial Offices.

The Libei Armored Cavalry 离北铁骑

The Libei Armored Cavalry is a heavy cavalry established by Xiao Fangxu to counter external foes at the northern front during the Yongyi era, when the Biansha Horsemen repeatedly assaulted Luoxia Pass. Currently commanded by Xiao Jiming, the Heir of Libei.

The Qidong Garrison Troops 启东守备军

Under the command of Qi Zhuyin, the Qidong Commandery Garrison Troops are stationed across five commanderies. They watch over the Qidong territories in the southern regions of the Zhou empire, which are led by the Qi Clan.

The Biansha Horsemen 边沙骑兵

The Biansha Horsemen are the aggressor forces against the empire of Zhou. The story begins with the aftermath of the war, where the Biansha Horsemen ravaged the six prefectures of Zhongbo and left them piled high with bodies. Also referred to in derogatory form as the "Biansha baldies."

The Twenty-Four Yamen 二十四衙门

Collectively refers to the Twelve Directorates, Four Offices, and Eight Services under which eunuchs serve.

NAMES GUIDE

NAMES, HONORIFICS, AND TITLES

Courtesy Names vs Given Names

Usually made up of two characters, a courtesy name is given to an individual when they come of age. Traditionally, this was at the age of twenty during one's crowning ceremony, but it can also be presented when an elder or teacher deems the recipient worthy. Though generally a male-only tradition, there is historical precedent for women adopting a courtesy name after marriage. Courtesy names were a tradition reserved for the upper class.

It was considered disrespectful for one's peers of the same generation to address someone by their given name, especially in formal or written communication. Use of one's given name was reserved only for elders, close friends, and spouses.

This practice is no longer used in modern China but is commonly seen in historically inspired media. As such, many characters have more than one name. Its implementation in novels is irregular and is often treated malleably for the sake of storytelling.

Diminutives, nicknames, and name tags

A-: Friendly diminutive. Always a prefix. Usually for monosyllabic names, or one syllable out of a two-syllable name.

XIAO-: A diminutive prefix meaning "little."

-ER: An affectionate diminutive suffix added to names, literally "son" or "child." Not to be confused with Xiao Chiye's nickname, Xiao Er, in which "er" (二) means "second."

-LANG: A suffix meaning young man. A term of address often used toward one's lover or husband.

LAO-: A diminutive prefix meaning "old."

-ZI: Affectionate suffix meaning "son" or "child."

-XIONG: A word meaning elder brother. It can be attached as a suffix to address an older male peer.

Family

DI/DIDI: Younger brother or a younger male friend.

GE/GEGE/DAGE: Older brother or an older male friend.

JIE/JIEJIE: Older sister or an older female friend.

-SHU: A suffix meaning "uncle." Can be used to address unrelated older men.

Martial Arts and Tutelage

SHIFU: Teacher or master, usually used when referring to the martial arts.

SHIXIONG: Older martial brother, used for older disciples or classmates.

SHIDI: Younger martial brother, used for younger disciples or classmates.

SHISHU: Martial uncle, used to address someone who studied under the same master (or shifu) as one's own master.

SHINIANG: The wife of one's shifu.

XIANSHENG: Teacher of academics.

Other

GONGZI: Young man from an affluent household.

-NIANGNIANG: Term of address for the empress or an imperial concubine, can be standalone or attached to a name as a suffix.

-GONGGONG: Term of address for a eunuch.

SHIZI: Title for the heir apparent of a feudal prince.

LAO-ZUZONG: Literally "old ancestor," an intimate and respectful term of address from a junior eunuch to a more senior eunuch.

GLOSSARY

GLOSSARY

CONCUBINES AND THE IMPERIAL HAREM: In ancient China, it was common practice for a wealthy man to take women as concubines in addition to his wife. They were expected to live with him and bear him children. Generally speaking, a greater number of concubines correlated to higher social status; hence a wealthy merchant might have two or three concubines, while an emperor might have tens or even a hundred.

The imperial harem had its own ranking system. The exact details vary over the course of history, but can generally be divided into three overarching ranks: the empress, consorts, and concubines. The status of a prince or princess's mother is an important factor in their status in the imperial family, in addition to birth order and their own personal merits. Given the patrilineal rules of succession, the birth of a son could also elevate the mother's status.

CUT-SLEEVE: A slang term for a gay man, which comes from a tale about Emperor Ai's love for, and relationship with, a male court official in the Han dynasty. The emperor was called to the morning assembly, but his lover was asleep on his robe. Rather than wake him, the emperor cut off his own sleeve.

IMPERIAL EXAMINATION SYSTEM: The system of examinations in ancient China that qualified someone for official service. It was intended to be a meritocratic system that allowed common civilians to rise up in society as a countering force to the nobility, but the extent to which this was true varied across time.

The imperial examination system was split into various levels. In the Ming and Qing dynasties, these were the provincial exam, metropolitan exam, and the palace exam. The top scholars at each examination level were known as the Jieyuan, Huiyuan, and Zhuangyuan respectively, and a scholar who emerged top at all three levels was known as the Sanyuan, or Triple Yuan, scholar.

KOWTOW: The kowtow (叩头 / "knock head") is an act of prostration where one kneels and bows low enough that their forehead touches the ground. A show of deep respect and reverence that can also be used to beg, plead, or show sincerity; in severe circumstances, it's common for the supplicant's forehead to end up bloody and bruised.

LAWFUL AND COMMON BIRTH HIERARCHY: Upper-class men in ancient China often took multiple wives. Only one would be the official wife, and her lawful sons would take precedence over the common sons of the concubines. Sons of lawful birth were prioritized in matters of inheritance. They also had higher social status and often received better treatment compared to the other common sons born to concubines or mistresses.

OFFICIALS: Civil and military officials were classified in nine hierarchic grades, with grade one being the highest rank. Their salaries ranged according to their rank. Referral by someone in a position of power, such as a noble, a eunuch, or another official, was the traditional path to becoming a court official. Another path, which later gained popularity as a way of combatting corruption and political cliques, was going through the imperial examination.

OFFICIALS OF COMMON BACKGROUNDS: Despite coming from affluent, possibly landowning, families, these officials were said to be from "common backgrounds" because they were the first court officials in their family. This is in direct contrast to the noble officials, who consolidated their power over time by forming a familial network with other officials and using their influence to raise their younger generations to officialdom.

QINGGONG: Literally "lightness technique," qinggong (轻功) refers to the martial arts skill of moving swiftly and lightly from one point to another, often so nimbly it looks like one is flying through the air. In wuxia and xianxia settings, characters use qinggong to leap great distances and heights.

YAMEN: An administrative office or department, or residence of a government official. For example, that of a local district magistrate or prefectural prefect. This is not the same as the Twenty-Four Yamen run by the eunuchs.

YELLOW REGISTER: In the Ming and Qing dynasties, households were classified and recorded into the Huangce (黃冊) or yellow registers according to their occupations, which remained unchanged from one generation to the next. These records provided information for taxation, as well as corvée and military conscription. Households were mainly divided into three categories: civilian, military, and trades, with civilians further divided into subcategories like scholars, farmers, or builders. Apart from the "good civilians" or 良民, there also existed a permanent underclass of slaves or 贱籍, who were born into their class or relegated as punishment for crime.

Tang Jiu Qing is an internationally renowned author who writes for the
novel serialization website JJWXC. She
started the web serialization of *Ballad of
Sword and Wine: Qiang Jin Jiu*, in 2018.
Her published works include *Nan Chan*
and *Time Limited Hunt*, among others.